ANDREI BITOV

Life in Windy Weather

Short Stories

Edited by Priscilla Meyer

Ardis, Ann Arbor

Copyright © 1986 by Ardis Publishers
All rights reserved under International and Pan-American
Copyright Conventions.
Printed in the United States of America

Translated from the original Russian

Ardis Publishers
2901 Heatherway
Ann Arbor, Michigan 48104

Library of Congress Cataloging in Publication Data

Bitov, Andrei.
Life in windy weather.

Translated from the Russian.
Contents: The big balloon—The leg—The idler—[etc.]
1. Bitov, Andrei—Translations, English. I. Meyer,
Priscilla. II. Title.
PG3479.4.I8A2   1986   891.73'44   85-19931
ISBN 0-88233-691-6 (alk. paper)

Cover photograph: Andrei Bitov and his daughter Anya. Toksovo, 1971.

Contents

Editor's Introduction   7
Acknowledgments   13
Preface   15
Autobiography   17

APOTHECARY ISLAND

The Big Balloon   *(Phyllis Lee)*   23
The Leg (Apothecary Island)   *(Janice Hoff)*   35

The Idler   *(Greta Slobin)*   47
Penelope (Nevsky Prospect)   *(Philip Swoboda)*   65

Infantiev   *(Carol Avins)*   81
The Soldier (From the Memoirs of the
            Monakhov Family) *(Priscilla Meyer)*   93
A Country Place
Life in Windy Weather   *(Carol G. Luplow & Richard Luplow)* 117
Notes from the Corner   *(Jascha Stewart)* 145

THE LOVER
A Novel with Ellipses

The Door   *(Marge Ferry)* 189
The Garden   *(Vera Kalina)* 197
The Third Story (The Image)   *(Greta Slobin)* 245
The Forest   *(Helena Goscilo)* 269
The Taste   *(Priscilla Meyer)* 335

Afterword   365

Introduction

Leningrad today is still very much the St. Petersburg of Pushkin, Gogol and Dostoevsky. Nevsky Prospect, its wide central avenue, brims with a continual stream of people flowing to and from the Neva river, past the churches, over the bridges, crossing the canals that provided the setting for so many of the classics of Russian literature. The hero of Gogol's "Nose" dashes into the Kazan cathedral, Pushkin's Evgeny is pursued by the Bronze Horseman—and the city itself has mythic stature. Designed at the behest of Peter the Great on Western European models, St. Petersburg was founded in 1703 on a marsh. This, together with the geometricity of its grid structure, caused Russians to perceive it as an imposition of a foreign, artificial order on Russian chaos, a chaos epitomized by Moscow which had grown in a more organic way. Dostoevsky called St. Petersburg "the most fantastic city," and Andrei Bely made the myth the core of his novel *Petersburg* (1914). This is the Leningrad where Andrei Bitov was born and grew up, a city of literary associations which inform his experience and his writing.

Bitov speaks mostly about Pushkin and Gogol, yet in important ways he is responding particularly to Dostoevsky. Dostoevsky discovers a fantastic world in everyday existence; the diseased vision of his heroes reveals the diseased nature of reality. Bitov too concentrates on his hero's vision, but both the hero and his reality are everyday, while it is the mode of perception that is rendered extraordinary.

But Bitov acknowledges no influences on his work. The scene in "The Idler" in which the young hero projects his guilt onto a fallen horse would remind anyone who has read *Crime and Punishment* of Raskolnikov's dream of the peasant beating the mare, yet Bitov is surprised at the comparison ("It's funny, everyone asks about that horse"). While he has of course read *Crime and Punishment,* Bitov explains the similarity by a kind of collective unconscious: the ideas, myths and symbols of a culture are in the air, and the fallen horse is part of a shared imagery.

The 1960s had begun a new period in Soviet literature with the emergence of many young writers who produced what came to be known as "Young Prose." They wrote short stories about the problems of their contemporaries who were growing up, unlike their fathers' generation, in conditions of peace and prosperity. The leaders of "Young Prose," Aksyonov and Gladilin, were from Moscow; Bitov, who began to publish a few years later than they, is very much a Leningrad writer. While he too discusses the problems of adolescence, he does so in a characteristically abstract and psychological way. His focus on "thought about thought" (the phrase comes from a favorable review by Lev Anninsky, a Soviet critic) caused conservatives to attack him for excessive subjectivity, preoccupation with personal trivia, and lack of moral purpose, all of which is antithetical to the Soviet view that literature must educate the reader to be a better member of society. But as Bitov's stories have appeared, the sincerity of his search for spiritual values and the high quality of his art have been increasingly recognized. Most of the stories in this collection have been published in Moscow under the title *Days of Man* (1976).

The Lover and *Apothecary Island* (named for an area of Leningrad) are comprised of stories written over a ten year period. They chronicle the development of Alexei Monakhov (*monakh* in Russian means "monk," and the name suggests a special sort of isolation) and of Bitov himself. Monakhov is to a large degree an autobiographical hero; while there is a well-defined distance between author and persona, it is a distance created by the author's greater insight and self-irony, rather than by a difference of world views. The settings of the stories too are taken from Bitov's life. His aunt's enormous desk ("The Garden") now stands in his apartment on Nevsky Prospect, and he can show you the meadow near his in-laws' dacha ("Life in Windy Weather") where Alexei stops with his son (in fact, as becomes clear in "Notes from the Corner," Bitov has a daughter, but in "Life in Windy Weather" he makes her a boy so that he can explore the parallel relationships of two pairs of fathers and sons: Monakhov and his father; Monakhov and his son).

The subject of the book is the growth of Monakhov's self-awareness, a growth which gradually, though never totally, bridges the distance between Bitov and his hero. Monakhov suffers from a sort of automatism, living in a dream-like state and refusing to make his thoughts fully conscious. He allows himself to steal from his aunt without acknowledging it to himself ("The Garden"), to behave badly to a girl without admitting his own selfishness ("Penelope"), and to live in cranky isolation in the midst of his family ("Life in Windy Weather").

The early stories establish Monakhov's character, and its origins; the later describe a series of awakenings through which he begins to break out of his self-preoccupation. A poignant moment in childhood begins the book; in "The Big Balloon" the purity and vividness of a child's vision, told with fairy-tale simplicity, is set against a harsh postwar background. "The Leg" shows the early stages of hypersensitivity that contribute to Monakhov's isolation: he struggles home on his injured leg, facing humiliation by his peers and reprimand from his family much the same way as in "The Door," almost ten years later, he waits for his girlfriend Asya all alone on the stairwell, trying to lessen the pain with another rationalizing monologue to himself.

"The Garden" and "The Idler" are stories of adolescence. Monakhov is on the verge of realizing that he is allowing himself the egotism of adolescence in the name of preserving the ideals of childhood; he begins to notice the escapist nature of his fantasies and the dangerous consequences of relating to the world the way children do. Bitov does not idealize childhood—children can be as cruel to each other as adults—but he sees it as a stage of life at which no discrepancy has yet developed between the inner self and the masks put on for the benefit of others. Children are capable of total, unselfconscious absorption in life, and so are still proof against the deadening artificialities of the adult world. Alexei's boss's excitement over the American stapler ("The Idler") is empty and perverted in contrast to the little boy's involvement in the snow city he builds in the park. But Alexei belongs to neither world: the boy refuses to play with this "uncle," and the boss scolds him for sloppy work. The problem is to reconcile the demands of responsible adulthood with the values represented by childhood.

Monakhov's parents serve throughout the novel as a point of calibration of his emotional growth. In the first half of the book he weighs his actions against their potential disapproval, but in the second he is finally responsible only to himself, so that the revelations he experiences are capable of changing him. In "Penelope" Alexei is able to realize that he has betrayed both the heroine and himself. He watches a movie of *The Odyssey* with a girl he meets in the theater—she is thereby associated with the model of fidelity, Penelope—but disposes of her unfeelingly because of her bizarre appearance which suggests recent release from prison. His interaction with her makes him think about his own reactions and about his habitual unwillingness to make such thoughts fully conscious. Thought about thought is Bitov's main concern. In "The Image" Monakhov realizes the subjectivity of love, a realization begun at the end of "The Garden" and only fully believed some ten years later when he meets Asya by chance after long separation. Her reality as an individual is irrelevant, Monakhov realizes: well-defined but flat, lacking any concerns but the most immediate and self-serving, Asya is rendered almost as a caricature of the Other Woman, the side of the coin which has Mother/Wife as its obverse. Asya, like the nameless wife and mother, also has a real-life prototype, but Bitov is almost exclusively interested in his hero's inner world; as with Dostoevsky, the only "reality" the reader can establish is the hero's construction of his own perceptions.

In "A Country Place," Monakhov, now a husband, a father, and a writer, is placed in a space he has to define for himself without reacting to an external event or others' demands. In "Notes from the Corner," we hear directly from him as an author; in "Life in Windy Weather," we see him as the hero who tries to find meaning and inner stability, the absence of which has caused awkwardness with his father, irritation with his wife and over his work, and inattention to his son. It is through his one-year-old son that he finds a new peace, this time not by joining the child in his game as in "The Idler," but by relearning his perception of the world. Monakhov finally understands the mutual dependency of father and son, and attains an adult self-image which is independent of the roles other people construct for him—in "The Idler" his boss's and parents'; in "Penelope" the audience's in the theater. In "Life in Windy Weather" Alexei creates an acceptable version of himself through his fiction and finds meaning in a religious-artistic perception of the natural world which he sees manifest in the pleasures of daily family life and in his work as love. As a writer, Monakhov can reconcile fantasy and subjective reality, which he has associated with childhood, with the "reality" of adulthood. Bitov suggests that fiction is a means of renovating perception analogous to seeing life through the eyes of a child (a Romantic idea similarly presented in stories by Yury Olesha, but again Bitov denies any direct relationship).

But, as suggested in "The Forest," an aesthetic perception fails to resolve the central Oedipal conflict that pervades Bitov's stories. Monakhov's relationship to his mother and father is elegantly analyzed in the implicit parallel to the situation with his girlfriend Natalya, whose two admirers, Zyablikov and Lenechka, are cast by Monakhov into roles that suit his own drama. When Monakhov first encounters the somewhat older Zyablikov on the street, he imagines that Zyablikov wants to beat him up. Later when he meets him at Natalya's he accords him undue admiration and tries to impress and placate him. Finally, Monakhov decides that Zyablikov is sleeping with Natalya, which allows Monakhov to leave in a righteous huff, though he is the one who has behaved badly. Lenechka, in juxtaposition, is younger—Natalya herself calls him her "son"—but he is nonetheless her suitor, deeply in love with her. Monakhov is confused: is Lenechka his peer and rival, or is he a son to Monakhov? This confusion of age and role reflects the Oedipal ambivalence that is the source of Monakhov's inability to decide whether to spend the last days of his trip with his mother, his wife, or his girlfriend. Throughout these stories, guilty ambivalence absorbs him so that he never does justice to any of his women, whether mother, either wife, or girlfriend.

Monakhov's second wife's grandmother in "The Taste" is the only woman whose image is uncontaminated by Monakhov's inner struggles. As an idealized representative of the old Russian aristocracy, she is, even in death, pitted against the mercilessly graceless bureaucracy of the materialist society which destroyed the values she cherished. The church where she spends her last night on earth is thematically allied to Pasternak's grave in Peredelkino: poetry and religion provide the only salvation from a sordid world in which lasting truth and faithfulness have been undermined. Thus "The Taste" illuminates the pair of deaths in "Infantiev" and "The Soldier," the first involving the growth of spiritual values, and the second in which literature provides the key to the hero's soul.

"Infantiev" and "The Soldier" form an epilogue in flashback form with members of the older generation as the nominal heroes. Asya's father (Infantiev) is even more emotionally isolated than Monakhov. Only with the death of his wife does he begin to perceive the whole level of existence of the unspoken, the emotional, even of the mystical, that he had totally rejected all his life. Alexei's Uncle Dickens ("The Soldier") is another isolated old man: the epilogue presents two possible variations of Monakhov's future, were he to neglect the struggle for self-awareness. When Uncle Dickens dies, Alexei comes into possession of some short stories the old man had written in his youth, and the circle is complete: Alexei gains insight into Dickens as an independent person, no longer distorted by Alexei's need of him, just as Bitov creates Alexei for the reader in a process which attains self-awareness for all three—author, hero and reader. The commentary on the nature of prose fiction in "The Soldier" sensitizes us to the implicit discussion of the function of literature throughout the book. Because finally, Andrei Bitov's real hero is literature. His novel *Pushkin House* is dedicated to the Russian literary tradition, the preservation of which provides the essential meaning of Bitov's works.

Priscilla Meyer
Middletown
1976, 1980, 1983

Acknowledgments

The stories contained in this collection appear here in English for the first time, with the exception of "Infantiev" and "Life in Windy Weather" which received advance publication in two Ardis anthologies of contemporary Russian prose. Most of *The Lover* as well as "The Soldier" were published in Russian in *Dni cheloveka* (Molodaya gvardiya, 1976), except for "The Taste" which appeared in *Literaturnaya Gruziya* (no. 1, 1983). The majority of stories from *Apothecary Island* were published in *Aptekarskii ostrov* (Sovetskii pisatel', 1968). "A Country Place" is contained in *Obraz zhizni* (Molodaya gvardiya, 1972).

The following people contributed translations to this volume:
Carol Avins, "Infantiev"
Marge Ferry, "The Door"
Helena Goscilo, "The Forest"
Janice Hoff, "The Leg"
Vera Kalina, "The Garden"
Phyllis Lee, "The Big Balloon"
Carol G. Luplow and Richard Luplow, "Life in Windy Weather"
Priscilla Meyer, "The Soldier" and "The Taste"
Jascha Stewart, "Notes from the Corner"
Greta Slobin, "The Idler" and "The Image"
Philip Swoboda, "Penelope"

I would like to thank Wesleyan University for grants which supported manuscript preparation, and Mary Lou Nelles for years of meticulous help.

Preface

I began with very short stories, from 18 to 200 words long. Gradually they became longer and longer, approaching a novella. But the novella also began to get longer.

The stories collected here are my best; I haven't written any more short stories since these. One day I sat down to write the next story to test my strength, intending after that to stop writing and live—I sat down to my story and just couldn't finish it until it had turned into a novel. Since then, no matter how many times I try, I get everything but a short story. I don't believe the genre exists at all.

The stories are ordered by the date of composition and by the age of the heroes, and these, my only stories hint at a novel. The hero—childhood—youth—love—children—death: a biographical novel with an insufficiently sharp, but nonetheless inchoate plot.

What I wanted to say in each of these stories I have already forgotten, but what I have said is not for me to judge. I could, of course, easily make up what they're about right now. I would even like to remember what they were about *then* and *there* as written by *that* person, but I won't. The past is utterly defenseless against our attempts to reorganize it. I think that for aesthetic reasons it is better not to disturb it.

Perhaps these stories, my proto-novel, were in part about how a person is unable to evaluate the *present,* tied as he is to the undigested past.

Andrei Bitov
April, 1973

Autobiography

I was born May 27th, 1937 in Leningrad. My parents were also born there. And my grandparents. And some great great great grandparents. Three generations is the maximum life of a name: I can't ask my grandmother what her grandfather's name was because my grandmother too is gone. This is somewhat strange: I know thousands of peoples' names, but I don't know the name of someone whose blood comprises one eighth of my own. But, thank God, I know my parents, and they are alive.

The first memory of my life is war. That permitted me in my youth to consider myself part of the "war generation." Now I no longer romanticize this circumstance, but it's a fact, if the one fact in our time is that war. The first (the most difficult, they say) year of the blockade I lived in Leningrad, and I remember surprisingly peaceful and everyday scenes (after all, I had no earlier recollections) like: corpses, bomb sites, half a meter of ice in the hall, and that catastrophic little piece of bread the size of a postage stamp, our daily ration. In March of 1942 my mother managed to take my brother and me via the "road of life" (the ice was flooded with melted snow, the car rode like a boat, I enjoyed the splashing) to evacuation in the Urals, and later in Tashkent. In 1944 we returned to Leningrad and I entered the first grade. I remember all this, but as if not about myself, but about some other boy. In my later work very little of this appears directly: two stories—"The Big Balloon" and "Apothecary Island"—contain something about childhood in wartime.

At times it seems that my adolescence followed immediately after my childhood, as if I had slept through boyhood: going to school in the dark mornings. What was important about it was perhaps the separate schooling for boys and girls: my first love came right after I finished high school and, as a result of the absence of sisters and female cousins, that love was the first woman I had known. To this first love I dedicated the stories "The Door," "The Garden," and "The Image."

Besides separate schooling, it was home, the family, that was important. In big cities after the war there were no such families. My grandmother was the head of the family, after her—three of her grown children, their families, then her grandchildren, I among them, of whom there were fifteen. They all lived together in one household in one big apartment. The house was a whole world and comprised my whole life, and it strengthened a certain isolationism in me which was quite in keeping with the spirit of the times, as was separate schooling. The household justified this isolation, providing an abundance of the best, the finest, people, painlessly dividing my life into two indisputable, a priori categories: my own personal world and the external one.

The existence of the outside world occurred to me suddenly, abruptly— the end of school, love, what to do? I think I was rather unprepared for life since I sincerely regarded receiving my passport in 1953 as a festive occasion. This was because, being a native Leningrader, I had cleverly managed to be born on the day Petersburg was founded, and so I received my passport on the same day the city had its 250th birthday. I eagerly expected there to be a national celebration somehow in my honor. But a date is arbitrary, time does not respect chronometry: the anniversary was celebrated only two years later, and then not on the right day and not in the right month.

From that moment begins my "biography" of the sort that appears on dust jackets, as if before a person began to write his life had no form. And like everyone else, I can list a dozen jobs which I not only didn't keep but didn't even loiter at. This negative phenomenon is called "flightiness," but I am justified in part by the fact that I changed occupations not always by my own will and each time didn't know whether I would have to take up this or that unexpected profession for my whole life because my life did not fully depend on me.

I didn't even think about literature, about art. My big family didn't have to keep up with the latest to consider itself cultured. Its tastes were independent and distant from the times: the most contemporary writer was Leonid Andreev, the most recent composer—Rakhmaninov. It was possible for me simply not to suspect the possibility of the existence of contemporary art, now, at this very second. I invented "physical culture" for myself, words which came into use ten years later, and diligently hardened my muscles, not yet knowing what I might need them for. Not having cultivated any refined tastes in me, my wonderful mother infected me with space, traveling with me every year from the time I was ten around our broad borders. Not knowing what to do next, I thought this love for displacement sufficient reason for entering the geological research department of the Mining Institute. Having encountered the exact technical sciences, I studied with extraordinary unwillingness, my muscles already burdened and bored me, my first love passed, and I really didn't know what to do with myself. But here I encountered a surprise no less abrupt than life after school: for the first time I was witness to the possibility of the contemporary expression of contemporary reality. It was 1956 and, by chance, I saw Fellini's *La Strada*. The very fact of this possibility revealed the possibility. And everything somehow started rolling inexorably all by itself. Everything coincided.

At the Mining Institute there was a literary society of amateur student poets and I happened to go to one of their meetings. This society was outstanding in its own way (out of it came such poets as Alexander Kushner and G. Gorbovsky), and I was simply astounded that there existed people who wrote about what they were feeling and seeing. They asked me if I was writing anything, and already I couldn't imagine not belonging to this world I had so instantly taken root in, I would have hanged myself, shot myself... but I had never written a line. Out of terror that I might be thrown out, I babbled some verses by my older brother written in the style of Severyanin—and they kept me in the group. Thus my literary career began with plagiarism. Out of fear of being exposed, I began writing poems designed to be no worse than my brother's. For my first efforts I was praised indulgently, for my brother's poems—destroyed. As a result of this recognition I began to write very bad poems with such passion that I let my studies go completely and was expelled from the institute.

And it was then I became a stevedore, a lathe operator, a soldier. I served in the army in construction units, where I was employed in the most varied professions. Missing my fiancee and continuing to scribble poems like a machine gun, I got into a nervous state and was demobilized. However I had seen some kind of life, experienced a bit, acquired some prosaic minimum.... And then came a major turning point, a different relationship to life: in the fall of 1958 I got married, was reinstated in my institute, gave up writing poetry and began writing prose. And that's what I've been writing ever since. I wrote stories during lectures, but no longer neglected the institute, and summer work on expeditions gave me material and experience. My impressions of these summers are the basis for my first books.

In 1962 I finally finished the Mining Institute, my daughter was born, I signed an agreement for my first book, and my first film scenario—and this was a new, in some sense a final, turning point. I dashed between working expeditions, my family, and literature, and finally was forced to choose.

In 1963 my biography ends, I became a professional in the sense that my sole occupation is literature and I have no other means of existence—what follows is not biography but books, which feed me not by my writing them but by being published: *The Big Balloon* (1963), *Such a Long Childhood* (1965), *A Summer Place* (1967), *Apothecary Island* (1968), *Life's Image* (1972).

These little collections are now being made into two big, complete books: *Days of Man,* a book of psychological stories about an urban hero living in the city, that is, what I've been able to convey that's new about my contemporary; *Seven Journeys,* a collection of all sorts of travels united by the development of the traveler, a book about another life, about space, about the swallowing up of time.*

To these two books a new novel has now been added, *Pushkin House,* written for "Soviet Writer" publishers.** This book is the most important. And these three big books are the total to date. They bring something to

---

* Both were published in Moscow in 1976.
**Published in full only by Ardis Publishers (in Russian) in 1978.

completion—my first conscious decade, 1962-1972. Now I'm more in a state of planning, of beginnings, than of completions. I have begun a quasi-English novel, *The Teacher of Symmetry,* and a theoretical dissertation, "Relationships between Author and Hero." I think these two sprouts will occupy me for two years. And then we'll see.

January 1974

Apothecary Island

The Big Balloon

Papa was shaving. He did this thoroughly. He checked his lathery cheek with his index finger, guided the razor over the cheek, touched the newly-shaven place, and wiped the razor and his finger on a piece of newspaper. He inflated first his left cheek, then the right one, sucked in his lower lip, and managed to sing during the process. Papa was now pressing his pants. He spat on his fingers and slapped the underside of the iron; he spat a mouthful of water on his pants, and still continued to sing.

Asya was on pins and needles. She was sitting on the edge of the sofa, hands placed on knees and spine straightened, trying as hard as possible to show how willing she was to "wait patiently." A pet, a prewar puppy, one-legged and swarthy, lay behind her, lonely and idle. Asya sat, and then jumped up, ran up to the window sill, and then—leapt up, lay herself stomach down on it. The window overlooked the courtyard, and there everything was grey and empty. The sky above was a brilliant blue. Because of this, the courtyard seemed even emptier. A little boy ran by, squealing "You're it, you're it!" He vanished behind the gate. From the gate a rumble was heard. It sounded like waves.

Asya slipped down from the window sill, and again found her place on the edge of the sofa to "wait patiently." Papa was already in his pants and busy stuffing his pockets. "When will I buy myself a jacket?" Papa said as he put on an off-brown tunic. Once more he looked at himself in the mirror, for some reason frowned, pursed his lips and knit his brows; preserving that stern and beautiful expression, he turned to Asya. Still glancing at himself sideways into the mirror, he said:

"Well, let's go, Aga."

They went out through the gateway and stopped, adjusting themselves to the light and the noise. Like an endless grey ribbon—above which there were patches of slogans—above which was an extremely blue sky—a parade stretched out along the street. And like river banks, people were for the moment motionless, watching the paraders. The sun poured down on Asya and Papa, and they squinted. And Asya's red hair sparkled in the sun. Papa looked at her and said:

"You are my flag for today."

He stood for a little while longer watching the parade, and started to hurry. There was a garden by the house, and he led Asya there. It was a very convenient garden: two steps and the child is in fresh air, and out of danger, and you don't need to cross any streets.

"Well, Aga...you play here. And I'm going, I have to. To a certain place."

And he turned around. And he walked off.

He left, and Asya immediately heard: "Little Red Riding Hood's here!" Little boys ran up to her, pulled her braids, and she pulled someone's nose, and they called her over to come jump on the blimp.* But this was all so uninteresting today: both the blimp which, half-deflated, lay like an enormous pudgy cookie on the vacant lot behind the debris and was so much fun to jump on, and the debris itself, which began right behind the garden. And Asya again found herself on the street.

The columns marched on and on. And on the sidewalk there was business. On the left they were selling red and green paper balloons on sticks; on the right two gypsies, trading in balloons, were fighting over the balloons. Or rather, fighting over the poor dark blue rind that you can blow up to become a blue balloon. They stretched the rind in opposite directions; they pulled, first one, then the other, as if they were sawing.

"It's my balloon!"

"No, it's not yours!"

"It's not your balloon!"

"No, it's mine!"

The skin burst. No more balloon.

And then they fought over the area of the sidewalk: whose it was, who came and occupied it first. And again they could not come to an agreement.

The columns marched on and on. Asya suddenly wished she could march with the others in such a column. Maybe carry something, or maybe sing. But most of all, just march in a column. Of course, they were all strangers there. And Asya began to waver. Just take one step—and there she'd be in the column, marching with everybody. And she didn't take the step. Because of this, her heart beat faster and faster. Just one step...

Ding-boom-ding!—as if somewhere far away a bell resounded— and Asya was already in the ranks and marching with everybody. Nobody was surprised and nobody asked questions. She was marching with these very many strangers, and somehow, because of this, something jumped up inside, joyful, puppy-like, and she herself wanted to jump. But Asya didn't jump.

And there from the side, outstripping the column, marched a very serious soldier...and there was something amazing about him! On his head was a helmet with earflaps, on his shoulders a metal box (obviously very complicated equipment), and rising from the box—an iron rod, which jutted out above his head. The soldier marched like that, serious and important, and

---

* Blimps were anchored around cities for protection against bombing raids during World War II.

he was like a man that is to be looked at: he didn't see anything around him. He marched on, as if from a different world, immersed in something, on the edge of the column, outdistancing it. Ding-boom-ding!—resounded both from somewhere inside Asya, and at the same time as if from far away, and she also was outdistancing the column on one edge, right behind the soldier.

She kept up with him with difficulty, colliding with the paraders, running around them, and for some reason worrying that he would notice her. And so they moved on for a while along the column, until suddenly the soldier turned down a side street. It was void of people, and after such a crowded street, it seemed especially empty and quiet. The sun split the street lengthwise: one side was flooded with sun, on the other—with ledges—there were sharp shadows. They walked along the shady side, and the other side seemed strange—bright; and the emptiness, and the silence and the flags from house to house also seemed strange. The soldier crossed over to the sunny side, and suddenly noticed Asya rushing after him. He paused—and Asya stopped short, not knowing where to escape to on such an empty street, and wondering what would happen now.

"What is it, little girl?" said the soldier, and he turned up one of his earflaps. Asya was silent. The soldier laughed and reached into his pocket. He got something out, and turned it around in his hands. "Here"—he reached out to Asya. Asya stepped back and looked at him mistrustfully. "Here, take it," the soldier said again, and stepped up to her. "It's like your hair." Asya was frightened and took it mechanically, all the while staring him in the face. Behind his head the iron rod quivered. The soldier laughed and walked off. Asya looked in her hand. It was a little spool of red wire, thin as a hair, and silky. Asya lifted her head, and looked around for the soldier. He was already quite far away, and was now turning in to the gateway of a big grey house. By the very gate he turned around, saw Asya, and waved to her as if beckoning to her from far away. And he disappeared. Asya walked slowly toward the house. The gateway had unwieldy wooden gates, joined together. Asya paused and examined them. She saw a flat bar in the middle, where the gates separated, and a rectangle on the bottom of one of the gates (the soldier had probably gone in here). And here in the other gate was a little window, and from there someone peered out and said: "What do you want here? Run along, you hoyden, run along..." Frightened, Asya ran off, turned down one of the streets, and again started walking. She calmed down completely and walked along some unfamiliar street, and on the left there was a park behind a beautiful lattice, and on the right there was a very long building with white columns, and in front there was a church cupola, and there was not one demolished building on this street. And not one person. Asya walked on, clutching the reel in her fist and stroking the silky wire with one finger. She walked on and didn't recognize these places. She tried to imagine which side their street was on, the one on which she had marched with the column and on which their house stood. And she wasn't very successful.

And maybe this wasn't her city at all—so sunny, beautiful, and empty. But a different, a completely different one...a magical city. And such unexpected things happen here! Such, such...she couldn't even imagine what kind of things... And then from a side street emerged a woman, holding an infant in her arms, and above...above...in the blue sky—a huge (such huge ones don't exist!) red balloon. Ding-boom-ding! Ding-boom-ding!—persistently, and from somewhere now quite near Asya, a bell rang out. A balloon...with a gold ship on it. The balloon pulled on the string in the woman's hands and strained upwards.

Ding-boom-ding! Ding-boom-ding!

Asya didn't even notice how she found herself right in front of the woman with the infant, and stopped short. She didn't even see them—she only saw the big, round, and wonderful balloon, but such huge ones don't even exist. The woman with the infant also stopped. And they stood like this, facing one another. "What do you want, little girl?" the woman asked. She was well-dressed and beautiful, furry. "The balloon," said Asya.

"What do you mean, the balloon?" said the furry woman. "It's Lyuka's balloon. Isn't that so, Lyuka? she said, butting her baby with her nose. "We bought it. We liked it very much, and we bought it." She wasn't speaking to Asya anymore, but to the baby: "Lyuka loves balloons like that." Lyuka sat in the arms of his furry mother, rosy and indifferent like a Chinese idol, and stared blankly at Asya. "So, little girl, this balloon is ours. And Lyuka and I must run now because our pa-pa is coming home soon." And she, after butting the indifferent Lyuka with her nose again, wanted to move on. But Asya was still standing in front of her, and—Ding-boom-ding!—the very biggest balloon in the world, the roundest, and the reddest, was the only thing that existed.

"What's the matter with you, little girl? Let us by..." the woman drawled discontentedly, stepping towards Asya.

"Auntie! Auntie!" shouted Asya.

"What, little girl?" sternly said the furry auntie.

"Where did you get it?" said Asya, and for some reason "it" came out a whisper.

"Lyuka and I will tell you," said the auntie, suddenly softening. "You just go down this street and turn down the first street on the right. Walk down that, and it's very close. Notlong Street. Not Long... No, it's not like that. It's just the name. There's a bright green house there. It's the only one that's so green. You'll see it right away. Besides, it has those stone women standing by the gates. Well, go into the courtyard, and there, straight ahead, is the entrance. The third floor... And now Lyuka and I have to run-run-run. Ooh, my precious!"—she butted Lyuka and really did run, but only for a few steps, and then she began to walk. And disappeared.

Asya quickly, and as if in a dream, found and didn't find the place—she divined both Notlong Street and the green house with the white stone women, and entered the courtyard. The courtyard was strange. The house on the inside was also green, but dark, peeling. And in the middle of the courtyard, enclosed by a round lattice, big old trees grew in a ring, and they looked as if they had joined hands. And in the very middle there was a round fountain, and in the middle of the fountain there was a beautiful white bird. Asya saw the entrance straight ahead, right across the square, and headed through the square. There were benches there, and they were all taken. Asya was already going through the entrance when she heard a squeaky voice: "Little girl! Little girl!" Asya stopped and turned around. "Come here, little girl," said an old lady from one of the benches. Asya went back to her. "You've come for a balloon?" the old lady said, and tapped the ground with her crutch. "Yes," said Asya in an embarrassed voice, amazed that the old lady could have known. "You'll be after me," the old lady said. "Do you want a balloon too?" wondered Asya. "We're all here for balloons," said the people on the benches.

Asya found herself a place on the wooden railing that enclosed the lawn. On the lawn lay last year's brown leaves. Asya did not quite understand what was happening to her. She cautiously stole a glace at the old lady. This one sat with her chin on her crutch. Asya looked away. She was a bit scared. And it was now certain that—Ding-boom-ding!—this was not her city, but an emerald or some other such kind of city. And perhaps she was dreaming all of this. She stole another glance at the old lady. The old lady was still there. She was saying something to her neighbor. "Now I shall find something out," thought Asya, and she listened to them.

"And so the house is on fire," the old lady was saying, "and I keep going up and down, up and down; I drag out whatever I can. And my son still doesn't come home, doesn't come home. And it's already dark out. Only the snow-drifts are white. And the house is burning ... and then HE appeared. So black ... gloomy ... I carry things out, and HE takes them. And my son is still not home. And I'm old, what will I do with HIM? I'm afraid of him. What does he care? I carry things out, and HE takes them. And so he took it all. And then my son came, but nothing was left: HE took it all. Only one samovar was left behind. I had stuck it in a snow-drift. It was silver ..."

Ding-boom-ding ...

"It's all true," thought Asya. "That's the way it is ..."

"Mmm, yes," her neighbor was saying. "Times were hard."

"And how are they now? And how are they now?" the old lady exclaimed in a ringing and rapid voice. "Just a balloon—and it costs thirty rubles!"

"Thirty rubles!"—this news pierced Asya. She had somehow not even thought about this, so strange had everything around her seemed.

Thirty rubles! ...

Asya jumped up.

"Granny! Granny!"

"What, my child?"

"Is there a Portovy Prospect in this city?"

"What do you mean, child? It's right nearby. Why do you want to know?"

"Oh!" joyfully exclaimed Asya, "I live there!"

"What a strange girl, isn't she?" the woman said to her neighbor. "As soon as you go out, child, turn right and walk on and on, straight ahead. And you'll find your street."

"Granny, will I have time?" said Asya, alarmed.

"Where are you hurrying to?"

"When I get back—will there still be balloons?"

"Well, I really don't know, child. This I can't tell you for sure. I don't know. You just hurry, hurry..."

And Asya did hurry. And she also easily found her street. Yes, it was her street. Just like it. There were many people as before, but the columns were already gone. It was still rather far from home. Asya ran—balloon! balloon!—and breathlessly flew up the stairs.

Papa wasn't home. In desperation, Asya sank onto the sofa, and then quickly jumped up: there won't be enough time, she'll be late... She rushed into the kitchen. There, by the stove, Marya Karpovna, steaming and angry, was pottering about. Immense, she lightly flew about the kitchen, fiercely crashing tureens and stew-pots, as if they were alive and it were possible to get angry at them. And it was almost impossible to catch sight of her hands, so quickly did they dart about.

"What do you want here? Go away, go away..." barked Marya Karpovna, not stopping her darting about.

"Aunt Marya, please can I have..." Asya said, plaintively stretching her words, "Papa isn't home, he'll give it back to you tonight, please can I have... Honest, I promise, Papa would have bought it for me, only he isn't home."

"In again, out again... What do you want?"

"Give me thirty rubles till tonight..."

"Thirty rubles! Look what she wants. I should suddenly up and give thirty rubles to some little girl..." Marya Karpovna was saying, smacking dough with her red and swollen hands. "What do you want it for?"

"A balloon like this!" said Asya, and she waved her hands to show what the balloon was like.

"Helium, is that it?"

"Yes," already rejoicing, said Asya.

"And these thirty rubles are for a balloon!" Marya Karpovna was horrified. "Thirty rubles, some joke, they sure soak you! You've got to work hard for thirty rubles... Some money!"

"Please, Auntie Marya... Papa will give it back to you tonight."

"Tonight, you say? True enough, it's not much money nowadays! Two ice creams—and that's the end of your money. Ekh..."

She dried her hands on her apron, and in a waddle, hobbled into her room. She returned with a red bill.

"After all, it's a treat for the child," she was saying, looking at the thirty ruble note. "After all, it's a holiday...How can one not pamper you, my unfortunate orphan...Oy, it's burning! Oh Lord in heaven!"—she raced to the stove, and then to Asya:

"Here, take it and run, before I change my mind..."

"Oh Lord in heaven, a holiday!..." snarled Marya Karpovna, snatching the hot saucepan, and throwing off the lid with a clatter. "Some have holidays, and some..."

But Asya was already rushing down Portovy Prospect, clutching the note in her fist, running around people, squeezing through, slipping through the crowd, her red head flashing.

The green house. The big white women. The round garden in the courtyard. And nobody in the garden. And the old woman wasn't there. "I'm late, I'm late..." her blood hammered in her head. Asya flew up to the third floor. It was a good thing that it was clear which door it was. There was only one. The other was boarded up.

With a swooping motion, Asya rang the bell. And then she got frightened. To ring at a strange door—formerly she would have felt shy and perhaps would not have dared at all. Asya had not yet recovered her breath, and her breathing and her heart hammered over the entire landing.

The door was not opened for a long time.

It was opened by a stout, flabby woman, still not old, and amazingly white. Everything about her sank downwards: her cheeks, her figure. It seemed as if she had melted. Her hair was tousled, she was out of breath, and very, very white.

"What do you want?" she asked rudely.

"A balloon...Do you have balloons?" said Asya, unclenching her whitened fist. "Here."

So she stood, facing the big white woman, holding out the red bunched-up bill in her palm.

The woman eyed all this: both Asya and the bill.

"We don't have any balloons here!" she said, and slammed the door.

And Asya's head spun a little; everything was drifting somewhere to the right, to the right. Something inside sank down with a dying motion, as in an elevator. Asya gripped the bannister. Then from a white cloud emerged, in the reverse order from which they had vanished: bannister, staircase, ceiling, landing, door, and the bell on the door. "And what about the balloon? The biggest in the world...the roundest...and the gold ship on it?"

There was no balloon. But there couldn't be no balloon. That much Asya understood. And she didn't move from the spot.

So she stood for about an hour. A number of people descended and ascended the stairs, and Asya turned away from them. She wanted to ring again, but she couldn't. She only looked at the narrow slit of the mail box and at the five little holes underneath it, and quietly repeated: "And now...it will open...One, two, three...Thre-e-e...Right now..." She took the spool out of her pocket, stroked the silky wire and said, this time more slowly: "On-nnn-e, two-o-o-o..."

Behind the door laughter was heard, and the door was flung open. Neat and gay, the same big white woman appeared, with a garbage pail.

"You're still here, little girl?" she said, already significantly more gently. "There aren't any balloons. We had some, but they're all gone already. Go home, go on..."

And she began to descend the stairs.

Asya didn't believe her. She stroked the silky wire and was now certain that there had to be a balloon. When the woman came back with the empty pail and saw Asya in the same spot, meeting her with an intent look, she suddenly turned even whiter and her left cheek twitched.

"And you're still standing here?..." she said. "I'd be glad to give you ten of them...But there aren't any. Oh you, my poor thing...What am I going to do with you? Oh, yes, good heavens!!" she suddenly exclaimed. There is one, there is! Only it has a defect...Its side got a little burnt...Wait, I'll be right back...In a wink. I'll just fill it up. There's still some left. Wait..." And hurriedly she disappeared behind the door, and left the door half-open.

Ding-boom-ding! Ding-boom-ding!—from far away the sound of the bell approached. Closer, closer. Something ripped open inside Asya, burst, and she sobbed.

And the woman reappeared carrying a huge red balloon in front of her. And here was the gold ship too...

Ding-boom-ding!

Asya, seeing nothing, stepped forward with outstretched arms, and took the balloon by the string.

The woman smiled.

"Take it dear, take it..."

Asya extended the red bunched-up bill on her palm.

The happiness disappeared from the face of the woman. Some kind of shadow stole across her crestfallen face. All this in one second. She took Asya's thirty ruble note, and, not raising her eyes, quietly slipped behind the door.

Asya went down the stairs. Ding-boom-ding! rang out inside her. Ding-boom-ding! She wound up the string and took the balloon in her hands from both sides. Her arms could scarcely encircle it. She pressed the balloon lightly and felt that beneath her hands it was resilient, almost alive. She put light pressure on the balloon with her fingertips, all five in turn, as if she were playing a scale, and ding-boom-ding, ding-boom-ding!

Then she noticed that the balloon was not quite round: in one spot it looked as if it were drawn together by a thread. And there was a big red patch on one side. But all this was insignificant and couldn't dismay her. Ding-boom-ding!—this was her enormous red balloon with a gold ship on it!

She walked down her street smiling and didn't see anything around her. The balloon tugged on the string, and when she lifted her head, it floated above her, enormous and red in the blue sky.

"Little girl, where did they get you such a wonderful balloon?" she was asked.

"I got it myself," she said.

"Where, then?" they asked her.

"There aren't any left," she said.

Here was her home. Here was the garden from which she had set out that morning. From all ends of the garden, little boys flew up to her.

"Little Red Riding Hood's here!" they shouted. And they suddenly became quiet. Did they also hear ding-boom-ding? Asya stood in the center, bursting with pride.

"Where did you get it?" one of them said, quietly and admiringly. "On Notlong Street," said Asya. "On Notlong! On Notlong!" the children suddenly hooted. "Maybe Notshort? Maybe Notwide? Maybe Oblong?"—they shouted and jumped and made a lot of noise around her. Someone jumped up and pinched the balloon. The rubber squeaked between his fingers. Asya suddenly understood what was going to happen, turned white and stepped back. But there were also little boys behind her. They too were jumping and hooting, and wanted to grab the balloon. Asya stretched her arm upward and raised herself up on her tip toes. "Don't, don't!"—she shouted—"It's my balloon. Mine! You can't, don't!" But someone had already grabbed her by the sleeve; someone had pulled her braid. "Little Red Riding Hood!" they shouted. Asya was frightened, terrified. The outstretched arm with the balloon ached. And then Asya felt that she was squeezing something in the fist of her other hand. The spool! "I'll give you something better! This is better... this is much better!" she said, offering the spool with the red wire to them. With a cry, they all threw themselves upon the spool. They almost tore off Asya's arm. But she had already run away, away from the garden—with the balloon, with the balloon. It was safe, safe! She ran up to her floor; she was panting, and the key wasn't going in the slot, and the balloon was in the way.

Eleonora Leonidovna and her son were coming down the stairs. The son screamed: "A balloon! I waa-ant it!"

"That's the girl's balloon," Eleonora told him. "Can't you see? Asechka," she cooed, "where did they get you such a wonderful balloon?"

"I got it myself," said Asya. "And there aren't any left."

"I wa-ant it! I waa-nt it!" monotonously and indifferently droned the son.

"Hush, hush," said Eleonora Leonidovna to her son. "Asechka, tell me where, and perhaps we'll go tomorrow...."

"On Notlong Street, but I don't remember the number of the building or the apartment number either," said Asya, and laughed.

"Don't joke, don't joke, little girl," said Eleonora Leonidovna, "I'm still older than you are."

"No, seriously, on Notlong Street. It's not like that, it's just the name. And the building is green and has big white ladies, and there's a garden inside, and there's a fountain with a bird."

"You ought to be ashamed, child," said Eleonora Leonidovna, and she began to go down the stairs.

Asya managed to open the door, and, hugging the balloon, she carried it into the apartment. At last it was safe. Marya Karpovna, already completely boiled, peeped out from the kitchen.

"And there it is, the dear!" she said. "What's this—it got burnt on one side? And there too..." she looked at Asya. "Ah, what a wonderful balloon you have!" she then said. "The best...I've never seen one like it."

Asya, folding the balloon in her arms, carefully opened the door to her room and walked in. Papa was still not there. She weighted the string down on the middle of a round table with the iron, and turned on the light. The balloon tugged on the string and rocked in the center of the room, enormous and red. Ding-boom-ding!—an unknown flower.

Asya marched around the table, raising her arms and legs high, and sang.

But there was no one to show it to: Papa was still not home.

The room she shared with Papa was narrow and small, and it suddenly occured to Asya that there was little air in it for the balloon. That's how enormous it was, that balloon. She opened the window, fastened the string to the latch, and let the balloon out into the street.

Outside the window, the balloon was like a flag. "Now you have enough air," said Asya, and sat down on the couch. And then she realized how tired she was.

She just had to wait and show it.... She sat and from time to time looked out the window. Outside the window swayed the balloon, and it was the biggest and roundest in the world.

Asya was already beginning to doze off when Papa came home.

He came in, sad and tired, and sat down next to her.

"How good it is to be home!" he said.

And Asya looked out the window—the balloon! And all the happiness, falling asleep together with her, awoke, and because there was someone to share it with, doubled. And she told all about it...

"And that's all," she said.

"Ah, you, my little flag," said Papa, and stroked her hair. "This is the most remarkable balloon I have ever seen in my life."

And Asya fell asleep, and she dreamed of how she got a package from Mama in the children's home. Inside, there was a pair of red pants. Mama had thought that Asya was still as fat as she used to be and that she had grown in two years, and the pants turned out very big for Asya. They hung below her knees and stuck out from under her skirt. And Asya couldn't take a step because of these damned turkeys. She's going along and they, hissing threateningly, slowly move away from the fences, and keep coming closer, and there are more and more of them, covering the whole street. And these nasty birds stretch out their bare necks, and their repulsive red beaks quivering, reach out towards her pants. And they hiss louder and more repulsively. And Asya runs. And they run after her, grabbing her pants and nipping her painfully on the legs. And they hiss. And she can't go any faster—her pants are slipping down...

And here they are, these turkeys, they are the little boys from her courtyard, they are the two gypsies, they peck, they jump, they tear her biggest and reddest balloon.

"No! No!" Asya shouts, and wakes up. In fright, she looks out the window.

Ding-boom-ding!

Papa sits nearby and looks at Asya. And Papa smiles at her.

And Asya suddenly remembers what she wanted to ask him all along.

"Papa, do you know where Notlong Street is?"

"No, Aga, I don't know."

"And you've never heard of it?"

"No... why do you ask?"

Asya looks out the window—and suddenly smiles. At something only she knows...

Ding-boom-ding!

1961

The Leg

(Apothecary Island)

"The clouds with their weight will open the gate
And God will enter with a spoon to stir the milk"
—S. Krasovitsky

To G. Gorbovsky

"Well, Monk, are you coming with us or not?"

Second-grader Monakhov wavered.

Today was Papa's birthday, and Mama had said, "As soon as you come home from school, get to your homework right away, and then tidy up everything very carefully before Papa gets home from work. That will be the best present."

His father's birthday—that Monakhov understood. But before him, serious and presenting a solid front, stood the boys, silently waiting and almost testing him.

...It was three months now since he had returned from evacuation and started at the school. Monakhov would leave with everyone after class, and everyone would split up into groups and go off in groups, while these two boys always went in a direction no one else went, and Monakhov would remain alone and walk alone. His bookbag would become heavy and alien, and Monakhov would be depressed.

He kept wanting to make friends, and did not succeed; somehow he wasn't needed, and at his age that seemed more important than anything. He had to start something, and Monakhov had chosen these two. He tried to be obliging to them, flattered them, and gave them his lunch and cigarettes. They shrugged and indifferently collected the gifts. Monakhov was patient.

And now today they whispered together in the coatroom for a long time, while he stood on one side and knocked his bookbag against his knees with a nonchalant air. His heart was pounding. Monakhov was not remembering or thinking about anything at that moment—he just waited.

At the entrance to the coatroom there was a damp smell and a large puddle. The coatroom had been a bomb shelter not long before. Someone, passing by, hit Monakhov's bookbag, and it fell into the puddle. By the time

Monakhov realized what had happened, the offender was already gone. Monakhov wiped off his bag, swallowed the insult, and was mentally flooring his opponent with one blow to the temple, when he heard:

"So okay, we'll take you along, Monk."

The insult vanished, and something within him leaped for joy. And then, a shadow—the thought of home and of that birthday. He remembered and stopped at the gate of the school. Those two went on ahead and also stopped, waiting...

"So, Monk, are you coming with us or not?"

And they, serious, presenting a solid front, turned away and set off. And again he was pushed aside, just as in the lunchroom, just as in the coatroom, just as ... he was always so unhappy because of that! Today was his first hope that all this might be ended. Tomorrow would be too late. And it all had to happen this way! Would it have hurt his father to have been born tomorrow...?

And they were walking on, getting farther away, and Monakhov no longer existed for them...

...Now they walked together, but he walked behind. Snow collected in his boots and melted there and the leg-ties of his father's long underwear came undone again and the laces, now grown heavy, fell below his boots. Monakhov stumbled, but he couldn't stop and retie them because he didn't want to and was even afraid to lag behind. There was still a catch in his throat from joy and excitement. They walked between uneven snowy piles of wreckage from which peeked broken brick, some plaster and splinters. The first boy turned and said:

"There was a house here and a vampire lived in it. Didn't you know?"

"No-o," drawled Monakhov, and began to peer through the bricks, but nothing was there except the bricks—red and grey.

"He drank blood," said the first boy.

Monakhov stepped on one of his laces, and it tore off.

They wriggled under barbed wire. On the other side was a garden. Here there was no debris, the snow was even, and old trees stood, sparse and separate. Monakhov had never even heard that a few steps from the school and its yard, behind the snowy piles, there was a garden, a neat snow-white garden with black trees. They had hardly gone any distance, but already you couldn't see the piles and the wire couldn't be seen either. All around stood the sparse trees, everything was white, both the snow and the sky, and the sky was two steps away, all around. There were no edges or boundaries anywhere, and it was very quiet. They quietly collapsed in the snow, the three of them, in a line. And steam quietly flew out from their mouths, just as white as the sky. It was warm and damp.

Then a round pond with a round island in the middle appeared before them. On the island, in a circle, coming right up to the water, stood the same trees. The ring of black water was broken by white blocks of ice. They found a pole there, and first the two boys, and then Monakhov, as if in a dream, stood on an ice block, one with the pole; they pushed off and floated toward the island. The ice block sank slightly under them, and their boots got completely wet. It seemed to Monakhov that they floated for a long time; actually they only pushed away once and were already standing on the other shore. And the island was an islet, and beyond the trees, in the center of the islet, was a hill. They walked around it, the hill was a hillock, and one boy climbed on top, and on the hill they discovered an opening, blocked by snow. They dug away the snow with their hands, hurrying and gasping for breath; their hands burned and reddened, so that when they stopped digging, Monakhov fancied that his hands were bloody and remembered the vampire, but it was only melted snow dripping from them. Beneath the snow a door appeared, but it was bolted shut, and on the bolt hung a large lock, and it was all rusted through. Their hands became rusty-red, but the lock didn't open. They covered the opening with snow and agreed to return tomorrow with a tool.

Beyond the pond, a snow-covered bare and level expanse opened out, and beyond that to the left was some large, stepped structure, also snow-bound.

"A stadium," said one boy.

"Bleachers," said the other.

All these things were completely unknown to Monakhov, and he was all eyes. They walked around the bleachers—the bleachers seemed as high as a two-story house. The whole rear wall was broken open and the boards were torn away in many places. Here again there appeared to be ruins and piles. There were incomprehensible tall wire fences side by side. They stood, rusty and torn, with large irregular holes from which the wire hung down like a rag. Where the wire was whole, a dead crow had gotten stuck in one of the loops.

"Cages," said Monakhov.

"Idiot, it's a tennis court," they said.

They wriggled through the gap and found themselves under the bleachers. It was dark and smelled mouldy.

"Quiet!" the first boy said in a loud whisper.

They went on for several steps bent over, almost crawling, although there was a lot of room. His heart pounding, Monakhov stole along immediately behind, lightly and noiselessly, vigilantly peering into the darkness, and suddenly ran into someone's stomach. He lifted his eyes—they were both standing up straight and watching him.

"Got any cigarettes?" the first asked loudly.

Monakhov also straightened up and felt in his pocket.

They smoked, hiding the embers in their fists. You could see snow in the chinks between the steps, and flat chunks of it lay on the ground under the steps of the bleachers. Right there was a mass of all sorts of lumber: a heap of sawdust, scraps of plywood and roofing. On the column directly in front of his nose was scratched, "Ninka, come at eight." Monakhov remembered the basement in his house, how they had sent him there for firewood and how he had stumbled upon...and then had backed away. "I'm sorry," he had said, "I'm sorry." The recollection was dreadful and sweet.

"Hey, come here!" he heard.

His heart jumped, and Monakhov ran towards the shout.

There stood the first boy, and before him, heaped in a large pile, lay gas masks.

For some time they stood silently, turned to stone.

"Look at all these slingshots!" said one boy excitedly, and then they fell upon the pile. They unpacked the cases and tried to pull the masks onto their heads. The rubber was grey, with large spots of mould. The masks were stuck together and tore with the effort of putting them on.

"Some slingshots..." said one boy. "They're rotten."

But here, deep in the pile, there were some better ones. True, they were broken in places, but they did stay on your head. When the first boy succeeded in getting one on, he was astonishing and strange to look at: a small grey elephant in a dark shed.

"A trunk, a trunk!" they shouted.

Then that creature in the gas mask began to jump about clumsily, spreading his arms. It was impossible even to look at him, he was so funny. But he got tired of jumping: the heavy canister dangled on its hose and hit against his legs. He sat down suddenly, as if he had fallen, and began to pull at the canister. Then the others found suitable masks, and also put them on. Now the first boy pointed in their direction with his finger and rocked back and forth where he sat. An absurd gurgling babble was audible from under his mask. He was laughing. And all of them, having taken off the canisters, jumped about, and their trunks swayed back and forth.

And now the first boy, having torn off his mask, all red, shouted,

"Elephants! We're elephants!"

And he began to whirl the hose around above his head. It made the air whistle.

And they all tore off their masks—and then it all ended: the gas masks lost their novelty. Lost their novelty, like the door on the island. But now, the first boy exclaimed,

"Let's slide!"

"How?" they asked.

"On the pillars!"

They walked along beneath the bleachers and soon discovered a stairway. After scrambling up it, they found themselves on a platform made of two planks. From here, at an angle, descended smooth round pillars. The first boy, deftly swinging his leg over, found himself astride a pillar. There he sat, hugging the pillar tightly with his hands and feet. Then he relaxed his grip slightly, and quickly and smoothly slid down to the very bottom. After him came the second boy.

Monakhov was the last. He looked down; something froze within him.

"Come on! Come on!" shouted the boys below. And the first one had already climbed the stairs, and here he was alongside.

"Are you chicken?"

There was no choice. Monakhov climbed over and clutched the pillar convulsively. He tried to find a better hold, and suddenly started sliding down. Faster, faster. And now that he was down, he cheered up. It turned out to be so simple! Something skipped within him. The others slid down, and he climbed up again first.

And now he'll slide down! Better than everyone. He boldly swung his leg over and sat on the log. And then he realized he was sitting wrong. His imbalance became greater and greater, he convulsively clutched the log, but he kept sliding down, sliding to one side. And then—one instant—and he is hanging by his hands, his legs are dangling—and he is flying.

He turned his leg under himself when he fell—it was very painful. But he started to cry out of anger that he had fallen, not because of the pain.

Up above, holding onto the pillar, the boys watched. He sat there, clasping his leg, and rocked—he was soothing his leg. He tried not to look at the boys—he was ashamed. They slid down.

"What's the matter?" the first one asked.

He wanted to jump up, to say "nothing, nothing serious." He jumped up—and almost cried out with pain.

"It—it hurts," was all he managed to say.

"Well, well," said the second boy.

"I told you we shouldn't take him with us," the first one said.

"Clod," said the second.

This was unbearable to listen to, and anyway the pain suddenly began to melt away.

"It's nothing," said Monakhov. He was ashamed, and he didn't look at his companions. Tears always betrayed him. Really, he never cried because of pain. Only because of an insult. It was as if not he himself was crying but someone inside of him.

Without looking at his companions, he turned and headed toward the stairs.

"He'll fall again," the first boy said.

"Naw," said Monakhov. "I won't fall now. Falling is silly."

Now everything went perfectly. He slid down and down, and felt a light sense of sinking within him, and before him slid the smooth, polished log, and the boys standing above grew farther away. He climbed and climbed up the stairway, and that was much longer than the instant of flight. So they slid, and at first he felt as if he were in a dream, and then as if his dream had become reality—now he was a flier, now an acrobat, and, finally, it became simply a boring task: there was nothing complicated, attractive, or dangerous about it anymore, and climbing up the stairs each time was boring. Besides, he was now beginning to feel pain in his leg while on the stairs, first weak and then stronger.

The thought that it was probably late already stirred within him, and the more boring the sliding became and the worse his leg hurt, the more urgently the thought of home hammered, the thought that his parents were alarmed and that it was Papa's birthday and that he hadn't done his homework and had soiled his coat—a feeling of guilt. And a sense of the unavoidability of paying the penalty for all this freedom—all these feelings grew. But he couldn't be the first to say that it was time to go back, both because he feared more ridicule and because he hated himself for all this, as if it were a weakness. He was afraid to reveal it. Then too, everything that had happened today was so great that he wanted to hold onto it, but that feeling was passing and melting. And the thought of home hammered even more painfully: poor Mama, and Papa who will be angry and yell and maybe hit him, and then he'd begin to cry because of it.

And his leg hurt quite badly. But the boys seemed not to notice, and he, in despair, kept climbing the stairs and sliding down and down, silently now.

But the boys too were no longer excited, and were quiet.

And suddenly the first one said, as if with a great effort,

"Well, that's enough."

They all immediately came to life and began to talk, and again everything seemed extraordinary and joyful...

When they got out from under the bleachers, they saw that it had become very dark. White became grey and thickened before their eyes. They were struck by it all: the late hour, hunger, and exhaustion, and their soaking wet feet were freezing cold.

Now Monakhov saw that his companions had become as uneasy as he was. That encouraged him. They started off, but not along the same path by which they had come from school; they headed around the bleachers, toward a building showing white in the distance. There, so the first boy said, was a street, and it was easy to get anywhere you wanted from there.

"And how do I get to Apothecary?" Monakhov asked.

"Idiot, we'll come out on Apothecary," said the first boy.

"We have a trudge ahead of us, but you can go straight home," the second boy said irritably.

"Doesn't even know where his own street is!" said the first one. "Incredible!"

They went on ahead, while Monakhov limped along behind. Though at first walking had still been no problem—the pain was only aching, melting—it had now become very severe. He tried not to step on the sore leg, but that didn't work at all. He was even surprised that there was no way to walk with only one, healthy, leg. A step with one leg—and again with that one. It was really so strange: one leg forward and the other forward—that's two steps already.... But what if you take one step and one step...?... Everything was confused somehow. He simply couldn't understand why he couldn't manage to walk with one leg. Suddenly it seemed to work out. But that wasn't it either.

The Leg

He dragged the sore one up, and took a step with the healthy one. That wasn't it, but it was easier that way. He walked that way for a while, until that became just as painful, until he was again pondering how to walk with one leg. He suddenly became confused about how he had to walk, foolishly switched feet, as if wanting to get into step with someone—and took a full step with his bad leg.

When he came to himself, he was standing near the white house that he had seen in the distance back at the bleachers. It was completely dark, and the boys were nowhere around. Nothing seemed to hurt. He stood on one leg. He had to take a step, and it really didn't hurt, but he was afraid to take a step. He simply couldn't believe that he could do it. It was as if he didn't know how to do it. He was about to try to transfer weight to the injured leg, and all the pain returned. It was as though everything became brighter, it was so painful. How, how, he wondered and suddenly realized that he was alone. Where were they? After all, they couldn't...? "Hey! Hey!" he shouted, and was surprised himself at how plaintively that came out. "Kids! Listen!" he shouted, as boldly as possible, even cheerfully.

Two figures floated out of the darkness. First one boy, then the second.... The first one had an arrogant, evil expression.

"Well, now what? Are you whining?" he said.

"Kids," Monakhov said, and it seemed to him that he spoke surprisingly simply and gallantly, "My leg's got something sort of..."

"Crybaby, crybaby," said the first boy. "Cry for me again, little crybaby..."

The second boy had a complaining expression.

"It's late already," he suddenly whined. "All because of you..."

"We give up on you," said the first one. "We would have been home long ago." And he whispered something in the other boy's ear.

"Well, are you just going to stand there? We don't intend to wait for you."

"I'm coming, I'm coming. I'll come right away," said Monakhov. "Only don't go away..."

Well then, leg.... So, let's walk. Now, please, he thought. And suddenly he took a step. Things went dark, but that passed quickly. And he took another step.

"Come on, come on," the first one turned around.

Leg, what's it to you? After all, there is only a little way left. Don't let me down. Think what the boys'll think.... Well then!

So he walked along with one leg, dragging the bad one behind him. Now the boys went off ahead and disappeared, now he saw them right in front of him, waiting, shifting back and forth. When he came close to them, the first one said something to him.

"Well, can't you walk any slower?"

The second boy's teeth were chattering, and he whined,

"I'm fr-frozen... I'll catch it..."

And they went off ahead again.

When he saw them again ahead of him, it was at an archway. Two large stone posts stood on the two sides, and it was light there. A strange light hung under the archway, and was swinging slightly. The deserted street lay ahead, with only every other light on it burning.

"There," said the first boy.

"You're already home, and we still have a lo-o-ong way to go-o-o," said the second one, and his complaining "o-o-o" seemed endless.

Monakhov realized that he would be left alone.

"But how do I get to my street?" he asked, trying to be as calm as possible.

"But this *is* your street," the first boy said.

"Mine...?"

"Oh, hell!... Yours, whose else? Apothecary!"

"Yes..." said Monakhov. "And my house?"

"There," he waved his hand, "You head that way..." This he said faintly and unclearly, and added something more, by now completely unintelligible.

They were gone. They crossed the street—and were gone.

Monakhov turned around and was surprised: the white house was two steps away. He looked at the street: was it Apothecary Prospect? He didn't recognize it. The name seemed strange to him. Why Apothecary? There were no drug-stores on it. Maybe because it was on Apothecary Island? But then why is the island called Apothecary!... True, it really did smell like medicine there. But how come?... On that side the houses were dark, their windows were not lit. Above the street lights the houses already blended with the night. On his side, there was a high lattice with cabbages which stretched into the distance and did not end, as far as he could see.

He even felt relieved when the boys left. Now he wasn't dependent on anyone. He knew the road home, and it wasn't far now. He'll get there by himself easily. And it's still not that late. He'll say he was delayed in school. They won't be angry for long, because of the guests. And, of course, he won't show anything. No one will even notice that there is anything wrong with his leg. They'll send him to bed, and he'll go right away. And lie down. He will lie in his bed. It will be comfy and soft. He'll look at the design of the wallpaper. And then he will fall asleep. And in his sleep, as always, it will all pass. And tomorrow he'll come home right after school—no one will even remember.

Suddenly he realized that, as before, he was standing still. "What am I doing?" he said to himself. "My mind wandered. I'll never get there that way. I would have been home long ago. What am I doing!"

And again he caught himself standing still. He had been scolding himself for a long time, and was standing still.

"Well, let's go... Well, come on, leg. We'll do this together. I will go—and you will go. I beg you..."

The Leg

The first step almost made him faint, but then, since he was already near the white building, everything cleared up and it was almost possible to walk. In any case, holding on to the lattice, he took step after step.

Good work, leg! You're my very good leg. You're an amazingly wonderful, dear, leg. You walk along with me. You don't stop, even though it hurts you very much. Thank you, leg.

The pain began to increase, but by now he understood that he must not stop. And actually, the pain seemed to stop growing. It remained the same.

Dear, wonderful, excellent leg. Why do you hurt so much? Are you doing it on purpose? Does it hurt you too, not only me? Don't you understand that today is Papa's birthday, and we absolutely must get home... We're late as it is. Do you want to disappoint Papa on his birthday? I don't believe you, you're pretending to be naughty... Don't you want to congratulate him? He's always been so good to you. You shouldn't be so ungrateful. And I too have always been with you; I never abandoned you. But you? How do you respond to all this! How are you behaving today? I don't recognize you. Are you my leg? You belong to someone else, you're not my leg. I never had such a lousy leg. You are a rotten, stinking leg, and what you have done with my good leg! You envied it, and poisoned it, and then burned it in the oven, because you were afraid of me. But I found you.... See how I move you along the lattice—just drop dead!

> A crooked, crooked leg
> Wanted a drink from a keg
> A keg among the vats
> Covered with crummy rats

A crummy rat—that's who you are, you're not my leg at all. Just wait 'til I drag you home... Do you know what will happen to you? It would be better for you to reform yourself. After all, you need to, not me. Later you will thank me yourself. Be good, my dear, beloved leg... Just don't hurt, just, please, don't hurt! Look, if you want, I'll get on my knees. Just don't hurt... I'll give you three palaces—silver, gold, and diamond... I'll give them all to you. There you will be fed with the finest dishes and wines. Isn't all that enough for you?... Wonderful leg, you are the smartest and strongest leg in the world, everyone is afraid of you, can you really not pity me, your little pitiful slave? I was rude to you, I am very guilty toward you. Oh forgive me, please, my most great and exalted leg! I'll never do it again. You are a huge leg: you are bigger than that house. You hurt so much, you are so big. Is it really so difficult for you to endure a little bit? Look at how far you've already gone! There is just a little bit left now, and you are behaving so badly.

Understand, I'm not asking for myself, after all, if it weren't Papa's birthday, would I really have pestered you so? I've really never asked much of you. And I fed you, gave you drink, provided you with shoes. Are you really so ungrateful, my beloved leg, that you won't do me this small favor? Which, after all, is not even for me, but for my poor old parents, for whom I am the last support... They will die without me, weak and alone. Aren't you sorry, and will you allow them to perish? You really have a good heart; you're only pretending that you're wicked, but in reality you're very good, my leg. It's only someone who doesn't know you who would think that you're wicked and heartless. After all, I know you well... Do you agree? Only pride prevents you from admitting it... Don't hurt, my own dear little leg. For God's sake and for Christ's sake... Excuse me, I really didn't want to insult you then. Well, go on, go on. Here, you see, I already recognize our street. There, you see, our house... It's quite near. It's just that I never went this way and therefore didn't recognize the street before. But now I recognize it. Do you recognize it, leg? Just an absolute trifle left for us to go. So you'll get there, it won't cost you anything to do me this favor... I wouldn't have asked you, but after all, there is no one who could do that besides you. There are the factories, and over there the institute; no one is there in the evening. Therefore, you help me today, leg. After all, you won't betray me, like those... We will punish them tomorrow. They will beg, crawl on their knees—but they will get no mercy. We'll say to them: what right have you to beg, you have no conscience... You are to be punished, and only punished.

You see, leg, it is better for you to walk, not to hurt. Do you think it doesn't bother me to plead and beg? Just be aware that my patience too might run out. And then watch out! If you betray me, I'll find you all the same. And no matter how much you beg me, I will be pitiless. Because I hate you, leg! I am ready to tear you up with my teeth, to gnaw you, to trample you, to cut you to pieces, to grind you into a fine powder! I'll put you into a mortar and I'll pound you with a pestle. So that it would be painful, painful, terrifyingly painful, impossibly painful... Leg, my fine leg, my beloved, the most beloved of my legs, look, there is the house...

Only the yard and the stairs left for us to go... Now be good, let me get there like a man. ....
....
....
....
....

...He stood in his own front entryway, leaning against the wall. The light bulb there was unscrewed, and it was dark. Some light made its way down from the second-floor landing. His floor was the third. By now he was unable to go up. When he came into the entryway and realized that he was already home, walking became impossible. He cried quietly and rubbed his back against the wall. It was probably very late already, because no one was on the staircase.

Suddenly the outer door slammed, he shuddered, the second door opened—and he recognized the dark figure as his father.

He flattened himself against the wall. In the darkness he wasn't visible, and his father went on past without noticing him. His father slowly dragged himself up the stairs, and his lean back was bent like a wheel. "Papa!" the boy wanted to call out, but he didn't call out. And then a sharp self-pity and a certain piercing and pitying feeling for his father appeared in him. "Papa! Papa!" he wanted to call out and run to him. But he couldn't run. Or call out. And his father kept climbing, slowly, slowly, and suddenly he stopped in the middle of the flight. And he stood there, stoop-shouldered, without turning around or going ahead, for a long time. The light from the second floor illuminated him well now. His father took out a cigarette, struck a match, lowered his head to his palms. He turned and began to descend. He descended and stopped, looking in the boy's direction and not seeing him. The boy shrank. Now, for some reason, he remembered nothing but the ear-phones with which his father had hit him the day before yesterday. That was when be was learning to calculate on the abacus...His father was standing, was looking in his direction, and his face wasn't visible—only his lowered shoulders.

"Who's there?" his father said weakly.

The boy burst into tears.

"You?" said his father, somehow surprisingly calmly. "I have been looking for you."

He came directly up to the boy and suddenly screamed:

"Good-for-nothing!"

Somewhat uncertainly and awkwardly, with a lurch, he slapped the boy's face. His hand dropped immediately and his lips began to tremble.

"You could at least have thought of your mother! Okay, fine, you don't love me...I know...although on my birthday...But your mother!...Did you really...?" he stopped short and looked at the boy with fright.

The boy shielded himself with his elbow and began to sob harder.

"What's the matter with you? Talk! What have you done to yourself?"

"My l-leg..." was all the boy could say between sobs.

His father carried him up the stairs and opened the door. All this went on in a fog. Mama too. The only thing he felt clearly was the touch of his mother's hands and the coolness of the sheets.

Later a puffy man in a white smock leaned over him and did something with his leg, wound something around it. It was very painful—and then he felt on his forehead, the weak, pitiful, slightly trembling touch of his father's hand. He seized this hand—it was hot and dry, with swollen joints on the fingers—and pressed it to his cheek.

"Don't be angry, Papa..." he sobbed. "I did my homework. Honest, Papa..."

His father's lips began to tremble, and he turned away.

"Doctor," his father said. "What is it, doctor...?"

1962

The Idler

The boss said to me:

"No, Alyosha, this won't work. It won't do. I don't understand, Alyosha, what's on your mind? You give the impression of such a solid man, but how do you stand up to a test? That's how. Is the trial period ending? It is. And when it's over—what then? Phooey? (That's his way of joking.) So then, listen to me carefully..."

He's quite right about that. I do make this impression. I make very different impressions. That of a solid man too. I can't exactly see what I'm really like. Let's take a mirror, for example. After all, it's in front of a mirror that we understand how people see us. That's why we look at ourselves. But I rarely recognize myself in the mirror. Sometimes I stand before it, tall and slim, and my face is handsome, taut, the features—classical and sharp. Sometimes it's an impossibly fat pancake—you can't even tell whether there are features on it. And my face isn't simply wide, but boundless at times, and then I myself am short and fat. For some time I thought it was only I who was confused by that and that others saw me objectively, with such and such definite features belonging to me alone. Apparently not. The boss once said to me: "Excuse me, but what is the matter with you? Look how tall you are! Are you on stilts or something? You always used to be a shortie, didn't you?" At that point he had already known me for a month and saw me every day. Then, as it happened, I noticed this in everyone. I hadn't noticed and hadn't noticed—and then suddenly I noticed it. In everyone and everywhere. And not only that different people see me differently—but every one of them, individually, even my best friend. And there is one thing about me, it simply terrifies me. It's my ears. They are never noticed right away. But your every acquaintance will inevitably notice them sometime. It takes everyone a different amount of time. Some don't notice them for a very long time. And that's frightening. Just imagine that there is some large gathering where you want to make some sort of a favorable impression—and suddenly your friend, while talking to you perhaps about something quite serious, freezes in the middle of a word, looks at you with amazed eyes, his face becomes unrecognizable and he bursts out laughing. And only in the rare intervals when he, all red, attempts to inhale or exhale, you hear the whistling: "Ear-rss... Look at his ear-rs!" And then everyone freezes, everyone has amazed faces and they all hiss: "Ear-rs! Ear-rss!" And one fellow even said: "Hey, is your other one like that, too?" and took a look at the other side. So that we never see anything right away and we see everything in different ways. And it goes without saying that people are all different people. To say nothing of the different traits of character I see in my face when looking in the mirror. Here it is, strong-willed and tender, the face of Jack London. And here is the fanatical, burned out—all eyes—face of an Indian fakir. Here is the face of the champion, Yury Vlasov. Here is the face of Prince Myshkin. And here is a weak, dirty face with traces of depravity, the face of a man capable of any baseness. There are of course some objective traits, or, to be exact, those of the police files: eyes—hazel, hair—light brown, lips—thick. But then, who knows, maybe this isn't exact, either.

"Do you understand everything now?" says the boss. "Then do it all over again, as I said. Otherwise the devil knows what, Alyosha. Now, then, do you understand everything?"

Do I understand what? What am I supposed to do over? What was this hateful man talking to me about?

...I get up, take a bottle of ink, approach, all my movements are slowed down and merciless, I approach and pour out the bottle of ink on his bald spot. Well, do you understand?...

I am sitting next to him, I look at him with clear eyes and nod.

...I get up, reach slowly into my pocket, my piercing grey eyes squinting slightly. I keep shifting from toe to heel, and back from heel to toe. I slowly pull my hand out of my pocket, and there's a lemon-shaped grenade in my fist. "You see this?" I say and raise the grenade to his bluish nose. "And if I open my fist," I say, "neither you, nor this damn office will be here..."

I am sitting next to him, I look at him with clear eyes and nod.

...I get up, looking at him with my green, hate-filled eyes and throw the whole truth in his face. My voice trembles slightly from indignation. I am not like this, I say, he will not get this out of me. I will remain a human being, and if you're hoping to get some such thing out of me, take this!

"I see, I see," the boss says with a special, approvingly kind voice. "I can tell from your eyes that you understand."

What did he understand? What did he understand from my eyes? What am I supposed to do with all this in the end? From today on I shall dedicate myself...to what? I will not sleep for four nights and I will invent a new machine, which, all by itself, will remove all the boring corrections I'm supposed to make, but what corrections—I didn't even hear. Then I will denounce this boss, I will open everyone's eyes. I will treat people thoughtfully and nobly in his place. Then in three years, by titanic labor during sleepless nights, I will finish all the institutions I did not finish. I will get a doctorate, skipping the master's. I will become the director of a major scientific research institute. A completely new branch of science! And here I am in five years, a full professor, skipping the associate. Then I will remember the wretched boss, who will have completely sunken to the bottom, wallowing in drunkenness and debauchery. Nobly I will extend my hand to him and extricate him. And then we will work side by side...Never! For this I'll go without sleep for long sleepless nights? And won't live? Won't know simple human joys? O-o-oh, no. In order to become like you, even if more important? I won't do anything of the sort. I will not go without sleep for long sleepless nights!

"Are you figuring out how to start?"

How stealthily he sneaks up! Only scoundrels can have such an inaudible step. Just like... Why are you breaking into my world? Leave me alone at least for a moment! Constantly—you must, you must... And you may? Is there "You may?"

"Yes, I'm thinking."

"Don't think. Just start and think later."

"Oh?" I say in a dumb voice. "You think it's better that way?"

"A tested method," he says.

"Then, with a tested method?" I say.

"Yes. yes," he says angrily for some reason and leaves.

To hell with you! I can't stand the sight of you even after one month, and what happens later? The trial period will be over, I won't make it—thank God, anyway. At least I won't be seeing you. And when they fire me, I will become invisible. Invisible, I will go through your whole bureau of passes without a pass. At last no one will be checking me against a document—is that me? This time it really will be me, and I will go through, myself, freely. I'll go through, open all the safes, burn all the personal files, take all the strictly secret papers into the accounting office, put the accounting books in the secret safes, I will call the boss to the director, and the director to the management, then I'll go to the radio station and play the gayest records and will announce public dances...

Almost missed my turn for a good job again. Moving cabinets from the third floor to the first. Last time I was daydreaming and missed out, and once you miss out—that's it (for jobs like this we have a line a week ahead). So then I had to squirm at the instruction period for a whole hour. I get convulsions if the boss talks more than a minute. And then he chose me as his focus in the audience. I have this disgusting manner of listening attentively, looking as if I were. And if, as most often happens, I don't understand anything, then some devious force prompts me to nod "yes" and to stare with an even more penetrating gaze. Any speaker spots me in the auditorium immediately. And then try to turn off when he keeps staring at you all the time and you have already been nodding for half an hour, and your whole figure is one big understanding. And questions are expected precisely from me. It's all quite disgusting.

Thank God, I didn't miss the cabinets. Just think, what a joy—carrying cabinets...But it is a joy. There is something human in it. We carry the cabinets, it's both difficult and fun, and there is that chance of breaking one of them. "JUNK"—Jobs Urgent Necessary Klassified—"JUNK" our brave doctoral candidates joke in unison, happening into the corridor. It's really scary, too—something human appears only when there is JUNK, but ideally, even this shouldn't happen, right? But it really is JUNK. Why, one might ask, do we take out of the cabinets those fat folders which have been gathering dust for three years and stack them (neatly, don't mix them up!) in the corridor, bend ourselves double under the cabinets on the stairway and downstairs again stuff these cabinets, meaningful in their emptiness, with some bulging dusty junk. The folders themselves are not too bad, but what really amazes me, what seems mystical and simply does not fit into my brain are the looseleaf notebooks. LOOSELEAF... What a word! How people could think up something like that I don't understand. You have to invent it. The wheel, the flint—I understand—that's brilliant. But a looseleaf—it's some kind of a horror, a perversity of the brain! There's also the hole-puncher. Also a hellish invention. HOLE-PUNCHER, SOLE-MUNCHER... There is even a special little fork for picking out staples! Just recently one of our workers made a labor-saving proposal: in a prominent place, where the office corridors cross, make a box with cubbie holes for each department so that it won't be necessary for somebody there to sort some junk. And what's there to sort? ... To sort, yet!... The box was set up, the worker received a letter of thanks, a twenty-five ruble bonus, he was encouraged, so to speak, and satisfied and is now pondering some sort of atomic box. He wants to centralize all boxes. And so on. And I keep wanting to stick some piece of crap into this box, or to mix everything up, to switch things from one cubbie to another. However, were the boss to offer me a distraction, like punching holes with a hole-puncher in his stupid papers—that I'd do with great pleasure. It's absurd, of course, but still, some little white circles do fall out... Or, just recently some fellow brought an American stapler to the office. It's embarrassing, of course, but it provided amusement for a week: everything possible was stapled. You push—it's stapled, push—stapled. An atomic hole-puncher! And of course, the contemporary look, the stainless shines and there is all that American writing on it. We even brought some papers from home, took them through this damn bureau of passes, in order to staple them. Why? What for? Then this, too, was over, and the boss got excited and solicited the little machine for himself: the owner gave it away out of toadyism. Now he locks himself up in his office and plays. He doesn't have such a good time either... There is also the mania for giants: paper-clip giants, inkwell-cathedrals and thumbtacks the size of a half-dollar. The hierarchy of inkwells and sundry office luxuries is also interesting. Maybe you've got a runner to sign, so you can observe all this. There is the director inkwell, can you imagine, even the director's facial expression is the same! There is also the assistant inkwell. It seems that there is almost no difference between them—it, too, is luxurious, but still it's an assistant. And so on, and so forth, lower and lower. It's probably quite difficult for industry to manage such great variety, in order to provide an inkwell for everyone according to rank. But that there even is such an industry, that's what's so terrible! There is also the boss-inkwell, which I hate most. There is nothing worse than the middle rank inkwells! The whole horror of rabble-inkwells and boyar-inkwells is combined in it. But what's the use of talking! Even the recreation corner has its own recreation-inkwell... But there is still something good in all this crap, and the good is in how terribly exactly the crap is expressed, without any doubts. Just start moving cabinets and you will feel joy. But why?

The cabinets helped. There wasn't even any of that most terrible agony of the last quarter of an hour before the end of work. This quarter-of-an-hour is probably the same as slow roasting. But there wasn't any of that: simply, the bell rang.

That's how low man is! Only after loathing can he feel joy. I did have happy times, after all, but I didn't feel anything special at the time, didn't appreciate, didn't understand. There were, for example, the summer vacations from school. I keep remembering childhood more often, and get so sad. And it isn't that it was all rosy, or that I myself was all pure and good, and that now I am filthy and repulsive, it's not the innocence that's the point. I was alive, to the last tiny cell! But now, even if I am alive, it's only in moments, between something shameful and something loathsome. That's it, isn't it? Maybe it is the innocence, after all...?

And so I've been given a joy: leaving work. It's touching how everyone starts preparing so as to be completely ready when the bell rings. How everyone collects and puts away their office supplies, and the girls begin to put on make-up, and some of them who are going out somewhere today even put on their hair curlers and then a kerchief on top of that, and their heads under the kerchief seem angular. How strange it is when it's an eve of a holiday and all, but all the girls on the bus have these angular heads, even the conductress! And then I love all of them at once. And they're riding to work. And there is so much readiness for the holiday in them that how can one not understand that they are going some place wrong to do some unnecessary work. And what for? Even a child knows that. In order to "eat." This I know from school: "The workers labor from six in the morning, the farmers give you food, and you haven't done your homework again..."

And here's everyone all ready and dressed and buttoned up. And something sinks inside me already—and here's the bell. And I run down the staircase, flying past the watchman, faster, and my heart beats faster, and I grab the handle of the heavy door and squeeze myself out, and run, run as if it were New Year's and the summer vacation, as if I were a child again and as if all the holidays had fallen at once. I get out. No matter what the weather is, it is always beautiful, and the first breath—a joy. I am newborn, strong, as if there had not been a working day and you have just awakened having slept the night badly for some reason, but somehow you woke up fresh and not tired, and the day has just started. And there's also the blue sky and the sun and the dirty snow covered with the fresh, so light and white that its surface is barely perceptible. The red tram with a white roof goes around the bend by the office, screeching. I have to go through the square where there is a lot more snow, and white trees, and red, green and blue children digging, and all this red, blue, green—it's all covered with snow and alive. And the old ladies sit quietly on benches and it's quiet everywhere, although the tram screeches nearby going past our office, but it's quiet anyway because quiet is not at all the absence of sounds. And in front, in this same square, there stands a forsaken church and its cupola is so blue it dissolves in the sky.

And here is the black canal. I cross it and find myself on a main street. There are a lot of people here and for a while yet until the bustle affects me, I can walk along and look at the faces. Many people walk past me and I understand something about some of them, and they stop being strangers—and they pass by, they recede. Here you gain and lose easily and suddenly—that touch of an unknown life. Something isn't right here. Especially if it's girls. Then you feel the loss more sharply: a whole world—a look—and always passing by. It's so obvious why they have that look, and clothes, and walk, and it's so close—just stretch out a hand, and so complicated, so difficult to touch. And I imagine: in a rough transparent stone there are narrow canals cut out for everyone. Everyone has a lonely and merciless path, and one can only look with sadness and regret at another one-person passing on the other side of a transparent wall, also looking at you with sadness and regret, and we don't even stop, neither you nor she, we don't knock on the wall, and don't write on it with our fingers, and don't make signs—we pass by, and there is so much bitter experience of the impossible in this. One-person plus one-person—equals two one-persons. Especially if it's a woman...Especially if it's friends...Especially if it's children...Especially if it's old men...

Today is the old man's birthday. I must buy him something delicious. I go into the store and I buy chocolate-covered candies. Half a kilo. I go back. I see a girl—pretty, very pretty...

..."Here you are," I say and hand her a candy. She smiles and accepts. Such a good smile—that neither a thank you or anything else is needed. So I walk on and present each woman with one. As I walked I gave away the half-kilo. Didn't even have enough. And everyone smiled at me with singular, uncontrolled smiles. And I am happy, I don't even need anything else. That is, I need... But it's embarrassing really to give someone a candy and then make a pass. What is really nice—is to go by. It's beautiful. The smile, it's yours. And if you try to make a pass—then what? For the candy, or what? It's embarrassing.

But I walk on, and I keep thinking about giving out the candies, but I don't really do it. If I give them all away—what will be left for the old man? I don't eat them myself, either. Giving them away, of course, is more pleasant than eating them. I would even give them all away, but what if, I thought, that pretty one who might smile at me so wonderfully suddenly turns away her cute little face, all crooked and squeamish, and goes around me, and I just stand there with my candy in my hand and a ridiculous smile... Stupid! I wasn't going to make a pass at you. Stu-pid!... But still, it's true: a guy like that would give you a candy, and then keep bugging you and bugging you, as if it weren't a candy but Notre Dame Cathedral. The pretty ones, they do have this kind of experience. So you can't give them one... The men, those fools, have long ago spoiled my pleasure...

But there is still a way out! It turned out to be so simple! I kept walking and walking—and suddenly began to fly. Immediately higher than the houses. I am looking at everything from above and the flaps of my coat are flying. A beautiful woman was walking towards me simply. She kept walking and walked past me. She didn't even notice. And here I am flying. The flaps of my coat are flying and the wind is blowing my hair. I see the woman and dive down. When almost near the ground, I spread the flaps and land. And stand up right in front of the woman. "Where'd you come from?" she says with surprise. "From there," I answer and point upward. "Would you like to fly together?" "I would," she says. And we fly, holding hands. Wind, space, freedom!

But I am walking down the street, the woman had long since walked past me, I am walking along, and thinking that you might even freeze up there...

In the evening we go to the old man's. To my mother's father. My parents keep grooming and cleaning themselves with care and agitation. Mama is mad at Papa because, apparently, he had long ago eaten the jar of preserves which Mama was saving for the old man. Papa is mad at Mama because he, having eaten the preserves, managed to forget about it, but Mama brought it all to light and now Papa is embarrassed. I have been ready for a long while now and am wandering about aimlessly, bumping into my agitated parents. They yell at me a little and this way make up with each other. And the thought suddenly strikes me that they too are old. I look at them, at how nervous and agitated they are and how they want not to be late and how they will probably be ready an hour before leaving—and I suddenly feel like crying. God, what wouldn't I do to make them happy and satisfied. To make them not die, not die, not die! And how little they need... And I keep wandering about aimlessly and don't give them any peace. But I would finish a hundred colleges for you! I would become an engineer a hundred times. I would give you my word now, my word of honor, that, finally you will not have to worry about your son any more, but I have given you so many already... "Alyosha dear, we don't insist, we don't need it, we simply want you to be happy..." They, my old folks, are sure that they know how I am to be happy. Forgive me... We all want happiness for one another and forget about our own. And I think I see the transparent stone again, in which canals are carved for one-persons.

And our whole family is going to visit the old man. It's actually quite close. The old man's house is right opposite. From one entrance to the other, you just have to cross the street. But it so happens that there is no crossing here. It's fifty meters to the crossing and then fifty more. That too isn't far, really. But we always cross directly from entrance to entrance. It's a shame to have to go around. There's really no need to go around. But in the middle of the street there is often a policeman walking along the line. One doesn't feel like paying a fine, either. If there is no policeman—we cross. So we are crossing this time, and we are practically in the entrance already when I hear a whistle. It probably isn't even for us. And what if it is for us and the policeman noticed which entrance we went in?

...We are walking through the courtyard, it's a rather long one, and he is already coming in the entrance. He sees our backs. He takes big strides to overtake us. I really feel like turning around but I don't. We are already near the old man's door. He catches up with us here: "Citizen!... One, two, three...," he counts us, bending his fingers over. "Three rubles, if you please."

Here I turn and look at the policeman with such a heavy look..."Go away, go away," I say. He turns all limp. "Right away, right away," he says and leaves, downcast. He walks like a lunatic. Everyone is amazed. "Alyosha, dear! How did you do that?" exclaims everyone. "What do you mean...What are you talking about?" I make a puzzled face. "Nothing happened," I say. And everyone agrees immediately. I joke with ease and eveyone laughs at my joke. And I alone know who I really am...

Then we all shout, throw out our arms and kiss the old man. He is so solemn, so solicitous, the table is laid with such care, that I feel like crying again. Devil knows what's happening to me! I don't remember crying ever, not even once. Absentmindedly, I hand my candies to him, he embraces me with his light arms, not exactly laughing and not exactly sniffling on my lapel. "Excellent student, draughtsman," he says to me proudly, inaudibly, almost shyly, patting my shoulder. And Papa nods to him. And Mama nods. We go to the table and the old man, giggling, with a mysterious face and the motions of a magician extracts a bottle of brandy from Gods knows where. The brandy he always makes himself, and this is his pride. He himself can't have any, he only remembers what it used to be like. Papa can't have any either. The same, of course, goes for mother. The brandy is meant for me. The old man keeps slipping things onto my plate and watches me eat in rapture. But again I cannot, I cannot look at the trembling hands, light like dried petals... So that I am even ashamed of my incomprehensible sensitiveness. And it seems to me that his hands live their own life, and that no matter how the old man tries to be sprightly and lively, disregarding his age, his hands give him away... They live cautiously, quietly, carefully and there is in this an ineffable sort of beauty and deftness, the deftness with which he masters his trembling and feeble hands. And I understand that I love those hands madly. It is not for nothing that the old man is proud of his brandy. It really is fire. And it quickly makes its way to the head. "Just don't drink too much," says my father. And I see Papa's hands and Mama's hands—these hands will drive me mad! And I understand that my intentions to remain sober are lost and that I will drink all of this brandy. Mama is throwing reproachful glances at me but I am already raising my hand drunkedly: everything will be all right, don't worry. As for the old man and Papa, for probably forty years now that bit of formality which arose when the old man was against my mother's marriage has not disappeared from their conversation. It has all been smoothed over and forgotten, they are attached to each other, but this manner is probably still even dear to them. They talk about the cosmos and about the giant radio tower which is being built in our city and which will be 500 meters high. The old man is ecstatic and tells about the popular science articles which are his great hobby. Everyone is nuts about progress, even my dear old man. Except for my mother. It is all the same to her; she is wiser sometimes, and they—they are children. This is what remains of their masculinity. And I am now completely drunk. And the old man is so glad and so happy. That we came. He loves us. We are all he has. We love him. He is all we have. And these are all the other words which are the essence and which he does not say. What he does say is that take the nitrogen bomb, for example—not only the atomic bomb, but the hydrogen bomb is like gunpowder next to it. He seems to be saying this with terror. But it suddenly seems to me that this terror of his is feigned and that, actually, he even admires it. That a bomb like that will fall—and all that's alive will perish, but that even the windowpanes in houses will remain intact. And no contagion—come in, help yourself. "That's what's so terrifying," I say, "it would be better if nothing remained." And the old man—his eyes round—nods and doesn't understand. "You don't understand anything," I say. "But I've been through three wars," he says. "So you don't understand," I say. "And that's not all," says Papa, "furthermore," he says, "but this is secret," Papa says, "other elements have been found beyond the hundredth...!" So they, these elements, according to what Papa says, have exhibited such amazing explosive capacity that take a bomb the size of a walnut—and a continent's gone. Suppose some journalist brings it in in his pocket, drops it somewhere—and that's it. And rockets aren't necessary... "Aren't necessary?" I say. "Aren't necessary," Papa says. "But in general—are they necessary?" I say. "You puppy," Papa says, "I've been through the whole war." "So that's why you don't understand," I say. "Puppy!" Papa says. "And that's not all," says the old man, "if there were some anti-matter from the anti-world—then one pin head would suffice for the whole planet." "And I was told," I say, "of course this was in America... in one of the secret places there were five submarines, side by side. And on one of them a sailor was sent above to shovel the snow. But he refused categorically. Then they sent another one. It's his—the other's—brother, who was telling me. So he shovels, and under him, on the boat, a fire had started and just couldn't be stopped. And the commander isn't there—he's on shore. And the fellow upstairs still does not know anything (he is shovelling snow), but he just feels: there is something heating up under his feet—but he pays no attention to it. And suddenly, there's this ga-asp! The boat blew up. And everybody else with it, and the fellow who was shovelling was thrown up in the air and flew off a few kilometers—and straight into a pile of snow. And the captain was walking along the shore at this time and was just then passing a street light. His forehead bumped into the pole—and he fell dead on the spot. And there were no survivors. Only the one in the snow pile—he remained..." "What's this for?" asked Papa, surprised. "Just like that," I said, "and then," I said, "when this whole thing blew up, all the torpedoes scattered in all directions. So they hunted for them for God knows how long after that to catch them all..."

"You don't know how to drink," said Papa.

I sleep badly from the brandy. I am being chased, I run and for some reason barely move my feet. I scream and only open my mouth, then I am chasing someone, and there's some incomprehensible war, the Mongol invasion, they are riding around town on motorcycles, with lances balanced—horsemen!—and they break into our apartment, and leading them is the boss who is screaming that I made a mistake in counting the lances and it's no good, and he throws the lance into my chest, and I don't feel anything, only it breaks in half, and then I suddenly feel cool, many hands are stroking me at once, and I recognize my old folks' hands... Towards morning deep sleep takes over, and I am barely able to get up, and then only thanks to Mama. I force myself to have breakfast in order not to hurt her. And I already have to run, I am late, but I don't feel like either running or rushing. Mama is already worried about everything not being all right at my job, Alyosha dear, don't be angry, I just thought... you understand Papa and I want you to get everything in order, you know... O.K., I won't, I won't... And I begin to feel absolutely black, because Mama always senses so perfectly when something isn't all right with me. And because she is right as always, I especially feel like getting angry and protesting and proving that they don't understand anything and that I—will do it myself. In the past I was amazed how the old folks sense everything that has not even happened to me yet, even if I give them no clue and everything is covered up. And I rebelled against the logic of this presentiment. Now, though, I understand that this is love, but that doesn't make it easier, but a hundred times harder. And all that maturity of mine consists in my starting to feel responsibility, but I still can't manage it.

I get angry, I say that everything is all right, and I go to work. It's already unlikely that I won't be late. I have to run as fast as I can, and get there on time, get there on time. And I barely move my feet. Our office is exemplary, and no one is ever late. It's frightening to see how, at the last moment, old men burst into the entrance hall, running, breathing heavily, and with maniacal faces. The management invented a horrible way to fight tardiness. Not punishment, no. This would have been human, however cruel. Once a month, and on an unannounced day, all the management lines up in the entrance hall. The director, the secretary of the Party committee, and the department heads too. They arrive and form a row on each side one minute before the bell rings. They stand with immobile, mournful faces, like an honor guard. And the latecomer, passing by them, lowering his head, almost disappearing, so that you actually see how much a person diminishes, runs through, but actually drags through, slowly, painfully slowly. And in fact, we don't have latecomers.

No matter how I dragged myself, the bus appeared immediately, and I got mad at the bus for some reason because, having gotten on it, I again began to rush to get to work. A seat became free, I sat down and began to look out the window. And then I again felt cozy, warm and drowsy, and it seemed to me that this was the same bus which I haven't gotten off all my life. The day hadn't broken yet, altough it began to get grey.

I look out the window of the bus and see the lit-up windows of houses. There too people are rushing to work. And suddenly I see: in one window, on about the third floor, there's a woman. The window is well lit, and the woman is standing close to the window doing something. And next to her, crooked somehow, stands a wardrobe. One can see it very clearly. And then it seemed to me that the woman suddenly bent away and that there was some shadow coming from behind the wardrobe. But the bus, it's moving—and there's no more window. I take away this picture with me and look it over carefully. Otherwise you can't see—it flies by and that's it.

...And then I see definitely that the woman did not bend away, but swayed, and did not sway, but recoiled, and covered herself with her hand in order not to see or not to get hit. And the shadow from behind the wardrobe is a man in a black raincoat and a grey hat, and in his hand there's a knife. He raises the knife: that's why the woman swayed. If only we'd reach the stop...! I jump out, catch the first policeman. "There, there...," I say. "What's there?" says the policeman. "Murder!" "Where?" "There. I can show you." The policeman looks distrustful. "I saw it from the bus." And we go. Not this house, and not that one. There it is! And there's the window. "Aha, this window," says the policeman. The three of us, the policeman, the janitor, and I look at this window. "This one?" "Right." "This one here?" "No, that one." "Aha, that one," says the janitor. "That's apartment 46." "Let's go," says the policeman. And here's the third floor. And here's the door. Ring the bell. Ring again. "Uh-huh," says the policeman. We break in. First room. Second room. Third... She's stretched out. In a puddle of blood. The woman. I leave. I alone know who I really am...

...We break in. First room. Second room. Third. Last. No one. "Ekh!" says the policeman. "Broke in for nothing. A detective, yet..."

...And we go. Not this house, and not that one. And what if I don't find the house? Don't recognize it. Or if the light has been turned off in the window? What then. How embarrassing! "Ekh!" says the policeman. "You ought to be ashamed of disturbing busy people..."

...And maybe I only imagined it? And what if I didn't? But even if there's only one millionth of a chance—even then the alarm must be sounded. And what if I didn't imagine it? And indeed. She's stretched out. In a puddle of blood. A woman. On the third floor. Near the wardrobe which stands crooked?

... And what if I had really seen the whole picture clearly? Both the man and the knife? And we go. Not this house, and not that. I don't recognize it. I can't find it. Maybe the light has been turned off? "Ekh!" says the policeman. "Aren't you ashamed?"

And what if I had seen it and not believed it: how could that be? In a lit-up window? Can't be. It just seemed that way. And I would just calmly ride on. And forget. And on the following day they would find her there. Stretched out.

It got considerably lighter in the window. I look and see that I have passed my stop long ago. And now I am completely late. So late that it's better not to go to work at all. And suddenly I feel really really light. It isn't that simple: not to go, to refuse, not go. And for some reason it's very complicated until you do it. And again I feel little...I hide my big briefcase in the basement. And I ride in the streetcar to the final stop and back. Then I rush to the eleven o'clock show. Then I go for a walk somewhere beyond the Islands, look around. And I go home after the sixth lesson...

I get out at a far-away stop. Here the snow is clean and the sky is soft and grey. Here stands a lone, last house. And there is a wasteland. And in it a strange lonely pipe. And the horizon blends with the sky softly and imperceptibly, hard to say where: either within hand's reach or in infinity. I am going along a narrow path trampled in the snow, everything around is even and white, behind, the last house completely diminished, and ahead, the pipe keeps growing and growing, it's huge, and can't be reached. And it seems that I will walk like this endlessly in a state of peace and happiness. But soon I get tired of the pipe, and I turn back, without reaching it after all—back to the thicket of houses, to the city.

I enter the movie theater an hour before the show... How well I know all these people who came to the theater for the first show and an hour early too! The pale, tall adolescent, who is constantly stuffing his briefcase somewhere, and the lame, unshaven man with a worn face, and the two old ladies engaged in such important conversation, and this quiet couple as if in conspiracy, and the ticket lady (her face will change by the end of the day), and the cleaning woman, and the shavings which she sweeps so slowly and lazily, and the waitress arranging her display case, her soda water, her ice-cream and cookies!

How familiar and how forgotten all this is... Going to the toilet and there's already someone there, smoking, going up to him and asking for a light, although you've got matches in your pocket. And this moment when you're inhaling and haven't gone away from him yet, mumbling thanks and you're still looking at each other... And one girl, not quite a school girl nor a grown up, who walks somehow particularly alone and independent, and your eyes meet, and you keep thinking of going up to her and striking up a conversation but you won't do it, won't talk. And you retain only a sensation of mystery and loss. And this film, whose subject is quite unimportant...

And then I go out on the street, squinting from the bright daylight. The sun has come out. And the city has come alive. Lots of people, all in a hurry, all with businesslike faces. All going somewhere. And this means that that's it, that peace is over. I am overcome by the feeling of being at loose ends, of alienation and uselessness. I am depressed that I am not like everyone else, and the people hurrying past me, each one, brings it home to me: you have no right, you have no right. Suddenly I understand what a wise child I was when I went out to the Islands somewhere after the movie, where there are still few people, and those who are there have broken away and live a stolen life, like me. Now I understand too much—I cannot behave wisely and I don't go to the Islands.

I go to the clinic to get a sick leave certificate. I am not I anymore. I have to justify myself and preserve everything as it was with all my strength. I have to correct what the boss told me to, I have to cope with the trial period and finally, keep my job and not hurt my parents. I am ashamed and depressed that I am not like everyone else, that I am so weak and have no will power, and that I so much want but cannot force myself to be good, to be like everyone, so that I could be calm and righteous.

I go up the hospital staircase, nurses brush past me noiselessly, as if in a dream, they're still girls... They are so changed by the white smock and the white caps. They are not like themselves at all. Here, too, it's quiet and it's another quiet world. Or maybe these people are very sick and understand something because of that...? I sit in a round room taking my temperature. Next to me is a woman in a red sweater, with a child that keeps climbing on her knees, endlessly repeating the same movement, and keeps sliding down and keeps the woman from taking her temperature. An unwashed young man who seems especially quiet, because one has a strong feeling that he is not really like that, not quiet. He holds his hand in a dirty bandage like a pistol and rocks it like a baby. A kid, a schoolboy with a greenish insolent face, keeps flicking the thermometer from time to time, looking over his shoulder. He sees that I am watching him, but he is not afraid of me, it is not from me that he is hiding, and he winks at me, as to an accomplice. Ten minutes pass. I go up to the nurse and hand her the thermometer. My temperature is normal, and the nurse, middle-aged, strict, looks at me reproachfuly. And I feel ashamed and think: all these people here are sick, and it's serious, and only I am like this and just disturb these busy serious people for nothing. And suddenly I keenly want to get sick and have someone take care of me and feel sorry for me, and then I would be justified before everyone because I do have the right to be sick and then no one could demand anything of me. I feel like lying in a cool clean bed, like being asked how I feel, like looking out the window which one naked branch keeps knocking on and where sparrows live, and having long quiet talks with neighbors. And then I must, I must be cured!

At this point a strong wind blew in suddenly for some reason, and the windows flew open with a bang. A lump of icy air and of dry snow burst into the warm and quiet hospital air, it blew up somewhere in the middle of the room, everyone came alive and started talking. The wind banged the open window frame once again, and it overturned a big potted palm and the stool on which the plant was standing. I, the person with the normal temperature and also a man, went to the window and slammed it closed with force. The snow had gotten stuck in the grooves, and the window wouldn't close. I shoved off the snow with my hand, feeling my fingers going numb and the snow melting under them, and finally managed it. Then the nurse and I picked up the palm and reinstated it on the stool. I still smelled the snow and frost, and the skin of my face still preserved the sensation of coolness, and the reddened fingers ached sweetly. For some reason I was surprisingly pleased at having done all I did, and I was glad the nurse thanked me, and I went out on the stairs and went down to the cloak room.

I went through the hospital garden and came out on the Karpovka. The water was black under the bridge, and white further on, and separate logs had frozen into the ice. There was ice on the hunchbacked wooden bridge and a horse was helplessly scrambling up it. The wide, low cart with fat rubber wheels was mounted with metal screens with bottles, and the bottles were ringing. The horse's muzzle was grey from frost and huge balloons of steam were billowing out. The driver, red-faced and even more fat in his sheepskin, was urging the horse on threateningly. The cart was barely moving, the horse's legs were sliding out in all directions, and then the cart stopped. The horse, pushing with all four legs, slowly started sliding backward. The driver yelled with a fierce voice, the horse pulled forward with all her strength, and slowly, unbearably slowly, sank down on her side. She lay on her side, with her head thrown back, and neighed quietly. She was so guilty, that horse, and there was so much guilt and hurt on her face, that it was clear: she was crying... Something big and choking came up to my throat: better I should have been lying on this ice now, trying to get up, and I would have been hurt and insulted, and better I should have been pulling this cart all my life... She was lying on her side, and her other shaggy side was heaving convulsively, in spurts, and steam was coming from it. The driver was yelling and beating the horse's wet side with all his might. I hated him, and the sudden thought that he too probably loves her, knows her, feeds and cares for her, was unnatural and revolting. And here some young fellow, cheerfully ran up from the other side of where the driver was, and, saying something cheerful and bracing to the horse, began helping her to get up. Then I also ran up and other people too, and all of us, united by something grand and happy, put the horse up on her feet, and with all our strength, sliding and falling without noticing it, pulled the cart up the bridge, shouting something loud and joyful, and then the horse separated herself from our efforts and went off by herself from the middle of the hunchbacked bridge. The people dispersed, the first fellow went off somewhere, grinning, and I remained alone again, and something big which I had felt just then slipped away from me.

I walked and thought badly of myself. I wasn't the one to realize that it's no use standing around and feeling sorry, but that one should simply help the horse. And how simply and well the first fellow managed it. And I will probably never be able to do it like that... And I disliked him. But I felt grateful to all the people who understood together with me that the horse could be helped and who forgot everything else at that moment. And it's so great that they are capable of forgetting "everything else!" And it's impossible, I thought, that they should be in a bad mood now, that they would not look at their cares and bustling lightly after having helped the horse, and, I thought, they will spend this day well. Perhaps the sole true feeling of freedom comes when a person realizes that he has just behaved like a human being... And, I thought, for how little we are grateful to people. And we are happy when we meet a man who has not lost his human self. And how good it is, I thought, when in the face of something significant and serious many people bring out the human being in themselves...

Then I saw the horse again, how she lay on her side, heaving her other, steaming side, and threw back her grey muzzle and helplessly moved her legs. And I understood that the horse—is some quite remarkable person, for whom one feels like praying and crying, and that there is no sight sadder than that of a horse.

Fine. This is all fine. But there's no sick leave. And what's to be done next?

And suddenly such a depression came over me—that I didn't want to live. Something in me is arranged wrong. I have no right to walk among people and pretend I am like them. They should isolate me or something. Put me in prison...? Take me!

...So I am in prison and finally I understand something essential. This "something" has to exist... And it's like a key to everything, to everything... And here I've got this key.

And perhaps then I would stop feeling restless and would gain the power of seeing and understanding what's around me. I would understand the goal and the meaning. I would get everything out of myself and create everything I was capable of. And maybe I wouldn't even understand, but simply by some miracle, I would wake up early one morning in equilibrium and simplicity.

But I am not in prison. There are no walls, no bars. I am walking on grey, trampled snow. Houses, streets. If I want I can turn left, if I want—right, if I want—straight ahead.

I walk as if free... What is this?

I see a self-service beer bar and go in. Before this was just a bar, it had a permanent clientele, it had its own micro-neighborhood and micro-world, and everyone knew each other, there was noise and smoke and they drank vodka. Now there are counters made of disgusting grey marble and shining stainless automatic dispensers, and you can't smoke here and hard liquor is forbidden. But people couldn't part with this place, they keep going here as before, and they have preserved everything as it was before: the spirit of a bar hasn't left the place. They smoke and they drink vodka here, and here they live their finished lives. There's noise here and everyone knows everyone else. And apparently, even the bar management understands that it's useless to fight this. The red dispenser spits out my favorite "Volga" wine, and will spit it out as many times as I want it to. I want it, I don't remember how many times.

I go out, reeling, onto the street. It's dark already, and my soul is quiet and peaceful again. I am able not to remember anything. I find myself in a square between two houses. There are no street lights here, only some light comes from the windows, and it makes blue shadows on the snow. A little kid has built a snow city and is playing in it, riding his truck. I plunk down on a bench next to him. And he really does live in his snow city, I think. He is not playing, but living. I quite understand him. I myself am dying to crawl on all fours on the creaky dry snow now and live in this city. I don't even want to be a little kid again, I want to get even smaller. A completely tiny man, for whom this snow city is really a city and the houses—huge houses. Tiny, invisible to everyone, I walk along these snow-covered streets and scramble up the huge peaks over to the kid on all fours. He throws a suspicious, sideways look at me.

"Don't be afraid, little boy," I say, "I'm from this city too..."

He stares silently.

"We'll live here together," I say, and ridiculous drunken tears are streaming down my cheeks.

"Uncle, you're drunk," says the little boy.

"I'm not drunk," I say, "I won't cry. We'll live in this city. You'll hire me as a driver for your truck..."

"You can't be drunk behind the wheel," says the little boy seriously.

"I'm not drunk, I'll never do it again," I say.

And so I'm riding the truck, filled with snow, I crawl on all fours along the narrow streets of this snow city and I push the truck ahead of me.

"Uncle, you'll destroy my city..." says the little boy.

"I won't," I say, "I'm a tiny man. Next to me, you're a giant, and I'm so tiny that I can't destroy our city."

I bring the truck to a big snow house and unload it. I put the truck in the snow garage. The work is finished, now I can rest. I walk in the snow city for a long time and choose the house in which I'll live. I finally find it. It's a marvelous house, it just needs a bit of fixing up. I'll make an addition for our house. I am pottering about with the house for a long time and now it is ready. Now I can call the little boy. We will be very comfortable in this house together.

"Little boy, little boy," I call him. "Where are you?"

I return home. I feel sick. I am nauseous. And I understand everything already. I am just madly sick. I would like to drink up a bucket of thin jello, to undress and lie down on a white, just washed and scrubbed, wooden floor. And just lie there and feel its fresh wooden smell and come to myself... Where is this floor from in my memory?

I don't remember anything anymore. Early in the morning I open my eyes and I see myself undressed and in my bed. Next to me is Mama with a concerned, sad face. I am ashamed, madly ashamed and I'd like to disappear, dissolve into something, so that only a clean, unwrinkled bed would remain. Again I want to be invisible.

"Don't be upset, Alyosha," Mama says. "Everything will be all right. Your mama will always be near you..."

It's worse than killing—saying this. I feel that I will start crawling on the floor now and excusing myself, like a worm. I hate myself...

I force myself to eat my breakfast and get dressed to go to work. And all the time more than anything else I am afraid of meeting my mother's gaze. I know what it's like, this gaze, when reproach and reproof have already disappeared from it. I fear it, because then I feel despair. Dressed, with my eyes lowered, I go up to Mama, kiss her on the forehead.

"Forgive me, Mama," I say and hurriedly, almost like a thief, run out of the house.

I am riding on the bus, but this time I can't succeed in becoming either a flying man, or a hypnotist, or a detective... I only reminisce about this. And it's a strange thing that I discover, reminiscing. Some time in the past, and it seems to me that it was terribly long ago, I was simply flying, I was simply invisible, I performed heroic deeds and died from insult. And didn't even notice how I did it. But now, and it seems that this started a very long time ago, any one of my fantasies, empty and silly, ends sadly in the fantasy itself. And there's neither victory nor triumph in it. There's always doubt or disappointment and the expected sad result... And that's in the fantasy, empty and stupid... And this is what experience is? It's this, only disgustingly blown up, that will become maturity and wisdom? And I will age just as cleverly, unnoticeably rejecting this and that and saying: how naive and stupid I was then, how little did I know and understand—and at this I will feel calm and fulfilled. To hell with it, to hell with it...

And here I am at work again. And first thing I bump into the boss.

"How are things, Alyosha?" he says. "What happened to you?"

And I suddenly feel that I am unable to lie and I remain silent.

"Did you get sick?"

"No," I say.

"Then what happened?" says the boss in surprise.

"I just couldn't," I say and deviously think of how I am still telling the truth, that I really couldn't, and that I can say this phrase and remain honest.

The boss exercises his tact and doesn't question me any further. That's just what I was waiting for, I thought. I begin to feel ashamed, and try to get rid of this shame.

"And have you made the corrections?" asks the boss.

"I haven't had time," I say and comfort myself: "I really didn't have..."

"But how is that, Alyosha?" says the boss. "Let's go into my office."

I drag myself to his office. The boss plunks himself into his armchair and it resounds under him. I stand at the table and don't look at the boss. I notice an American looseleaf on his neat table and can't take my eyes off it.

"Well, tell me about it, Alyosha," the boss says in his special tender tone of voice.

I remain silent. The boss again exercises his famous tact and asks no further. Then he begins to talk.

"What is this, Alyosha? I know your father, you studied together with my son... You know my attitude to you. You are an intelligent, capable young man, you have a lot of talent... How is one to explain your attitude?"

I remain silent. I know: it's better if I don't talk. He probably really doesn't have a bad attitude towards me. He probably really would like to help me and let me stay, although I don't deserve to. He probably will give me more time so that I can prove myself. Better not give him any more words of honor. It's more honest. Better to remain silent and wait till he decides it all himself and lets me go, slapping me on the shoulder...

The boss maintains the silence for a while and continues:

"You're a grown man, Alyosha... You well remember your school graduating class... Kukharsky, Potyomkin and Myasnikov are already doctoral candidates, Moskvin and Nomokonov are research assistants at major and promising institutes. Zaporozhchenko is already a captain... And you, after all, were no less talented than they?"

He maintains the silence again and now speaks in a more jocular tone:

"The trial period is ending? It is. And what's the result? The result is phooey. I can, of course, give you another chance... But I must be certain..."

I am standing. I am silent. This is not a lie yet.

"So then, Alyosha..."

A quiet skirmish starts up inside me. Everything in the office smoothly slips aside. And all this dissolves. I don't see or hear anything more.

And what I see is the cactus on the window sill. Every one of its needles. It's green, but the needles are reddish. And in the window there's the sky, very blue for some reason. The snow glistens. The snow and the cactus. A red streetcar with a white roof bends around the turn. The streetcar and the cactus. And the cupola—so blue that it dissolves in the sky. The church and the cactus. Black-white trees... And that's the same square! I am always happy to see it after work...

And in the window pane, above the cactus, there's a bubble. It's amazing what's in this bubble! The sky, and the snow, and the streetcar and the trees, and the cupola—it's all inside it. It's all tiny, strangely elongated and somehow especially bright. The snow city is in it. Someone lives there, someone completely tiny... I wonder, what do I look like to him from there?

1961-62

Penelope

(Nevsky Prospect)

They had still not brought the money from the bank. It ought to be here by 3 o'clock at the earliest. Monakhov was happy that he had succeeded in finding everything out so cleverly without having a run-in with his superiors. He did not have to put on a look of cheerfulness, yes, everything was in order, yes, if nothing happened they would succeed in fulfilling the plan this month... or, if on the contrary his superiors should press him, then complain about supply, about organization. On the whole he had succeeded in not doing all that.

Returning from the accounts department, he once again edged past the enormous black sofa which occupied the corridor. There was no one sitting on the sofa, and that was also surprising; after all, it was payday. Everybody probably knew that the money was held up, he alone didn't know. There was always something or other he didn't know, and then a boss would emerge through the doors, one of many pairs of these black doors, some boss or other of his, who would shake hands with him: "But what are you here for? Didn't you know?" Monakhov passed the big sofa. Farther on were the two most dangerous doors of all, one across from the other: one of his superiors might very well dart out of each, but no one darted out. He walked down the surprisingly empty corridor, past still more doors, already less dangerous—but it was as if no one was there—past the cabinets full of files which had been dragged out into the corridor, past the men's and ladies' rooms, past... but he was already descending the stairs, barely keeping himself from taking the steps two at a time, and he did not bound down them also because suddenly, there at the bottom of the stairs, on the landing, was his superior: hello, comrade Monakhov; they shake hands; and where are you off to...? To have a smoke, just to smoke, you see: and he didn't run at all, but walked without hurrying—I like, you know, to have a smoke, in the open air, when there's plenty of time. But he was already out on the street, and there—if only to get past this narrow back alley: you're not likely to meet anyone there...

And he didn't.

He walked along Nevsky Prospect, and things were quite fine. The sun was out. And the air was especially clear. he loved the Nevsky most of all in the fall, although along this section, where he was walking, there weren't even any trees—still, on the Nevsky, it was fall. He continued walking, and for a little while more he considered why it was, how it had come about, that he lived out his life this way and experienced these various feelings, as in the corridor, on the staircase and in that back alley, but it was not the kind of weather to be thinking for any length of time about *that*. Still, he thought it strange that these sensations already arose so mechanically, that you don't even think about them, that they pass as if part of a dream, unpleasant and rotten, and then it is as if they had never been. He thought about all this, but, as it were, in passing, so that it didn't bother him in the least, and what he arrived at was this: that at this point you don't even recall it, as though it were a dream, as though it had been some time very long ago. In any case, by the time he was crossing Sadovaya Street, he wasn't thinking about any such thing anymore, indeed, he wasn't thinking about anything at all.

There were women and girls walking by here, of course; it was possible to watch them. This girl-watching was also mechanical, to the point where it seemed strange. That is, it was not like being seventeen, at an age when each girl is a mystery and each one might be yours. Look, dammit, you know very well, after all, that in principle every one of them ... but it's impossible, if only because there's only one of you and you're not seventeen. I mean, if not a million, isn't it all the same whether it's one or ten. Might as well be one. He thought about this also in passing, as though he hadn't even thought about it. So he walked along and looked at the women and girls as he was used to doing, simply that. And there weren't even all that many of them. After all, it was a weekday and during business hours.

All in all, he felt very good, walking this way along Nevsky Prospect, his beloved fall Nevsky, glancing from side to side—how clear the air was! Walking along like this gave him a feeling of freedom, of wide open spaces.

He didn't understand whence came this glorious sense of wellbeing, for which, it seemed, there were no grounds: anyway, in three hours he had to return to the office, and after that ride back to his hole, to his division, to distribute money to the workers and worry about, for example, the disappearance of key number 19, because of which—God, what idiocy—he would not be able to turn on some oil-burners out there, which if not turned on, would, in turn ... but to think about such things was perverse, for while he really did feel so good right now, he instinctively understood that by thinking such thoughts he could dispel this feeling of his, lose it, and therefore it was better not to think about anything of the sort. As before, he was scarcely aware of what he was thinking: his recollections, the thought they had called up, his thoughts about that thought, and finally the thought that it was better not to think about any of it—it was as though he had never even had any of these thoughts at all. But it now occurred to him that, while he was not particularly excited at the prospect of making anyone's acquaintance at the moment, still, it would pay to dress better, because having come in from the country wearing a jacket and boots, he had not stopped by his house, and now no one would give him as much as a second look, he did all the looking. This was a most comforting and detailed idea to dwell upon; nevertheless, he didn't want to stop by the house, because—well, he was a grown man—it would be kind of stupid to stop and change clothes and then in three hours to stop and change back so he could return to the country—all that just so somebody would look at you. In any case, he didn't look like a provincial, and as far as being inconspicuous, lord! What a thing to worry about! One could think about it, even about all that, but, crossing the Fontanka Canal, even these thoughts seemed too critical to linger over, and then worries about dress were really too trivial to linger over anymore.

In any case, and here I will be precise, crossing Liteyny Prospect, Monakhov had already ceased to think abut anything at all, even in the most casual way; not even a sense of shame remained, or so much as an "as though"—he did not think, he did not remember, nothing gnawed at him, or pulled on him. By now, only his beloved fall Nevsky remained, and the people passing, whom you could watch, and the houses you could recognize, and the sensation of gaiety did not disappear.

But you can't go on like this either for long. With effort, half an hour. Something or other begins to give, there's something to be attended to. You've got to do something with almost three hours, after all. What with there being nowhere, really, to go. Go home? There wasn't anyone there, or any reason to go. Anyway, what was there to do at home? And inasmuch as it didn't suit him to do any thinking in this kind of weather, a billboard turned up—so it's the Colosseum, wide-screen cinema. They were showing *Ulysses,* the wanderings, it was, of this guy Ulysses. That's Homer, the *Iliad*. Never read it. Sophocles, Euripides. Heraclitus, Herotodus. Demosthenes. The barrel. Spartacus Giovanioli. Romulus and Remus. Men of genius. A name. People don't read them, but everyone knows the name. And what we do read, we don't even know the names. No men of genius, those. Yet the geniuses we don't read. One can think about all that too—in a casual way.

By this time, Monakhov had already gotten a ticket. One, please. That's a hell of a pleasure—getting a ticket for a bad movie on a weekday and during working hours.

He phoned home. Mama? Well, see, I've got to wait here at the office... I doubt if I'll manage today... Yes, I've got to go right away... well, of course... I will, I will... no really, I'm not cold, I feel fine...

When Monakhov emerged from the dark box-office and stepped out onto the Nevsky again—he even squinted, so bright was the light, so clear the sky. It's pretty stupid, he thought, to go to a movie when the weather was like this, when it would be better to go to some park, if only to the Summer Gardens or the Mikhailovsky.

But at this point, again, somewhere in the storerooms of his brain into which the light hardly filtered, it flashed that you could sit in the park and think, perhaps, happy thoughts, but then—you stand up and walk around and forget your happy thoughts. This seemed somehow to be pointless, and even a bit of a drag—you sit and reflect, yet however beautiful your thoughts may be, in itself, thinking things out is in the last analysis unsatisfying. This painful idea slid through Monakhov's mind like a snake, leaving no tracks. And Monakhov turned off the Nevsky, so sunny on this autumn day, and, maintaining his inner equilibrium undisturbed, passed into the dark entryway to the wide-screened cinema. The Colosseum, wasn't it?

Yes, he also thought about how this movie would inevitably be idiotic. At first he hoped that it was just a title, the business about Ulysses, but that it was about some Italian peasant, or American travelling salesman, or poor French kid, and he was the one, the peasant, the salesman, the kid, who did the wandering as though he were Ulysses, though actually it was in our time: cars and long limousines drove up to their cafes and then a solitary figure, rain, a turned-up collar, cigarettes, then these outdoor shots in black and white, a wasteland, petroleum storage tanks on the horizon, leaves on the asphalt and the black trees of empty parks, but as soon as he glanced at the stills posted up in the glass case it became clear; it was not a matter of "as though" he were Ulysses, but it actually *was* Ulysses, in all, so to speak, his ancient half-dress, it was in technicolor, no less—and it even left a bitter taste in his mouth, this anticipation of the farce he was going to see. But in the end, he would go into the theater all the same. And all the same he would enjoy it, however much he might deride it later. Because the jerks who make these films have some way of getting hold of something inside you, so that only for appearance's sake, only to uphold your standards of taste, you will deride it, when actually you will enjoy it. Because there is a banal sort of sentimentality on which these jerks zero in. There is in everyone. He was thinking about just this most clearly of all at the moment. He had thought the matter through up to this very point more than once, and, if there had been someone next to him who could have understood, he would even have spoken to him about it right off. He had been thinking about it just when that elusive thought about the park, namely, that it wouldn't be worth it anyway to sit down there (in the park), had slid through his head. The same snake mentioned above.

And so he passes into the dark entryway of the theater and this is virtually the first sentence of the story which I was intending to write. And now at last I am starting out with this sentence, but for the sake of still another sentence, the sole sentence I know and the one which ought to come at virtually the very end. Thus, you see, I am getting on to the start of the story, and even if I'm not ashamed of what I've written so far, trembling seizes me now, because I'm getting down to it. He passes in, and doesn't think about anything, for as to the park, it was as though he hadn't thought about it, while as to the movie, he had already thought it through before then.

Monakhov passed into the entryway of the theater together with a number of other people. Because there were five or ten minutes left and people were already gathering. The sun, in a wedge, shone into the entryway, and he was just crossing the dividing line with most of him still in the shadows, when he heard—and to this I can attest, that it was precisely this he heard—he heard, behind his back, behind his left, that is, his right shoulder, someone say, someone's voice say,

"Brutes! Ugh, brutes."

Monakhov didn't turn around, and, to be precise, he hadn't even caught the words, he merely understood that behind him, off to the right, there was a young, female voice.

This voice repeated:

"Ugh, brutes! Brutes!"

Monakhov turned around, and though he was careful not to stare, he caught sight of a smallish and rather solidly-built figure, and a young face which was not unattractive, framed in short, light-colored hair. The girl was almost next to him, and having turned just the slightest bit, he said, in an utterly mechanical fashion, without thinking,

"Are you talking to me?"

For some reason, this had been uttered not to himself, but out loud, loudly enough that the girl heard it; yet it had happened so involuntarily and naturally, that he himself was pleased with how he had done it. He rarely succeeded in such things. It is possible that he would never have uttered any such things if he had not been ashamed to recognize his own helplessness.

The girl glanced at him. There was neither indignation nor a desire to get past him in that glance, which also could not fail to surprise him. The girl said:

"Of course not!"

Monakhov skipped a step and found himself next to her. He couldn't very well make a point of looking her over; however, thus far he hadn't detected anything unpleasant about her. He couldn't examine her better because somehow he must contrive not to stamp out the spark of this light conversation, which, considering his, Monakhov's, savoir faire, would not be hard to do. And he said:

"And I thought you were talking to me..."

And he broke into careless laughter. Well, "broke into laughter" isn't exactly the word—more like "emitted a sort of half-snort."

"Oh, of course not," the girl said in a friendly way. And he would have been obliged to repeat, "And I thought you were talking to me..." because there was absolutely nothing else in his head, and that's what he would have said, if the girl had not added:

"Of course not... To such a nice guy..."

Now things were taking a new turn. He had not expected this. And this inspired him, and he said:

"A guy can look nice—and be a brute."

Just get a look at him, so tall and broad-shouldered, having just barely turned his head and inclined it in her direction—she, so small and solid—and he, smiling broadly, but with the air of a man of the world, added in a slightly ironic tone, which was meant to signify that *he* knew, and which furthermore was meant to signify a certain complicity on both their parts: so to speak, they both knew, and so, with all this in his voice, he added,

"Or am I wrong?"

But it must be said that at the very same time when he had already said "A guy can look nice—and be a brute," and when he had already prepared the follow-up line, and the intonation for that follow-up line, except he had not yet succeeded in actually following up—the two of them had already stepped out of the entryway into the light of the courtyard. Here something unusual and indecorous in his companion showed itself to Monakhov, but he was not yet able to say precisely what. But it was already too late not to say, "Or am I wrong"—he said it. But whatever it was that he had noticed in the light and hadn't yet figured out had already begun to put him on his guard.

As if she had sensed this, the girl said,

"Could it be?"—here she paused—"with eyes like that?"—and she gave him a glance which was both devoted and admiring, one might even say amorous, or inviting ... who the devil knows how it was she glanced at him.

At this point Monakhov began to feel torn in half: one half which, as it were, no one saw, already, as it were, slept with this girl, and no one, as is proper, saw them, but the other half dug in its heels and dropped behind, people stared at this other half, many people, going into the theater they looked and condemned, this second half of him was ashamed and uncomfortable, it wanted to efface itself, to disappear.

But they were already approaching the ticket-taker. As is proper, he let her go ahead of him—as they say, ladies before gentlemen—the girl slipped her ticket to the collector, but as for him, having dropped behind as though to let her go in ahead of him, he was all ready to run off with his ticket—the hell with it, this film—and head off to, say, the Summer Gardens or Mikhailovsky Park; he had already stopped in uncertainty at the doorway where he was supposed to surrender his ticket, but he received a shove from behind, because everyone had to get into the theater, while the girl, as she was handing over her ticket, just looked at him, so that she went into the lobby backwards—at this point there was nowhere to go; it seemed as if he were just pausing for some reason, well, as if he were searching for his ticket which he had stuck somewhere—it was in his fist, his ticket—and then they tore off his stub, and he found himself standing in the lobby next to the girl, clearly illumined and in full view of everybody.

The situation was something out of the same dream in which you suddenly find yourself without your trousers. You stand up, to take a typical example, to get off the bus, but it turns out you don't have any trousers on. A quilted jacket, for example, but no trousers. There was certainly something of that dream in this situation, especially because there is even something delightful about that dream. And there was in this situation, too: for some reason, he didn't run away from the girl in spite of it all, and there he stood, next to her; he had seen everything now—but he didn't leave. He just keeps on walking, trouserless, the length of the bus. What he had seen was that her hair was styled short—and it was not as though it were really a hairdo, rather it was like hair that had recently grown out; moreover, it was so bleached as to be almost brittle; that—there was a blazer, close-fitting, as though it were a man's sport jacket with turned-down, old-fashioned lapels which resembled dogs' ears, and beneath the jacket—a cowboy shirt, again, like a man's, which had not been laundered for a long time; well, then there was a sort of skirt, of course—a skirt; but on her feet, these impossible things: with the heels worn down, shapeless—and no stockings. Well, of course, who says that... And so he stands next to her, and no one is going to interpret it in the right way, that he found himself standing here just by chance and that he is just simply standing there—what with her gazing at him like this. And actually somewhere inside he didn't even want to leave. And since he didn't want to go, he said,

"So who were you calling brutes?"

"Well what else can you call them? Brutes, that's just what they are. A really poor old lady was standing in line, and they stole her money, twenty rubles. They should only know who they're stealing from... an old lady, poor, standing in line..."

"Well, yes," he said, "I understand. Really. Standing in line..."

"What did I say that for? Good Lord!" he thought, in agony. Something inside him writhed with discomfort. "Some old lady... cretin. Wherever you look there's a cretin."

The girl experienced a different sort of discomfort. It was as though everything underneath her jacket and skirt had gotten hitched up and askew, and now she tried to get it all back to its proper place. She took hold of her skirt and her jacket, and, while gripping the garments she had taken hold of, she twisted her whole body, her torso and her hips, and for a short while everything seemed to have settled in its proper place. Until the next time. She did not feel uncomfortable about doing this in full view of everybody. Apparently Monakhov was feeling embarrassed enough about it for both of them. That, of course, was the case. In any case, if they were not to go their separate ways altogether, they must go somewhere and get out of sight, and there, in the auditorium, where the lights had already been turned off, thought Monakhov, all these problems would disappear.

They moved forward, and he suddenly felt her take his arm. She did so rather forcefully; the gesture was meant to be noticed. The snack bar appeared. Various people were already sitting there drinking soft drinks or beer. The audience. This was definitely not the place where Monakhov wanted to show himself just now. "Audience," he thought venomously. But the girl had already said the following:

"I really want something to eat. I still haven't had breakfast today."

At this juncture, things stood (thank God!) like this: Monakhov had only one ruble on him. So he could say something like "Even if I had the money, I couldn't eat anything," but instead he said with relief:

"As ill luck would have it, I don't have any money."

"I have enough for a sandwich," she said.

In they went, to the snack bar. At this point, there was nothing to be done. Because Monakhov could do anything now, but there was one thing he couldn't do: show the girl that he was embarrassed to be seen with her. They made their way among the tables of the tiny snack bar; it seemed to him to take forever. During this brief time, ponderous thoughts rose in his brain, thoughts big and rustling. Like owls. These thoughts, these owls, were connected with the same subject as before; yet earlier he had been but dimly aware of them. Now, however, they stood out more sharply in his mind; at the very least, it would no longer do to doubt their existence. Did they exist, or didn't they? They did. These thoughts concerned the girl: why was he ashamed of her, ashamed even to walk beside her? How shameful it was, that he was more ashamed of someone in front of others than he was ashamed of himself in front of his own conscience. Monakhov could arrive at no other explanation of this fact than this one: in the latter case, no one else is looking. That's a pretty sordid way of looking at it, thought Monakhov. Be that as it may, this explanation of his struck him ever more forcefully the longer the owls flew about in his brain.

"Wouldn't you know it!" he said. "Today's the day I get paid, but I only get the money in two hours. I'll have plenty of cash then, but right now—not a thing."

"Why did I say that?" flashed through his mind. But the girl asked:

"What do you do for a living?"

Monakhov faltered: he wanted to pick out a simpler job for himself than he had, but none occurred to him.

"I'm the head of one detachment...on an expedition, that is," he said, realized he was boasting, and added: "The money's good enough." He wanted to add something more, but he managed to stop with this last, and merely repeated "But today, you see, I don't have any. I'm sorry."

"You can have half of mine," said the girl.

"Oh no," he said: "I can find a ruble anyway."

"Then what's the problem," said the girl.

A humiliating thought struck Monakhov, making him feel more like a swine than ever...For her, maybe, a ruble is a whole day's earnings. This thought of his made him angry, for he sensed keenly enough how low-down such a thought was, and how old-fashioned besides.

They were seated at one of the little tables. The girl had gone through two whole sandwiches. And a bottle of beer with each. As the girl silently ate, Monakhov began to feel desperate—even to talk with her would have been better—so it was absolutely incomprehensible why he was sitting here with her and somehow bound to her: he could not walk away—it all had the persistence of a dream. His present thought was: since he was here, sitting with her, he ought to be decent about it. He did not, however, find this decency in himself at the moment. And then he got furious: on whom or on what was he so dependent now, that he found himself fettered in this way? On these people at the other tables? But why, exactly? It was then that he began to understand how little control he had in taking a single step, in making a single motion, in uttering a single word: though day after day he might live his life assured that his movements, words, and acts were his own—still, they were not. It was then that it began to dawn on him that, evidently, the whole of his life was of such a character that he had so little control today. And somewhere very far away was that tail end to which he would have had to go back and relive his life anew for him to be free now. This thought circled above him, but the girl had now eaten everything; she laughed, sipped her beer, and said:

"You've got to get me a job. You can, can't you?"

Monakhov was distracted by her question, and gladly left off thinking what he had been thinking. In a tone of voice which even conveyed a seriousness and earnestness which he would have been hard-pressed to explain had he been conscious of it, he said,

"Why not? Sure I can. But only as a cook. We need a cook."

"It's all the same to me," said the girl. "A job's a job."

Monakhov suddenly realized what he was saying. What am I doing? ... This will never do...

"It's only thirty rubles," he said, retreating.

"That's O.K. by me," said the girl, "a job's a job." She put her hand on his knee and, leaning on it, she bent towards him:

"You'll arrange it?"

"Why not?" faltered Monakhov. "But what kind of work do you do?" Even with her, this transition to the informal "you" was for Monakhov like being on a roller coaster: it took his breath away.

"Oh," she said, "I can do plenty of things. I can operate a lathe, I'm a house painter, a cook, and—(all this time she had not withdrawn her hand from Monakhov's knee)—a woman..." She broke out laughing.

Monakhov laughed too. Right about now was when he stood up on the bus, turned out to be trouserless, and started walking up the aisle. His heart sank. Yet for some reason, it had gotten easier. The girl watched him, and kept her hand on his knee. In the meantime, some little demon inside Monakhov just went limp. It was as though he couldn't see anything anymore. He just said

"I'll have to check it all out," he said.

"So you'll take me?" asked the girl.

"It's possible," he said, and wanted to ask something, or add something, or at least think of something—but at that moment the bell rang. The girl stood up, took his hand, and, laughing, pulled him out of his chair, and they went towards the auditorium.

They had tickets to seats at opposite ends of the auditorium. They stood in the aisle, waiting as everyone took their seats. She held his hand and wouldn't let go. Once again, things had gotten unbearable. He was pierced, or so it seemed to him, by the glances of the whole auditorium. Everyone was trying to get seated in their places: oh well, there wouldn't be any seats left vacant—it was awful to imagine himself being obliged to ask someone to trade places, while everyone exchanged looks. But she held him back, people took their seats, and they continued to stand in the aisle.

They managed to sit down together once the lights had gone out. Or rather, she had managed. She took his hand right away. It was a short subject about Chinese vases. Very many Chinese vases. At last he felt calm, almost cheerful. Because they were no longer standing in the aisle, it was dark, and no one could see him, Monakhov. It was really quite pleasant to feel her close to him in the darkness. And he liked the vases.

"Really beautiful," she said.

"Really."

"I bet you'd like to have one like that in your house," she said.

"You could spend your whole life working, and not make enough to buy a vase like that..." he said suddenly, surprising himself. Even as he spoke, he felt disgusted, but he got the whole sentence out anyway. He didn't like to let things like that escape: to utter someone else's words out loud. But at this point she said something which evened the score:

"What do you think of abstract painting?"

For a few moments he was stunned. He gaped at her.

"It's okay," he said. My God, he thought, so it's come to this. What kind of terrible experiences has she had that she starts talking to me about abstract painting?

"I had a friend once..." she said, pressing his hand.

What tormented him now most of all was the prospect of their being turned out of their seats after the short subject. Then it would begin all over again, and they would be sticking out in the aisle. If only there won't be an intermission, he thought. Then they wouldn't have to get up. If only they don't switch on the lights. Sometimes they don't.

The short ended, the lights went on, and they had to get up from their seats.

"We'll have to go to our reserved seats," he said.

"Let's go, then," she replied. And she led him by the hand to hers.

All the neighboring seats were filled.

"Look, you see, there's only one seat." he said.

"We'll sit together on the one, then," said the girl. She actually sat down and, scrunching over, made room on the single chair. She tugged at his hand. There were people sitting on both sides of her; they were watching; and Monakhov had never felt worse.

"No," he said. "I won't sit like that."

"You'll have plenty of room," she said.

"No," he said, "not like that."

The lights went out.

"Sit down," the girl whispered loudly.

The fellow next to her stood up. Here comes a scene, thought Monakhov, by now indifferent.

"You take my seat," the fellow said, "and I'll go sit in yours."

They exchanged tickets, and this decent fellow walked off. ·

Once again, Monakhov breathed easier. Once again, he felt almost cheerful. On the screen, the idiotic charade in Greek costume had begun, just as he had imagined it. Sharp-nosed Penelope did not want to get married, she was waiting for Ulysses. The girl placed Monakhov's hand on her own knee. Penelope's suitors conducted themselves disgracefully, though it was not exactly clear why. They insulted Ulysses' and Penelope's son, an unpretentious youth. A duck-nosed Antinoös appeared, who behaved like a man. Compared to the intentionally worthless suitors, he was simply charming. A lovely guy. Very strong, too. He symbolized temptation. The girl stroked herself with Monakhov's hand. At last Ulysses himself appeared, a red-haired superman, though a little on the fat side for a superman. The real thing, nonetheless.

The film was beginning to absorb him. As he gazed at Penelope, Monakhov's interest in the girl's knee waned. Even though Penelope was not all that strikingly beautiful. But this was only on account of the fact that we judge beauty in the movies differently from beauty in everyday life. For real life, Penelope was pretty attractive. But when she changed the color of her hair and became Circe, you could say she really got much better looking. The girl, it seemed, was equally interested in Ulysses. As if by agreement, they released each other's hands.

Monakhov watched, and thought about various things. However ineptly this box-office smash was put together, despite all its school-boy overdoneness, still, Homer was clearly not famous for nothing. If nothing else, just the basic plot has so much in it. But there was no getting away from the grotesqueness of this whole effort from a purely human point of view, though there was something strangely similar to the original in it. Not without reason is it said that we live in an epic period. Only it is not pomposity which is the measure of epic stature. Take a look at wily Ulysses—what a low-down, treacherous fellow they make him. The perfect modern playboy. The epitome of selflessness—to tie yourself to the mast so as to listen to the Sirens. That kind of selflessness is nothing more than a taste for thrills: he enjoys doing it. He asked somebody to tie him down... so that, when all the points were added up, it was Ulysses who had won. Anyway, the Sirens' song was unimaginatively done too, of course. Obviously the electric guitar was the best idea they could come up with. And then Ulysses gets completely inhumane when he says to this young girl, the daughter of some king or other: I now remember everything, I must go; but I will bring away with me these tears of yours.

Football in ancient Greece—that wasn't so bad. Wine for that one-eyed devil Polyphemus—they managed to wade through that bit well enough. Only it was too bad that the poor creature got his eye burned out, and that he didn't crush the heroes. And then it was totally uninspired how they filmed those specimens from the kingdom of the dead. What a stroke of genius to have one of the dead come forward and say how there, in that kingdom, things are worse than bad. He doesn't say anything more, just that things are awfully bad there. It was just this kind of restraint in the use of special effects, these descriptions in no way frightening in themselves—which really frightened you. This sort of thing had probably been Homer's idea. But just then—the screen filled up with some kind of cold mist, and everyone's face turned green... Generally speaking, it was a brutal epoch, this Hellas of yore. Powerful little guys. But no one really human. In our day, in the present epoch, true humanity is finally able to surface. Chaplin, for example. While back then—as though that was what they needed, as if that was the best part of a person—they bragged about their muscles. While in the essential things they were extraordinary weaklings.

But then comes the really bad part. With the bow. Ulysses just stands there, as though he is supposed to figure something out when he is dressed like a beggar and the suitors splash wine on him. No, as it turned out, he was simply waiting for the moment when he could best make short work of them, as though he would be justified in taking his cruel revenge on them by their vileness; nothing more. Even though he was a swine himself—and remained a swine. Only Ulysses—the swine-hero, the king of the hill—is justified, the blind genius Homer has sympathy for him. That's how it is.

Still, for the most part, you don't think about that. You watch. And you feel like Ulysses—just as strong, brave, and handsome. He doesn't go under, and he doesn't get killed. Women love him. They love you in the image of Ulysses. And everything ends happily for you. And you embrace faithful Penelope, who by chance did not make a cuckold of you. And the lights come on. And you have to go out of the theater. Into your everyday epic actuality.

Monakhov was very surprised when he found the girl next to him. Recollections of her, like strange shadows, flickered in his brain. It all seemed so far away. As he came out into the light and took a puff on a cigarette, and the other people emerged—they were walking side by side, but that was a bad dream—he was afraid to glance at her, lest she become someone real. Not Penelope. All the same, you're a bit of a Ulysses, emerging from the theater.

In this painful daylight he didn't know what to do. But as for walking side by side with the girl onto sunny Nevsky Prospect—that was impossible. Good Lord, what had made him shoot off his mouth?

The girl looked at Monakhov; she did it quite simply, without any challenge in that look—and didn't take his arm. They passed into the same tunnel-like entryway where they had first caught sight of each other. The girl walked at his side and glanced at him out of the corner of her eye. It was as though she understood that Monakhov shunned her; but she still hoped...

Monakhov walked beside her in stony silence.

"Well, how did you like the movie?" she said, casting a quick glance at him.

"It was all right," he said, as though forcing his words through a sieve.

"And the woman?"

"What woman?"

"Penelope?"

"She was all right..."

"Would you like to have a woman like Penelope?"

Monakhov was overwhelmed with misery and compassion. He hesitantly touched her hand. But this gesture was not understood; it was slurred, incomplete. The girl glanced at him out of the corner of her eye, waiting for something...

But the blazing sunlight struck their eyes.

They went out onto the Nevsky. Well-dressed people were passing. Women, among others. Girls. Monakhov stopped. And she, small and bedraggled, stayed at his side. Somebody looked at them. Somebody said something, he was sure. He himself hadn't heard. But he was positive somebody had said something.

"What?" he said mechanically still not knowing what he should do, and glanced sharply at the girl.

She looked around, as though she didn't understand where she was. There was something childlike about her expression now; it was perplexed and piercing at the same time. She was, it seemed, ashamed of herself, she felt guilty—that was what her face expressed. All these people, the passers-by and he, Monakhov, were in the right, while she—was not. The world had cast her out—that was what her face expressed. And were it not for him, Monakhov—her expression would have been quite different. Monakhov understood all this now in one single sensation. But this insight was too weighty for the Monakhovian consciousness to handle—it burst in upon him and immediately toppled over. Anyway, the central fact remained, that he was ashamed to stand next to her on Nevsky Prospect. And when these two things were taken together, Monakhov felt terrible.

Just then he caught sight of something in her hand he hadn't seen before. Some green material. Where would she have gotten hold of that...he wondered. The green thing was a little knitted cap. The cap was full of hair-curlers. The girl took the hair-curlers out of the cap and stuffed them into her various pockets. Her jacket was close-fitting, and the pockets bulged in an unsightly way. When the cap had been emptied, the girl pulled it onto her head and assiduously hid her short hair beneath it. It was hard to imagine where she'd dug up this treasure. It was awful to look at—Monakhov didn't know where to escape to. Just inside the entrance of a nearby building, he spotted a telephone booth; he mumbled something indistinguishable, and zipped over to it.

From this vantage point, the girl was not to be seen. Panting, he dropped a coin in the slot. The coin vanished. He dropped another one in. He kept an eye on the door: the girl was not to be seen. The second coin vanished. Two girls, quite young, one of them rather pretty, came up behind him and stopped. They stood waiting for him to finish with the phone. The girl was not to be seen. Monakhov got out of the phone booth. The girls took his place, chattering. He hadn't the strength to go out onto the Nevsky. He drew back farther into the dark hallway. He turned around—through the glass doors he could see a sunny rectangle of Nevsky Prospect. People passed. Across the street stood a house. Cars drove by. Suddenly, right in the middle of the rectangle, as in a picture frame or a snapshot, the girl appeared. She was very easy to pick out, all lit up. He was in shadow. She doesn't see me, thought Monakhov. But it was clear that she saw him too. Otherwise, she wouldn't have been looking as she was. Her gaze was somehow very tranquil, very understanding, not at all reproachful. To go out there, onto the Nevsky, was beyond his strength. He beckoned to her from the hallway. With a finger. Convulsively, surreptitiously—almost as though he was not beckoning to her at all, but had merely jerked his hand for some unknown reason. All this time, the girls had been on the phone. But she stood in her frame and didn't move. Monakhov glared at the girls and retreated still deeper into the shadows. She didn't move—she just watched. What's the point of doing that? What's the point... thought Monakhov, who beckoned again, this time more decisively. The girls fluttered out onto the Nevsky. She hesitated, it seemed, and then came forward.

"Well, what is it?" she said. There was something constrained and dejected in her manner.

He stood silent as though concentrating.

"What's to be done about a job for you?" he asked.

"You'd know better than me," she said indifferently.

"Well, anyway, what's to be done?" he said, rubbing his forehead as though to indicate he was thinking it over. Good Lord, he thought, will this really never end...? So far she hadn't even said anything; why did I have to bring that up again? What am I going to do? I'm not going to do anything, anything for her, even if I could!

"Yes, what's to be done?"

This somehow had to be brought to an end. Just say: I'm sorry, it was a rotten thing to do, of course, but everything I said was just a lot of talk. I can't help you in any way.

"I'll try," he said. "Since you don't have a passport, it will be pretty hard, of course, but I'll try."

What a swine I've become! he thought hopelessly.

"And how will I find you?" she asked, with the same sad woodenness and alienation.

"Saints and devils, help me!" he thought, and said:

"I'm going out to the place where we work today. I won't be in town. Look, come right on out there yourself. It's Kilometer 53, on the railway. That's what the station's called. Ask for our camp. Anybody will tell you."

"... What time? What time should you come out there?" he scratched his chin. "It will have to be sometime during working hours. Before five. Come on Thursday. I'll be at the camp."

The girl, it seemed, had understood something. The wrinkles on her forehead relaxed.

"I'll be sure to come," she said.

"Yes, come," said Monakhov softly, with difficulty, swallowing the ends of his words. "I can't guarantee anything, but you can always try. Well, you go along now. I've got to make another phone call." And he began to stare at the floor. He scratched his chin again.

The girl glanced at him with surprise.

"See you later." She said this somehow strangely, half-questioningly, and her voice reached him as if from far away.

Monakhov lifted his eyes—she was walking away. She walked away for what seemed like a thousand years. Small, in her jacket and cap, she grew dark as she approached the glass doors. All the while, she was silhouetted in that sunny frame—out there was the Nevsky, people walked by, across the street stood a house, cars drove past. The girl walked away, and didn't turn around. It seemed as though she ought to turn around. But she didn't. He must cry out, he must stop her—but Monakhov was not in any condition even to imagine such a thing. How... will I ever live with this? he thought in agony, and at the same time, he waited—if only she'd hurry and finally get to the end of the hallway. And it would all be over. But she kept on walking in the rectangle, growing darker as she approached the glass doors—and suddenly, she disappeared, she was gone.

Monakhov remained standing in the hallway. He waited a little while. He went out onto the Nevsky. The sun. The girl wasn't there. He suddenly felt so empty and light, it was as though he could take off into the air, like a released balloon. He almost choked—so furiously, with a whistle, had he gulped down the wonderful autumn air. His fear passed. He suddenly realized it had gone, and it was only then he realized that the fear had been there. Everything began coming back to him in waves. He started to feel sick. Nothing and no one could help him. Where was it, that station at Kilometer 53, where he had never even been?... Had she understood, or not? He recalled her parting expression and decided that she'd understood. This thought did not relieve him. He walked on, and it seemed to him that everyone saw him, all lit up by the sun, and that everything that had happened was written all over his face.

... I do this kind of thing every day! More or less, but every day, thought Monakhov.

And it was like a long-forgotten feeling to think, not offhandedly, not "as it were," not forgetting, not while half-asleep.

1962

Infantiev

To R. Gabriadze

No one knew exactly when Infantiev had begun working at the Research Institute, if only because it was his job to keep track of such things. It seemed that he had always worked there. Oddly enough, no one had given him much thought or notice all those long years. People would just say that he knew his job.

Infantiev was suddenly noticed when he became head of the department.

It was really then, too, that people began forming an opinion about Infantiev's relations with his wife. She had worked in the same institute, though long ago, right after the war, and only briefly. But few of those old colleagues were left: in the past few years that generation had been pensioned off one after another—and besides, by now their memories were failing. They remembered that she was younger than Infantiev, slender, good-looking, dark, and another trivial thing—that she wore hoop earings, like a gypsy. They remembered that she had been gay, vivacious, though there didn't seem to be anything you would reprove her for. Beyond that, nothing concrete. Especially since no one had seen her since those days, and no one knew what she was like now. But none of them had grown any younger over the years...

Anyway, they regretted not having paid more attention at the time. Because from his colleagues' point of view, Infantiev's relations with his wife were not good. One could tell that just by the way he talked to her on the phone. In the first place, he addressed her with the formal "you" and called her Natalya Vladimirovna. In the second place, his responses were curt and rough: "What else do you want? No, no, no! I'm busy. Yes. Yes..." In the third place—they were just not good.

One would have liked to know more, but Infantiev was rather sullen and solitary by nature and shared his thoughts with no one. What had happened between them over the years, what had brought them to this state?—one could only guess.

But one day these guesses became quite beside the point.

One day the phone on Infantiev's oceanic desk rang, and Infantiev, calmly picking up the receiver, suddenly changed completely and said: "Yes, Natochka...How are you feeling, darling?...I'll be right there..."and immediately got his things together and, without a word to anyone, rushed out of the room. His visitors were extremely alarmed. Rumors instantly flew through the institute. And then every single person remembered that Infantiev had not been himself lately. For the past month—no, two—no, one and a half—I remember it well—when we were on the cultural expedition... That is, they were all simply amazed that they hadn't figured it out at once. After all, during the past month or two he had so often taken off and disappeared in the middle of a work-day! Some said that Infantiev had always been a secretive person—and there was nothing strange about it. Others said they were sorry for him—such a misfortune—though what misfortune, they didn't yet know.

That was how everything looked from the outside.

And the misfortune was that Infantiev's wife had breast cancer. It had happened six months before. Infantiev understood that it was not only painful and dangerous, but that for a woman it was something more. He pitied his wife and, when she came home after the operation, tried to make her forget as quickly as possible what she had gone through. This he understood in his own way: he tried not to let her get depressed and preoccupied with her illness, and therefore acted as though nothing had happened. His wife was to take care of the household as before. And if he saw her sitting in a daze, defeated, looking into space, he immediately thought up something to keep her busy or divert her. "Sew a button on for me," he would say, for instance. But this, of course, also involved the desire to preserve the long-standing order of things. However, not everything worked out exactly as before. For example Infantiev concealed from his wife the fact that their daughter had left college. He knew how much that meant to his wife. Before he never would have kept something from her just because it might be painful and she had to be spared—but now he did. As a result it was almost a harder time for the daughter than for anyone else. And as a result she didn't fully comprehend the family's grief—it wasn't only because of her youth. And Infantiev was shaken even more by this all happening at once: first his wife, now his daughter.

And then his wife was so sick that the approach "Everything as it used to be, and don't let her lose heart" no longer worked, and she found herself again in the hospital.

There they no longer tried to do anything for her. And fairly soon Infantiev and his daughter walked to the hospital to bring Natalya Vladimirovna home. Natalya Vladimirovna would not agree to ride home for anything, no matter what the vehicle: the smell of cars made her choke and feel nauseous. This was called "metastases to the lung." So they went on foot. It was rather far, and he and his daughter really carried her the whole way, holding her on each side by the arm. It was clear and frosty, and from the clear smoke-colored sky fell a sparse, light snow, one flake at a time.

After that—Natasha, Natochka, darling—she didn't get up any more. Their daughter went out somewhere every morning—as far as Mama was concerned, to the college. And Infantiev, Infantiev...he, a short, thin man, with slicked-down, greying, really all-grey hair and bright, vacant eyes—Natasha, Natochka, darling—they heard how he would talk on the phone and then take off: I'm coming, right away. Of course, by this time nothing would work, it was impossible to keep his wife from seeing that she was sick, or to pretend and say that everything was as before. Natasha, Natochka, darling...

They buried her in a very beautiful cemetery, the best in the city. It had long been like a museum, and burials took place there in exceptional cases. Infantiev had enough connections to arrange it. The cemetery overlooked a lake: a high, hilly bank, covered with pines. And along the slope, down to the lake, among the pines, were graves, graves. At the top of the hill was a cathedral built long ago. It was a remarkable cemetery: it didn't make a depressing impression at all, but rather one of aliveness—a fine sad feeling, perhaps, or even joyful. The main thing was that the graves, though close together, were not fenced in but spread down the slope. The whole view—the slope, the pines, the lake, and the distant wooded shore opposite, and the parachute tower to the right—one saw all this even before the graves. And if the sky were clear, and it was sunny, and the pines rustled, and puffs of clouds were reflected in the water—there was no death here. And the sun went down behind that distant shore, and its rays, already horizontal, illuminated the whole slope, all the graves, the whole cemetery, until dusk fell.

It was bright here somehow, and open.

When they buried her there was some definite sort of weather, but he couldn't recall what. He remembered that the weather had been distinctive, but whether it had been joyous or sad—that he didn't remember.

As a whole, when he pictured it afterwards, that day took the form of a dotted line or a queue: it had three dashes, three pictures, three bullets—the rest he didn't remember—three frames of a lost film. But even these threes found no place in his consciousness, they ripped apart and therefore seemed to be not about him, Infantiev, but about some other person, one who looked very much like him but still wasn't he. Infantiev always imagined these pictures with some degree of perplexity. They turned up in his brain independent of his will, suddenly, always only three together and only in that order...

It was easy to say: he felt lost..."Where's grandmother? Where's grandmother?" they suddenly began saying. It seemed to Infantiev that everyone had turned to him, was looking at him, asking him alone. "All right, I'll go," he said, and ran back along the narrow path among the graves. The path, along which their procession had just squeezed with difficulty, was now deserted. Infantiev ran along the path, which was strewn with bright yellow sand, and the farther he got from his group, the more he felt seized by a strange and indistinct excitement. He ran just as a boy entrusted by adults with an errand, breathless with responsibility and confidence—such a forgotten feeling—and at the same time, of course, he was running away from the procession, because what was happening there was something obviously remote which had nothing to do with him, and it made no sense that he was taking part, had to take part in the strange proceedings of those people with the long box, which held... no, of course not!... some unknown thing. Infantiev was running away.

And suddenly he seemed to stumble, and he froze in precarious imbalance, leaning forward, the way he had been running, but didn't fall. The procession was advancing towards him, and Infantiev hurriedly retreated to the side of the path, stood in a little gutter, on last year's leaves, caught someone's censuring, reproving look and dropped his eyes. He hadn't run away at all, but had made a circle and ended up again in his own procession. Carefully lifting his gaze, he saw in front of him a priest—walking ahead of everyone with an absurd expression of both vanity and laziness on his broad face, waving a censer, walking with a sort of weighted step, slower than he wanted to, as though afraid of slipping ahead of the canopy which was being carried right behind him, and of the coffin, which they carried behind the canopy. All of a sudden Infantiev could say to himself the word "coffin," because he had realized with relief that it was another procession, not his, that his mind had simply blanked for a moment—it had been stupid even to think it was. Of course it wasn't his procession—they wouldn't have had a priest... Some fragments had suddenly coalesced in his brain, he instantly understood everything and impatiently shifted from one foot to the other while the procession passed, and as soon as it had passed, an illuminated clearing with a flowerbed in the middle opened up to him, a clearing bounded by that same old church whose blue cupola could be seen from all over. And the gates of the church were open. Infantiev ran across the clearing and made the steps in two bounds, the flaps of his wide-open coat flying. After reaching the top he stopped short, unable after the light to make out anything in the dark depths of the church. The flaps of his coat subsided, and, as though folding his wings, he quietly stole inside. He had probably not once in his life been in a church; he said of himself "never been inside." With an unconscious movement he raised his head and looked up. Dust-filled light was coming down, he couldn't make out anything else. Recollecting himself, Infantiev lowered his head and took his hands out of his coat pockets. Having taken them out, he didn't know what to do with them, where to put them. He made out a small crowd of dark figures, silhouettes, grouped around the center—and again it was a coffin. A narrow column of light slashed the whole shadowy mass in two. "Like a sword..," Infantiev said to himself. He still fussed with his hands, first folding them on his stomach, then behind his back, then rubbing them stealthily with his handkerchief. People were crowding around, almost swirling, falling into the narrow ray—swirling, like dusk-filled light. "They share a common grief...," thought Infantiev haltingly. He noticed with surprise that all these people felt much freer than he himself. "They believe, after all, and I don't...", Infantiev said to himself with surprise, noticing the absence of the trepidation and silence he had expected to see here. On the contrary, there was a hum of voices and disorder. These people with a common grief behaved, it seemed to Infantiev, too freely. One person alone was overcome with grief, almost wailing—an old woman with a ravaged face. And someone else blew his nose loudly, two people carried on a lively exchange, a heavy old lady knelt down and took a very long time getting settled, rustling and fussing. Some bundle was being passed around. They were waiting for something. An absurd idea suddenly became clear to Infantiev—he had been observing it all during the past few days, but understood things only now. Maybe it hadn't been absurd—but what shattered now was a certain imprecise notion which Infantiev had somehow had, namely, that people experience grief communally, identically, jointly, that profound grief has only one manifestation. But now, observing this disorder surrounding the coffin (though what they were waiting for Infantiev had no idea), observing this disorder and even a seemingly irreverent impatience, and noticing in himself, an unbeliever, somehow even more reverence and trepidation than could be seen on the faces of the believers, not knowing where to put his hands, Infantiev forgot about everything and wondered at it all—and suddenly he saw grandmother. Black, indistinguishable from the other old women, she was standing right at the coffin, her spare little head softly bent to one side, regularly lifting a lump of handkerchief to the same eye and slowly moving her lips. Infantiev strode quickly, the flaps of his coat again stirred—as though he had lifted his wings. He walked around those dark figures, who suddenly seemed stationary to him as he approached grandmother. "Really," he repeated to himself with faint perplexity. "At a stranger's coffin... really," he kept saying, for the first time in his life calling his mother-in-law "mamenka," not "mama," but "mamenka." "It's embarrassing," he said, blushing for some reason. "They're waiting for us." Grandmother, finally recognizing him, began to fuss about, hid her lump of handkerchief in her sleeve and was already moving away from the coffin sideways, her eyes lowered, when all at once a seemingly common sigh and hush spread over everyone—a man in a cassock had come out. "A priest... a clergyman..."—Infantiev didn't know what to call him. A beautiful deep voice drifted upward in the narrow, dust-filled column of light. And the people standing there suddenly astounded Infantiev. The disorder had vanished, and instantly there arose that very communality which Infantiev had so naively grown to expect among a people sharing a common grief. And now they seemed to lean and reach simultaneously to one side, in mutual silence, hearkening. They suddenly froze, oriented in one direction and purpose, they were now something whole, unified, But in this there was no longer any grief, and that amazed Infantiev even more.

Then followed the second picture. He stood at the edge, he had to be the first to throw in a handful of earth. Everyone seemed to have withdrawn, vanished, they were no more. He stood at the edge, and before him there was nothing. Only an even light suddenly flooded all around, the sun had broken through. And Infantiev kept standing motionless at the edge and seemed to be listening to music. It descended on him together with the light, drawn-out and slow, unchanging and as though endlessly repeating. From above a light snow suddenly began to fall, and the people withdrew and dispersed as though on wings. And this snow and sun, and the drawn-out musical sound, and a kind of boundless scattering from it, as from the center of an explosion, the flight, the retreat from it of all the remaining people into a distant, constantly accelerating and whirling infinity, as though someone had blown on a dandelion and it had scattered in all directions... And he kept standing and standing at the edge, and before him nothing—a milky void, and snow and sun coming from somwhere above but it wasn't clear from where, and the strange scattering of whirling faces behind his back and their retreat into infinity—and suddenly the earth landed with a damp sound on the lid. Light, light, light...

And now the third... When Infantiev, prodded and supported by someone, was supposed to go back, apparently, home... Now Natalya Vladimirovna was no more. Infantiev stood at the very bottom of the slope, almost at the water. A strip of yellow sand—and the lake. There were no graves before him, only her dark mound. And then, when he turned (they turned him) to go back, up the slope, he suddenly caught sight of the next grave and felt surprise. He stood still, dully looking it over. It was enclosed by a wire mesh with a roof—not exactly either a hut or a veranda. In the hut was a beautiful gravestone, a small obelisk at its head. Set into the obelisk was the portrait of a young man with a mustache and a pleasant, intelligent face. But judging by the gravestone, he had died at the age of fifty-two, so that he was unlikely to have looked that good. It was probably an earlier photograph. Next to the gravestone was a neat little bench; everything was extremely well-kept. And on the gravestone, and this was the most surprising of all, a live sparrow was pecking open a piece of candy.

For a long time after the funeral Infantiev could not bring himself to visit his wife's grave. Only in the spring, when the snow had melted and there was an extraordinary day, he went to see about the monument.

As he rode, and he rode for a long time, on the tram, and had already passed the city limits, and it would soon be time to get off, clouds blew in from somewhere and it darkened. Infantiev noticed this suddenly: it had been sunny—now it was dusk. He was surprised that he hadn't noticed it earlier, and sensing his surprise, he realized that all through the long trip he had been as if submerged somewhere. That is, now he couldn't remember either that he had been riding, or what he had seen out the window, or who had gotten on at the stops. And now he realized that he hadn't been thinking about anything that one could get that absorbed and submerged in (in what? where?). Yes, actually, in the generally-accepted sense, he hadn't been thinking. But had been completely engulfed? And then he remembered by what. And immediately felt embarrassed and even blushed and turned around, to the right and left, as though someone might have noticed something. But the passengers suspected nothing. And anyway there were only three of them. And the conductor was dozing. In fact, it was foolish of Infantiev to have looked around. He realized that now, that nothing was written on his face.

If not for that sudden darkening, thought Infantiev, I wouldn't have noticed anything particular about myself but would simply have gotten off and forgotten everything that happened in my brain during the long ride. Imagine... This is all absurd.

...Such a long ride—and Nata, suddenly she got on the tram, and through the windows, on both sides of the tram,—sky (the tram was crawling uphill), and pines, they rustled, and she got on,—slender, noiseless. She got on, and—what was it?—suddenly he felt terrified. No, she was alive. But just because of the sun, and the sky, and the pines, and the tram crawling uphill, he cried out, but, strangely,—he was silent. His mouth merely opened slightly and he was silent. And she raised a finger to her lips and looked at him and came towards him. Noiselessly. But none of the passengers even paid any attention: the woman looked out the window, the man dozed. And Nata came up and said: "Well, how are you?" And he wanted to say that things were bad, everything was bad, wrong... "Not bad," he said, "we miss you." "That's good," she said, "that's good." But Infantiev felt somehow strangely that everything was normal, natural, and, at the same time, that this couldn't be, it was impossible that there could exist some sort of "there." But it was so simple and necessary—"there"... "So, how is it there?" he asked, for some reason timidly and in a whisper. "What's it like there?" he asked with unusual curiosity, fear, and respect, special respect for a person who knows about it for sure, and in a moment he too, Infantiev, would finally find out the truth. "What's it like there?" asked Infantiev. "Look," she said and pointed out the window. He looked out the window: there was a blue sky (the tram was crawling uphill). "Yes," he sighed. He turned around and Nata was gone.

Well, if now it was the dim light that had made him suddenly notice these things about himself, he had to admit that it had happened before this, too... He would be sitting at home and think: that Nata died, it's so absurd that it couldn't be. And especially the funeral, the cemetery—all that was over (because it was unnatural for such things to linger on), it was over, and that's why Nata somehow or other simply hadn't been around for a long time. He would be sitting at the table—and wouldn't turn around, because suddenly the thought would pierce him: why shouldn't she walk in right now, just like that—walk in and sit down beside him; he wouldn't have been surprised. And just then the doorbell would ring. Infantiev grew pale, went to the door, opened it—no one. And in his dreams too it had happened, more than once. Not so often, but more than once. She came to the house, and he alone saw her. Their daughter didn't see her, and the neighbors didn't see her. And they chatted about the house, and a sort of unusual calm and wisdom came to him then; Nata walked from room to room, talked, but only he saw it, the others didn't. And he and Nata had an agreement, she had wanted it: she would come, but he must tell no one, no one...

Odd: on the way there was sunshine, when he arrived—stormclouds. The cemetery had grown dark, and he realized fully what an amazing cemetery it was: even now it wasn't gloomy. It was simply twilight, and the pines were rustling. He went down the steep bank, along the narrow path among the graves—and he was on the shore. The lake seemed very calm and dark. Though it was smooth, it slapped for some reason against the smooth sand. Infantiev was surprised at how calmly he looked at the grave. Of course, he was slowed down, and his eyes kept getting fixed elsewhere. And it could be, too, that he wasn't admitting to himself that Nata was under this stone. Of course, to admit it would also be unnatural. After all, it was just a place, just a memory, just a possession: that was the only reason one could even go to a cemetery. Infantiev noticed that at the next grave, the conspicuous one, with the little house, someone was standing, a woman. He stood there, more at the lake than at the grave, and he felt so good and calm, he felt free of motion and of thought—and suddenly thunder cracked right over the lake and along the water, and the first round and sparse drops rolled up into gray beads on the sand. Completely mechanically Infantiev looked at the sky. The movement was simple and absurd, because where would it be from, if not the sky? As he looked up, the drops started beating down faster, and he heard someone call to him. He shivered and looked over at the next grave. The woman stood facing him, waving her hand and saying: "Come over here, come on. You'll get wet." Infantiev went over. "I have a roof," she said. "Come on inside." And as soon as he had gone into the mesh hut it began to pour. Infantiev thanked her and looked around. A bicycle was leaning against one of the wire walls and large raindrops beat on its seat. And then Infantiev was totally stunned: on the wide, low gravestone, laid out in a circle, were pieces of candy. "Mishka the Polar Bear" brand. Infantiev stole a look at the woman. But everything was normal: she had a very calm, even soothing face, and she was Infantiev's age. He glanced at her and then looked away. "Today's a holiday for us," she said. Infantiev was beginning to feel uneasy. It had grown completely dark, it was thundering, and lightning seemed to be striking at the black bosom of the lake. The whole mesh hut was enveloped in rain, and streams of water coursed through the mesh, leaving only a small square in the center dry. It was all stormy and cheerful, what was going on outside. But this strange woman here with the candy. Was she all there...? "What holiday?" he asked, to be on the safe side. "Misha's birthday," she said, and pointed to the portrait of the man with the mustache and, glancing at Infantiev, began quickly, as though breaking into a run: "He was a polar explorer, that's why 'Mishka the Polar Bear,' I put a big bear on the gravestone for him, but it was stolen, there, there are the footprints, after that I made a fence that could be locked, it was such a beautiful bear, white..."

The sky burst right over the lake. A gap opened, and through it broke the sun. Clouds covered the sky as before, and the rain poured down, and the pines rustled heavily. But everything had been amazingly transformed. The rain glittered and burrowed into the sand, and the sun, like a projector, illuminated the wet pines, and the gravestones shone, and, mottled, the lake gleamed. It was already thundering somewhere farther on. Infantiev even said:

"Wonderful."

"Yes," said the woman, "Misha and I love this place very much."

"Especially Misha..." thought Infantiev and suddenly blushed painfully.

"Oh, I didn't explain to you," the woman began in that racing way. "Misha used to tell me, when we were getting to know each other, how the fog was pitch black, he ran smack into a polar bear, he was crawling, crawling, suddenly he felt something: what was this wet, warm thing? And it was a bear's nose, and the bear didn't do anything to him and walked away, so that's why I put a bear on the gravestone, with its nose to the portrait..."

"Yes," said Infantiev, "that's how it is..."

"Help yourself," said the woman. "Take a piece of candy, go on."

"Oh, I couldn't..." said Infantiev.

They sat on the little bench near the gravestone. Infantiev chewed the candy. The gap in the sky spread—and already half the sky was clear, and everything gleamed freshly washed. And Infantiev grew extremely uneasy. Because earlier it had been raining, and then there had been a reason why he was in this cage listening to this woman, but now the rain had stopped and it made no sense. And much of the woman's story made no sense. Judging by appearances, she came here almost every day, and had bought a bicycle especially for that purpose. She had wanted a motor scooter, but was a little afraid—it would be stolen, even at a cemetery. So she understood, then, that it might be stolen? And she understood, then, that this was, after all, a cemetery? She erects this whole monument, brings candy, and yet said herself that they had lived apart for many years. He somehow didn't catch exactly how she had put it. Maybe he was on an expedition? No, she hadn't said that. The woman went on running along slender, merging words, and Infantiev felt out of his element: here was an entire life, the entire story, and he—what was he doing here...? and was she even normal...? and the rain had stopped. He chewed the candy, and that too made him feel awkward. But not to chew and only to listen—that was even worse. The candy... how delicious it was! And suddenly he wondered: how many years had he gone without eating any? He couldn't even remember the last time. Only candy from his childhood came to mind. But he could have some every day... And this woman... Despite the fact that he felt awkward and couldn't follow what she was saying, for some reason he needed very much to listen to her confused and merging words, and what she was talking about was also very important and even close to him. As far as continuity was concerned, nothing she said made any sense. And at the same time the most important thing, the essence, reached Infantiev for the first time. And it occurred to him that probably all his life he had listened to a lot of things that he could have understood but hadn't. Because he had taken understanding to mean only distinct sequence, only the following of one thing from another. And right now that running, non-sequential story was exactly what he needed, because, discarding continuity, it conveyed an essence. Infantiev even began to fidget on the bench—what he was thinking and understanding at that moment was too complicated and inexpressible. And maybe this time he shouldn't try to formulate what it was and then it would be more precise...

The woman looked over toward Natalya Vladimirovna's grave...

"Did your wife use your last name?" she asked thoughtfully.

Infantiev hesitated in confusion before confirming, "Yes..."

"So your father was a priest?" the woman looked pleased.

"What makes you say that?" Infantiev was taken aback.

"Of course he was..!" and again the woman began rushing off in her pattering spech. "Figure it out... You're Russian, after all, aren't you Russian?"

"Of course," Infantiev said irritably.

"But the root of your name," the woman ran along without hearing him, "is more French... Spanish, even. The Infante is the royal child, the heir. But you're probably not from Spain..."

"That's for sure," Infantiev was glad to hear at least something that made sense. "I was born here."

"And your father?"

"On the Volga..." said Infantiev. "Near Astrakhan... Wait a minute," he brightened, "I think he actually did go to a seminary for a while...! But what he did then, afterwards," Infantiev caught himself, "had nothing to do with that. He was a repairman." Infantiev was annoyed.

"There, you see, you see!" the woman was triumphant. "That means your grandfather was a priest."

"He was not," Infantiev slammed the subject shut. "Where did you get that from?"

"Of course he was, of course he was! It's so interesting...!" the woman exclaimed. "It's just those old-time Russian provincial priests who used to make up such strange last names for themselves. When the main clerical names were already taken—Preobrazhensky (Transfiguration), Voskresensky (Resurrection), Uspensky (Assumption), Bogoyavlensky (Epiphany)...-then they began thinking up much stranger ones, anything as long as it sounded nice: for example, I'm friends with a priest named Phenomenov... just like you're Infantiev."

"Oh," Infantiev had nothing to say. But then he hit on something: "Like in the circus."

"Exactly, exactly! Performers' names too...," the woman was delighted. "What a fine observation! In the circus they're more often Italian, but they also had Almazovs (Diamonds), Izumrudovs (Emeralds). Exactly. I never thought of that. It's interesting—Monakhov (Monk) is such an actor's name, but it must come from a line of priests. Probably the father was a priest, the son an actor. Can you imagine the drama? The conflict?"

"Yes, but my grandfather was not a priest." Infantiev took on the look of a safe.

"He was, he was! I assure you! He was a country priest out there on the Volga somewhere. And your great-grandfather and great-great grandfather as well... And your father was sent to a seminary too, though he didn't finish, as you say. Otherwise you just could not have a name like that. Or do you insist that you come from a family of wrestlers?"

"What do you mean? That's a good one... What are you driving at, anyway?" Infantiev was flustered.

"The circus!" the woman burst out laughing.

Infantiev stuck a piece of candy in his mouth and shut it.

And the woman went on running along slender and merging words which told how she had rushed in a taxi across the whole Soviet Union after learning of her husband's death, how she had no money and, besides, her apartment had been robbed, and how she had collected money from her friends, and how it had all gone for the monument, and how she had a son, a schoolboy, and how hard, hard, hard, and how much happiness, happiness, and something so very incomprehensible and most clear of all was at the end, but it couldn't be retained, couldn't be remembered—could only be felt, and, perhaps, the memory of his own feeling...

"Yes," sighed Infantiev. "That's how it is."

"And my son is grown up now...," she said.

Infantiev suddenly realized how many years had passed since that time, how long ago everything was that the woman had been talking about, and that it was now, amazingly right now.

It was as if the woman understood what Infantiev was thinking about.

"It seems to me that I commune with him," she said. "Rather, it doesn't seem so—I do."

"Yes," said Infantiev and, not really understanding, he glanced at her.

"I know, " said the woman, "your grief is greater. It happened to you recently..."

"Yes," said Infantiev simply. "It's so empty..."

"And with me, if I feel bad, I always come here and have a talk with him. He quiets me for a bit and I feel better."

"You probably believe in God...?" Infantiev asked in a whisper, and carefully glanced at the blue cupola.

The woman noticed his glance and smiled for some reason "Oh, no," she said. "I've never even been there." And she also glanced at the cupola.

"I have," Infantiev sighed. "By chance... It's strange, somehow... What can you do...?" he mumbled, by now completely meaninglessly. "So, you talk to each other?"

"Don't be surprised," said the woman. "I'm a highly educated person. But what is it, then, if not communing?"

"Well, yes," said Infantiev, "I just hadn't thought of it that way yet."

"Especially since he's not even there," she said, and pointed to the gravestone.

"What...?"

"Isn't it so that yours isn't there either? It's only a monument, a memory...and the place is beautiful."

"Mine isn't there either," agreed Infantiev.

"They're alive, of course," said the woman. "Otherwise how could we talk to them?"

"I somehow hadn't thought to look at it that way," Infantiev said slowly, with surprise.

"He even comes to see me..."

"You too?!" exclaimed Infantiev.

* * *

He rode home, the tram crept downhill. The sky had grown pale and dark, there were pines along the ridge, and through the pines flashed the red sun.

"Yes, I hadn't thought of it that way," Infantiev kept repeating. "I wondered what it was. And this is what it turns out to be?"

1961-1965

The Soldier

(From the Memoirs of the Monakhov Family)

The past is so changeable! Perhaps for the first time I catch myself thinking thoughts which will soon become habitual and seem as if they had been obvious for a long time... It would seem that I myself am changing, have changed, one could say, have changed my views. But these are all nuances, intonations, immaterial—the past, immobile in its facts, has frozen forever; people who have passed through my life have stiffened there in irreparable poses. But no! Not only my views... the past itself has changed. Completely different people have inhabited it; that which was not to be forgotten—is just what has been forgotten. Lord! I have passed by friends and loved ones without noticing, and now that I look back and approach them—what impassable passions and pains the waters have closed over as if they had never existed!

Here's a man who seemed not to have existed at all in my life. But now suddenly he has become much more important than people I've spent years and time with. Only one generation has to appear after yours for you to become a devotee of your own time. And you draw other designs on the past, other functions and meanings on the face of the future.

Here's a man who reminded me by his devotion to his epoch of an example of another faithfulness, a faithfulness which inevitably awaits me: to my own time, to my epoch, to myself.

This man returns me to that time in which he got stuck, where I discern a figure which at that time I somehow never attributed (or was still not capable of attributing) significance to... But now he is more distinct than he was then, although he is long gone.

His nephew and I went to the same school. Actually, Alexei only called him uncle—it turned out that they weren't related at all. But about that later... What can I say about Alexei Monakhov? Once we were friends, then parted without having quarreled. But during those years in question, we grew up too similarly: we finished school and entered the institute.

We can't say with certainty what forms us and when. Alexei had his first suit made in nineteen fifty-six on a pattern from an English magazine from nineteen fifty-six, and that suit looked so well on him that he conquered his first heart, or rather, that first heart conquered him, Asya...

The Neighbor

...Once Alexei came home from the institute—both halves of the doors to the apartment were open—and saw an unfamiliar old man who, moving drily and angrily, was directing the removal of such things, so familiar since childhood (the things we are intimate with), as the oval mirror in the frame of gold-black grape vines; the table lamp, formerly kerosene (enamel and bronze); the etagere with the two carved Negro cupids (they're the augurs) and a long, polished mahogany night table on which in his childhood Alexei used to play soccer with wads of paper, and the wads would skid particularly well... The old man was swearing foully at the janitor who had gotten the table stuck in the doorway; he leapt over the table and with trembling, angry hands showed him how to carry the table out. The janitor listened to him gaily and dumbly.

Here Alexei espied his father and mother eagerly and gaily bustling about, almost like the janitor. They seemed to be looking the old man in the mouth, and his swearing, so forbidden in the family, caressed their ears. They had smooth, clean faces, almost the same as in their wedding photograph; the kind of faces, it turns out, that people turn to each other with relief at the first possibility of love... That love, unconcealed, unrepressed, undistorted by experience—that pure expression—struck Alexei in the faces of his parents. And the possibility was youth. Much later Alexei understood that their love for the old man was so suddenly simple and joyous because in its pure disinterestedness it was almost the only means for love in the Monakhov family, that is, of love for each other.

"Well, Alexei! This is Uncle Dickens!" Alexei felt a rough, hot hand, saw a white, porcelain cuff, an agate cuff link... "Hold this!"—and Alexei held the oval mirror in his arms, taking it by the golden cluster of grapes; for a second he was reflected in it—the reflection taunted him with clumsiness and health, and here he distinguished the old man with a word forgotten through disuse, "refinement," but if a word is forgotten or doesn't yet exist, there exists nonetheless a mute sensation, a hesitation, a catching of the eye: the unnamed is surprising.

Alexei was surprised that even ordinary repellent traits were attractive in the old man in their extreme form. Everything became attractive: fastidiousness, dryness, abruptness—underworld aristocracy... And the blue suit with thin stripes sticking out on the dry body like a blouse, out of style by about twenty years, which looked as if it had been lying in a trunk all these years, folded in four like a letter, and which preserved above all precisely these four crossed folds—this suit, it seemed, would come into fashion only the following season: it was so elegant (Alexei's English suit was made for cows and was the size of a cow); and the cherry boots with the anti-fashionable tips and cracked laquer; and the shirt... Lord! no one ever has a white shirt—it can never be absolutely clean, that's the trouble...! and the pin in the tie—for Alexei it was a diamond of the first water shining in it. The face... Alexei had already fallen in love with Uncle Dickens. He was extraordinarily clean, Uncle Dickens. And it wasn't that he had "washed up," that was clear at once: he was always clean, there was a visible absence of any smell... which was strange, considering his camp life. He was extraordinarily thin and dark; every last silver thread was so carefully parted (later at Uncle Dickens' Alexei noticed a special silver brush for this purpose); his mouth folded into an extraordinary satiric accordion—Uncle Dickens never got around to having some teeth put in; while his eyes—almond, broadly set, huge, although Mongolian—were, there's no other way to say it, like a horse's, snorting and flaring... To the cumbersomeness of the portrait one should add that Uncle Dickens himself was dried out and miniature, though it was impossible to call him small... "Where are you going, you bum," he yelled, sticking his fist in the janitor's rib, and his voice was surprisingly Russian.

These pieces of furniture, so part of the family to Alexei, turned out in fact to be Uncle Dickens'. That is, his whole life had been such that he had things, but had no home...

Uncle Dickens, or Uncle Mitya, called Dickens only because he loved him and read and reread him all his life (and also for something else which can't be put into words), fought in all the wars, and the rest of the time, in short intervals, built things (he was an outstanding specialist in acoustics and resonance and was always needed someplace). In World War I, a youth, an ensign, he was a tsarist officer. In the Civil War he became a Red officer, was demobilized after everyone else and was going to go into an administrative unit but was recalled to emergency construction in Siberia just before Alexei was born. There as a regular officer he was again mobilized and fought in Khalchin-Gol, the Finnish war, World War II... "And the Japanese," Uncle Dickens would add after some thought. Finally demobilized, he arrived in his native city with these three pieces of furniture which he'd picked up somewhere... But someone had long ago taken his apartment, and he gave them to "sit around" to the Monakhovs who, after returning from evacuation, had nothing left besides an empty apartment and a grandmother who had somehow survived in it. Having given them to them to "sit around," he once had a soft moment and gave this "furniture" to the Monakhovs in a burst of generosity, but soon got an apartment on the floor above. Then he said the Monakhovs, who meanwhile had acquired some things, should give him his presents to "sit around temporarily." He was at this time working at his peaceful and pleasing occupation—tuning pianos, and already was considered a great specialist ("Uncle Mitya has absolute pitch," Mama would say) when suddenly he left his apartment empty and uninhabited, again hastily summoned to some construction where something threatened to collapse without him.

Now, at his final return, Uncle Mitya didn't even mention that he hadn't ever managed to furnish his apartment, and his first communication to the Monakhovs after their separation was an enumeration of the possessions he had given them for temporary storage. This enumeration included a worn suitcase containing suspenders and toilet articles, all listed, such as: a Gillette razor, a set of hair brushes, and several reproductions cut out of old journals. Enumerating all this and scolding Alexei's mother for having ironed on his end table thereby ruining the immaculateness of its surface, he took all his property and carried it up a floor.

Alexei's mother was genuinely happy when she would tell about how Uncle Mitya had actually taken back things he had given to them... And Uncle Mitya's stinginess, even greediness, which had other petty pretexts for appearing—they too were endearing traits in the eyes of the Monakhovs. And Uncle Dickens himself, venomously setting his toothless mouth, liked to emphasize that yes, he was stingy, but like the son of a Kazan innkeeper... And here he attributed to himself the famous anecdote about the cabbage soup and the fly-raisin, that this had allegedly happened to his father... he would get drunk quickly, filled to the gills with the home brew of life, he would exaggerate about the barkeeper... and Alexei was always surprised that with Uncle Mitya even his faults were qualities and one could love them. A personality.

The air in their apartment seemed to move, as if they had emptied a room piled with furniture that they'd always remembered but forgotten, taken the torn Viennese chairs to the dachas where they had stood out in the rain, and here they'd washed the window and it turned out to look out right onto the garden... Evenings Uncle Mitya would come with his decanter (the monogram "N" with a line under it), and everyone would gather in the kitchen. Alexei didn't remember their ever having been together, although there had always been the three of them... Even his father, apparently willingly, would leave his study, the dark bridge-head of footsteps, and listen to the sharp and empty babble of Uncle Mitya with obvious pleasure. It was as if all his life in his study, listening to his own footsteps, he had been concealing a secret idleness, and was pining away in there from it. With Uncle Mitya his father almost stopped squinting... His mother would look at Uncle Mitya with loving smiles, and when she would look away, via the sugar bowl or a spoon at his father or Alexei, she would still not have had time to change her expression, and this light would flow out to them too, and, shifting their gazes from Uncle Mitya briefly to each other, none of them would have changed their expressions, and they grew happy from these half-expressions of semi-warmth caught midway, and, not understanding, not recognizing this happiness, they would wink to each other with love, as if to say, what a fine person Uncle Mitya is... Alexei's house thawed out, and it seemed it was precisely the homeless Uncle Mitya who made them a home. Uncle Mitya was allowed a great deal, more than anyone else, and more than he would allow himself. For some reason we need that—to allow another to know everything about oneself...

Once when Uncle Mitya had said something very well and exactly, and Mama had laughed so happily, but father—so unnaturally, at a time when Alexei himself was so unhappy (from jealousy, always the same Asya)—Alexei thought, looking at his father with hatred, that his real father was Uncle Mitya.

Mama had a "young" photo of Uncle Mitya, prewar, with a loving inscription—handsome, elegant, a noble lady-killer... Alexei stood in front of the mirror with the photograph, made a face and—was completely convinced. Uncle Mitya was only older than his father by about ten years, Alexei reasoned, as if he were contracting an unequal marriage. And actually, in his lean bakedness and wiryness, and mainly, in the transparentness of his malice, Uncle Mitya was younger than his well-fed, successful father. He tried on the patronymic: Alexei Dmitrievich—no worse than Konstantinovich...

And it wasn't that Uncle Mitya would say anything special. He was fine, getting drunk, all the more precise and sober in his evaluations. "Crap"—that was the summation on one occasion, but the room almost seemed to brighten up from Uncle Mitya's summations because each time there was no doubt: he was exactly right. Like every unusual alcoholic, he possessed a particular humor of gesture, grin, grunt—all this fully replaced speech and was always clever. It was as if he were sorting over this and that, and we were witnesses of his thought, we knew what he wanted to say, but having sorted them over, didn't say this or that because neither this, that or the other was worth it—he would grunt at just the right moment, and everyone would laugh the happy laughter of mutual understanding. And because even the weather had now "become crap," Alexei felt free and gay, I don't know even how to explain such an effect...

I hope we'll be able in part to explain this "effect" in the next chapter.

Bleak House

Familyless Uncle Dickens could be that easily essential to the Monakhov family because he had, small as it was, his *own* home.

Alexei liked it at Uncle Dickens'. He liked it when, sitting him on the "settee," thrusting some "pornography" at him for inspection, Uncle Dickens would go out to the kitchen to make "camp tea" and Alexei would remain alone. This little room was made for running off to secretly in childhood, despite its being forbidden. Exactly—Uncle Dickens' little apartment was just like a forbidden book in childhood.

It was funny in all respects, cut off from a big apartment into a separate one ("divided")—it was so small, it got so little in the dividing process of the so-called "communal" space (that was not included in the order) and there was so much of everything in it that couldn't possibly fit but was essential for a bachelor gentleman such as Uncle Dickens. There was so much of everything in it that couldn't possibly fit that it was as if everything had coasted around, pushing each other out: in place of the bathroom was a little kitchen, in place of the "john" ("toilet" is a more indecent word than "john," Uncle Dickens always said)—a shower; the commode, being last, had nowhere to go and stood in the entry under the coat rack (it's unclear how Uncle Dickens convinced the technical inspector, but he was good at talking to *them*, they submitted to him willingly). So that the first thing one saw upon entering was the commode, however, of an unusual whiteness and refinement—that "liberty" line Uncle Dickens loved was present in its langourous morning curves. Who sat on it? Uncle Dickens insisted that "people," and now he himself, in his own words, sat on it, curtained off by an old moth-eaten nobleman's fur coat, also acquired by some chance—but we never found him at this occupation. It seemed he had no physical needs at all: he didn't sleep, didn't eat, didn't anything else. He went to extremes in this: "Don't spit when you brush your teeth!" he once admonished Alexei. He only drank and washed.

And everything about the old man was distinguished by the incredible cleanliness of conscious egoism: the floor was scrubbed in village style, and at home Uncle Dickens often went around barefoot—and when Alexei once expressed delight at this irreproachableness, Uncle Dickens frowned characteristically and said "You simply don't know what it is to get up in the morning..." And actually, one had only to find Uncle Dickens once in the first half of the day, in his grey stubble, pacing barefoot about his crowded apartment in snow-white shorts and a fluffy Orenburg shawl thrown over his shoulders, incessantly drinking tea (he never got drunk before evening; before "eighteen hundred hours" he never drank anything else) and incessantly sniffing: "Don't you think something stinks in here?"—the first thing you heard entering—to understand what his cleanliness meant to Uncle Dickens, although he never spoke about the trenches and dugouts of war, or about the barracks of construction sites. But he worried about it unnecessarily—there was never any stink in his apartment. It was its own standard of the absence of stink. Alexei had only himself to sniff.

Uncle Dickens had everything—he even had a "fireplace." Actually, not a fireplace, but a "pot-bellied stove," true, a very compact and sensible one, which he had carried with him throughout the entire last war. Because the only thing Uncle Dickens could not arrange in order and correspondence was his chamber pot. He never had enough air, and he was terrified of stink— that's why the windows were open wide; and he always shivered and shook incredibly ("A shiverer," Mama would say, "Uncle Dickens is a shiverer")—

that's why his "fireplace" roared. He went around the house either barefoot or in felt boots. But he never was able to reconcile his circulation with his surroundings.

Thus one could find him in the mornings in his study: barefoot, with the window wide open, in his fluffy Orenburg shawl and shorts, his back to the blazing "fireplace," in his hands an open volume—of Dal's dictionary, or "Bleak House" or "War and Peace"—and he was so fine, one could love him (he never demanded it), that Alexei always felt, childishly, that Uncle Dickens was reading a different "War and Peace" than everyone else, not in the sense that he read it in his own way, but that he actually had a different book called "War and Peace" with a different Natasha, a different Bolkonsky, also by Tolstoy, but by a different Tolstoy... And it's true: it couldn't have been the same book.

Everything connected with Uncle Mitya underwent an unexpected revitalization for Alexei... Even things which belonged to everyone, for example history—one had only to place Uncle Mitya in it—and it took on an unusual optical effect: Alexei began to see it as if it actually existed. It was as if it didn't get dark around Uncle Mitya: he was like silver dipped in the water of time—the special usefulness of such water, Alexei remembered, was proclaimed by his grandmother... Alexei began to see things as if he had never written school compositions, seen movies, as if he hadn't taken courses in history... And one couldn't say that Uncle Mitya told a lot of stories—but, strange to say, he had only to use the words "Civil War" or "World War II" for it to really be the "Civil War" or "World War II," and it was as if Alexei himself saw Uncle Mitya in them. Not to mention the Finnish or the Japanese—for Alexei that was sailboats and islands—mind-boggling exoticism, with the bittersweet aftertaste of envy, that exists or had existed for someone, it wasn't made up. Alexei himself was not so distant from the last war, everyone around had fought in it, but time passed, the war receded, and the witnesses and participants began to tell about it as if they themselves were not completely sure: did all this actually happen? Although they, of course, were convinced and knew that it had, but—time...

Uncle Mitya, such an uncommon character, could create a fact by simple word usage. And Alexei would swallow his saliva, feeling the metallic taste of genuineness in his mouth: it happened, it happened, nonetheless all this had happened. It was as if Uncle Mitya himself, because he was so unusual and unprecedented, underlined with his exceptional example the significantly greater reality and possibility of even the most distant, even the most impossible things—because it was easier to imagine anything than to imagine Uncle Mitya himself, but there he was, before your very eyes. Well, he was the one, they say, that's how it was: he'd shot a panicker himself with a pistol during an attack, and from the word "attack" Alexei felt as cold and empty as Uncle Mitya had—after success, alone in the dug-out next to the empty bunk of the soldier he'd shot. He was the one who had bored a hole in a famous dam in such a precise spot that it removed all the vibration and stress and instead of collapsing is standing to this day, toothy as an organ, resounding correctly and exactly, and the construction is not disorder and rubbish but a work of art. This is what it was: it was as if Uncle Mitya didn't even remember the struggle, the petty rubbish of the barbs, the exhaustion, the rages, but only the result remained, the completion—and there was no need to think about it any more: it had happened, it was done, it was past. The wind blew in the revolutionary archways, blew the crests from the piles of sand, the horses pawed the ground and whinnied, Uncle Mitya raised his collar, a bullet flew past, life passed... There is no sweeter banality than the one that belongs to you, there is no greater man than the one who proposes that we believe in that which we already believe, but, it seems we want to so badly... Lord, how many times have people fallen in love on this Earth!—but again and again someone is able to, able to use the same words, and in the same, the self-same sense...

It was a different "War and Peace" in Uncle Mitya's hands.

At three o'clock he would begin to come to life—to shave, wash, perfume himself, tie his tie. It was a pleasure to watch—though there was no one to see. Alexei was once honored to be present at Uncle Dickens' toilet—and could never forget it: the sight had its own accuracy and ritual beauty, although Uncle Dickens was not a fetishist. His toilet was a story about the nature of things, and, it seemed, he was in contact with the very concept of each thing, and not with its material form. When he would put on a shirt, it was as if he understood the shirt, he tied his tie—it was as if he understood the tie. By five o'clock he would be entirely ready. At 7:30 he would go (on foot, he didn't acknowledge public transport, and saved on taxis) to the hotel "Europe." Greeting everyone (everyone already knew him), he would go up to the "roof" and arrive just at the evening opening (after the afternoon break)—get into the empty room to the freshly-ironed tablecloths, blue from whiteness, to the waiters, not yet overworked and therefore still civil, to the daylight which poured evenly through the glass roof. Here he dined and drank his first glass. He would finish drinking at the Monakhovs'.

His life was understandable to everyone. He lived on modest means—"the rentier of my own fate," he would say of himself. Occasionally he would tune someone's piano, and he lived, not lacking for anything on principle. Not for anything or anyone. "Need and crap are synonyms," he used to say.

And so, the heart of this funny apartment was the study—not in the same heavy, production sense as Alexei's father's, but in the lost and now out-of-use sense: a study where a man, a gentleman, is alone, writes letters, leafs through a novel, simply lies down—and Alexei liked to stay there for a minute alone, on the settee, created to be uncomfortable to sit on, to leaf through a monograph, let's say, on Beardsley, sweet and small as a child's sin, to examine the forbidden room missed in childhood. And the books he took and returned to Uncle Dickens (which served as the pretext for his visits) were also a fulfilment of childhood: "Aphrodite," "Atlantis," "The Green Hat," when should they be read, if not under a blanket with a flashlight?...

He was right to take his things back from us, thought Alexei, with difficulty making out his immobile image from a distance in the oval mirror, as if it reflected a former, young Alexei. Above the long, low, end table on a pink wall with broad white stripes (the wallpaper from some play) were two paintings by Puvis de Chavannes ("Pooey-deshan"—a single child's word), Uncle Dickens' favorite artist—one could look at them long and dumbly, like the cracks and wallpaper from the bed during angina holidays... Closer to the window was a small upright piano on which Uncle Dickens played a potpourri of Griboedov waltzes. In the far corner in the shadows stood various junk: a three-legged spiral stand for a wash bowl with the bowl, and a mirror sticking up crookedly above it; behind it, in the very corner leaned a cot, folded like a centipede, which Uncle Dickens had carried with him practically from his first war or construction project and on which he slept to this day. How Uncle Dickens managed to open it alone Alexei couldn't understand, because if he were present at this procedure he absolutely had to help: to hold it, restrain it, stretch it out—and then they barely managed it even between the two of them. "Not like that, you fool!" Uncle Dickens raged, which referred not to the cot but to Alexei. The fact that it nonetheless did unfold was some kind of childhood wonder: when out of an armful of sticks a many-legged construction, delicate as an arched bridge, quivering and rickety as a bonfire, would suddenly unfold like an accordion and over it, on slats and hooks, a Kiplingesque tarpaulin would be stretched, consisting of patches, the carefulness of which would have caused any widow to burst into tears.

Even to enumerate a few of the things standing along one of the study walls, that is, opposite Alexei sitting on the settee, presents a complicated problem because of the possibility of the easy and involuntary immersion in each of these few objects—all these were "things belonging to one person" (it's not clear which of those five words to emphasize—each one is stressed), that is, to Uncle Dickens. The old man had taste. Not in the now current sense of better than others, or "not any worse than anyone else" or—in order not to be laughable or outmoded; not this contemporary layered taste—no, he had his own, personal taste, in some ways high, in some ways low, decadent (his love of "Liberty") and not ashamed of itself, respecting itself—that is, not slavish, not snobbish... He liked the things surrounding him—that was the basic condition of his taste. And they stood in his room that way: with taste and as they fell—there was no assigning of things to their places. It was as if they had been brought in one by one... Uncle Dickens would say "Here... no, put it here, and this one—over here, not like that, crap! sideways, sideways, you bum! and where'd that junk come from? It's mine?... let it be. Should the cupboard be where the piano is?... Maybe it's better that way?... Oh all right, stay there!" and he would go out to wash his hands again, come back shaking them carefully and would find the towel hanging on the three-legged table over the non-functioning, because it was peacetime, basin...

"Where's the lamp? Where did it go?" Alexei thought slowly and found it to the left behind his shoulder—of course, next to the "fireplace."... then he looked at the door: it was time for Uncle Dickens to return—and he came in, carrying a small tempered nickle tea kettle.

The Ordeal

...This business with his father Alexei just couldn't endure by himself.

On that memorable day Alexei went into Uncle Dickens' with the despair of a last hope. We don't go for help telling ourselves that we no longer believe in the possibility of help, but—we just go, and go precisely to the place where we can still expect it, we go with an outstretched hand, like beggars—we get a handshake, they give us a hand... The handshake so natural (a form of greeting!)—"And that's all!"...—from the threshold disappoints us. "Him too..." we think bitterly. "Him too..."

So it was with Alexei. He expected something, although what was good about "Uncle Dickens" was that you knew in advance everything you could expect of him, it was as if he warned you first thing: this, that and the other—and nothing more. But Alexei took the leap... It seemed like something out of the theater to him, something out of the Stanislavsky method... With him—so distressed, with sunken cheeks, having borne everything in silence, and they—two of a kind, who had endured everything, never asking anyone for help... And here Uncle Mitya, who never betrayed any feeling because nothing is ever serious for anyone, would understand that for Alexei this was real, put out his hand, spare, masculine, and say a wise word (only "Uncle Dickens" could say one)... tfoo! Then, with the accumulation of a tear, along with its sympathetic sting, it would emerge that Uncle Mitya was in reality Alexei's father... At this point there would be such confusion, such an apotheosis, that even the Moscow Art Theater couldn't play it.

Actually, as soon as he saw Alexei in the doorway, Uncle Mitya understood something—a subtle man. It was as if he didn't even want to let him in. Then he did let him in because he probably couldn't think up any reason not to let him in. "But I'm going out soon," he said from the inertia of some preceding, omitted phrase and probably hated himself for the one he did say, because he quickly turned away, stamped, and dashed into the room in front of Alexei. After the first quick and immediately scared look in the doorway, Alexei didn't manage to catch his eye again.

Uncle Mitya was very nervous, that was clear, Alexei had never seen him like that. His glance skidded about absentmindedly and kept managing somehow to avoid Alexei, not to catch his eye, and Alexei felt that this glance left a curling trace around the room the color of egg white, a rubber braid. Uncle Mitya of course could not and was not getting ready to go out: he was in his morning, dismantled state and, for technical reasons, could only get his squeaking parts together in two hours at the soonest—but he wasn't even thinking of going out. All the more since his "fireplace" was roaring and on the settee lay an open volume of Dal's dictionary—Uncle Dickens' everyday reading (he liked to delight in the brevity, the pithiness, of the definitions of "that Swede"). Catching Alexei's glance, Uncle Mitya became even more embarrassed, bustled up to Dal, and tried their usual game... "Tell me as briefly and exactly as possible what a lorgnette is." "Well," Alexei responded limply, "it's something in between binoculars and eyeglasses, they are held to the eyes at theater and at balls..." "That's brief!" Uncle Mitya raged and glanced at Dal. "Glasses with a handle—that's all!"

He ran angrily around the room, and perhaps because it seemed to him that Alexei was about to open his mouth, he would seize whatever was at hand spastically and begin to speak, too fast, interrupting himself, and losing the thread, which was also not his way. In short, he didn't know how to behave, which was unthinkable for Uncle Dickens, at least in the eyes of Alexei, for whom he was behavior itself, its standard. He could at least say to Alexei in the only intonation suitable to the occasion which he did so well: "You're crap, Alexei" or "But he's crap!" (about his father)—and comfort a distressed soul. But he didn't even say that, but began to curse someone (Alexei didn't understand who), and so insistently and dumbly that Alexei felt sick, almost ashamed, he almost wanted to defend "him," so defenseless, from Uncle Mitya. But apparently Uncle Mitya seemed to get more and more disgusting and unbearable to himself as well: he couldn't keep it up, and finally said the long-awaited "That's crap!" but here too rang false and ran off to make tea and disappeared, it seemed, forever.

Alexei indifferently gazed around the study always so dear to his heart—but this time nothing touched him. He looked at everything with boredom, the way one looks at a book read in childhood. Even himself he found lonely and old. Somehow he suddenly thought that Uncle Mitya wasn't "great" to anyone except himself, Alexei, and hadn't been all his life. Despite all his exceptional qualities... "Glasses with a handle..." Uncle Dickens... The nickname suddenly seemed very exact to Alexei, expressing something besides what he suspected. That was it, not Dickens, but Uncle... Here Alexei forgot what he meant. Because suddenly he remembered the first frightened glance which Uncle Mitya had met him with. And at this moment, as never before in his life, not with anyone, he vividly imagined his separate existence. It was a striking sensation—Uncle Mitya stood before him in the doorway, an old man losing his strength a drop a day... Dignity, a longing for dignity, was Uncle Mitya's last passion, the last possibility of his life, and he hardly had the strength to preserve at least its appearance. For this it was essential to him not to need anyone so that no one would need him, because the slightest dependence, the slightest responsibilities of love would immediately have sent him to the bottom, so heavy, already almost waterlogged; he would not have withstood even the slightest burden of feelings: he would burst, disintegrate, fly to flinders—the dry, sharp, tiny flinders of which he was composed...

Alexei felt this not exactly in words, but very fully, in its total volume, as if he were no longer Alexei, but was Uncle Mitya himself—he felt such anguish, terror and confusion inside himself, examining the image erected in his memory as if he were seeing it right now for the first time. Lord, thought Alexei, what a terrifying life he lives! And he, Alexei, had come to him for love, wisdom, pity... How he had dared, a well-fed, fat, healthy, young, dumb nonentity! Alexei went to extemes: Uncle Mitya's egoism seemed noble to him. At least, it was far better and purer than the indecent overflowings of the soul which Alexei had just been indulging in...

In this assessment Alexei was partially correct: Can one really subject another person to that danger of not having the strength, of not withstanding, not coping with what people heap on him...? As it is, haven't I piled enough on him...? Uncle Dickens, father, grandfather—Uncle Mitya played all these roles... Alexei imagined to himself, entering into the image, how nauseating and humiliating it had been for Uncle Mitya when he'd lied just now, saying he was in a hurry (for the first time! How scared he'd been, poor man...), when he avoided Alexei's eyes and babbled something...Don't be afraid, Uncle Mitya, I won't do it, I won't pile my burden on your weak, frail little shoulders, I won't subject you to the danger of humiliation at your own weakness and inability to cope with life with dignity...I will protect you...

That's almost how Alexei spoke to himself, already, unfortunately, self-conscious and touched by himself. And, one should give him his due, not once in his life had he yet been so subtle, exact, sensitive—so intelligent. For a second, Alexei was a genuinely mature person, only to forget about it shortly thereafter for many years, almost forever. It's possible that this insight was unusually perceptive of Alexei, preceding the fact and therefore not teaching him anything, although it's strange...

Looking at the floor, apprehensively, Uncle Mitya came in—Alexei was right. And, convinced of it, Alexei cruelly got up and said: "Good bye, I have to go," and probably precisely in that moment of satisfaction at his own intelligence and pleasure at his action, the experience of his recent insight was taken away from him almost forever, as premature, undeserved. He had already received "his reward..."

Uncle Mitya raised his wide-spaced eyes to him, filled with the light of inner surprise, looked at him for a second and said nothing. He accompanied him to the door.

"And how can he be my father...How can he be father, son and holy ghost?" Alexei said, laughing sardonically at his own recent stupidity, as if he were an upperclassman to himself. "My father should be precisely the way he is and no other. And I am his son...it's frightening—but true...and Uncle Dickens—what children could he have!...He died a hundred years ago... Glasses with a handle."

Alexei felt he had overtaken Uncle Mitya too.
But here he exaggerated.
Couldn't he imagine that Uncle Mitya might be ashamed... or disgusted at someone other than himself?

First Death

Alexei lived, and no one of his had ever died. They buried his grandmother without him, and anyway he was still a child. Now they were dying one after the other, as if by agreement. Just as classmates rapidly get married and have their first babies: all Annas or Andreis... and suddenly, surprise, they just as rapidly start dying off.

They found Uncle Dickens in a cold and clean apartment, by the extinguished "fireplace," with his hand on his throat—he had been tying his tie. He was already entirely ready "for dinner"—he lay decked out and ready for his coffin. No one had to do anything, no one had to "fuss," as he would have said. This explained still another aspect of Uncle Dickens' mania for cleanliness—readiness for death at any moment. An old officer...

His funeral was totally unlike the triumphal mockery of grandfather Monakhov. Despite its poverty and smallness, it produced a very touching, and not a gloomy impression. The weather was unusually clear and Dickens' corner of the cemetery was light. There was almost no one at the funeral, just the Monakhovs and the janitor Koptelov (he whispered to Alexei that he had served under Dmitri Ivanovich during the last war—however, they had no further conversation). Mama cried a lot, and, late and breathless, a teary beauty appeared with a wreath from the waiters of "the roof." He was "one of us," Uncle Dickens, and he liked that.

In short, for Alexei it was the first time a close person had died. With his grandfather everything had been different: the death had been overshadowed by enthusiasm over the birth of a great man. That payment is always demanded for greatness—humanity. No one was interested that grandfather had been a person. Grandfather had been a dolphin or whatever you like, but not a person. With Uncle Dickens it was the opposite: nothing besides the person had died in him, but nothing had remained afterwards either, nothing had been born, and this emptiness between death and birth had not been filled with anything, had been unfillable. With the death of Uncle Dickens—Uncle Dickens disappeared.

And that was a loss. Only now could it be fully realized what Uncle Dickens had been for the Monakhov family and what it had been and not been—for him. Uncle Dickens was not at all a great man in the generally accepted "weighty" sense, but we want to emphasize his peculiar and exceptional greatness, the greatness of the awareness of his own "size."

He was not a strong and not an impressive person, he had very little of everything, but he had no pretentions and didn't encroach on anything belonging to others. On the other hand, he remembered himself all his life, and at a time when everyone forgot everything, he never forgot his "little bit." There was no reason to prefer the Monakhov family to many others, including his own possible family, but this particular family happened in his life, and, since that was the case, he never changed it. This devotion was devotion to himself, which is what makes it of a higher sort than, say, a dog's. In some sense the Monakhov family consumed Uncle Dickens, used him with its love, and in so doing, drained his love to the bottom. But, as we already said, he had very little of everything, though that—was everything. So he entered their nest, and served as cement. They, strong and healthy, started using him easily, not noticing how and when it happened, supposing that they enhanced his loneliness with their love. On his way from the Civil War to World War II on the sturdy and invisible fishing-line of his fate, he got caught in the Monakhov's pond, and stayed there, being a man filled with genuine nobility. During his rare civilian vacations, in the rare intervals between campaigns and distant construction sites, he barely managed to carry off his little sack of accumulated warmth when they would summon him again, when it was already time to leave... Thus he expended himself in trivia, as in a family. Nothing was left for him. He got nothing from it. The Monakhovs nodded, yawning before going to sleep, and said in Uncle Dickens' warm wake that yes, every person should have a place to "come home to"... They were well-read people.

Dickens' Prose

They thought that Uncle Dickens had no family, but, too late for the funeral, his sister, a retired teacher, arrived from Yoshkar-Oly. Someone even remembered that Uncle Dickens had once said something about there being a sister... They had even all argued whether or not he had said something. But there was the sister, sitting in the Monakhov's kitchen, embarrassedly and noisily drinking tea from a saucer: her little fingers were fat and stubborn. She firmly refused everything except tea. She was shy and embarrassed; Mama was particularly courteous—Alexei smiled, looking at them. She was "of another breed," as Mama later said of her. And in fact it looked as if a pointer had a dachshund sister, or perhaps his mother, either a Bashkir or a Chuvash. Uncle Mitya had also once said something about that too... The Monakhovs also argued about whether she was a Chuvash. But the sister finally got into Uncle Mitya's apartment and immediately, with a tenacious and frightened glance, photographed the material valuables...

The retired schoolteacher didn't miss a thing, took everything down to the last nail off to Yoshkar-Oly. And no matter now much the Monakhovs said to her: at least leave the piano, that they'd buy the piano, that it wouldn't survive the move—her lips would become more and more of a thread, and she would not allow herself to be cheated: the piano sailed off to Yoshkar-Oly. It seems it really didn't ride off but sailed off because it turned out to be cheaper that way, and she was in no hurry. Curiously, she too had no family.

Even Puvis de Chavannes, no matter how much Alexei explained to her that it was only a reproduction not worth a kopek but was dear to him as a memory... she twitched at the word "kopek" and wouldn't give it up either. Well yes, as a memory... One had only to remember Uncle Dickens' stories about family greed... Later discussing the teacher, the Monakhovs remembered them.

Alexei was only able to spirit away "Atlantis" while the teacher was watching Alexei's mama whom she had from the very beginning regarded with inexplicable fixedness. He re-read it and was touched... "On that quiet moonlit night de Saint Avis killed Morangea..."

But she gave Alexei Uncle Dickens' papers with ease. Mama, however, took them away and locked them up. Alexei wasn't sure that she didn't read them when she was alone. However, she gave Alexei two notebooks "as a specialist." Look, perhaps you'll be interested... These were Uncle Dickens' compositions.

One notebook was called "Poems," the other—"Novellas." Alexei felt shame and the pain of love, reading them... He naturally "evaluated" Uncle Dickens by notions cultivated in childhood. However, this evaluation was not completely caddish, but many-leveled and complex: a low satisfaction at the near-fall of an idol was replaced by disillusionment (not in the idol but at the fall), and the disillusionment—by steadfast tenderness. The pain at the crumbling of an old image turned out to be easy and swift, but the construction of a new one was light and joyful, certain and final: as if it were the true one. In the final analysis, Alexei only came to love this image the more strongly now that it could no longer acquire new features.

The poems were indisputable: unbelievably weak and naive—but through them too flitted Dickens' untainted soul. (With prose, making evaluations is more complicated... It's harder to evaluate as categorically as poetry: poetry and non-poetry—it's as if there is no middle ground. In prose something always turns out to be expressed: either the author's intentions, or the author himself... As a document at least, it always has some particular interest.) We even like Uncle Dickens' prose, and we value it higher than Alexei, who is still not completely free of snobbism. In this case one can't ask Alexei's opinion even though he is more of a professional specialist in that field than, let's say, we are.

He can't judge objectively because the reading of the prose of Uncle Dickens is for him more a direct, personal experience than the average reader's experience. He has different associations than the ones experienced by the prose itself. For him, for example, the slight opening of the curtain which always exists between generations was a shock. Thus a young man, himself reaching the age of a personal life and plunging into it head first suddenly asks himself the naive question: wait, can it be the same for other people? and, looking for an answer, remembers (who else can a person that young remember?) his parents and discovers that in that sense he knows nothing at all about them: did they love, did they suffer, what were they and perhaps even are they for themselves and for each other when he, for example, isn't there? Do they too really... etc. That is, he, already, it would seem, an adult, faces the problem of understanding by himself everything in the forms presented to him by time, or else the previous generation will get old and depart without having showed its hand to him: did it live at all?—leaving him a lifelong supply of childhood images and experiences of the life of adults. That is probably extraordinary, and here there is a secret, inviolable and holy—guarded. Because even the completely logical certainty that others are the same remains empty and lifeless, unfruitful. It's this, perhaps at the price of suffering, which allows a person to live his own life further...

So, when Alexei read Uncle Dickens' compositions, it was as if this curtain fluttered in the breeze, and a corner turned up a bit... he didn't find any "details" in the tawdry sense there, but the image of an old, wise person with some higher experience expressed only in his behavior where every gesture is final and summary, crowning a long series—such an image swayed severely, revealing an infinite childishness, naiveté, sentimentality, absence of taste and strength. But this image was at once newly plastered and painted into being touching: people used to be purer and nobler, people used to be different, they used to be more naive, fearful and full of ideas—that is what individuality is in the real, not in the "professional" sense ("to become an individual")—all these "people used to be" reduced to one departed Uncle Dickens.

Here an effect is observed which brings us to one easy thought about the nature of prose, and we can't refrain from this suggestion...

This effect is contained in the fact that, suddenly, stumbling upon the page of a person we know well or are even close to but who we didn't know "did some writing," and reading it with incomprehensible greed, we at once begin to know many times more about him than we did up to then by spending time with him. And it's not a matter of some secret or jealous facts. The example of a page on which we would find no such facts as objects of curiosity or jealousy is the proof. In this case nothing obscures anything for us, and we learn even more about the author. That unconquerable curiosity with which we pick up such a page is nothing other than a thirst to learn an "objective" secret—the secret of what it's like when you're not there, but that kind of secret is the cloud on which we live. What will we learn from this page if there is no gossip on it? Style. The "secret" we talked about contains style, and not plot ("jealous facts").

Besides the problems and facts the author chooses to elaborate, the resulting prose will always to a greater degree reflect his intentions, which are revealed independently of the author, irrationally, almost mystically, like some substance...(we have experienced unexpected surprises at this phenomenon). A person taking a pen in hand for the first time, still embarrassed by this unexpected summons, still defending himself from his possible fiasco with a careless sardonic smile (although no one sees him, he deliberately chooses the moment), but in fact instinctively (health!) terrified at what will happen not to it (to prose) but to him... this person has already encountered the phenomenon of literature: whether he wants to or not, he will reveal his secret. From this moment he can always be exposed and found out, caught: he is visible, seeable, he is on display. Because style is as exact, as unique a print of the soul as a fingerprint is the passport of a criminal.

And here we come to our long cherished thought that there is no such thing as talent—there is only the person. No such separate thing as "talent," like height, weight, eye color, exists, but people exist: good and bad, smart and stupid, people and nonpeople. So the good and the smart are talented and the bad and the stupid are not. And if a person has intelligence and heart and he wants to tell the world what he has, then he will unavoidably be verbally talented, if only he believes in himself. Because the word is the most exact weapon given to man and no one yet (which constantly comforts us) has ever managed to hide anything in the word; if he lies, his word gives him away, and if he knows the truth and tells it, then the word comes to him. It is not man who finds the word, but the word which finds man. The word will always find a pure man—and he will be, even if just for a moment, talented. In this sense we know only one thing about "talent": that it, as they say, is "from God."

That is why it is so awkward, so terrifying, so shameful and dangerous to learn of a close person that he "does some writing." That is why we must take the first opportunity to find out about it... To write is in general shameful. A professional is protected at least by the fact that he has been going around naked for a long time and has become hardened and tempered in his shamelessness. He has already said, blurted out, revealed so much about himself that he has already diminished the absolute unexpectedness of the information about man that is literature. And we again know nothing about him. A person always has the goal of being invisible (a defense) to others, and there are only two means to this end: absolute closedness and total openness. The latter—is a writer. About him we know everything and nothing. That is why (with the same uncontrollable greed as looking at someone else's page) they begin establishing who an author was after his death so doggedly: letters, memoirs, medical certificates—and are never successful. This person, having lived so openly, so on view, so on display, turned out to be the most hidden, the most invisible and took his secret to the grave.

For it to be so, writers have to be geniuses: amateurs—crystal pure and honest.

In the notebook "Novellas" there were about ten little pieces. They were all written at the front in the summer and fall of 1944. The smallest was little more than 100 words long, the largest—not more than three pages.

Here is the novella whose events obviously served as the inspiration for the whole cycle—"Loneliness." The hero ("He") comes to town on leave and goes to his beloved ("She") to tell her once more (without hope and expectations) of his love. "I know," she said quietly. Containing his excitement, but already in a calm voice, as if not giving his words any importance, he added:

"I've come from the front—and am leaving again for the front."

He said this—and went out of the room."

Then he wanders around the town all day, stands the whole night on the bridge... "And only at noon, when the sun had already climbed high in the sky—he got on the train and went off to the front."

Uncle Mitya lived a very lonesome life! We regard his independence with even greater respect. Here's where he meets an orphan on the roads of war ("The Little Girl"): "... I have neither bread, nor a kopek, just as you probably have neither close ones nor relatives who could shelter you... My poor little thing! Come with me along this straight road. We won't turn to the left or to the right... We have nowhere to turn, my poor little sister! We have neither friends nor home—not even a little copper kopek."

Then there are novellas showing that in bowing to life, the man did not become a sceptic or a cynic... His hate for the Germans, the Hitlerites, during the war was so sincere and simple: "No bird of prey, no hungry animal would peck at or eat that garbage" or "What did that wretched cur, that vile German scum, think, fulfilling the command of his executioner masters?" And his sympathy and pain was so unconditional and disinterested: "I stand by the window and look at these ashes—and my heart is flooded with blood."

And here are both qualities mixed, an alloy: "... this still more arrests your attention, and, looking more intently, you already see clearly that it's a 'Fritz,' struck down by a bullet in the course of his work.

This figure, by the naturalness of its very pose (he was repairing wires) stuns you, shocks with its vitality, and evokes, in the final analysis, a feeling of disgust and deep hatred."

That "in the final analysis" is extraordinary! We too believe that Uncle Dickens was a real soldier. The loneliness of his fate, unrequited love, eternal war, pain for his fatherland—how few pure and strong lines it takes to paint his self-portrait! Sensitive and romantic... and we, perhaps for the first time, accept and forgive romanticism—to do that it took only crystal purity.

Uncle Dickens' prose indisputably expresses him more than he—it. He probably didn't even suspect how much it expressed him... But for us he himself is so fine that he is better than any, even the most powerful prose, and we are grateful to Prose that it expressed him to us.

For a clean person clean paper is no waste...

I append the novellas of Uncle Dickens.

The Snowstorm

It was long ago—in the days of my distant youth when I was in love with a certain girl. They called her Nastenka. Perhaps she was not as beautiful and not as good, perhaps not even as intelligent as others, but I loved her as only the ardent heart of a young man can love. I loved her madly, passionately, furiously—I loved her, as they say, to the point of crime—and at the same time felt all the hopelessness of my dreams, all the pointlessness of my outbursts.

I was poor, even very poor—and this kept me from realizing my hopes and being more daring and decisive. Finally, not having the strength to contain my passion and honest intentions any longer, I fell at Nastenka's feet, asking for her hand and heart.

Nastenka was not surprised, nor outraged, and did not fall into my arms. She only answered "Go to Papa. I can't without Papa."

Hard as it was for me, I was nonetheless compelled to do it.

As was to be expected, I received a refusal. A severe refusal, categoric.

I was incensed, insulted—I was ready to shoot myself from grief—and suddenly chance or fate herself came to my aid, gave me hope with her golden rays, and propelled me on the path of seeking my happiness by another road.

My friend, my best school friend, inspired me to "steal" my bride, marry her secretly against the wishes of her parents... I like a madman seized this idea, ran to Nastenka and shared my plan with her—Nastenka was terribly afraid, waved her hands, but in the end agreed and even got interested in the future journey.

Everything was ready for the appointed hour. Both the covered carriage with a pair of sturdy horses and the faithful coachman. Here I am sitting in the carriage with Nastenka and we're driving to a village 40-50 versts from our town. We arrive silently, sadly, and suddenly bad weather blew up, a snowstorm started swirling along the roads, swept all the paths and crossroads... The snow piles up, the wind... In a word a blizzard, a snowstorm struck, and God's world became invisible.

Nastenka gets nervous, bites her lips, but is silent and doesn't ask any questions. I sit restraining myself from fury, ready to bite the throat of every creature we might meet—wild animal, a horse, ready to break the windows in the carriage* and strangle the hateful storm with my own hands.

I urge on the coachman, swear at him, am furious—but the horses stand still or barely move and the blizzard sweeps our traces and my carriage more and more mercilessly.

It had already gotten dark when we drove into some completely unknown village. The blizzard had died down. The snow had stopped falling. The moon was rising in the sky, a big, light moon like a silver ruble or a dinner plate.

---

* We are not sure that this equipage is correctly named by the author (A.B.)

Nastenka cried and asked to go home. "I want to go to Mama, I want to go home," she sniffed every minute, and firmly demanded we return.

And I... I understood the inconsolability of real grief, the irreparableness of the situation—I was crushed by unhappiness, deceived by pitiless fate—and could no longer manage the terror which had seized me.

By night we got to the town with difficulty. Nastenka got out of the carriage, not even saying good-bye to me.

From that time on I saw her no more. The memory of the ill-fated adventure to this day lives in my heart, disturbs me and makes me relive the past.

Even now I see Nastenka as if she were before me, sitting in the carriage, wrapped in a fur coat and crying very quietly. I see her blue eyes, the confused look on her dear little face—I see the beautiful, childishly capricious lips trembling from nervousness—and I see the tears, bright as crystal, breaking out from under her thick dark eyelashes.

It was long ago, very long ago, when I was young and in love—and, like all young people in love, I had to earn forgiveness for my irresponsibility and wild youthful outbursts. But I never asked forgiveness and didn't even look for sympathy in anyone's eyes. And now—I'm too old to change my habits and tastes.

And still—it's all very sad, my dear reader.

And we are so taken by the charm of this tale that we can't refrain from appending another little novella, although everything is quite clear without it. But you won't have another chance to read it, and so we append another one here... (This is the last novella in the cycle: everything began with arrival and departure and ended with return).

The Mirror

After many years of travelings and wanderings, I happened to come to a place where people lived huddled together in their scanty households.

I was received hospitably and put in a little house which seemed comfortable and cozy to me.

By some strange chance there turned out to be a fireplace in the room—and this put me all the more in a good mood. At last I can rest and set myself in order!...

I lit the fire and began to warm myself. A pleasant drowsiness overcame me. I tried not to think of anything, not to think at all—it was so pleasant sitting by the fire—but all sorts of images awoke memories, stole into my mind, churned about like worms and gradually irritated my nerves.

I remembered the past, my friends, a beloved woman. I remembered days of bitter disappointment, unrealized hopes, of loneliness...

All this seemed so distant, long forgotten now—and only my heart still beat in my breast making me relive what I had lived through.

Yes, yes! You're right, my poor, weary suffering heart, I still love that woman—and no years of separation can stifle my feelings and passion.

I still want to love, to dream, to hope, I still thirst to be caressed by the hand of the woman I love, I'm not too old not to have wonderful desires—and don't paths cross on life's way sooner or later, and don't rivers overflow their shores in spring?...

Everything changes in life—times, people, feelings. Perhaps the one I still love to this day will make me happy with her smile and tenderness.

Thus I sat by the fire remembering the past and dreaming, as in the past, about happiness.

Suddenly I saw a mirror on the wall, took it down—and...my hand trembled. An old face with grey hair, with a high, bald forehead, with dim, deeply sunken eyes looked at me.

No, no!—that's not my face, that's not I. I didn't believe it, didn't recognize it—I was shocked by the cruel change.

A bitter, somehow sly smile slipped across the face of the old man and made me shudder.

I laughed out loud—and with revulsion and hatred heaved the mirror into the fire.

"Let everything burn—the gilded frame, old age, and the fantasies!"

I drank a glass of cold coffee and lay down to sleep in a warm, soft bed for the first time in long years of traveling and wandering.

To the bright memory of Azary Ivanovich Ivanov (1895-1958) the author dedicates this entire story about the old soldier.

Editor's Note

The subtitle to "The Soldier"—"From the Memoirs of the Monakhov Family"—alerts the reader to the fact that he is dealing with a fragment of a larger work. "The Soldier" is part of a chapter from Bitov's novel *Pushkin House*. Uncle Dickens' past was rewritten for "The Soldier," where Dickens is "summoned to some construction where something threated to collapse without him" (page 96). In *Pushkin House* Dickens returns from exile, not a construction project.

A Country Place

Life in Windy Weather

To Alexander Kushner

Finally they moved.

He was as usual struck by how overgrown the garden had become and how the lot itself seemed to have shrunk, and the dacha, hidden by undergrowth, seemed less bulky than it had last year. The trees, recently small, now reached to the windows of the second floor. The dacha, still unfinished, had already begun to get dilapidated, the frame, not yet trimmed, had gotten still blacker, and the entire dacha, which had stuck out so awkwardly and tastelessly before, now seemed to have made itself at home, to have taken root, and for the first time he liked it.

The doors opened poorly, and it was half-dark inside, like evening. The windows were shielded on the outside by winter shutters, and the sunlight, piercing through the cracks, clearly delineated one board of the shutters from another and just as neatly drew lines along the floor.

"Alyosha, if you don't need me anymore, I'll go..." his father said uncertainly, and by his tone of voice Alexei knew that his father was vacillating between staying to help him get settled and not really feeling much like staying. "I'd like to go back while the traffic is still light..."

"Of course, go ahead," said Alexei, carefully stepping on a strip of sunlight. "Thanks for bringing us."

As he accompanied his father to the car, he thought that the dacha, which would probably never be finished, somehow corresponded perfectly to this "limousine," which would never be a decent car. If his wife's parents had a sort of country house, then his father had a sort of car. In this way there was established a sort of balance.

The car finally started and his father drove off.

Alexei went back to the house. His wife was cooking cereal for their son. He was standing up in his crib, and he stamped his bare foot and joyfully held out his stocking to no one in particular. Alexei thought about the simple and for him unusual things which had to be done: undoing the shutters, chopping firewood, heating the house, and something stretched his mouth toward his ears in that kind of smile which arises somehow apart from our own will, which we cannot restrain.

He did not sleep soundly that night, as always in a new place. He woke up early, and he was so free that he even felt at a loss. His wife, as in town, was busy with their son and had even more to do than usual. But he found himself with so much time that it was hard to get through it all. The move to the dacha was for him a real resettlement: all the parameters of his existence had changed, and the most important of these was time. As he lounged about, he turned on the radio: the announcer was giving the program for the day, and the thoroughness with which he stated the time made Alexei smile ironically. He looked at his watch—it had stopped. "Moscow time is zero hours, zero minutes, zero seconds," Alexei said.

Distances too had changed. Suddenly he no longer had to be somewhere by a specified time, he no longer had to wait for buses which sometimes were late and sometimes didn't open their doors,—he was now totally independent in his movements, and distances which in town were inescapably connected with some means of transportation could here be traversed only on foot. In this sense he had suddenly become the owner of his own personal means of transportation—if he wanted to he went, if he didn't he didn't; he left his terminal when he had a good mind to, and in all this he was independent. After loitering about the house a bit and lighting the stove for his wife, he went out to take a walk and broke trails to the lake and the store, marvelling all the while at this new means of movement, and when he again found himself at home it was, as before, early: in town he would still be sleeping. This excessive amount of time stretching out before him made him wary. "Okay, I can finally get down to work...," he said uncertainly, and with unusual care, not regretting the time, even somehow wishing that it would race by with its usual speed and would stop being so very relative, he set about preparing a working place for himself.

He chose the second floor, which was not yet finished, and carried up a table, a chair, and his simple equipment. During this time again no time passed at all. As before, it was like a becalmed sea which he had to sail across but he seemed to have forgotten how to sail.

He sat down at the table, and he got bored. He couldn't imagine a better place to work in, but he didn't feel like working. The four windows looked out in all four directions of the compass. They were level with the treetops, and the branches probably would have knocked against the glass if they had not been kept back by the small balconies; the branches perhaps knocked against the balusters of the balconies, but he couldn't hear it.

So he sat, thinking hostilely about his work, when he suddenly discovered that the weather outside had turned bad. The wind forcefully swooped down on his study; everything began to creak, to squeak; it felt as if a sailing ship had just set out, plunging through the water. The first large drops hit the north window; a real squall swooped in with them; the leaves of the trees which had covered the windows, turned inside out like an umbrella, turned silver, and seemed to be streaming. Alexei gladly yielded to the feeling that his study was actually taking off into the air, and then it was no longer the wind but the study which raced along with such speed that it cleaved the air and caused the wind to rush by—trees, forests, mountains flashed past the windows, merging together into an indistinguishable strip. The study howled in the gusts, and merging with it, he felt its stress, the straining of all its rafters, columns, piles, which Alexei called to himself first masts, then musical strings, as he called the whole of it first a ship, then an organ. The bad weather filled his abode with a kind of special coziness, and he wouldn't have wanted to change anything, to adjust anything in it. The jutting ribs of the house, the slag underfoot, the spiderwebs everywhere, and the clumps of dusty rubbish—everything seemed just as it ought to be.

Suddenly the wind fell, the foliage stopped flashing past the window, and a heavy shower clattered on the roof. Alexei raised his head and as if for the first time saw that there was no ceiling above him—just the roof. In places it rose in sharp angles, in places descended in obtuse arches (as he called them to himself), and then his entire dwelling took on the appearance of a cathedral, which merged in his mind with the image of the organ... But the study no longer howled, since the wind had stopped, and the roof simply jingled under the blows of the shower; the shower turned out to be a huge hailstorm; Alexei went over to the window and saw the hailstones jumping about on the floor of the balcony and said to himself that they were the size of eggs, chicken eggs, although they were no larger than bonbons. The sounds changed around him, and along with the jingling of the roof slating above him he heard other, brisk, sounds, rather like a ripping sound, and looking around, he saw water dripping from the roof into little rusty tin cans placed here and there about the room. A feeling of constancy and stability came upon him as he looked at these little cans standing here, just as they had in past years exactly in the places where the roof was leaking. The sense of all this could have become the beginning of his work, but drops began to fall onto his table, on his papers, infrequent drops, but large ones. He wandered about the second floor with the table in his hands, trying it out in various corners, but in these too there were some small leaks. He sought a waterproof spot by trial and error, by touch as it were, and had just about found one when he heard his wife, who had just discovered the rain, cry out from down below. She had apparently been sleeping until now, and she cried out that something of hers outside in the yard would get wet. Alexei went downstairs, muttered to her, "You always leave everything outside," and went out into the yard. But it had already stopped raining, and Alexei came out just in time to see it suddenly come to a stop: to see the newly colored swollen leaves swaying, each leaf more separate than before the rain; to see each leaf suddenly begin to stir in the still, thick air, and as if coming alive, bend down and straighten up its back and roll a large diamond drop off itself like a heavy burden; to see it breathe with joy and relief and offer itself up to a ray of sun which had just broken through and seemed, like the leaves, to be glowing with health.

In this way the days flowed by. Time was motionless, yet the days passed. And it was strange, looking back, to see how many of them had already passed. And he couldn't get at all used to the fact that the passage of time could be seen only by looking back and only in large sections, whereas at any present moment it was motionless. But as for work, he just couldn't get anything done. When he went to bed he couldn't understand where the time had disappeared to.

Whereas in town he woke up every morning with a feeling that yesterday evening had not been entirely normal, that is, he had chattered about God knows what, something superfluous or personal, had done some awkward and shameful things (what, exactly, he couldn't quite recall, as if he had been drunk); whereas every morning his first feeling was one of shame at the previous evening, and while dressing he immediately brushed this feeling aside and it disappeared, and then the day followed, bustling and unthinking, right up to the next "not-entirely-normal-evening," and just a brief spark of awareness had to flare up the next morning and fade away as he pulled on his trousers,—whereas in town everything was just like that, in the country everything was quite different.

In the country, on the contrary, in the family circle, in the sun, air, and water, he outwardly relaxed, grew younger, and in general began to look better. It was peaceful here, and he managed very sensibly either to complete his affairs or lay them aside—specifically so as in the country at least, to be able to live peacefully and work on what he considered it his duty to work on.

At the same time, now that he had finally escaped from the city, where he labored, cursing its bustle, knowing in minutest detail and loving to expose all its nuances, now that he was able to do all those things he couldn't usually do, somehow instead of joy and activity he felt only a kind of significant emptiness which he had nothing to fill with, because now he didn't feel like doing the things he had planned on filling it with, for which he had been trying to create this emptiness. And besides, he had to some extent gotten tired of the eternal struggle and bother with himself, and consequently he found it boring by now to berate himself for laziness and idleness, to denounce, to flagellate himself, and nevertheless still not move a muscle, and then after all this to think about the whole complex—and so he didn't think about it.

At times he even felt a certain satisfaction at this state of affairs. Consciously he had already understood for a long time (this was very like the way he felt and understood the fuss and bustle, these understandings were directly related) that the main thing is simply *to live,* to be alive, and therefore no matter what your condition is—fruitful or unfruitful—as long as you are *alive,* not benumbed, and trying to accomplish things... but what does it mean to try to accomplish things: if you're not alive you won't accomplish anything anyway.

This state of idleness revealed to him, for example, that he had a son.

Floundering about in the sea of time, he stayed home more and more and constantly saw his son nearby, a being so completely alive that it made him ashamed of all that was lifeless in himself, and especially of such a lifeless thing as the establishment and then the living through of this very lifelessness in himself. Such a taking-stock and comparison of himself with his son occurred in town too when, worn out by the fuss and bustle and unhappy after bothersome meetings and conversations which were so long that they caused him to lose all touch with reality, he would suddenly find himself at home and would see his son, whom he had not remembered once all day, break into a joyful smile at this arrival. At such times he felt simultaneously a kind of meaningful ebb and flow: an ebb away from his day, a flow toward his son. But in town this always happened somehow in passing, it didn't enter his consciousness, his feelings, he just somehow quickly got used to it: well, so, he's home and here's his son—nothing surprising in that... And the usual insane evening would begin.

But in the country, whether because he saw more trees and living things—cows and horses, calves and foals—or whether the air was healthier, or whether he stayed home more and spent more time with his son, he began to look at his son differently.

He would be thinking about his son and suddenly he would understand things for which he had somehow, without noticing it when it had happened, lost his taste or sensitivity, things unusually simple and eternal in their simplicity: joy and pleasure, for example. Sometimes, bored by his idleness and thinking about the city, he would suddenly hear some foolish cooing sound from his son and he would turn around and see his outstretched hand and his face lit up with joy at the mere fact that they saw and recognized one another... Then Alexei felt his lifeless cloud fly away from him and something amazingly happy and light unfold in his breast, something which can be called many things and can be called love. He was truly grateful to his son for so generously sharing his life with him, for radiating life, and the unconsciousness of this gift did not detract from Alexei's gratitude, but rather confirmed it. He would be filled with amazement, a naive and simple amazement, when he watched his son. And as he came closer to the truth of this primitive nature and to belief in it, it was without the least bit of even good-natured self-mockery that he had such thoughts as: How did he get to be like that? He's alive and already has everything? Hands, and eyes, and even ears? And he looks like his father?

The knowledge of how children come into being did not damp his feelings, he discarded this knowledge as not explaining anything, and then the phenomenon of his son amazed him even more—where was he from? No really, if you think it through to the end, where was he from? Or the helplessness and weakness of his son struck Alexei: the fact, for example, that it would take nothing at all to kill him, you could do it with one finger and there's the end of life in this little body!—how does so much life find room in such a small body? He was amazed at the youth of his son, at the tenderness of his skin—what a used-up piece of junk he was in comparison with his son! And the exactions of weakness struck Alexei: if it happens, for example, that his son needs something, simply needs it, wants it, he doesn't doubt in the least that everyone will obey him, will submit to him, while his son's dependence on them, his parents, is only imaginary: in actual fact the parents are dependent on him, obey him and fulfill his wishes, serve him.

Every day Alexei went for walks with his son, pushing him in his stroller. His son was already trying to walk, and once Alexei took him out of the stroller and his son held onto it and for the first time walked down the street with his father. It was windy, which made the sky seem high and the sun unusually small and distant. The couple they bought milk from was turning hay in a meadow, and either their children or grandchildren, or the children or grandchildren of summer residents, were turning somersaults in the hay; a train rumbled in the distance. And Alexei walked more slowly than he had ever walked before because for the first time, side by side with him, for some reason raising his unsteady little legs high, walked his son. And perhaps just because he was walking so slowly Alexei heeded and absorbed everything around much more intensely, minutely, palpably than usual, as if the life around him or in him had become much more concentrated at every foot of the way: every breath, every starling house, or bush, or chip in the dust of the road... And suddenly his son became unusually excited, and forgetting that he could not yet walk without support, he abandoned the stroller and stepped off to the side. He stretched his hand out to what he saw before him and said all the words he knew: "Mama, papa, wawa, goo, all." "All, all, all!" he said joyfully, pointing to what he saw. He saw a cat running across the road: an unfamiliar creature, but a living one. It was an uninteresting cat, plain and sedate; it had obviously lived a long time on this earth and was completely unaffected by his son's radiance. It neither stopped nor quickened its pace; it was not in the least affected by such rapt attention, and surprising Alexei by the constancy and measuredness of its movements it disappeared into the bushes on its own business. Alexei managed to pick up his son, who had taken the step so selflessly in the joy of learning. And suddenly he felt and understood his son as never before and remembered something long past and long forgotten about himself.

Truly, he had never seen so much life, joy, and pleasure so completely and fully embodied that they, and not flesh, seemed to be the basic material essence of his son's being. And then Alexei was even more amazed as he discovered in this so joyful babbling, in these so clear and loving eyes, not joy at all, but sadness, a sadness placed there by nature itself, along with the joy.

In this way the son was helping his father to sail across time and come to land at evening.

Still, the fact that he was doing nothing tormented him terribly. Then he would remember the bustling city, which he had so recently cursed, as a place full of life, a place outside of which he couldn't accomplish a thing. Then he would feel like going into town (though he wasn't always concretely aware of this, since it contradicted his summer schedule). And then unfinished matters would somehow all by themselves begin to be recalled, perhaps not very significant matters, but all the same, until he got them done they would give him no peace and he would not enjoy his freedom because of these trifles. And then he would begin (and this was almost activity) to make little lists of these matters, large and small, which kept cropping up and piling up, gladly and even lovingly including the merest trifles. He would rewrite these lists in various sequences: by importance, by time, by convenience of itinerary. He would elaborate points and make remarks in parentheses: "mustn't forget to ask," "mustn't forget to say," "pretend you forgot." After which he would remember one more thing, perhaps the most important of all, and would have to rewrite the list again to insert this matter in its proper place.

He would play around with these lists for a while and then begin to explain to his wife that he absolutely had to make a trip into town. His wife of course said he didn't need to go, that he already had so little time for relaxation and work, that this was all just a waste of time. He realized that her words were just, even recognized his own words in hers, and he began, as was completely natural, to get irritated, and like a child he rebelled not against the meaning of the words but against the logic by which they had arrived at these words; it was the logic which seemed especially unfounded and unjust, and irritated him more than anything else. They argued each point and then each went his own way: his wife to take care of the house, he to lie somewhere in the sun. But then, like people who love each other and know each other too well, they forgot their quarrel. Neither argued any longer about the trip to the city, at some point or other it simply began to be talked about as something already understood; the day was set, his wife gradually remembered more and more new errands: what to buy, what to bring from home,—the list grew and became much too large to be completed in one day's trip. But this didn't bother either one of them, because it was somehow clear to both that there was really nothing to take care of, that he simply needed to go to the city in order to see once more that everything there was bustle and delirium, and then to return satisfied, charged up, and perhaps begin to do something.

What always happened, though, was this. In town he would manage to get some item on his wife's list done and half of his own and return cheerful and raring to go and sit down to work the next day. Only the next day he didn't sit down to work, didn't get himself moving. This impulse to get moving, for which town was supposed to be the external stimulus, just completely faded away.

When all this became a steadily and clearly recurring cycle, Alexei became unbearable. Whereas in the city he was calm and balanced in the mornings (that was when yesterday appeared to him as something vague, half-forgotten, and insane), now it was the other way around. He would calm down only toward evening, and after involuntarily oversleeping he would wake up an irritable crank, almost sick—and his wife would bear the brunt of it. This was apparently a substitute for the work which he should have started each morning. And only towards evening, when the day was almost over and he could calmly live with the thought that there was no use starting anything anymore today, better to start tomorrow, "sleep on it"—only then did he become the very nice person that he was in reality. In the morning and afternoon, though, he was a real fury (a fury because he was irritable in an unmasculine way), and everything seemed part of an evil design: any little trifle—his socks, his razor, matches—opposed him, hid somewhere; sharp corners appeared where they had never been before; something would fall; something would squeak; mosquitoes attacked him by surprise everywhere; little persecutions, dirty tricks, annoyances were stuffed into every little nook and cranny; everything stealthily carried on an absurd guerilla warfare with him. Everything raised protest, hatred and anger in him.

By the end of the day the abundance of irritations, recollections, associations, thoughts, and ideas would leave him tired out. And then—here the only thing lacking would be some act of reckless despair, just throwing up his hands and giving up on the whole thing—he would pull out from his store of ideas one, arbitrarily selected, carelessly toss it about, savor it a bit, and present it to his wife at teatime, getting overly excited and agitated in his need to somehow rid himself of these feelings. His idea would be pretty good, but it wouldn't solve anything. While in general it would be on a rather high level, it was nevertheless on a scale with those in most idle conversations: the conversations of neighbors, of his wife's relatives, or of his father. As a rule some external impulse would give rise to an idea, a political one for example; then he could generalize and attack, extinguish his creative ardor, and calm himself down. He would hardly be making any real effort and would once more come to a halt on that difficult ascent towards work and come sliding back down the slope, so that tomorrow he would be able to pass and overcome the same moment of inertia and then ascent as yesterday and the day before, perhaps even gradually immersing himself in the matter inch by inch, but again coming no nearer to actually reaching his goal. He would take up the newspaper, look at it as if nothing were there, and say, for example:

"It's not quite clear what sort of meaning they've attached now to the word 'formalism.' I still understand it in its everyday sense that's forgotten now—'He's a formalist in matters of honor,' for example. If you can't pay a debt at cards—then it's a bullet in the head. That is, a strict adherence to certain principles, rules, forms, which are presented to us, nurtured in us, exist before us—an adherence which is often contrary even to common sense. In this case formalism is something conservative which has existed for a long time and become permanent and static. Academicism, then, is the highest degree of formalism. There cannot be formalism in something newly formed, something that has just come into being—this is a new form. Perhaps they're using 'formalism' for 'unjustified form,' or, as they say, for form which doesn't correspond to reality? But if one literally compares art with reality, that is compares them formally, then art has always been completely conventional and has never been a copy of reality. Not to mention the fact that art itself is reality anyway... Take even such an obvious phrase, for example, as: 'Ivan Ivanovich thought such-and-such and such-and-such,'—that is just such a conventionality! Almost an abstraction. Who knows what he was thinking!... In and of itself true art has not only never aspired to conventionality, but has always been most anxious to avoid it. To free oneself from the shackles of conventionality, of ossification, is precisely what one can call formalism, to free oneself and come closer to the living truth—this is the mechanism by which new forms are born. It is simply a liberation from forms which are past, confining, or incapable of expressing what is new—an emancipation, an escape into open space, a coming closer to that which is alive. Calling this formalism is just like calling black white."

The idea would be sometimes intelligent, sometimes stupid; sometimes precise, sometimes not so precise; sometimes original, sometimes unoriginal; on the average—well, an idea. Having expounded it, he would gradually regain his sense of time and place; the room which had blurred while he spoke would come back into focus, and the objects become clearly visible. He would nervously look at his wife's face and read approval of the idea in it, then he would calm down and feel a certain pleasant drainedness, as if he had done some real work. Having closed up shop for the day, as if having rounded up the whole unruly herd of his thoughts into the enclosure and lowered the bar with a clang, and for the last time having looked back over his shoulder at all that motley mess, that bellowing, bleating mass, he would return, tired and satisfied, to his hut to sleep, to remember nothing until morning.

One day he awoke and at that precise moment his petty, irritable, splintered world fell on him and entered into him. This happened before there was even any concrete reason for it, as if this petty irritation stood at the head of his bed, watched over him, kept guard, waited for him to open his eyes and his soul. At night this irritation apparently slept, all curled up next to his slippers like a domestic pet. Alexei felt tired and desperate. "I'll go into town," he said. "When?" asked his wife. "Right now."

They argued—but these days it didn't do any good to argue with him: they shouted—and his son began to cry, and they stopped talking. Finally his wife wanted to be left alone and Alexei got permission to go to town with the absolute condition that he bring from home the night table which his wife couldn't live without. In this way the permission was rather more like an order to bring the night table than permission, and this conciliated his wife. Alexei was already feeling as if he were in the city, and even an order to bring back the sideboard couldn't have deterred him.

But as it happened, just as he was about to leave for the station his father unexpectedly arrived and brought with him the very night table in question.

And so on the one hand he didn't need to go in by train, which was always so crowded, but on the other his wife no longer agreed to his going since the night table had already been brought and no new errand had come up. His wife again said that he had no reason at all to go and that she really ought to check out why he kept spending so much time in town. This was a mistake because he was in the clear and now he had a good reason to get all upset and quarrel with her. The advantage was on his side. His wife lost the skirmish.

He left feeling relieved. The quarrel had eased his tension. He felt a pleasant emptiness inside following his spasm of irritation. They left for the station along the rough country road. A strong wind raced along the rails to the city. The car waddled like a duck, and the wind outstripped it. He saw the train platform, from which the wind seemed to have blown all the people. A train had just left. The picture was sad and chilly; it calmed one. For some reason he imagined a girl standing on the platform with her back to the wind, imagined her figure: her dress pressed to her back by the wind, the bubble of her skirt blown forward, her hair streaming in front of her. It wasn't his wife. He didn't choose any face for her. There was in fact no such girl, but there certainly might have been, so he wasn't imagining anything extraordinary. A kind of bittersweet feeling filled his mouth at the whole picture and at the image of the girl in the wind, a feeling which fully corresponded to a general bittersweet sensation he was experiencing and which he called to himself "acerb."

He could already recall the quarrel very calmly. It's strange, he thought, how easily and convincingly I dispelled her suspicions, even though I didn't try to prove anything, since I really don't have anything to prove—I'm not seeing anyone. And how unsure and difficult it would have been if I hadn't been blameless at that moment. The main thing is that there are the same grounds for suspicion in both cases. But if I had had something to hide, it would have seemed unconvincing to me the way I go to town just to go, and I would have begun to spin tales in order to hide something, but I really would be giving myself away.... All life with people seemed to Alexei to be a structure of suspicion and ignorance, and he pictured this structure as composed of interconnected rods, like steel fittings, or like a thick net in which the threads going in one direction are suspicions and the cross threads are ignorance, and when these threads intersect, in the knots... He got confused, the image didn't work any further. No, we really don't know anything about one another, continued Alexei, we could live together for a hundred years and still not know, only make guesses; our deductions are merely castles in the air, and these castles... It only seems as if these castles refer to other people, but they're really about oneself. We do, of course, know really—but almost nothing with total certainty. And we keep wanting that total certainty, we keep on trying to find out for sure, and from this mechanism doubt arises— from our trying to make sure for ourselves, trying to feel it. Situations are stereotyped and repeat themselves endlessly, every one of them can be interpreted different ways, each one can arouse suspicion, and only one in a hundred has any basis for suspicion. Because of that one percent we suspect all one hundred percent. If we could be cynical with a machine-mind cynicism, then we would never be found out. We always give ourselves away, always call suspicion on ourselves, even though we could dissolve our guilt in the sea of those very situations when we weren't guilty. And we wouldn't even have to lie. But that's not the way people are... He again recalled the quarrel and thought that his wife hadn't really seriously suspected anything, that she even knew for sure that he was going into town just to go. She had said it without cause, just to insult him... After all, insults are always unfounded. She had no grounds, but what about a reason? He sensed perhaps that there was a reason, but was afraid to think about it. And after all, if there really had been something going on in town, thought Alexei, disgressing, and if she had really known about it, then she wouldn't have said anything to him, she would have let him go without a quarrel, would have held off, gathered proof, and there would always be too little proof, and she would have kept on waiting for that next, decisive piece of evidence which would make everything clear, but this decisive piece of evidence would never turn up and would not even exist... poor woman!

Suddenly the car seemed to wake up and jerked forward, stopped swaying—they had come out onto the highway. People passed them, coming from the village heading toward the station, and Alexei was amazed at how many kept coming and coming, yet no one at all was on the platform. His father also cheered up on the smooth road, felt freer behind the wheel. A dog ran toward them and his father said:

"Have you ever noticed how all animals run a bit sideways?"

"Yes, I've noticed," said Alexei and could feel the tone of dissatisfaction in his voice which always appeared in conversations with his father. In this case he was a bit irritated by his saying "all animals," since it was not "all animals" but one dog that had run by. But he caught this mild irritation in himself and was already mulling over the irritation and condemning himself for it. Of course his father always talked somewhat unnaturally, that is, he talked not because he had something to say but just to make conversation, and this, moreover, was always colored by a certain intellectuality and emotionality of tone which was bound to be irritating. But now he often felt that his father really couldn't talk any other way and that in his inconsequential conversations there was a rather terrifying loneliness which made him try, in his inability to communicate, to retain at least the symbol of communication. Alexei glanced cautiously at his father, and suddenly saw how very old his father was, and a painful sense of resemblance, kinship, of the inevitability of likeness passed through him like a slender needle.

"Alyosha," his father said, wanting to talk. But the son was silent and his father had to begin again, had to overcome the awkwardness of having nothing in particular to begin with, since he didn't know what to say to his son so as to make the conversation arise naturally; so he said: "You know, it suddenly occurred to me, I don't know why..."

Alexei, continuing to note that day's feelings for his father, was touched by this maneuver and said to help him (which he would never have done another time):

"What occurred to you?"

"Have you ever heard the name Viksel?"

"No."

"How can that be? He's a famous scientist. A corresponding member of the Academy?" he said questioningly. But his son seemed not to have heard the question and the father continued: "We studied together. I hadn't seen him for thirty years, and then I ran into him the day before yesterday... He's a big man now." His father sighed and again paused for his son's answer.

His son hummed something to himself and remained silent.

"Well, and now," his father said with a sigh, "he's in communications. Head of the institute. His institute has become extremely important now..." His father's face took on a mysterious look. "Because in this war it won't be the first day that will be most crucial, but the second..."

Alexei smiled ironically.

"And why's that?"

"Well, you see," his father answered, coming alive, "I didn't know this myself, I read it somewhere recently." His father's voice began to flow smoothly, almost like a lecturer's. "You see, the primary blow will be delivered on the first day, and then on the second day the war itself, strictly speaking, will begin, and then..." His father paused meaningfully, and then like water breaking through a dam his words began to flow still more easily and rapidly. "Communications will be the most important and difficult thing of all, since it will be difficult from a practical point of view to command not only the army, but a platoon as well—so everything depends on communications! Because there may be as much as several kilometers between soldiers..."

"That's silly, Papa," said Alexei amiably and softly, amazing himself at his tone and at the fact that today he wasn't getting all worked up at such talk, although usually it took a whole lot less to make him flare up and get impertinent with his father.

"Why so?" asked his father, half-attacking, half-defending himself. He looked perplexed, as if he didn't know whether to feel insulted already or whether to force his son to say something obviously insulting.

"Why," his son answered calmly and affectionately, "would you need these communications on the second day when on the first no one would be left alive anyway?"

This was not like the usual course of such conversations—no squabbling had arisen—and his father was flustered.

"Well, if that's so..." he agreed uncertainly. And he fell silent. He was half-glad that his son was so restrained and polite today, and half-sorry that no conversation had ensued.

They drove for a while in silence. His father tried to think of a new topic, and not finding one, took up his most pointed and cunning subject: his son's work and affairs. Alexei continued to think about his father with the same sadness and tenderness and was not at all irritated (and this was a complete exception to the rule) when his father stepped into his field and began to make up some absurd thing. Yet usually Alexei could not endure the opinions of unqualified people, especially of his relatives and least of all of his father—it was out of some twisted thirst for communication that his father would say these things which were so important to Alexei simply to say them, even deliberately said them. And Alexei thought: why does Father deliberately say these things? After all, he always gets upset when his son gives him an impertinent reply, and Alexei always does get impertinent at such talk, like a little boy. The main thing is, his father knows all this; he is, after all, an intelligent man...And as he thought about all this Alexei began to understand better his father's awful loneliness. Namely, that over the long years the sweet feeling of insult had in its own way become dear to his father. "And just what have I said this time? No one ever..." And after this his father would almost be able to stop thinking about things, to shed his responsibility and train his blindness to a fine point.

Alexei thought about all this while his father told him in a calm voice things which always irritated him and led to quarrels...Alexei thought that these constant squabbles occurred only with his father, and not with others, precisely because of their closeness and lack of indifference to each other, because of his desire for equality between them. It's simple and easy with those you're indifferent to only because, justifiably or not, you set yourself above them—you feel an inexplicable superiority, and so you forgive them. Or rather, you ignore them. But his father is not his equal, so he's got to be forgiven. This was a childish atavism, this desire for equality. There could be no equality here. There was rather a reverse equality, a different dependence—one of father on son; and perhaps there had always been this very dependence. "And it's the same with me and my son," thought Alexei "exactly the same..."

They were driving through a forest, and the road was quiet, there was no breeze: it felt like a warm summer day—and suddenly they drove out into an open space. There were fields, ploughed lands; he caught a brief glimpse of a bumpy country road next to a barn standing askew, and an emaciated, wild-eyed cow looked askance from a roadside ditch; further on the fields stopped suddenly, there were meadows and scanty shrubs blown about by the wind, and nothing more, not even any cars coming from the opposite direction. The wind cleared the horizon and a deep blue forest, the height of grass, rose in the distance with a strange clarity. Alexei lazily looked out the window and thought how unusually close and comprehensible this inexpressive wasteland felt to him. An affectionate, cool, calm feeling settled in Alexei when his glance, without straining, slid along this smooth space and encountered almost nothing to linger over. His glance was like a slender, suddenly animated thread which connected him with nature, and two scale weights hung on the thread of his glance: he himself and the wasteland—on one level, in complete balance... The grass touselled by the wind, the rusty little puddle in the grass, the solitary crooked little pine bent over it—all were dear to Alexei. His glance kept moving, never clinging to one thing—he felt spacious, it was like a deep sigh. The slow, indiscernible gradation of shades of green, blue, gray, the elusive pale beauty of the wasteland entered Alexei and filled him with a melancholy joy, a pleasant, vague regret. It was this cool beauty which now seemed to him to be the most authentic kind of beauty. This had not been so even recently, he thought, just recently I might have said: what a dull place! And he felt somehow surprised as he recalled that just five minutes before they had passed a lovely pine grove like the ones Shishkin loved to paint, and Alexei had not even noticed it, just as he had never noticed the wasteland before. Alexei thought how little experience and how much effort were needed in order to perceive vivid beauty, to perceive what is usually meant by beauty. He remembered the sharp colors of the South which had so delighted him at one time—and now they seemed so lifeless, inauthentic, like paper flowers. "I am a northerner," he thought almost proudly. "If I ever go someplace for a vacation, I'll go to the tundra... I really must go to the tundra in the spring!" he said to himself excitedly, and he cheerfully straightened up on the car seat and glanced sidelong at his father.

Although before his father had habitually and unconsciously started quarrels with his son, he was now suddenly glad that no quarrel had occurred, and was grateful to his son for this and loved him. It was pleasant for his father to be sitting behind the wheel of his own car, earned by his own work, even though it was a small car—but then not everyone had one, especially now. How outrageous of them to raise the price: just think, a "Zaporozhets," just an old junkheap, and still... But here he was behind the wheel of his own car and next to him was his son, no one could say that his son had achieved little in his life. I was still just a kid when I was his age, didn't think about much of anything, while he's such a talented man, and well known... And it was obvious how pleased he was to have heard in that one sentence Alexei had addressed to him the word "Papa," and how much he would like to hear it more often. "And here I am waiting for the time when my son will say 'Papa' to me," Alexei was thinking, "I need that as much as he does..." The father was flattering his son and in doing this it was again obvious how well he actually knew what irritated his son and what pleased him. Because once again he was saying unnecessary things which in principle should be unacceptable to his son, only now these things pleased his son. His son understood that the conversation had not changed at all in the way it worked, but now he thought: what can you do, the form of father's conversation is so unsuccessful, but its essence is the most beautiful thing in the world—love.

So they drove along the windy clear wasteland, and the forest remained on the horizon like a low deep blue brush. When the highway began to bear left the forest began to get closer, to grow; hills appeared and the road went up and down. They came to a long straight rise and could no longer see anything. When they got to the top they found themselves at a railroad crossing. The barrier was up: the switchman's hut looked through its red window at the sunset; in the distance below the rails disappeared around a bend in a curve that resembled a sabre: a train might appear any time on its blade—and there was no one in sight. The wind rose again here with new strength and tossed the grass and shrubs in all directions; it slapped against the windows like a hail of slaps in the face... This crossing destroyed one's sense of time and seemed drawn-out. And Alexei looked about now in the same way that he had looked at the empty platform at the beginning of their journey. Beyond the crossing they saw the forest right near by, and beyond the forest one sensed the beginning of the suburbs.

Then, looking above the forest with the feeling inspired in him by the crossing, with the picture opening before it and the wind rushing all about it, looking about sadly and lazily, he suddenly saw something rising over the forest which he had never seen before, yet which seemed so familiar—a silent puffy ring on a slender gray stalk opening out like a bud and a fire, thick as kasha, slowly turning about within it. His father wouldn't be able to see it as his eyes were glued to the road, and the son, in a voice which amazed even himself by its strange calm, a calm which itself produced fear, said, "It's war, Father."

Now they would have to brake sharply, turn around, and rush back, away from the city, to get his wife and son... Alexei imagined how the four of them would drive and drive along empty roads, going further and further away from the dead city... But no, the shock wave would reach them at this crossing, they would not even have time to turn around. And the car would fly like a speck of dust and they would no longer feel anything inside this speck of dust... The radius of destruction... Or maybe they would have time to stop and jump out, fall face down in a ditch at the side of the road. Whirling about in the air, their "limousine" would take off above them, or the hut from the crossing would float past above them, maintaining its orientation in space with uncertain ease, and only then would they crawl out of the ditch into a strange and empty silence which even in daylight would create a feeling of eternal darkness, as if parts of the earth were gone... But no...

Alexei's daydream passed instantaneously and calmly. At another time it had occurred repeatedly, so by now it had lost its sharpness, was habitual and did not frighten him. At one time it had been agonizing: during periods of prolonged, forced separations it had meant the destruction of everything dear to him in his distant home city and his own empty, useless preservation. But now, suddenly feeling the edge of the usual crater hollowed out by this once agonizing daydream, he lightly slid into it: comfortably, without lingering over it in his consciousness, several pictures passed before him in a single moment—and that was all... They were driving in the same car, along the same road. If he had stopped his daydream, focussed on it, then the only thing that would have struck him in it would probably have been its banality, and his strongest feeling would have been relief at the thought that nothing is actually written on our faces and that at least some of our stupidities remain hidden and we don't have to blush over them... But now the car was coming out of the forest, which they had seemed to rush through surprisingly quickly. Because the forest had lain so blue so long on the horizon, because it had taken them so long to get to it, it felt as if the forest should have been more endless... And they found themselves already at the fork in the road by the automobile inspection post, and turning left again, they began to enter the suburb.

His father passed the inspection post all scrunched down as usual, trying to make himself unseen, and when the red motorcycles grazing at the side of the road remained where they were he livened up, straightened up, became unnaturally dashing, cursed the inspection "cops," and hitting on one of his other habitual targets for his too frequent and therefore harmless abuse, he continued to talk about them in an excited tone of voice that demanded sympathy and censure on the part of his son; his son easily and readily agreed with him and said yes, that's true, since the subject of conversation made no difference to him. The father was again grateful to his son, glanced sideways at him deferentially, as if evaluating his son, apparently again and again noting with pleasure that his high evaluation was in no way excessive, but if anything an underestimation... Alexei saw his father in the rear-view mirror looking at him and tried to look nonchalant and important.

"You're getting gray already," his father said. (This phrase always signified a final peace and gratitude and for some reason always pleased his son).

"Yes," his son said carelessly, "I have been for a long time."

In this visit to town, as in all the others, Alexei didn't get anything done and felt especially strongly how senseless and unnecessary were the supposed affairs which had brought him there. All day he rushed from place to place, found one person in and another out, met someone else just to set the next (also unnecessary) meeting, and suddenly, or so it seemed, found himself in a long narrow room with almost no furniture, among strangers. It was dark outside, Alexei should have returned to the dacha long ago, his wife would be getting nervous and annoyed there, and there was absolutely no point in his being here... Three good-looking girls, strangers to him, were sitting on the floor on mats, their expressive legs crossed; a tall fellow, also a stranger, was pushing buttons on a tape-recorder; one other fellow, the host, he at least was an acquaintance—a schoolmate he hadn't seen in ages, so of course he would come across him today—he wandered about the room, now turning off the light so that only the green eye of the tape recorder remained on, now turning the light on again so that everybody squinted in confusion and looked unnaturally pale; and the only bottle of vodka had been drunk up; and all the cigarettes were gone... Alexei sat in his corner on a pile of books feeling strangely sad, and just couldn't budge from his place even though he should have left long ago for the dacha, just sat there as if waiting for something. His sadness was almost shameful yet sweet, and it reminded him of something—he didn't know just what, as if he were at one of those first school parties with girls. Lonely—but unable to leave. The host again turned on the light and got out an air pistol from somewhere. They started target-shooting—the target was the cover of a German magazine—there was a dinosaur on the cover. Alexei suddenly got unusually interested, and with childish excitement grabbed the pistol: "Give it to me! Give it to me!"—and then he just couldn't hand it over to anyone else: "One more shot! Just one more!" "You know," his friend laughed, "that's just the way it was with me... When I first got this pistol I shot from morning to night, till I was utterly worn out. Wasted all my time on it. If only someone had taken it away from me!..." "Lend it to me," said Alexei with childish fervor. But his friend immediately refused and wouldn't let him have it. Alexei wouldn't give in: "No, lend it to me. Just for a while. I'll give it back... Just for a few days and then I'll give it back... You were planning on coming out to the dacha anyway, you can get it back then..." His friend finally seemed to tire of the argument and, coldly raising his eyebrows, he agreed. Alexei immediately grabbed the toy and left, hardly saying goodbye.

When he arrived at the dacha he didn't show his wife the pistol—he went to bed. And the next morning he took it up to his study on the second floor, hiding it in his shirt. Alexei admired it for a long time and then opened the barrel, enjoying the opposition of the spring of the cock and the coolness of the steel. He put in a lead pellet and shot at the rusty can standing on the floor. He hit it. He kept shooting for a long time at the little cans placed about in case of rain. The cans jangled and jumped, the pellets glanced off in various directions. Alexei placed one can on top of another and then another on top of them, and the cans rolled around on the floor.

His wife quietly stole up to him, attracted by the strange sounds. She was surprised. She joined him in the shooting.

Alexei crawled around the floor picking up the pellets. They kept rolling away and disappearing. Each time they shot, fewer of them remained.

Thus the day passed.

On the next day Alexei shot for a while again in the morning until he could find only one pellet. He shot it—and there were none left.

Alexei went downstairs and aimlessly wandered around the yard. Again he went upstairs, again he took up the pistol and looked at it for a long time, stroking its lustreless, burnished surface. Looking out the north window he pensively raised the pistol to his temple. The barrel immediately found a place for itself, falling into a sort of recess which seemed made for it. He suddenly remembered the humorous words of his platoon commander: "Every man has a natural recess in his shoulder for a rifle butt." With a bemused chuckle he lowered the pistol, and for a moment more he continued to feel the cold circle on his temple. Alexei opened the barrel and cocked the pistol without a pellet. Again he laid it to his temple and slowly pulled the trigger. There was a hollow little bang and Alexei felt a slight pain. "A toy," he thought dully, turning the pistol about and staring at it with surprise and mistrust. "A toy pistol... And my toy temple." His glance slid over to the pile of clean paper. "And my toy desk." Alexei looked up at the roof. "And a toy house." A spider fell from above and began to sway in front of his nose, dangling up and down. "A toy spider," Alexei said aloud.

Alexei got up and wandered around his second floor for a long time with the pistol hanging in his slackened hand. He stuck the pistol under a pile of rags in the corner, looked at the pile with seeming satisfaction, and then immediately forgot completely about it.

To his wife's surprise Alexei suddenly became quiet and even-tempered. He wandered about the house more absentminded than usual and didn't answer questions right away, as if answering to a call from a distance. When he bumped into something he didn't even get mad, just smiled absent-mindedly and guilty. The variety of projects he thought of tormented him and he just couldn't decide which to take up first. And if he forced himself by great effort to settle on just one thing chosen at random, he still didn't know where to begin; too many things rose up before him, too many things filled his head to the bursting point—and all his tormenting idleness suddenly turned out to be extremely full. At times he would be distracted from all this and then would begin to feel a tenderness for everything, would begin to live. This joy would be communicated to his wife, too and they would feel unusually grateful to one another.

When he finally sat down at his desk it was Saturday, getting on toward evening. It didn't work out though because relatives came on Saturday to spend the day on Sunday. He was already feeling feverish, thoughts teemed, and despairing of ordering them, he finally steeled himself, jumped in as if into cold water,—and it turned out that there really wasn't such chaos, the chaos turned to strength, everything was becoming ripe, indispensable, unique, and he was swimming, swimming... when something made him look out the window and he saw his smiling relatives coming up the path. He looked at them without recognition, as if remaining invisible to them, but they had already seen him and were waving. When he heard the commotion and exclamations below and he knew that he too should be standing in the doorway greeting them, his thoughts began to scatter and became disorderly again. For a brief moment he tried to force them back, restrain them, not let them go—but they scattered. He felt this physically, as if in his brain, in his cranium, a thought was crawling away... and giving up trying to restore any of them, he hurriedly went downstairs.

He stood in the doorway, smiling affectionately and quietly to everyone, while his relatives unburdened themselves in the passageway of all their bags and bundles and exchanged some rather unclear and too joyful exclamations with him and his wife. "Well, how's the work coming?" was all he made out. It was his father-in-law who said that to him. "Not bad," Alexei said ironically. But his irony was devoid of venom, he wasn't irritated now—and this too was the result of his period of idleness, when he had convinced himself that he was in no way better than anyone else, and his occupation was the same as everyone else's, and there was no call to make a cult of it. In addition, the feeling remained that now he had finally begun and would continue no matter how much he was interrupted, that his work had gotten underway. Basically everything was fine, although physically he didn't feel too well: he had a fever and the small of his back ached—this unslaked desire. Well, what of it, they're not to blame, they would have come anyway—he had forgotten...

Having put down their things, they went into the house. Alexei conversed with his father-in-law on phenological and political subjects, made tea ("Where did you learn to make such marvelous tea!" his mother-in-law said ecstatically), paid attention to his guests: the duty of hospitality was his— and he fulfilled it. There was some confusion as to who were the guests and who the hosts: the owners of the house had come as guests, and he, a guest in their home, received them now as host. Whether because of this or because they were relatives, but not blood-related, life in the house turned into a cumbersome and distorted ritual.

All the rest of Saturday was taken up with tea drinking. They all poured for one another, handed each other saucers and spoons, here, do try this cookie or have some of this candy; from time to time someone took the teapot to be refilled with hot tea and this provided a brief respite, a halt, and then it all began again with renewed vigor. It became even harder to tell who was whose guest. But then, fortunately, it was time to go to bed.

Sunday was something else again. A disguised war was waged in the kitchen, near the baby's crib, and outside in the yard. The whole thing was made more complicated and confused by etiquette, politeness, and the friendly way they treated each other: all this served as a kind of battle shield or fortification—the Trojan horse with a communal apartment placed inside it, noisy squabbling baked into a sweet dough. Breakfast went off comparatively easily, but only because dinner lay ahead, for which all forces were being martialled. With the approach of the dinner hour the war moved into battle, the battle into a bloody slaughter. Their son, to whom everyone gave such loving attention, sometimes fell into the dense encirclement where they kept tearing him away from one another, cooing to him all the while, and at other times he was abandoned by everyone and found himself with no supervision at all. It was precisely because of this that no one was nearby when he got into his mother's powder, scattered it about, smeared it on himself, and ate some of it. Then mother and daughter, wife and mother-in-law, mother and grandmother—all quarreled a bit about who was to blame.

Finally dinner too passed, the relatives began to get ready for the return to town, and Alexei, tired and sated, afraid of the impending final battle known as "preparations for the road," simply fled, explaining that his son had not yet had his stroll.

He put his child in the stroller and pushed him about the village. Outside the gates of his own home it immediately seemed to him that it was still Saturday and no relatives had come or would be coming. Again he felt in himself that trembling which he had experienced yesterday on his second floor, that world which had arisen in him then, had pulsed, had come alive, had seized him and borne him away—he joyfully felt the same smooth swaying and as always thought with surprise and ecstasy that it hadn't broken off, hadn't stopped, that it could still happen to him. He tenderly thought about his wife, the dacha, and his relatives, and he glanced at his son. The latter sat in the stroller: fat, grasping the hand rails, looking at the world. What was he thinking about? He does, after all, think... "There are three things," thought Alexei, "which no one knows about, and everything that we know about them is only what we or other people have imagined and then affirmatively repeated so many times in the form of opinions that they seem real... Those three things are what, and more important, how a child thinks, because he cannot yet talk and when he can he won't remember how he thought; what a man thinks in his last moment, when life is coming to an end in him and he can no longer tell anyone anything; and thirdly, and this at every stage of life, what does a man—any man, Mr. Ivan So-and-So Ivanov—what does this man think who is someone else and not you..." Alexei pushed the stroller along the uneven, awkward side streets and he wasn't so much looking and seeing for himself as he was watching how his son looked and saw. Even though he didn't know what his child was thinking, it seemed to him as if an absolutely certain link was being established between them. And furthermore, it was he who was the subordinate one in this relationship, not his son, it was he who saw through his son's eyes. His vision had seemed sharper since yesterday, but now with his son, with his son's eyes, everything seemed even more sharply focussed.

He took his son around the village as if around a huge ABC book... They would see a stream and he would say to his son: "See, a stream?" His son would look at the stream, and Alexei would say, "This is a stream," and it really was a stream. He would say to his son, "There's a goat," and it really was a goat. He would say to his son, there's a tree, a boy, a house,—and it all really was just what he said it was. Alexei would not have been able to explain just then what was going on and what was happening to him. He felt a kind of genius in this nominative simplicity of things and words, and he felt as if he were on some higher threshold beyond which everything truly begins, and that few had probably ever stood on such a threshold of a new logic, a new thought process, a new world. He saw a cow. "There's a cow, and there's her son—a calf," this was all so; and further on, beyond the cow, lay a swampy meadow with such smooth young greenery that it seemed like something one could not touch, like an emanation perhaps. In the meadow strange little flowers in the form of white cotton balls were growing as if they had just surfaced onto the green, thick, and yet airy surface. The meadow was empty, and only somewhere in the center a small boy, made still smaller by the distance, stood bent over, apparently picking these white flowers; but from the distance it looked as if he wasn't picking flowers but was stroking the meadow's surface, which was as impalpable as the sky. He stood there, apparently barefooted, not afraid to get his feet wet, and not afraid of falling through: there was, after all, a quagmire under the covering there—he was apparently too light; and beyond the meadow stretched an embankment, and a locomotive raced, chugging along, piping its tune with amusing diligence, now hiding behind bushes, now reappearing; it worked like a fussy old man, looking small in the distance, and behind it stretched an endless line of cars which seemed oddly not to coincide with its hurry. Even though it was far away everything was clearly visible, as always happens on these last windy days—each car or platform was visible. Alexei felt like counting the cars and was too lazy to count them, and he didn't. Here was the meadow, the boy, the train . . . And all this was really so—the meadow and the boy and the train, and the cow with her calf, and he with his son . . . All this for a prolonged moment fell into a straight line and formed a kind of axis, and this was perhaps the greatest truth of all those that he so persistently sought and had sometimes found. The seemingly accidental symmetry by which his son stretched out his arm in the direction of the train, and the cow chewed its cud standing with its head in the opposite direction in which the train was going, and the meadow, and the boy stroking the meadow, and finally the train—and all of this as if lying on one axis which coincided with his gaze and the wind, united by the cupola of the sky, as by a legate, and brought to a completion within him, Alexei—all of this and the seemingly endless continuation of the axis beyond visible bounds—the feeling of this symmetry was the happiest of all feelings. It was a pinnacle, a summit, an explosion, and in the next moment, whether the train left or the boy moved from his place or the cow... the axis fell apart, and Alexei felt a blissful emptiness: he existed now in the greenery of the meadow, in the boy in the meadow, in the train moving away, in the sky, in his son, in each and every thing. His life exploded, sprayed out, and seemed to flow away and fill everything with meaning and life. He felt like a god, nowhere and in everything, embracing and permeating the world.

 He suddenly found himself standing by a meadow he had seen a thousand times before, holding the stroller while his son babbled something. Then as if by the reversal of a strip of film in which they play back an explosion, where all the fragments fly back and the smoke and flame flow back, thicker, and disappear like a genie into a bottle and only a smooth space remains as if nothing had exploded, Alexei separated himself off into a tiny point in space and felt as if he were drunk. He turned back, pushing before him his likeness, his eyes, his joy; he opened the gate and walked along the path in the garden; and he came alongside a flowerbed—of all flowerbeds this one was the most accidental. It was about the size of a plate, and nestled right next to the path, because it had only just been made and hadn't been planned at all. His mother-in-law, his wife's mother, his son's grandma, had made it today on some unclear inspiration, repeating all the while, "My grandson's flowerbed, my grandson's flowerbed." It was sentimental, but sentimentality toward children had ceased to seem reprehensible to Alexei when his own child had appeared, and on the contrary was somehow right and understandable. They came up to the flowerbed and Alexei said, "Here is a flowerbed, it's your flowerbed, these are your flowers..." He paused, squatted down, bent towards himself a yellow flower with pendant buds and couldn't remember its name. He bent it over so it would be closer to his son: his son immediately stretched out his arms to the flower, his little hands, his little finger-petals, his little petals, petal to petal—he reached out and then hesitated, not sure whether to touch it. Alexei was moved by this desire and fear, by these hands, and he said, "Here's a little flower, it's just like you, it's your brother..." He wasn't quite sure if he was right to call the flower "brother," and he muttered, "It's your sister"... Suddenly he had the feeling that someone was watching him, a feeling which destroyed and broke up everything, and he pretended that he had bent over in order to take his son out of the stroller, and when he straightened up with his son in his arms he saw his friend smiling to him from the porch and then recalled with consternation that he himself had invited him to come.

"I'm not alone," said his friend and pointed to the veranda, where Alexei saw his wife. He didn't understand, but then saw a girl, whom he recognized as an old acquaintance, looking out from behind his wife, and she smiled and waved to him. He and his friend went over to the others on the veranda. Alexei gave his son to his wife, and while everyone talked excitedly back and forth in greeting he thought about how he had known them separately, the two friends, but had never seen them together, and what could it mean that they had arrived together? And it seemed to him that they hadn't "just happened to meet on the platform." His son started crying because of all the strangers and the unusual noise, his wife said they should go up to Alexei's study and that she would join them as soon as she had fed their son and put him to sleep.

They went upstairs and everyone was delighted with his second floor—his study with the spiderwebs; his friend was openly flattering him, although with a friendly coarseness, while the girl expressed herself in a way he would like most: without saying anything she simply glanced about with approval and satisfaction, as if she had already thoroughly and with interest thought about it all, about Alexei and his country abode, and was now pleased that everything was just as she had thought it would be and had not disappointed her; and Alexei, looking at everything through their eyes, was pleased both with his study and with himself.

Although Alexei mainly addressed his friend, and the girl was silent, she kept coming more and more to his attention. From time to time he watched her take something from his table and examine it, then put it back, or watched her listening to the conversation, or moving about carefully, avoiding the cobwebs, or watched her smile. There was in her simultaneously a kind of freedom and embarrassment which lent to her presence here a shade of personal concern that was more than just curiosity, and this concern flattered Alexei. And there was in her movements a sense of acceptance of the whole place, Alexei included, that made her presence here seem to him at once natural and eternal, as if she should stay and his friend should leave. The fact that Alexei had never seen them together and had not heard about them aroused in him a child's sense of the presence of lovers, a long-forgotten and mysterious feeling. He used to feel this way, for example, when his older brother had company and Alexei would sit quietly in a corner and try to figure out which beautiful girl was with his brother, and in general who was with whom, and then they would send him to bed and he couldn't sleep, but would listen to the noise in the next room and remember the girl who had come up to him, "Is this your brother? What a nice boy..." and had stroked his head; he didn't sleep and figured out how much younger he was than she and whether he could marry her when he grew up, and came to the conclusion that of course he could, that a seven-year difference is nothing. Or another feeling, when he was a bit older and was ready for love—a feeling he would suddenly get from two people sitting at a table—not the kind who noisily emphasize their liaison and find that pleasurable, but two quiet people who sat apart, who had a secret, a collusion, a telepathy, and Alexei had no proof of this, but it was so. Such a bond between two people in a sea of lives, each separate from the other, seemed to him in his childhood such an impossible, higher, inaccessible happiness, and he felt all this now—not as strongly, but something like a glimmer of his childhood feeling, and there was something genuine in it.

Moreover, as he watched her it began to seem to him that he had once been with her, that there had been something between them, and a compact hung between Alexei and her over his friend. This feeling was pleasant, somewhat troubling, because he really began to recall a bare room, and twilight, and an ashtray made out of a can on the windowsill. Had it happened or not? Perhaps he had dreamed it? But no, it hadn't happened, he wouldn't have forgotten it; most likely he'd made it up... But no, a kind of agreement, some kind of thread stretched between them, and both felt it, he knew it and she did too. But all the same it wasn't just empathy, there was something with a touch of recollection, and he just couldn't put his finger on it.

They chatted for a while in his study and they went out onto the balcony. The low sun illuminated them on one side. The long slanting shadows of the railings arranged their geometry on the floor. The wind which had blown strongly for three days shook the trees, but the balcony was on the side away from the wind and it wasn't windy there, it was just continually sensed: heard and seen. And they sat on the sun-warmed boards and continued their conversation about something or other. His friend was relating something. Alexei listened and didn't listen to him. His wife joined them, having finally gotten their son to sleep. But this didn't interrupt Alexei's feelings, it even strengthened them. The bond between him and the girl was not broken, he felt its pull, and he felt something unusual and slightly romantic in the fact that they had made no visible efforts to support it, had done nothing specifically directed toward it; there were no glances, no poses, and a feeling rather like gratitude arose in him for the fact that she made not a single movement which would break their thread. And it was good that there was no growing excitement or tension, everything remained undisturbed, their bond grew stronger as if apart from their desire, and it was even as if they tried to subdue it. And this gave rise to a feeling of ease and naturalness in him, of something very rare after which you would feel no repentance or shame. As if everything had already happened, but only ease and gratitude remained in consequence, and seldom had he felt such ease—never, in fact.

They conversed pleasantly about this and that. About schoolmates and acquaintances, who had seen whom, although no one had seen anyone—it was vacation time. About various things, what seems like what in the light of today's events, although nothing was like anything, and there were no events—it was vacation time.

They had already run out of conversation and gradually began to feel awkward, to look silently at the view from the balcony—which was not, however, very interesting—when his friend said that here she, meaning his girlfriend, was trying in vain to hide from everyone the lovely songs she had brought along with her. Sing them, sing them, they begged her. "I'm not hiding them, I'll sing them," said the girl. And she sang simply and naturally, even interestingly, seeming to take advantage of the fact that she really had no voice and using that to good effect. Alexei was deeply moved, because he decided that she was singing for him. And so he hardly remembered anything of the three or four songs which really were good. Only the beginning of one of them. This song even distracted him from his sweet fantasies. The two-syllable words at the end of each line were sung with a double stress which made the words sound broken up, like splintered pieces of word-goblets and word-cups. This imparted to the song an even wilder quality than the strange text, the elusive motif, and the lack of rhyme.

> Such a mighty tem-pest
> Fell upon our is-land,
> Tore from homes the roof-tops,
> Like foam from milk too fro-thy.

The songs were sung—they again fell silent. And when his son started screaming below, they jumped up almost joyfully, gladly stretching and moving their legs, and began to talk too loudly and animatedly, without any transition from the silence.

His son immediately calmed down when he saw the people. It turned out that he had been screaming simply because he wanted company. He got company and now he treated even the strangers cordially. He walked about the room going from person to person, or rather, didn't walk, but seemed to fall out of one person's arms and into another's, because between the time that one person let him go and another caught him he had only to take one independent step, and down he went.

And so, as he was enjoying himself together with his son, Alexei suddenly turned around, as if someone had called him, and caught the gaze of the girl. He immediately felt that her gaze hid in it a certain nuance, and because she had apparently been watching Alexei for a long time and now glanced away too quickly, as if it were giving her away, this nuance became an absolute certainty to Alexei—and he became embarrassed. He leaned back on the couch; his head receded into the twilight: from here he could observe and come to himself.

He felt a kind of childishly despairing sinking feeling each time he looked at the girl (now she tried hard not to look at him, and this, of course, gave Alexei renewed confirmation), and he felt a childish resolve to do something as yet unknown even to himself, something sweet in its non-fatal, savory peril. Because of this he could not have felt freer, more unfettered, and he continued to lie there, hiding his head in the shadows. Then he discovered something that would save him: it was a piece of fluff, like dandelion fluff, which had stuck to his knee. "For good luck,"—he remembered this omen from Pioneer camp days. The fluff suggested an action, and the action freed him of his awkwardness: he set the fluff on his extended finger, glanced at the girl as if hinting at what his wish was, and carefully blew. The fluff flew up to the ceiling; it was clearly visible and disappeared only right at the ceiling, merging with the chalky surface. Alexei persistently scrutinized the empty air and suddenly discovered the fluff lower than where he had expected to find it,—it was falling at a measured pace. Then his son noticed it too: he squealed and stretched out his hand, started to talk incomprehensibly. "Just think," said Alexei with simple pride, "such a little thing, a little piece of fluff, and he already notices it..." He caught the fluff and blew it again...

Whether everyone, like Alexei, saw the fluff through the eyes of childhood, or whether his son had communicated his view of things, everyone was unusually carried away. The fluff flew up sharply and slowly fell, now merging and disappearing, now becoming visible, as it marked out in the air an invisible striped pattern of light and shade. Alexei looked about with a foolish expression on his face, and then the one to discover it first yelled, "There it is, over there!" Each time his son saw the fluff he became even more excited; confusion and perplexity fell like a blind over his face when he lost it from sight, and an even stronger excitement then replaced this perplexity. This intensifying of feelings in his son from repetition, rather than the quieting down which Alexei felt corresponded to human nature, pleasantly surprised him. The fluff again disappeared. "There it is! I see it!" Alexei recognized the girl's voice, was distracted, and suddenly saw everything from a detached point of view. In this light his son remained the same to him. The rest, supposedly adults, sat with half-opened mouths and vague smiles; their looks crossed, joining somewhere in the center of the room at an almost invisible and immobile point, and they were very tense, as if they were at a seance where the movement of the fluff was communicated by a common telepathic effort. There was such enthusiasm on their faces that they seemed possessed, almost ecstatic, as if they were testing fate, as if they were betting a fortune... Because he saw them all seeming to reveal themselves in their most defenseless and absurd essence, Alexei felt the abasement, gratitude, and awkwardness of the voyeur. He caught the fluff and held it back. For a moment those present seemed to return to reality, and when he noted the first gleam of recognition he said, "After all, we are adults..." Everyone laughed without embarrassment, and then he realized that he had exaggerated, as always, and as always this was unpleasant to him. "Well, we have to go now," said his friend, and this "we" cut Alexei to the quick and sobered him up.

...He went with them to the station to see them off, feeling bored and depressed. But everything had happened as it had to happen: from the very beginning it was clear they would leave together, but Alexei felt injustice and hurt in the fact that here they were leaving together, they would arrive in town where they would go somewhere and stay together... Alexei felt something like jealousy, but he wouldn't have admitted it to himself. He felt even sadder because it was beginning to seem as if he himself had thought up the whole thing about the meaningful bond between himself and her, that there had been nothing of the sort, that she in any case hadn't felt any of this, and he perhaps had given himself away by some absurd gestures; and she all the while had been laughing at him, and when she was alone with his friend they would laugh at him together... This was humiliating—to have to change one's perception so sharply: just before he had been experiencing a radiant feeling, another feeling from childhood, long-forgotten.

And so they silently made their way to the station. The wind nudged them from behind and urged them on. The air was amazingly transparent—all the distances seemed outlined. The red sun lay on the horizon and permeated everything through and through, as if piercing objects in its way. Several long, narrow clouds seemed stuck into the sun, like red arrows or red feathers. A withered tree near a warehouse for construction equipment, a misshapen snag, looked eerie and beautiful—black on the red sunset—so beautiful that it would be tasteless in a picture. Actually it was a cold day, a cold wind was blowing, and perhaps for this reason there were no people there at all, and those who were there had frozen immobile in the wind, and it seemed that it was precisely they who created the feeling of desertedness, and if they hadn't been there, the feeling wouldn't be. The wind raced along the tracks, chased chips and rubbish from where the freight cars were unloaded, and also—and this seemed endless to him when he saw it—the wind chased a large piece of cardboard with jagged edges: the wind turned it over, the piece stood up, stopped still for a moment, then slapped against the embankment and rolled on, raising dust; then it turned over again and for a short but seemingly very prolonged moment it stopped still and tremblingly opposed the wind. As before they were silent as they stood now on the platform. The train came and they shook hands; for some reason his friend thrust his hand out first (the pistol jutted out stupidly from under his arm), and then she gave him hers. And somehow she gave him her hand and squeezed his and looked at him as if he were still being a fool, but there had been something, there would be something, and he felt a pang and tried to restrain himself, but couldn't—his eyes clouded over and he saw only dimly, and was afraid he might blink out a tear. The train started up, they waved from their car—she waved, but he didn't see his friend, he had disappeared with his pistol, had dissolved, no longer existed. And the train carried her off in the same direction as the wind blew, that is—toward town.

He stood there a while longer and was happy. The thought that he would certainly see her in the city vaguely remained in him. Then with a sudden sharp tenderness he thought about his wife and son, about the house he was now returning to, and again about his wife, that he would see her now as if after a long separation...

He slowly wandered back, against the wind, past the warehouse and the freight cars which were being unloaded, and rubbish flew into his face—"Such a mighty tem-pest"—he crossed the tracks, and in crossing the tracks there was such loneliness in all this emptiness, this windblown space all around— "Fell upon our is-land"—a feeling of isolation from the world seized him, and this was pleasant; an island ... really an island ...! A smooth sandbar, a yellow turbid sea, and huts on slender legs, and roofs of broad stiff leaves—"And tore from homes the roof-tops"—the wind chased a large piece of cardboard: it stood up, stopped still for a moment, then slapped against the embankment and rolled on, raising dust; then it turned over again and for a short but seemingly very prolonged moment it stopped still and tremblingly opposed the wind...

And here was his quiet home, and the roof was whole. His home, his fortress,—the second floor... Alexei remembered how his study had flown in the hailstorm, and how the hailstorm had beaten down all the cornshoots... "And it tore from homes the roof-tops, like foam from milk too fro-thy..." A chill passed through him. He went up to the second floor—he was shivering...

In the evenings, when, quite drained, and with a light, unreal ringing in his head he would come downstairs and drink tea with his wife, he thought that this was precisely what is called happiness. He turned on the radio, and a French woman sang her song, the tea was strong and hot, his wife, his eternal companion, sometimes sewed, sometimes drank tea with him—was nearby, and Alexei had no need to leave her for any place, and his son was not yet asleep and offered him a toy... And to Alexei it seemed that he would remember this peace and quiet all his life—after all, who knows what direction life might still take.

1963-1964

Notes From The Corner

"They told me I was too young... So I said: it's not my fault. And now I walk around thinking: I could write about this, and about that. And about that... But then it's terrifying, I'll be walking along and—what can I write about? What? That's my business?! About this..? But why exactly that? Or about that..? It's just pointless."

"The Bus" (1961)

The Corner

June 18th

    I had a dream. It seemed to be some kind of a meeting. The space, as always in dreams, was undefined: a hall or a basement, one I'd either been in many times or was in for the first time—maybe the Writers' Union or the housing department. But it was as if I didn't know anyone... In short, a hybrid from dream and memory of something very familiar and something completely unfamiliar.

    The people were the same as the hall. The meeting, by all appearances, had an ideological tone. Some were incensed about something, someone was betraying someone, someone else was busy climbing the ladder; who and how I don't remember, just that it was all disgusting. In the hall there seemed to be no windows or else they were shuttered, blocked or caulked tightly; it was half dark, and the light was weak, dirty yellow, and people were sitting the way they do in a village club, on long simple benches—hunched and indistinguishable, merged.

    And then it was as if they all turn toward me and I, quietly standing somewhere far away from the presidium by the wall, become the *center*. As if the Chairman points at me from the stage, as if someone whispers hotly in my ear, inciting me to something (I can't manage to turn around to face him—he's always behind me...), someone very familiar, maybe even one of my friends but it's still not clear who. And it becomes clear to me that they're demanding that I "speak out": you're always silent, you get by without saying anything, but what do you think? Isn't that true? So be brave... And I am incapable of pulling myself away from the wall and already sense that if they force me, I won't be able to hide in the bushes, to fudge it, say yes and no, not lie but not tell the truth—I won't get away with an indefinite jelly of fear and the desire to remain "honest" this time. And I'll say everything I possibly can within the bounds of my ability and my necessity, condition and education, fear and reproach.

I'm still standing by the wall. Someone's whispering in my ear, pushing me; something turns cold and sinks in me from fear and decisiveness; fragments of opening phrases and variants of beginnings interspersed with spasms of terror flash through my mind at a furious rate... and suddenly I'm standing on the stage on that amateurs' rostrum. In front of me and slightly below me is the hall hidden in darkness, silent and breathing. I can't see it and I speak. I speak astonishingly, in a trance of truthfulness and blindness, like someone who has decided to leap, but whose soul cries out and freezes in flight... Perhaps I'm speaking unintelligently but in any case it is enough to alarm me and the audience. I can't remember what I said, no matter how I tried later—only two things:

"If S.B. were to be moved to China, he would play the role of V.A., and if V.A. were to be transferred to the US, he would play the role of S.B. Then where is literature? We're not talking about them..."

And the other:

"... If millions of whatever it is, be it Jews or artists or simply live people, were to be collected and led off somewhere under convoy to a cliff to be shot, to be destroyed, and one of them (it's not hard to make a mistake on such a large scale!) suddenly turned out not to be a Jew but an Urdmurt, not to be an artist but a plumber, not to be alive but a corpse, then he would yell: 'What an injustice!' I'm not speaking on his behalf..."

And so I've finsihed, I'm walking along the narrow passage between the benches, and all around there is such silence, tension and breathing, as if there were no exit where I'm going, but a grave, a cliff, nonexistence. I walk and I wake up more with each step.

And having awakened, I see the sun behind the shades and across the room the little bed of my Annushka: she's already awake, enthusiastically and efficiently pulling at her diaper and gurgling with pleasure. Somehow she senses that I'm looking at her, turns from her diaper and looks at me, recognizes me—it crosses her face as a visible movement, recognition spreads; delighted, she says to me for the first time: "Pa-Pa."

June 21

When we say injustice, we always mean some kind of social process. Whether you've been jailed or you've been shot, or deprived of expected or deserved rights or privileges, or your work has been interfered with, it always involves some stretch of time before the tragic resolution; some quantity of people, participants; some forces, external, internal, have gotten involved.

Everything changes its color if you imagine the terrifying outcome occurring suddenly and immediately, crushing you in such a fragment of a second that you don't have time to feel anything, you're deprived of your previous afflictions, of the false logic which you can't even begin to imagine, of the surrounding society, of the vicious bits of paper with signatures, and of the long-drawn-out-ness. Then it turns out that it is precisely this process leading to the result that we call injustice, and not the outcome itself, which is rather fate, destiny, the end. We go through exhausting gyrations in certain social spheres when we realize the approach of the terrifying outcome, when we recognize the forces of evil in the social sphere, their implacable logic, which consists only in the absence of logic, in the irreversible strength of the execution of the instructions (when the execution coincides with our interests, usually there's no talk of injustice, but the mechanism of these forces is the same: it doesn't matter that they coincide, since they don't correspond to our interest). If it weren't for these gyrations which we perceive as merely the external mechanism of implacable forces, this gyration that you can't even comprehend, everything would turn into *chance*.

Imagine, a person comes up to you, you've never seen him, you don't recognize him, you have no connection to him (just as, by the way, with any functionary), and reaching you, he shoots you... Perhaps you die instantly. Then your loved ones will say "How absurd, what an absurd accident, just yesterday he was joking..." If you don't die instantly, then you too will say to yourself as you're suffering, "How annoying to die so suddenly because of some absurd accident," and in any case you'll depart this world, cut off from the reason for it long before your death.

And even now, imagining it, I often omit the process which we experience as injustice, abbreviate it as a brief tremor and imagine the result directly: absurd, terrifying, savage, stupid, accidental—all right, but what does this have to do with injustice?

Is it because there is no sentence, or because they didn't inform you of it? Is it because you don't agree with it, or is it because you don't recognize the right of precisely this court to pronounce it on you? Or that you're afraid to die, or that you're not prepared for it? Because there is no reason, or because you haven't understood it?

But even if we deny ourselves the possibility of grasping the essence of things and descend a level lower, satisfied with merely external and social categories, injustice will still seem too refined and rational a concept for the world as it is understood and structured on this level (or, as we say in such an instance, for the *contemporary* world). The essence suddenly turns out to be (if all other variations which are qualitatively indistinguishable on this level are suppressed) that an unknown man can come up and shoot you down at any time of the day or night, at any point in space, and eradicate your parameters.

This is beautifully expressed in Kafka's work, although this same external category for him would be the discourse. For him it's incidental, as though it were self-evident—one of the cross sections of the image he has created...

That's why his novel is called *The Trial* and all the action, all the hero's suffering, is the process of the trial, and the denouement is simply fate, simply murder, and, at first glance, they are not even interrelated.

August 10th

You bump into old words... Some months ago I suddenly wanted to write a poem and, of course, didn't risk it. Then yesterday it came back to me. There weren't enough words and so I did not and will not write it, but something like a prose translation remains:

> Suddenly you will see what you see every day and it will penetrate you and fill you with despair—an attack of pity, helplessness and love. People, small and touching, will suddenly be running along as you watch, apparently going about their affairs, we'll go do this and we'll go do that. They'll get on a bus and get off it. Some will go in one direction, others in the opposite, some will stop by the newspaper stand, others will stand in line. Someone is building something—he makes his contribution—while someone else is blind drunk, and then a slight rain begins to fall. People run along, their trajectories joining, intersecting, dispersing; buses and trams cut the web of their movement, driving over your warm trail. It's even surprising the acrobatic precision with which each follows his own path—without injury or disaster. And observing this dexterity will intensify your feeling to an unbearable point: Lord, why, where are they going?! And you'll stop, paralyzed, feeling the insubordination of your arms and your legs, and the idea will come to you—almost seriously—that these connections will never again be restored, that the channel by which the Pavlovian commands of the cortex direct your body to move has been blocked; and the people will continue their chaotic running around as you watch. Preoccupied, purposeful, they are actually going nowhere. "Like ants," you'll say to yourself, "like ants..," and you'll come home. And if this feeling stays with you long enough that you bring it home, then, perhaps, you'll sit down and write, feel uplifted, as if experiencing an illumination, and you'll write: like ants, like ants... You'll live some more and one day you'll reread that and exclaim, grinning wryly and superciliously, God, what a fool I was! I didn't understand anything, not the least thing... and have I managed to understand anything now? (since I understood so little so very recently). It isn't that way at all and these words are wrong, and it's hopeless to the point of embarrassment! A certain pride will soften you, you'll live some more and think some more

and one day you'll become so wise that your very wisdom will become unbearable to you and, with arms dangling as if you were tired, you'll gaze down from wisdom's heights, unsure whether your arm or leg will ever again respond to the least of your commands. You'll see how the people run about, intersecting and tangling their trajectories. Suddenly you'll see that these are molecules jumping from light shocks, overcoming inertia in short, straight leaps. And the shock was: buy some sausage, then stop at the pharmacy and after that a sharp turn in the other direction...So they're jumping and intersecting, indicating their straight leaps with short dashes. And then backwards, but then to the side and another to the other side, one shock, another, a fifth, and you can no longer define the direction. You're in their motion—the labyrinth, chaos—and everyone is safe and sound, and the beauty of their movement, of their complete naturalness as if they were in the jungle amongst the beasts and the lianas, will intensify your sensation. "Why, where are they going?" you'll say. Brownian motion, Brownian motion...you'll repeat. And you'll go home and, provided your brain is still capable of retaining the sensation, you'll jot down: Brownian motion, Brownian motion...Like ants, you want to write, like ants...

One of the lies which dooms man to incongruousness and to suffering is that an idea is capable of transforming the world. The world is transformed, but not by the idea. There are always ideas. People who have no words use them, and then it seems to them that their actions are filled with content and purposefulness. There is always some legendary personality who provides the idea by which we, comrades, are now living and are made happy...and that's how it all comes about: it turns out that all humanity developed purposefully and meaningfully and the idea of that eminent personality is the fruit of this progression. From this idea has arisen that wonderful and, at last, just and meaningful world in which we, ever grateful to the idea, are living... Thus has it always been, you might say, for all people and in all times. And even honest people, having grown up in this atmosphere of double dealing and card sharpery, learned to fit into the proper order of action and of thought about such things so that in the beginning was the idea and then the effect and under no circumstances was it the opposite way around. In this deception there seemed to be a kind of power over the world, its subordination to you—and you were the lord of nature, the peak, the garland, the halo.

One bumps into old words...That's how mankind lives: deceiving itself. Some deceive only themselves—these are honest people. Some deceive themselves and others, or others and then themselves—these are dishonest people, the exploiters and expropriators, the politicians and potentates, the tyrants and fanatics. That's how mankind lives: deceiving itself. The operatic, romantic tyrant deceives only others. This is not human, though, and so doesn't happen. The everyday, petty tyrant deceives himself a little in the beginning, then deceives others a great deal and, in the end, once more himself—but just a bit. The wise man deceives neither himself nor others; he understands. For this reason he can't do anything, even speak; he is an unknown because, incapable of action, he doesn't reveal himself, is invisible, ceases to exist. He is also not human and therefore nonexistent. The artist, the poor wretch, goes hot and cold, hot and cold his whole life long. as long as his talent is alive. He lives like a man: deceiving himself, and in this state creates and then deceives others too. What's more, he suddenly discovers the deception, suffers and becomes a wise man (for a short while). Then he can do nothing, inasmuch as a wise man is nonexistent, invisible, isn't there, so the artist returns to life by means of a new deception, which is never new, and the cycle begins anew. He lives, turning over ideas which are never new, he lives creating likenesses of himself and likenesses of his world and deceiving people by justifying their existence, not as that of beasts or of birds to whom the Lord gave life, but as that of the beginning of the rational, of the garland, of the halo. He lives only in moments of wisdom and enchantment, allowing into his consciousness the idea that the Idea is incapable of transforming the world. Then once again he becomes stupid so as to continue his life and business. He lives, throwing new ideas into the world, ideas as old as the world, and even the simple fact that deaf, dumb, and blind people arm themselves with these ideas, ruining them with a single breath, turning them into cudgels and always, without fail, murdering him, because they only need one idea and he might go and give birth to another, even this never kills the artist. He brings his fruits and drops them in the earth and they bring forth new fruits, not better, not worse, similarly wonderful and unrepeatable and differing only in that they exist in the present time, just as though they had merely been "translated into modern language." But this is only because they are born each time like a word that has been uttered for the first time.

August 11th

Old words...Let's put it this way: human efforts are vain and futile. Vanity of vanities. I've had my fun with this vanity, my internal struggle with it, and with its cult, in fashion at the moment among members of the elite. This word has been resurrected on many lips and its rebirth is connected with a certain general animation in this recent, and, alas, all-too-brief period. This word evidenced a certain level of spiritual life among the elite and it would have been nice for it not to have disappeared so soon. But within the circle of spiritual experience and concepts described by this word, its use and the excitement about it testify to a faith in progress, the surroundings, and the continuing resolution of social problems. The word doesn't transcend the sphere of everyday sensations and is therefore ignorant and optimistic. It somehow suggests the existence, to the degree that it is non-directional and contentless, of a high meaning and loftier goal, which is always very abstract, elevated and vague for everyone. It seems to summon us to a pure life, to honest service and to a high goal, while actually it is all governed by gain and the increase in the Coefficient of Useless Action. Without vanity it is possible to do so much more so much better and still receive the same first prize, the abstract and forceful presentation of which still serves to stimulate that impulse, even if there isn't really any prize, because each of us already has his own. So that this fuss about vanity, its cult, since it became in a way a passport to spiritual life, and each praises himself for his martyrdom in the battle against it, still doesn't lead out of the narrow region of social movements in opposition to which it emerged.

That's enough about vanity. Futility is another affair. This word has unexpectedly taken on meaning for me and all my experience has anchored itself at its shore. There's not much use in talking about it, of course. It's almost a perversion to try in a period of artistically hopeless wisdom to create anything whatever based on one's personal situation. This would be disgusting, unless it naturally emanated from the nature of the artist who, the more he wanted to sell himself, the less he was able to. Wisdom is double-edged: it can't exist in any desired higher sense if there exists an attempt to express it. Of course, the desire to say something profound about futility is self-contradicting because this would be possible only if there were a deep consciousness of futility itself, and such a consciousness precludes the possibility and capability of expressing it. But I want to live and will try to suppress this disconcerting idea quickly. What's more, if it suddenly turns out that a circle of my friends would find what I am now writing close to their own thoughts, and empathize and be thankful to me for the frontier of sincerity and expressiveness I have tried to attain, then, even if only one or two understand and turn out to be in the same phase, my whole situation and writing will be transformed into its complete antithesis. And I will receive satisfaction and further assurance that my work isn't useless but, on the contrary, directed and essential. I'll be able to maintain both enthusiasm and self-esteem and a small superiority over everyone, a jaunty step, and the desire to work and work—How much I can still do!—it's just a phase; this too shall pass. I'll let down the blinds of consciousness so that nothing will interfere with my doing what I can at this moment. This will be a happy state. When I leave the house of those friends who have appreciated what I've done, there'll be no taxi and I'll go home on foot with several novels milling in my brain, competing for the right to be the first. Everything will be wonderful, the same excitement and vanity will still trouble me and prevent my writing all those wonderful novels. I don't think my obliging and still-healthy consciousness would permit me never to surface out of the hopelessness of the things I've suddenly understood. What vile words has man not yet thought up for the designation of these shifts, of these incessant betrayals of the truth, of these cowardly escapes into lies? Mankind speaks two languages—only two! With what joy, having overcome the torture of consciousness and having felt newly capable of life, do we recall words and are stunned by their precision: he overcame himself, he fought with himself, he came to terms with himself; strength of character, strength of will, a service to the people, a sacred task... Returning through the empty streets with a buoyant step, how we look at the girl then as she hurries home alone! We are newly capable of inseminating and incapable of love, it seems to me. Immersed in ourselves, we take pleasure in ourselves, our being is open to life and to delight, we're ready for battle! And you'll review all the physiological explanations of your recent condition, denying their essence and truth. You'll address yourself as if you were the indifferent and affectionate nurse who surrounds us in this world disguised as love, and you'll say to yourself, as she used to say: you're tired, you've been tired, you're having bad luck, you've had bad luck, so your situation is understandable. You'll bury this period with words which have already been spoiled so that it will be impossible to remember. "Fatalism," you'll smile wryly, "pessimism." To risk the image, it's as though there were two seasons in our consciousness: summer and winter. With a bit of preparation, it would probably be possible to distinguish both fall and spring. I'm not sufficiently full of life at the moment to hop up and down over an image and delight in it. But, all the same, spring is the beginning of summer, and fall the beginning of winter. That evening of the buoyant return home from the understanding, appreciative friends can be considered as spring. After that comes summer. Now—let's call it winter, but not quite, because here I am writing this empty blather. Well, not winter then, but fall. That isn't what I wanted to say. We speak with different words according to the seasons of the year in our consciousness (this year, of course, has nothing in common with the astronomical year). And in daily life and work we are obliged to renounce those few words of that other language which live a deep and eternal life. Of course, we create spiritual values—that's why these words are essential; we shake them, but use them, recognize them at the bottom of the puddle, by the dark and rotting memories of our winter consciousness. Distant and sated, we ourselves erase these eternal words, so that in the next winter of hopelessness and hindsight about our past we'll once more be ashamed to see what we exchanged them for. We live and speak and do in a different language of a sleeping, sated consciousness. How willingly we reiterate that pages composed with inspiration are helpless and weak and the other way around—that that which has been written with coldness and indifference, almost with boredom, appears to be the peak of our inspiration. We are so serene when we swim in the language and words that are within our grasp.

    I began, however, to speak of futility and I'm saying just anything, keeping the subject at arm's length because there aren't enough of these words, I don't know them. I have none of the word-keys for the painful and intense feeling I have now, and it's shameful to substitute lock picks and a crowbar.

Anyway, inevitably I will now write about exactly this and only about this. About futility. I write this useless and harmful opus and, when you get right down to it, I want to get out of it as soon as possible. Somewhere on the opposite bank of my consciousness is a big fish that I'm secretly hoping to catch. I want to lure it. I am going to write and write while that fish, lured, comes closer, and then I'll be able to pull it out. Somewhere I'd get all tangled up in the lines, having tied them all together, and, already despairing, confusing their order and interrelationship, pull on the first one that comes to hand. Then somehow suddenly by a miracle I'd wind up with the right line, the one with the right fish, and everything will come together and take form so that in the end I'll come to a real affirmation which will fill me with a belief in the necessity of continuing my efforts. I'll swim across, fly over, land, and come out on the shore in complete certainty that this is not that old one, but a wholly different land I've been heading towards, where at last I'll go forward. And all this only because the shore is the opposite one. At first, it won't hit me that there is no qualitative difference in their opposition, that they're only reversed and that they represent, as before, equilibrium and disequilibrium.

I was writing about the seasons of our consciousness. It had already become difficult for me to withstand the tension of full expression and I wanted to read what I'd written to my wife and calm myself down for today. But my wife had to cook the kasha and wouldn't be able to listen until later, so I went out on the balcony, lit up a cigarette and stared at the trees and houses. Unbeknown to my conscious will, it happened that I gazed like a wise serpent. It is impossible to separate what seems to us to be and what is actuality, what is pose, what is false beauty, and what is natural, and to what degree pose and false beauty are present—isn't it to the degree that they not only subvert nature but replace it? Standing there, thinking about the seasons of our consciousness, I saw a tree which was right in front of my nose and I thought about seasons in general. I had just rejected this image, looking at the tree, when I imagined its potential growth. I imagined life and nature in their cycles as an unending series of spheres embracing each other. They are completely similar; the difference is the quantitative one of the time and space of their existence and not of the coincidence of the phases of the cycle. But everywhere the completion of the cycle is death. Our disinclination to accept this changes nothing. It comes naturally out of our position as constant witnesses of the development of life's laws and as the discoverers of them. We ourselves are subject to these laws and don't want to acknowledge their application to us. We arbitrarily designate as the heights of development those moments at which we are in the best of positions. In this way we again begin to believe in progress, in the intentionality of development, and to take the desired for the actual. We don't want to admit that that which we consider the height of development is only a point separated out by us arbitrarily from its continuum, and that for nature it's all the same whether things are good for us or not, that nature will not stop at this point but will go onward mercilessly.

We call this unfairness or see a decline so we can hope that it will change into advance, so that after old age will come youth, and after fall summer ... Yes, everything repeats itself but we won't be there to see it, we're one-time observers, ephemera, and we don't like it. But nature has no goal—it is unending and eternal in its deaths. And winter is the end of the cycle—not summer, which is so agreeable to us. And death is the end of each individual, not maturity. And the development of our consciousness tends towards its own winter. Consciousness alone has deprived us of the submissiveness of the beasts and we added suffering ourselves. Consciousness—a contradiction of itself, out of egoism, out of having an "I," began to desire something impossible in nature—stopping points. We want to stretch something into infinity that exists in nature in the form of finite and unendingly-repeated small and large cycles, stopping at the points we like. Our consciousness allows us to know pleasure and to wish for its infinity; we want it but we don't get it! We don't! We want the lives of our loved ones and they die. We want unending love and yet love ends in our very selves. We want some kind of unending orgasm and yet are practically impotent ... We must, or maybe we had better never, understand that our perfectly natural internal resistance to and indignation with the implacability of nature cannot be taken as a proof of the existence of a goal, of meaning, or of progress. Our scrambling, overshadowed by the lie of the goal, is essential for the life of consciousness in nature but shouldn't be taken as a confirmation of our ideas, because the ideas gave rise to the scrambling, not nature. Winter naturally ends the year. Death naturally ends life. Humanity will naturally come to its end. As will the solar system. And this is not a tragedy in nature's view; there can only be the tragedy of a single individual, endowed with consciousness but unable to manage it. Consciousness also has its winters and its final winter, sufficiently far-off for the moment, though perhaps quite near. Perhaps the winter of consciousness is nearer than the winter of man.

August 18th

If such a view seems too black, you can simply begin the discussion from the other end, emphasizing that everything begins from birth, from spring, from the first joys of consciousness ... and truly—these are the forces of creation. This is how optimism and pessimism appear in daily life: it's where you look, at the beginning or the end of your book ... but either way, our salvations and defeats are only ephemera, they don't exist any more in nature than do any of our moral or spiritual categories. And nothing in nature changes because of our view of her, no matter from what vantage point we observe. When I spoke about death, I felt no despair; I was attempting to see things as coldly and naturally as nature does. I wasn't upset and I don't need to justify myself.

If I was speaking of death as a natural completion of any process, then, first of all, I was speaking of what everyone already knows and which, at the same time, can never be known by a living person. The very concept of death is only the construction of our consciousness, the result of an individual protest that disregards the obvious—that in nature this thing is equivalent to any other phenomenon, it has none of the nuances or aftertaste which we may feel—there is only unavoidability. Secondly, if I was speaking not only about the innumerable deaths of infinitely small magnitude in nature (a human life is sufficiently long that man becomes witness to them and even loses count of them, and these atoms of death are also obvious to everyone yet equally knowable) but also of the general, final all-encompassing death, then, in the first place, I meant not the final death but rather just the deaths in that sphere which I can imagine, extending them into infinity. In the second place, I was talking more about the tendency towards final death and not really about the definitive death, absolute equilibrium and absolute zero. We cannot be witnesses to that; it is far too removed from us and we don't need it anyway. Compassion for the coming generations, for these witnesses to the cooling of the sun, is alien to us, what's more, it's stupid. Mankind will come to naught much sooner from the crisis and death of consciousness—but we are capable of feeling the tendency that all living matter has towards death, even towards the final death: this tendency is in us, in our brain and in the sum of our consciousness. It is possible to go on shaking these thoughts endlessly, to feel as though you've been cured, to take pleasure in the grass and the sunshine: what a spring! how wonderful life is! You'll keep going out to sit on the porch until death itself. But all this is still just an escape from our ridiculous fear and a gladness in the face of what seemed impossible; one more time we've escaped and again there is the impossibility of simply saying: yes, that's the way things are. I use the word "tendency" because I once heard it used in a way that pleased me.

At the institute, while teaching us misunderstood and castrated dialectics, the instructor once said: we say that under capitalism the working masses descend ever deeper into impoverishment, even though we are aware that the standard of living in the developed capitalist countries is not only not falling, but is actually rising (the discussion was being conducted by then with the pretense of directness and openness: we were looking truth in the eyes and so on—a conversation of the end of the nineteen-fifties). We even know that this standard exceeds our own not merely as a given, but sometimes in terms of the rate of growth as well, as we saw in West Germany. So, if we speak of the increasing impoverishment of the working masses under capitalism, then we are speaking of the *tendency* towards this impoverishment... this is what the instructor said and that is how a new dialectical concept was implanted in my consciousness. Someone had probably earned a degree for such charming sophistry. The reputations and careers of the clever and creative big-wigs in these dead disciplines have always amazed me. Our liberals, for example, are up to their ears in all this: isn't there progress (granted, only partial, of course it's only a half-measure, they say with conviction, as though justifying themselves) in the formulation itself?... The fact that its application has become possible they see as progress, these first defenders of the status quo, these indispensble costume changers of the old into the new, who put make-up on corpses, these double speculators who don't even bother to be cynical as they amass the spoils; money-grubbers, wrapped in the banners of ideas, of progress and of the furthering of the new order, peeking out of there like lice from their cucoons or whatever you say in this ...botany.

In letting go and giving free rein to my malice, and not even so much to my malice which is a worn-out feeling in relation to them, as much as to my desire to be angry, I fulfilled a certain spiritual need just as formally as we, in our rare flashes of life, have grown accustomed to fulfilling all needs, including love. We must now return to our theme, although it's already completely lost in this confusion. I comfort myself with the thought that if these pages are bound together by anything, it will surface without my efforts, though admittedly as a result of them, and that only in that way could something come out that I haven't discovered in myself or haven't already expressed. Having comforted myself with that, let's continue.

As I foresaw when I was writing about this on the preceding pages, my writing has turned into its own antithesis, since I've already met friends who not only read these pages but responded to them with understanding. This prescience of mine does not, however, fill me with pride. With sadness I realize that joy of the kind which followed, for example, the short story "People I Know" (1959) is no longer possible. In that story, I described the death of one character whom I regularly encountered and had observed since childhood. A few days later, I saw this character lying down exactly as I had pictured him, with the same bustle around him as I had just described. A definite pride inflated me almost to bursting and I told everyone I met who understood me and who knew me. I clothed this new story within the story in a sort of mystical horror, as though I were ashamed of the deed, as though I were insisting by doing this that writing in general (and my own in particular) can take on such concreteness and solidity that it can happen in real life, and therefore you should never write about living people, and you should certainly never kill them in stories. I also created the image not only of a powerful storyteller, but also of a man capable of being so shaken and stunned that he can't get over his pain, as though the recollection of my "murder" tormented me and wouldn't leave me. I don't castigate myself these days, not at all. I was completely sincere in my game and believed in it, and after all it wasn't only a game, there was also what had really happened that I was telling everyone about at the time, only it was weak, just a bit weak, and I dramatized it in my exposition and repetition. We intensify our feelings by expressing them, after all. Especially in writing. Perhaps this is what creativity is. Hence the eternal cliché that books are lies (here we have in mind not the ideological spectrum—which is always a lie—but the purely commonplace, as it is understood by the average reader. I'm speaking, of course, only about honest literature). From the fact of the intensification of feelings by their expression comes another commonplace argument—that the artist is only wonderful in his work, while in life—if only you knew this skunk in real life...! So, I was sincere in my distortion and exaggeration of the real history within the story, and my desire to boast about the incident seems to me to be evidence of those untapped forces that now only inspire envy. In essence, I was boasting by playing up my shock and my mystical horror and thereby associating myself with Flaubert, who felt symptoms of poisoning when poisoning Madame Bovary, and with Pushkin who cried or rejoiced over the unexpected actions of his heroes, and, although I didn't say so myself, I felt myself to be their equal. This bothers me all the more now that, reexamining that moment when I saw the realization of my own story in life, I see that the scene was in no way similar to the one I had described except for one detail: the worn-out, beat-up shoes of the deceased. After all, I used to see those shoes on that character all the time and they had always been worn-out. But this detail, this one coincident point was sufficient, together with my unacknowledged internal desire, to wholly merge the two pictures at all points. Apparently, I very much wanted this to happen. And then another thing was nice—the moment when I encountered my character alive and well a little while afterwards (apparently it had only been a seizure). When I saw him again, two feelings almost equal in size and intensity conflicted within me, highlighting each other. One, the most sincere, which I tried to ignore and suppress, was the disappointment that this character hadn't actually died, killed by the power of my imagination. The other, cultivated and forced, which I couldn't ignore without revealing a certain internal dishonesty, was the feeling that I should experience some kind of relief and joy, since I had been delivered from that alleged torment of conscience that I had so willingly and bitterly talked about. There's no getting around it, the disappointment was simply stronger, although at the time I didn't let myself admit it and am acknowledging it literally this minute, as I recall it for no particular reason and, in turn, distort it all in the name of a new design. But I didn't start talking about him for nothing, or, more precisely, not without an internal motivation, because the intensification of feelings in narration and, consequently, their distortion and falsehood, very much concerns me now. And the shame, to all appearances the stupid shame, I feel because of this often comes close to paralyzing me in my writing. Especially as the path I have recently chosen consists in trying to write the truth about myself, as this is the sole truth of the truths accessible to me, and becomes all-encompassing if it is attained. To express in full a moment of one's own existence would be a pinnacle, and thinking this and trying for maximum sincerity, I keep catching myself in distortion and falsehood. Already acknowledging the impossibility of my own demands, I am all the same incapable of renouncing them to this day. Sweeping aside all the powerful devices once available to me that are clearly capable of creating an effect on the reader, even the select reader, I am all the more often unable to take up the pen because all the shapes converging around its tip make me feel ashamed...even this word "pen" I've just written—it's been a year and a half since I began writing directly at the typewriter and haven't been using a pen...But, well, maybe that's nonsense—these "pens"—if only it were just the "pens"!

Yes, so it doesn't make me at all proud to have known how I would dash around to my friends with these pages, demanding their compassion and their praise and of course giving them demerits if they didn't demonstrate this compassion ("giving demerits" is one of my least favorite traits, although I too sometimes am guilty of doing this: I'll say more about this when I start to talk about judgment, if I get that far). I knew that it would be like this and I'm far from believing that knowledge of one's weaknesses eliminates them. If it were otherwise, there would be no literature, or any living people and their geniuses. The knowledge of weaknesses, one's own, let's say, and even the struggle with them, never has done anything to eliminate them. Speculators of all epochs have sought to create ideal images of geniuses, of the dead ones, of course. Being dead, they were already powerless to amend anything. People are so blockheaded that they could no longer see what was alive in their creations, they only believed documents. They turned to diaries and correspondence to find in them living people similar to themselves so that they wouldn't despair in the face of their own weaknesses which (especially these days) seem to a young person to be his private curse, and makes him torture himself that he is the only one so spineless and weak, unlike everyone else. Every childhood seems to prove this view. Later on comes the torment (during the crises of opened eyes, when you discover that resemblance and replication are world-wide and it seems that you've been deceived, and, what's more, that they've been deceiving you your whole life: the world overwhelms you with its redundancy, its eternalness and its impurity), then begins the torment of being the same as everybody else, without the least recollection that you were just tormenting yourself for totally the opposite: you're the only one who is so bad in this regular world, the only one who can't come to grips with himself and attain the ideal, that you're the freak, different from the others. And then, getting used to it and failing to come to grips with yourself, you'll say (and this will be out of fatigue): we're all the same and each of us is unique. This one can live with. I'd like to say something about the incessant distortion of reality through the internal and social image of it—something more detailed and particular—below, if only we can make it to this "below."

Well, it doesn't really surprise me that this all happened as it did on the preceding pages, except perhaps, that it happened much earlier than I had planned. And I resumed my notes today after discharging completely through contact with my friends. But, after all, I know very well that today too—a Sunday with no rain—friends may come and the contact will take place again, the grounding and the discharge...And if I sat down on this particular day, while for a week before I was incapable of doing anything after the previous discharge, then isn't it because I'm rushing to add new pages so I can read them to the friends who will come today? But that's completely pointless.

I arrived in the city... Damn the city—I won't get to it anyway. I had just written about how friends would be coming today and they immediately materialized: they've arrived. And now I'm writing for no reason at all—so that my friend can film me with his wonderful movie camera as I work here in my attic. It's going to come out very nicely.

September 4th

Let's continue. I wasn't particularly pleased by my prediction that I would read these pages to my friends in the hope of sympathy, despite my awareness of the superfluousness of doing such a reading before I'd even finished writing, and this reminded me of the following story told me by a certain P. This P., whom I haven't seen in a long while, is a wonderful person in many respects and is himself a great ideological figure. I would even take him as a unit of measurement if it were necessary to measure the particular potential of a distinct category of people who prefer to influence others by words rather than deeds. It would be possible to design a machine that would listen to the successive loud-mouths and then spit out a card with a value: 10 P. or 0.000075 P. Let's not hurt anyone's feelings—to start off we could submit this text to it. This man, endowed with many talents and in any case, a very sensitive receiver of telepathic ideas (these days this has become a way to neutralize ignorance or to substitute for knowledge), also possesses an indisputable talent as a writer. I've never read any of his pieces and none of his friends I know can boast of having had that honor. He would show me an enormous basket crammed full of manuscripts (not a single one of my acquaintances could boast of having written that much), and, putting his hand into it, would pull out a single sheet at random on which there would always be the outline of one future project or another, and without looking at it, would begin to narrate. He could do this endlessly, or at least as long as you could sit there. Over the course of many years now I have not forgotten and often think about one detail from one of his long tales. The story was still in the form of an outline and took nearly an hour of uninterrupted narration. This detail, by its similarity to many of my own sufferings that have lost their keenness from repetition and become quiet, fleeting glimmers that no longer induce pain or pangs of conscience, like old age, callousness, a scab on incurable spiritual sores,—the similarity of this detail to much of my experience and, in particular, to the incident of prediction previously described, at first made me prick up my ears, and then, also beginning to fade, only depressed and distressed me... but it's already time to go on to the detail itself...

There was an old man who lived by himself in a room. He was completely alone and his room was neglected and empty, like a mystic's. The atmosphere there consisted of an amalgam of some cats, some odd girls who for some reason would come over and sleep with the old man, dark corridors, and a noiseless, inactive communal atmosphere which surrounded the lonely old man as though it were simply in the air, and this made the air into something other than air, a soup, some kind of culture medium, in which the microbe of his loneliness existed... Long descriptions of his uncomplicated routes to the hallway toilet and the kitchen which foreshadowed the action that kept not beginning gave a vivid impression of this culture medium, and all of this was transmitted exactly by an essence that arose organically, saturated with all the possible textures (so hard to convey in words) of the walls, floors, plastering, dust, textures of color, light, viscosity, density, touch, smell, etc.—another sort of soup of textures, unusually thick. So, this old man, spending the night alone one time, suddenly woke up and for a long while tried to understand a feeling not readily identifiable in texture before he realized that he wanted to eat. Then he remembered that he had some sausage in the kitchen and he set off on the journey that took many minutes from his bed to the kitchen. The journey became a real odyssey, thanks to the detailed descriptions of the sensations of surface and temperature of the floor in contact with the old man's bare feet, of the skin of the old man's feet in contact with this surface, the sensation of the cold handle of the door in the old man's hand and of the new floor in the hallway, then of the darkness of the corridor and of the lost sense of distance along the path he had traveled and of whether or not the kitchen would soon be reached in this darkness, and of the wallpaper which he touched, feeling along the wall as he guided his blind journey; the search with his hand for the light switch, the sudden illumination of the kitchen, the sensation of the kitchen floor, which changed from its having been lighted, the feeling of his long-john cuffs which bunched up with each step across this floor and so on and so forth and finally, the return trip, with the sausage, having again put out the light, once more in the darkness of the hallway and, perhaps because of the onset of the darkness again, or perhaps because the old man suddenly felt the awkwardness when he reached out to touch the walls, he suddenly discovered in one hand (in the other he held the sausage), a cold, heavy tea kettle. Then he remembers how he took the kettle and filled it under the spout and he doesn't understand right away why he did this... And suddenly the oppressive feeling of his own agedness pierces him, as it hits him that without ever once having thought about it, he's already known that after the salty sausage he was going to want to drink, and, without any conscious thought or idea, not even realizing it, he'd filled and carried away the kettle so he wouldn't have to go to the kitchen a second time, after he would have eaten the sausage and then gotten thirsty.

It seems I overdid the retelling and the connection is perhaps unclear, but I haven't got the energy to explain it further and want to go on now to something else, a sentence begun and abandoned many times about how I came to the city and met my friends, so I can finally part with it with a sigh, just as I parted a moment ago with the no-less tiresome repetition of the sentence about how the prediction of my premature reading of the first pages of "Notes" to my friends gave me no feeling of pride whatever.

And so, it seems, I arrived in the city. I met G. and K. by chance and we were very glad to see one another. Added to that was the fact that both of them, just as I met them, had suddenly received pleasing business news. The meeting and the news together—all this cheered us up to an unusual degree. Joyful affection and elation came over us; we had some drinks over at G.'s, then at my place, later at somebody's wedding, and would probably have gone over to K.'s to finish up if we hadn't run out of money and, more important, the stores hadn't closed. Our joy in one another, at least mine, was so great that it took away all the numbness out of which I write these notes, just like a swim in the ocean. It was as if from their presence the incentive and confidence in our work returned, the loneliness of it disappeared, and there was a sensation of strength and of what we'd already achieved. We drank and rejoiced and, as always when those who have lost faith find support and understanding contact with others, it wasn't so much the painful ideas and observations that were shared as it was a simple feeling of gratitude to one another. We blissfully yes-yessed, nodding at anything whatever, just from the feeling that we would always understand one another; we had only to meet more often, or maybe just never part. As always, when people are lonely and suddenly rejoice at meeting, we only nodded to each other like respectful Chinamen, as though grateful for each nod or sound or gesture, as though we were rubbing noses. We drank down our cheap wine. "This, that and the other," one of us said suddenly. We kissed and hugged him, thanks, we said, for saying "this, that and the other" to us, we too always thought so and were alone in our thoughts, but now we're not alone. Then he hugged and kissed us. "No, no, I thank you because you understood my this, that and the other and now I am not alone, I thank you," and then we all embraced each other and thanked one another, everyone nodded their heads and knocked foreheads in gratitude and it was as if we were rubbing noses and we drank again to this. And the other one said "this, that and thingamabob" and again everybody thanked him and he thanked everybody, and each was grateful that the other was grateful to him and then that they were grateful that he was grateful. Stupid people and half-wits have made jokes out of this—but it isn't really like that. And "boogly boo" I said, and we drank again and I was content with my boogly boo, which was just as good as both the "this, that and the other" and the "this, that and thingamabob" of my friends. "Really, we're nightmarishly patient," said K., and this was a spectacular phrase, it contained truth against all those who considered us impatient, as well as our confidence that we go on living no matter what and will still continue and still do something and contribute. And we drank and, grateful, rubbed noses.

It was then that the first thirty pages of this text were read aloud, and it was drunken G. who read them. And so well did he get across everything that I had written there, and much more, even to me, that I was amazed both by him and by myself and was moved and ready to hug and kiss everyone, but restrained myself out of authorial humility. Of G. and K., people who meant so much to me and to what I succeeded in understanding, you can't get off with a simple statement as I did in P.'s case. A lot more must be said about them and I'll try below to express what they and a few others did for me, but meanwhile I'll go on to another of those ideas that torment me and are connected directly with the origin of these notes and with my current condition. And this I will do tomorrow.

September 18th

I didn't do it the next day, or the day after that, and I won't do it today, two weeks later. My composition is coming out from under surveillance and siege. What I express in it overall I can't say, but I've already felt a change in intonation and mood several times since the first page and my narrative is becoming something of a journal. I never wrote that story and now I've started lying to myself about it, though I can comfort myself with the fact that it is turning out to be a special sort of diary and that it came into being organically.

The tone of tragic wisdom and universal abstraction has been replaced by conceptions more personal and elegiac. The last pages about the city are pure elegy. But now, half a month later, I can see that I was wrong to make my trip to the city into such a joyful event when I described the meeting with G. and K., because it wasn't only this meeting that took place in the city, in fact the meeting took very little place.

The city now makes me absolutely ill. I get colds in it. I suffocate there. I start to hate when I'm in it. I can't live in it. And I can't live without it. I come to the city out of touch with events and happenings, encounters and acquaintances, fresh intellectual crazes and the newest ideological eruptions. The writers' patrimony splashes about in its pond and I see just the foam and don't understand anything. I discover later, after several encounters and conversations, when my head has already started to ring and I'm getting dizzy, that I'm completely wrong about something and that somehow I see the world differently from everybody else and, most important, am perfectly incorrect in my orientation. I've gotten lost in this literary forest that I used to know so well and suddenly, although nothing has changed in it and all the pines and firs are standing in the same places, this forest is completely unrecognizable. I can't find the paths—it's as though they'd been covered by wind-fallen trees. It turns out I had a terribly wrong feeling for where my body was in time and space, and it's strange to find yourself standing in a place you thought was here and then have it wind up being way over there. I might never have noticed how I'd gotten lost if kind people hadn't pointed it out and explained. No, it's not as though they shouted it in my ear. I simply read it on their faces all of a sudden, and in their words: it crept in, just in passing, that I wasn't who I took myself to be and that I am not standing where I thought I was, that I don't think the thoughts I believe I'm thinking, nor do I think them in the manner that I thought I did. The times are entirely different from what I imagine them to be; let's say I think it's a fall morning when actually it's already a winter night. Or I think I'm standing on the corner of Nevsky and Zhelyabova and actually it's Bolshoi and Vvedenskaya and, what's worse, maybe it's not even this corner but a third, and the city may even be an entirely different one and the Party congress that just ended not the seventh but the twenty-seventh. As for me, I mistakenly introduce myself to strangers and act as though I were their acquaintance; no one has heard of me and no one knows me. I've never written anything and never taken part in life. And people speak to me only out of politeness and so as not to get mixed up with a madman. Well, my dear friend, is it pleasant to suddenly find all this out about yourself?

I thought I'd simply gone out to the dacha at Toksovo, where I'm living quietly with my wife and child, but it turns out that I've disappeared completely, slipped into a new existence, lost my ability to relate to people and am somewhere in the anti-world. And on top of that I'm trying to delve into our healthy Soviet world! What a strange idea! They're upset at the top—and with good reason. Why are you delving? You're dead, Sapozhkov, as the hero so wonderfully remarks in a story by my friend, Vadik Fedoseyenko. "You're dead, Sapozhkov," says the hero to his kindergarten playmate. "What are you talking for—dead people don't talk." "I'm not dead," answers Sapozhkov. Yes, you're dead, you're dead! What can you answer to that if there's no one to support you? You can begin to believe it. Especially since you've been burying yourself all year long. But no one knew about it. How did they ever sniff it out?

I sense another change in intonation—there's no whiff of elegy here. Here a furious, unjust intonation pulses within me, thoroughly alive, where I have no concern for the objective representation of the world in the merciless equilibrium in which it always exists, which means that the only excuse you can have for your own indignation is your own incomprehension. Joyfully embracing my own incomprehension, I will include an excerpt here which I wrote yesterday and today quickly attached with coarse thread and rough stitches to the preceding text that had lain around idle for half a month. I'll insert that appendage here and call it:

OPEN LETTER TO THE WRITER R.G. OF LENINGRAD AND TO READER V. K. OF TAGANROG

September 19th

In general, they're all busy burying me. Even my wife, even M.D. Not to mention such experienced undertakers as R. or D., although these are two very different morticians. Well, D.—he's fairly transparent—he thinks something like: Bitov will die as soon as his sexual confusion quiets down, or Bitov has become conceited and fussy and can't write because of his inflated condition, or Bitov's writer wife is suffocating him with her creativity. It's understandable for D. to think this way, because he's a person who, with the zeal of a first-grader, seeks all motivations in pathology. Those three or four motives out of which he believes he himself writes he considers to be common to all humanity. Therefore it's naturally incomprehensible to him how a man can write if he isn't short, isn't ugly, isn't Jewish and is successful with women. How can a man write who is externally so unlike a short, ugly-duckling kike who is unsuccessful with women, that is, so unlike D. himself? But R. is burying me for far more numerous and intricate reasons, although it should be said that he is enterring me with that same Protestant simplicity, without tassels or brocade, in a tight unplaned, pine coffin in which you can barely turn over—as if it weren't enough to be in a coffin—and you can't help getting splinters. Let's put it this way, at least: this man, in spite of his brains and talent, or perhaps because of his brains and talent, is organically incapable of seeing himself and incapable of relating to people, the thing he needs most, and therefore is unfaithful. And that's why he'll never acknowledge a single natural intention if it looks unseemly and why he rejects any awareness of his own unfaithfulness, which he explains by a newly-discovered imperfection in the object of his former love and present unfaithfulness. I don't know a single one of his former close friends whom he wouldn't slander that very second or, and this is a testimony to the really outstanding qualities of this character, a minute later. Well, so what, let them bury me. But I confess an unremitting love for both of them, all the more since it has withstood the knowledge that they don't talk about me the way I'd like and even talk about me behind my back. My love for them has been shaken, of course, but it has nonetheless endured and, if you take into account that no matter how wise an artist might be there is one situation in which he will never be unkind or objective: when someone else is unkind and unobjective towards the artist himself, then I really do love them tenderly. Both D. with all his Odessa shenanigans and R. with his petty-official baseness.

Everyone is burying me, Mama and Papa too. Mama, because I'm getting out from under her influence. Papa, because the principles of my existence in a way cancel out those of his own. And both are burying me because the image they create or created in advance of me and of my life has nothing to do with me in practice, living in today's world. There's not a thing you can do about it, be it ever so sad, and one is obliged to establish less intimate, more formal relations, because nothing can effect the transformation of the desired into the real, and even if you spent your whole life trying to exchange the image of me that exists in their consciousness for the real me, this would only be the birth of a new, fresh torture—the beginning of discrepancies with the me of tomorrow. I love Mama and Papa.

How is my wife burying me? It is practically impossible to put into words, it is at such an undeveloped, alive and changeable beginning stage. Let's say that it is for the moment expressed most clearly in all sorts of mutual dissatisfactions. Perhaps it wouldn't have been this way, but it's only natural—my wife being a writer. The dissatisfactions, in other words arguments, which arise on utterly petty pretexts (the source is always communal and social—lines, crowdedness or the lack of money), tend toward insult. It's as simple as a fight with flying dishes and damaged furniture. In the beginning, the objects closest at hand, most durable and least valuable fly to the floor, that is, those which won't be ruined by such treatment or which you don't care about... I've always been surprised by the effective subconscious calculation of this so-called temporary insanity. Then, unless for example, a little bird comes flitting into the room and dispels and refreshes everything with his joyful chirping, drawing the attention of the combatants to the nature of their activity when outside the windows are so many causes for joy and exultation, if instead the events continue to develop and the insanity gains momentum, turning from an infant into a grown man, when it's already impossible to find appropriate objects close at hand because everything that was formerly close at hand is now underfoot and to bend down for something in order to launch it again would mean to turn a serious matter into a parody, there comes a certain moment of confusion because it's imperative you find something and now you'd like something heavier. It seems a shame to throw the crystal vase next to you, especially because this surely would be the end, the ejaculation of the wet dream, the discharge; and here the perversion comes into play—the inability to sacrifice the vase becomes an even greater desire to humiliate and hurt the partner, maybe by throwing a bowl of hot soup at him, which is cheap but effective, particularly when the soup has cooled a bit and you can get away without burns. You can fling the cat at him or the floor rag, macaroni, soap, cheese, a moustrap with mouse, dirty underpants, peed-in diapers or a volume of Rabelais—big and heavy—who might've written an entire volume of lists of things suitable for flinging during an argument. The role of all the above-listed items is easily played for my wife and myself for everyday use as if specially made for the purpose and costs absolutely nothing—it's our "writerdom," a thing, as D. would understand, fully equivalent to kike-ness, ugliness or shortness. All kinds of things come to mind here—for example, that what the sober man has on his mind the drunkard has on his tongue. Did they have to say it so meanly and then, on top of that, call it "folk wisdom"? It's simply insulting... It's possible to work by the principle of inversion—to call you ugly if you're handsome, dim-witted if you're intellectual, a hack if you're talented, or a stool pigeon when you're pure as snow. You can save yourself labor and just call a spade a spade, call a Jew "yid," a doctor "quack," a poet "scribbler," a writer "pisser."* And since we can both call the other "you pisser," this becomes uninteresting, so we go deeper into the analysis of each other's writing and into the differences between our creative identities: stinking realist, you can't imagine a single thing, my wife says to me; petty, primitive surrealist, you can't write a single truth, I can say. After this artillery fire it's possible to make up, that is, to say—well, of course you write better than anyone, you're the most talented of them all,—even more than I. Oh, come on, how could I ever be compared to you? the partner should then say. Intelligent, loving people—they talked it over and everything's okay. A quiet period. But how can we live with what "the drunkard has on his tongue;" how can we free ourselves later from the quiet sallies of this worm that reason tries to drive away: "what *is* on the sober man's mind?"

Essentially this is the same way all fellow writers bury each other, with the difference that they don't share the love of a husband and wife; there is neither the necessity of living in the same room after an argument, nor the one room which imbues the arguments with so tangible a form.

They say that in Moscow in the house on Herzen Street there's a respectable man, with the obligatory Jewish surname, who is in charge of writers' funerals. It really is a bothersome business and not everyone is up to the task—at any moment you've got to be ready for an all-hands-on-deck. He probably hasn't had a vacation in years—they won't let him go, afraid that they won't be able to manage without him. And once, no doubt, they did let him go and he'd packed his suitcase and laid the pyjamas on top, headed off to the train station with his ticket in his pocket and—bang, someone died—and not just anybody, but one of the real top brass—they caught up with him and brought him back. It was a famous man who knew everybody and had been on a first name, arm-in-arm basis with all of them. He looks at you just as though he were taking a measurement. By eye he guages you, accurate to the centimeter. Coffins probably have their sizes, just like galoshes. It's S., they tell him. "S.?" he says,—"Which one? We've got three. Ah, K., height number four, width three." He's not interested in young ones they say, doesn't appreciate them, doesn't notice them. But they're growing after all, the young ones... He's probably thinking—just a couple more years to retirement; he's planted a little berry plot not far away, three stops past the cemetery. But it's a mistake not to notice the young ones. Look at Sh. who had a heart attack, and G. with his stroke, and E., a chronic alcoholic, and V. sexually impotent, and A., a thinning of the brains. Of course, what kind of funerals will they have—there won't be all the pomp and honour, but all the same they have to be... buried.

---

* untranslatable pun: *pisa'tel'* (writer); *pi'satel'* (pisser).

Yes, if you get unused to the city and don't see people for ages, the people with whom you stand, as it were, in the same rank, living by the same thoughts, writing with the same ink—you look up and you've dropped behind, you're out of touch. You were sitting there peacefully scribbling away thinking you were doing something and meanwhile you got left behind. You come to town for some necessity, tearing yourself away from your labors, you've got to buy matches or salt, but everyone turns their backs on you and shows you their asses and when you greet them they get flustered and give their hands unwillingly, looking you over awkwardly and censoriously: what are you doing here... we buried you with all due ceremony and you pretend you are alive. You died a long time ago, kicked the bucket, you're no longer on our list, there's a new ammunition clip, we already fired you out, we turned our backs on you, don't breathe down our necks, you'll never catch up with us. But people are respectful, of course they don't show openly that you're dead, they have their composure, the contemplation of a corpse doesn't disturb their imagination or digestion, they don't bat an eyelid, they're used to it, they'll still worry deep down whether you intend to buttonhole them with questions for long, whether they'll still have to talk for long with people who've become superfluous when they're hurrying as it is. They're still alive, but they're polite after all, they won't say anything, they'll just shift from foot to foot and change their stance out of impatience, looking at the passing women, and when they find out that you only came in for salt and matches and then are going back, they calm down completely. Well, what do you know, they'll say to themselves, the old dearly-departed is just a novice in this affair, wanted a breath of air—a little adjustment problem—but he's disciplined, he knows that he has to go back to his coffin, it's okay, he'll get used to it—he'll come back one more time and that'll be it—he'll settle in . And they'll look at you just as though you'd turned to glass, they'll be convinced that you no longer exist, and they'll stick out a hand as though into nothingness and run off.

Now I don't go into town. Now I go for salt and matches to the place next door, the local cemetery supermarket, just as good. Exactly the same. Who's alive and who's dead—who can figure it out? Each thinks of himself as he wishes. I go to this supermarket and get depressed. I wonder, isn't there some way to buy these matches and the salt without having to go out at all? And what's the point of going out? What's the joy in all this writing? It's all just expenses. Look at this—matches a kopek and the salt—seven kopeks a pack all at once. My friends are silent and the publishers aren't biting. A kopek, another kopek and then seven more, and then another kopek—that's ten already. And this is only an image—matches and salt. Really just peanuts. But butter, meat? Bread these days too... And shaving—that too—you'll go broke just on soap and razor blades, and then only if you don't lose the brushes. The old beard just grows and grows, no matter how much you shave it. I would like to shave it off in one fell swoop, the whole length allotted to me for my lifetime, but no, it comes in day after day, like on a ration card, and you count the gray hairs one more time. How many boots alone do you wear out, how much paper do you use up, and then typists aren't free either... And in reward—what? You don't exist, you're dead, what a reward! Ah, if only you knew—it's all nothing but expenses...

So here it is bedtime. Time to lie down in my damp coffin. Twelve-thirty. Out the window is the pitch darkness and my typewriter and I are reflected in the glass. I'm dark in the glass, gloomy. I don't like myself. G.S. writes good stories. I don't even write anymore, I'm just a corpse, what can I do? My wife will finish it for me. I might have tried to paint or sing, or play Bach on my aunt's piano, but I don't know how. Now I can't see anything in my dark window pane—the electricity is interfering. Maybe I should turn it off and get used to the dark. But why? After all, I already know everything out the window very well anyway. Nights here in Toksovo the hoodlums are out. I'm probably quite visible in this window from out there. An easy target. Grab me and gun me down. As a preventive measure. So I don't take it into my head to come back to life. If it weren't so cold I'd run out to have a look at how well I'm visible from the street. But this is also senseless, because when I run out on the street, I'll no longer be at the table and all I'll see will be an empty room. And maybe that's how it really is, the room is empty. I wouldn't mind going along with the hoodlums now myself, following the obscure and animal impulse that would begin to toss within me at this: which garden to climb into, which window to smash?

I'm telling you, don't worry about me. If I'm dead I'm dead. I won't be resurrected. I don't want to be. There are no drafts in the coffin. And I don't want to overtake you. Much less breathe down your necks. I breathe down my own neck and step on my own heels; I chase myself and fall behind myself or overtake myself. That's the riddle of it. What's going on? Living on his own, running on his own, doesn't spit on anyone and doesn't persecute anyone. Well, Qwertyuiop, as M.D. wrote. It's as if I were playing the piano and had run a finger along the entire keyboard, giving out such a tr-r-r-r-r-r-r-illl.

That's all. Goodnight to you. Go ahead and feast yourselves on me, on what has been eaten off me. I don't need anything that can be bitten off me. I'm already smoothened, hardened; these days there aren't any extensions of me that are convenient for biting off. Take a bite and your teeth will slide off clacking. And I'll keep rolling along. Like a round loaf. I'll raise chickens at the dacha, tender reptiles—let them sing. Let the piglets grunt. Let the streptococci hop. The diplodoci crawl. Let the pale spirocetes dangle down here and there to complete the picture. And, as for the writers, God bless them, let them write, let them not sleep if that's what they like.

Rock-a-bye, how nice! Only now there'll be another bad dream. War again. Am I writing for nothing while my windows shake from the nearby shooting and in the mornings the wonderful marches resound amidst the rustling of the falling leaves? Or will those two grab me under the elbows again and say: come along now.

They're with me constantly. I already recognize them in my dreams. I even had tea with them recently. They came over and I offered them tea. They drank it, out of surprise. Suddenly they began indulging in confidences. I'd gotten them some bread as well... One was all pale, green, and complained to me of tapeworm. He couldn't eat any of that or any of this, the tapeworm disliked everything. Even hot tea was forbidden, it had to be cooled. I asked my mother-in-law about it in the morning and she said the best thing for this problem is camomile with dried mushroom spores stirred up in vodka. When I dream of them today, I'll give him this advice. It's also an excuse to have a drink, after all. Let him and his tapeworm drink it with the spores and his friend and I'll have the unadulterated stuff. It's a long time since I drank with anybody, at least with them I'll get to drink. And I won't put the wife to any expense. One of them can guard me while the other runs out for the vodka. Only, please, R., don't you come into my dreams. Because what's the idea, I dreamed you and you wouldn't shake my hand? I say to you: but why? and you answer: you know why. What kind of attitude is that! as S., the writer from T——, said. You can't explain the problem to a simple man. You didn't give me your hand and after you V.I. shook his dusty forelock and stuffed his hands in his pockets as deep as they would go. And then Shch. hides his short paws. We've gone ahead, he says, we're creating literature of the idea, we have a new system of coordinates, information-muckification and your system of coordinates is the old one; don't try to get into our good graces—you're still writing that "feelings and sensations" crap, you're already a dead man. Don't breathe down our necks again—there's just the three of us so far: me, B.I. and R. So if I do dream of you, it's that kind of thing, we'd better drink together—don't worry about your ulcer—it's okay in a dream.

But maybe I'll sleep without any dreams. And it might happen too that one day dreams will cease to be dreamed altogether. It's just possible. How are we to continue living, R......? You'll tell us how, of course. This way and that. But it turns out I know it all myself. After all, I used to have all kinds of silly fantasies about myself and loved to write about them. But now I don't have them anymore, those fantasies, I've begun to age. In the beginning I used to boast about my gray hairs and the teeth I'd lost, I was young. But since I started to notice that it wasn't just a matter of teeth and hair, I've stopped bragging. And yet, there is one fantasy out of them all that remains. It's as though ten or twenty years had gone by and here I am going along an unfamiliar street in some unknown little city in an unknown land. I'm gray, there are some manly wrinkles on my face, I'm in some old coat and I've got a bundle on a stick over my shoulder. I'm going along, but I've absolutely no one to go see. As though I had neither family, friends nor acquaintances, and as though I don't know the tongue in which everyone here is conversing. And I have no memories of anything. Just as though there never had been anything. There's only the fact that I am walking, gray and wrinkled, along this unfamiliar street. What happened to everything? And where am I going?

And what do I actually think will become of me? In the simple, daily, sense—how will my life turn out? I picture a war and the destruction of everything—that's one. If not that, then it's that they'll pick me up and I'll be in prison—that's two. If not that, then that I'll be dying of longing for my homeland in a rich house on the shores of a warm sea, famous and lacking all that I love—that's three. If not that... I can imagine anything at all, only there's one thing I never imagine, that I'll go on living for five, ten, thirty years just as I'm living now... This seems to me an impossibility beyond my power. The Greats no longer amaze me with what they wrote, but I'm amazed at how Dostoevsky died in his sixties and Tolstoy in his eighties?! How did they last so long!

There is already so little left to live, sang the forty-year-old Vertinsky, yet he too died in his eighties. And what was he—Vertinsky was small potatoes. If geniuses who found themselves in this world were given such insanely good health that they lived out their entire lives, for what and for whose sins did they suffer such torment?

Enough. Where are these tigers, Lord, as Lev Tolstoy said; look how long I've lived and still I haven't seen a single tiger. They wanted to record Tolstoy's voice on the just-invented phonograph. They asked him to say something to the children. And it will be preserved, thought the director, the great voice addressing the children, and the descendants. And what did old Lev say? "Children," he said, "be good, behave yourselves. Obey Mama and Papa. And most important, be good." And he didn't want to record any more of his voice on the phonograph. Well, if you think about that you'll figure it out.

Now with each page I write I keep wanting to finish, but to finish at the end of the page. But I keep beginning something I hadn't planned on writing, it slips over onto the following page and ends somewhere at the beginning of it. And again I stretch to the end of the page. And again it climbs over onto the next one. Here, reader... That's all. I don't want to do any more.

September 20th

I didn't end quite right yesterday anyway. Because when I wrote "Here, reader," it was the beginning of a sentence like this: "Here's reader V.K. from Taganrog who writes:"—but, having written the first two words of this phrase, I saw that it was the last line and that I was once more creeping over onto the next page, and I got frightened. I moved the carriage back a word and put in a comma, and it came out as direct address. I put three dots on the end of the address for significance. And there was still room enough to write "That's all, I don't want to do any more." It turned out okay.

And then I went to bed, but I was still revved up. The whole continuation was coming into my head, keeping me from falling asleep; clever little phrases would flare up and then go out without a trace. Of course I didn't really remember them and nowadays I don't have the silly habit of hopping up in my drawers to search for pencil and paper to catch these clever little firefly phrases. I have no feeling that something priceless is being lost forever. I'm not I.E. Let it be lost, I think, thank God. But I guess I was excited, everything in me was intensified. That's why I suddenly smelled the odor of dust. A sharp sort of smell as when the first nails of rain hammer the dust onto the street. "Where's that from?" I think. And immediately there's a clever little phrase: "What is it that smells to me of dust all the time?" And behind this one stands the amorphous mass of sentences in close ranks and one is already stepping forward to get in line with the first; in the remaining sentences, which I still can't make out, I discern a certain preparedness to appear in a defined succession and to form a whole coherent fragment that would begin: "What is it that always smells to me of dust?" The heck with you, I've given up on them, it's time to sleep. That's how bountiful I am, and it might have been not a bit worse than "How wonderful is the Dniepr"... I sniff, and it continues to smell of dust. But here in Toksovo there isn't even any dust. I lie there and the smell just streams into my nostrils, despite my head cold and my stopped-up nose. What could it be? I wonder. I start feeling around under my nose and I hear a light crackling and something like a tiny blue spark glitters in the pitch darkness. So it truly is fireflies... And suddenly I understand—it's the shirt that I put by the pillow so I wouldn't have to reach out for it in the cold tomorrow morning, but could just pull it on while staying warm (cf. the old man). The shirt I have is one of those warm modern ones made of orlon, a synthetic, so to speak. So this orlon electrifies while I'm wearing it during the day. Take it off and it discharges. This is the reason for the thunderstorm smell and the crackling and even for the sparks. Every time I take it off for the night I hear that crackling but this is the first time I've noticed the smell. My father, who's got a shirt just like this and who dearly loves the phenomena of nature, used to tell me that his crackled and gave off sparks and a smell of ozone. I knew that it crackled but I didn't believe the part about the sparks and the ozone, I thought he'd exaggerated out of his love for the study of inorganic nature and was thinking of Richmann, who was killed by lightning. But it turned out to be true. So that's how the senses and their organs are sharpened in the creative act!

Actually, if all these pages are a sort of open letter, then at the beginning it was more or less addressed to R. and now is becoming an answer to my Taganrog reader V.K., who has written me a letter. You see, he likes Leningrad very much although he's never been there. And he likes Leningraders very much; he got to know them in a skiing camp. People get to know each other in all kinds of camps, times change... Now, he writes, I would very much like to get to know you. His wanting to get acquainted is somewhat explained in the beginning of the letter where he describes how he read my little book: "I was still in bed, golden squares lay on the floor and I was praising you to the skies as if I were reviewing your book." Reader V.K. of

Taganrog would like to become acquainted with me and wants me to write him about how I began writing, what the stimulus was for that beginning, what themes most concern me, how I write, what I think about when I write and what feelings are aroused in me by "work on the word" (V.K.'s quotations)? Boredom, most often, dear V., and a certain unhappiness that I'm unable, that I no longer have the strength, having become a writer, to make myself till, load, or drill; that in all my life, having had a few jobs and written what I've written, not once did I *work,* and because of this have for a long time considered myself scum and derided myself, though I don't anymore. Aren't you obliging me, dear reader V.K. from Taganrog, to write much more in answer to you than I've written in all the time I've been writing, and still be unsure that I've recounted or explained anything at all?? Simplest of all (and perhaps there would be no less truth in this than in an entire volume) would be to refer you to the rambling letter of the preceding pages where I wrote about wanting to finish writing so that the page would end at the same time as the writing but kept creeping over and creeping over and I couldn't do a thing about it. So that's how I write and these are the feelings I experience. And once in a while when I've turned out the light and am lying down in the complete darkness of my damp coffin, it is given to me to sense that my shirt smells of thunderstorms and of the dust that the first nails of rain hammer onto the road. At last the page has ended where I was planning to stop.

October 4th (the House)

Pioneer time is beginning! I'm growing younger every minute. I've got to get busy: two Pioneer organizations want to receive some compositions from the Pioneers. One might wonder what I have to do with this? And it turns out that I'm the one who supplies these Pioneer compositions. Well, there's no point in putting up a smokescreen, there's no place to hide: I supply—so I supply, I'm no kid, I understand what I'm doing.

If a writer opens his eyes just a little wider, he catches himself involved in prostitution. That's why he doesn't open them. The Soviet writer squints. He says to his wife, keeping his eyes to the ground, examining the toe of his boot: I'm going out for a bit, I'll take a stroll, get some air ... while really he's on his way over to the House of Committees and Meetings. The blue plaques, the whispered-in corridors, the draughts from office to office, the acquaintances, some you greet, some you don't acknowledge and some you embarrass. And there are clients—editors, for the most part. They greet you as they see fit and you do the same. One likes you one way and another some other way. One would be glad to, but he can't. Another can, but he prefers blondes and you're a brunette. One likes them pure and young and modest and you lead him off to one side and, off to the side, offer yourself as just that kind. And another you lead off to the other side—he likes it peppery, in the mouth and in the ear, any way you can do it he likes it, and you try to seem his type. You'll suffer, of course. One finds you to be too virginal, the other that you're too much of a slut, but there's nothing to be done, it's the profession—you just grin and bear it. You meet a writer friend in the hall and you complain: you know I'm ready to do anything, but really, this way? I can't... what is it with him—it's not enough or what?

It's a tough profession, believe me!... But you knew yourself what you were in for. It's not all so simple. Look at Gypsies—as soon as they're born gypsies they get themselves all in a toil and moil over how to live without working, and so much energy is spent taking this route to avoid labor that it turns out to be harder than any labor ever could be. And while the gypsy may complain, he'll never want to change his lot. It's the same with a writer—even when it's unendurable for him, he is ready to do anything just to keep from being deprived of this very unendurability.

And everybody's squinting, as though they weren't selling themselves. A prostitute is rightfully insulted if you call her by that name. Early in the morning, writers lie in bed, saying: do you think I was always this kind of girl?... I wrote a novel, didn't you read it? I had a fiance', and people said he had talent, he took me into a certain place and asked: you want to meet a few of my friends? He took me to the editors and left me there, I went from hand to hand, he deflowered me, published me, and then dropped me. Let the others, he said, use you now, let them publish you. It's a sad tale, what can you say...? But there're so many of these tales you can't even force out a tear. you leave five rubles on the little table and fifty kopeks on the counter; there's nothing to be done, the merchandise is not returnable—put it on a shelf. A young girl will be horrified when she looks at a prostitute and will rejoice in her own purity while the prostitute will say: little fool, I too was once as pure as you. "You were never so pure!" the virginal maximalist will say indignantly. "It's impossible!" And both of them are right.

A professional is a professional, he takes pride in it. In writing, it's the opposite. Imagine a gigantic brothel, grand style, industrial scale, a corporation with plush pile runners on the stairways, an elevator, low polished furniture and white telephones, with both a production and a delivery department and not without its First Department*—and people going in and out, going off into offices, all after the same thing and all, imagine it, pretending that they didn't come here for that. It might seem funny and silly—but try sometime in a gesture of despair or in an agony of innocence to shout out what they have come for, and they'll lynch you. If you open your eyes, the picture you get is fantastical: everyone doing his thing openly and unabashedly—in the hallway, on the window sill, on the radiator, sitting, standing, in twos and in threes and solo—Sodom!—and somehow everyone

---

* The KGB office found in every Soviet enterprise.

seems not to see, doesn't notice, denies it, refutes it, no one acknowledges anything. You think you'll go out of your mind, when suddenly you're astonished: why this system is just brilliant! And, it's true, even if you were a genius you couldn't invent anything to combat the existing reality. But if you see this given reality then, like it or not, you've got to act accordingly. But you're required to act otherwise. What should you do? A declaration will save everything. Someone once understood that in the face of a given reality which, the moment you see it, topples everything, there is only one means of defense—to declare that this given doesn't exist. It doesn't exist, hm-hm. Here are two goats—an editor and a critic who are engaged in the act of sodomy right on the stairs. "It's an outrage, disgusting, how dare you!" "But we're hm—hm," And it sounds like a Turkish-Bushman phrasebook: "What is this?" "This is a brothel." "This is a brothel?" "No, this is the Great Soviet Bear and the house is hm-hm." "Who is that? Is that the messenger?" "No, that's the chief editor." "But aren't you free?" "Me? I'm not even here—I'm hm-hm." "You're hm-hm? But here you are, I can see you, I'm holding you by the lapel." "That's no lapel." "What? It's not a lapel?" "What's the matter, don't you understand the Russian language? I just said that I'm hm-hm."

And it's as though a fog had come down and covered everything, is he there or not? Tell me please, black is really white, isn't it? You understood me perfectly—you didn't understand a word I said. A cooling grammatical fog falls over everything: if it isn't the present in the past then it's the past perfect in the future. And the mystery of London fogs is related to the mystery of the English language: past perfect in the future and future perfect in the past. And suddenly the scales fall from your eyes, it's suddenly easy, as though the invisible, skilled hand of Filatov* has cut away your cataracts, and you run along the hallway with everyone at a skip, clenching the joyous shout in your teeth: I'm hm-hm too! Me too... It's time to admit to ourselves that there is a certain house we all go to. Not so very long ago, hypocrisy was not a Russian characteristic. But that was in a freer world. Some irony—to lose the latter once and for all in order to receive even more of the former. There is such a house! I am announcing this (God knows what kind it is) discovery. But I'm not beating my breast. There is such a house and people go there for one thing only and never admit it to themselves. All you have to do is go there on the fifth or the twentieth of the month, on the day they distribute the material benefits, and even better, if you really luck out, to find yourself in line at the little window they throw the bones out of—Lord, if your nose isn't permanently stopped up from the Leningrad mists, what an odor you'll smell there!! The printed page smells so delicious, translated into printed symbols, like spam and garlic cutlets... Damn, I'm beginning to forget that smell, and I want it so much... But the mountain won't come to Mohammed. It keeps not coming.

---

* A famous Soviet opthalmologist.

There's a house where we all meet. We're as equal in it as we are in the bath house. Whoever is still embarrassed covers himself with a bucket... and those who have clambered onto the top bench in the steam room don't come down. Go on, splash it on, more steam, steam! There are the old nags, worn out by the years, some powdered and rouged, others who've stopped using makeup. They go and they hate the young people. And the young people go there, pretending to be virigns. They go to see the ones who like them. There are people who like to deflower. "Look how he's putting it on," hiss the nags at the backs of the young ones, "we'll break you all the same." Just take a little more merciless look, a little more maximal look—and see how clear it is that everyone here is equal, mere excrement, that the very fact that they're here says it all. But no, what loftiness, what stratification! This one is a general and that one a meter-reader. Oh come on, you're all naked...! And the buckets don't have any distinguishing markings. But no, every bucket stands alone. Each one, no matter how low it may appear in the eyes of the other buckets, has its leaders and its scum; each one pretends to nobility and loyalty and all of them are indignant at the opposites—baseness and servility. The main thing is to cover themselves with a bucket and hm-hm! And like a legend (just get a taste and you'll understand its flavor and its deep significance), rumors are out about the two castes of hell and its deities. No one's even seen them—the names just keep coming up like the names of the apostles. They are the personification of the dream, its two poles, shadow without light and light without shadow: Kochetov and Solzhenitsyn. With Ehrenburg, an upstart, in between them. I scratch my forehead, fighting it off, it's a mirage, delirium, impossible...but sometimes it seems to me that they're all the same. Of course, it's seductive for a time, it's pleasant to wrap yourself up in the plaid blanket of Romanticism: black and white, hell and paradise, good and evil— how nice to see a dichotomous world neatly divided by such clear boundary between light and shadow, as though we were in an airless expanse, how seductive to measure our reality in terms of Dostoevsky's demons while Sologub's petty demon grimaces and scrapes his soles along the wallpaper, having become even pettier as he scattered and spread all over the world and finally settled into complete equilibrium...

Boys and girls go there still not knowing what it is they're selling; demonic youths go there who've already smelled themselves burning and have long since decided to run away but keep not running; the well-fed cynics go there, machines to whom nothing matters; the liberals go there, who keep brushing it all aside with their switches, thinking that the next time they wave them their twigs will bloom; the two-bit theory. They embrace Soviet dialectics: less is better, yes, better; the legal period and the illegal period— they are forever the bearers, they are forever the custodians, like people who don't know of matches, like priests in a cult, the keepers of fire, they carry in a basket, in a fieldbag, in briefcases, Camus and Kafka and never ignite them, and once more clamber to kiss the classics of revolution: the moment isn't ripe, quanitity is becoming quality. So they save up, consume, get fat and still there's no quality. And there won't be any. "And who needs it!" as G.G. says. And everyone squints, and they all pretend they aren't selling themselves.

A decent woman sleeps ten times with one man and an indecent woman once each with ten—according to Lachsness. With us it's amazing how everything is built on such fine distinctions that it takes extensive training to tell them apart. For example, you sleep with twenty and I only sleep with fifteen: I'm decent and you're not. There are decent circles and indecent circles. But each indecent circle has its own decent and indecent people, its own progressives and reactionaries. There's your fattened quantity! There is a decent man to associate with, a decent man to use, a decent editor, a decent member of the steering committee; there is a decent Party man and a decent stool pigeon, and there's a decent son of a bitch. We use them, dropping through to the bottom from level to level. And we gather on our own Olympus, drink tea and converse with Olympians, sure that on Olympus there aren't any microphones or tape recorders, no direct link with the other Olympus, and that there are two Olympias which have joined hands and wink at each other across the street. And again we rank ourselves on the scale of honesty and decency at this tea drinking ceremony.

And in that house the windows are misted over and steam hangs over it—you can see it from the side. But if there are people who go around it by the side, we don't know them.

Tomorrow, I'll sit down and do the Pioneers' work. I sat down to do it today but here I've gone and written something else. I sat down to do it yesterday too. It's the same old homework. I don't want to do it. You slump between the book *It Was Near Rovno* and the typewriter and feel like going woman chasing. And so what? One dear comrade has to put off freedom, debauchery and spiritual growth for a month. For a month you have to replace all this and counterbalance the absence. You have to practice self-discipline, take yourself in hand, take up excercising, vegetarianism, abstinence, moral hygiene, the study of foreign languages, fasting, exhaust yourself with labor so you can manage the situation without noticing anything.

October 5th (Anniversary)

Starting with the shirt that smelled of thunderstorm that time, the desire seems to have arisen in me to write something down the morning after about whatever I had been writing the evening before. A sort of morning meditation on evening themes. Today I was able to open my eyes, for the first time in a long while, as you open them in childhood. I had been sleeping soundly and opened my eyes immediately, not feeling in them any of the discomfort or hangover that burdens the morning of a neurasthenic. I discovered that it wasn't yet eight o'clock and that I'd slept only six hours, even less, but I didn't feel like sleeping anymore. I found in my mind a certain spaciousness and lucidity, for I recalled distinctly the sensations and impressions I'd had when I stopped writing and got ready for bed and before I fell asleep. Naturally, I neither heard nor saw anything while I was writing—I was giggling at my well-turned little phrases. I especially giggled at the sentence: "And young people go there, pretending to be virgins." Perhaps it was because I tittered over it so that today this sentence says practically nothing to me. I don't remember the rest of them. But everything that happened after I got up from the desk and what came after that I remember very well. I didn't force it, didn't repeat it in the growing drowsiness so I'd remember it in the morning, I didn't write it down in shorthand so I could decipher it with knitted brow the next day. I just opened my eyes today, which further bolstered and intensified the sensation that this morning was special, a kind I used to have, but, alas, have long since forgotten: like a five-year-old who goes to sleep knowing that tomorrow is a holiday, the New Year or his birthday, and who feels especially keenly the darkness of the room, the feel of the sheets, the taste of the pillow, and his entire skin still so pure it its every little cell ... and suddenly he snaps open his eyes, just as one sometimes opens a window with a decisive gesture, quickly and eagerly, to let in the fresh air, he opens his eyes with a kind of strong internal movement and sees the morning in his room and the white window, and immediately realizes: it's a holiday! I got up from the typewriter yesterday and once more saw nothing in the night windowpane except my own blind reflection with intensified shadows, sunken cheeks and eye sockets, looking skull-like at me. Then I suddenly heard the silence, and then the sounds in that silence: outside the rain had been coming down for some time. It really was coming, coming along beneath my windows, tramping, pulling slow feet out of the limp earth, scraping itself and blowing its nose. And with that compound feeling of childish fright, though now lighter and less intense, and with that grown-up's chuckle at myself, which arises from the fear of seeming naive, laughable or stupid even in one's own eyes, I didn't at first believe that it was rain and not someone walking beneath my windows, and that he was able to see me but I couldn't see him ... and, already really scared, I turned out the light and at first saw nothing. I got even more scared, and then saw the maple bough that drops to my window and the beginning of the path that heads away from my window, and even the sky turned out to be not a night sky, but whitish. I situated the sounds in the expanse beyond the window so that they became concrete and understandable, for example, the sound of water pouring from the roof into the rain barrel: this was him scraping on the door, because the rain barrel stands by the porch. The tramping I couldn't understand, but out of a habit of denying the supernatural in the everyday, of convincing myself that I'm living in a world of rational connections that are very simple and not mysterious if they're known, I explained to myself that it was just that I couldn't understand what was happening, but all this was actually produced by the air crunching as the water forced it out of the soil or something like that. In any case, I told myself, it's the rain and not anything else, which only reaffirmed my uncertainty about it. More than anything else I was calmed by the fact that the sky was whitish. And I went to sleep like a living person, not once having fixed or formulated my sensation, so that isn't why I remembered it and relived it when I woke up.

    Then I went out on the porch to relieve myself. The morning seemed surprisingly warm to me, perhaps because I had been expecting an icy cold too much. It's hard to explain any other way, because a man can't feel warm who has just waked up, climbed out of a warm bed wearing only his drawers, and gone out on a damp porch of an early October morning on the sixtieth parallel. The morning rose, whitish-gray, out of the bushes and grass in puffs of fog; it seemed the bushes were breathing freely and the steam, perhaps because of this, didn't feel dank but warm, like breath. The steam rose up in soft, melting tongues to the porch and, expended, seemed to lay its warm dog's muzzle on the lowest step. The sensation of the morning suddenly comingled with my sensation of the evening before, so clearly recalled at waking, and startled me by its comprehensible similarity. Without wanting to, and without trying to figure out what constituted this shared quality, as though I felt that unnecessary or superfluous, I just took it in, absorbed it, and this made me even happier. I was made happier of course by something else as well—my slow urination. I watched how my stream fell from the height of the porch and onto the earth, beating a small hole into it, and how steam was also rising over this hole. Having shaken my shoulders rapturously, I rushed back into the house to the warmth, dove under the blanket and with delight thawed myself out under it.

    I detected that scraping sound that gets louder at night, when the mice come alive behind the wallpaper. Mornings, they're usually quiet. Following the sound, I traced its source from behind the walls to the outside. There, above my window, I saw a bird. She's apparently got a nest there. She strode back and forth. I couldn't get a good look at her from my bed, the eaves were in the way and the bird behind them, and she flew in and out too swiftly. I thought it must be a swallow, but wasn't sure that they stay on here into October, after all, they're migratory birds. This bird also made me happy. There, I thought, not only mice, but birds too...

    Speaking of holidays, it seems to me, if I remember rightly, that today marks the fifth year that I've been writing prose. On this day I wrote my first story, "People Who Shave on Saturday." I'm very surprised that my head suddenly gave me back this date today. I don't remember dates as a rule, although from childhood I've tried to memorize them in some naive certainty that this would preserve the event in my memory that so excited me at the time. I still had too little experience to observe what memory does with our lives and how the resurrection of cherished events in our lives happens without our conscious efforts to resurrect them and, perhaps, in spite of these efforts. I've tried to memorize many dates in my life: the days I first met lovers and the days I first possessed them, the days of my achievements and victories; I would learn these days by rote and note them down on numerous slips of paper. At first the papers would get lost, and then the date would stop meaning anything to me and I'd lose the date. And now, I struggle to remember the years and establish the date in my memory plus or minus a year. And I haven't even gone far along the roads of memory. In the beginning, I cherished this date, October 5th, 1958; after all, it seemed to me that my beginning to write had saved me, had made my existence meaningful and so forth. I remembered this date today just in time—I reregistered these five years, which not so long ago seemed to me so distant; the desire I had to celebrate them arose from an understandable impatience with the flow of life and from that love of round figures which, no matter how relative they may be, create in our psyche the illusion of normal phases in our life. Just as when I'm reading a too-thick book, no matter how much I like it, I count up the number of pages I still have to read from time to time and determine the proportion of the part already read to that part remaining to be read, just as my father always wants to see the turn-over on his car's odometer, just as we like to notice how much time it takes us to do one thing or another. But even if one date or another is still able to excite us (and perhaps especially if a date can excite us) we, as a rule, miss it, forget it, like my father who, while keeping his eyes on the road, invariably misses the moment when his odometer goes from all nines to all zeroes. And it seems to me that my anniversary today would have left me indifferent if it hadn't been that I was able to open my eyes so easily this morning. And it leaves me indifferent anyway, as it has nothing to do with and doesn't merge with the joyful discovery of today's milky morning.

So no matter how I have qualified my anniversary, I celebrated it in my own way by writing these pages. I finished writing and ran out for the milk which I had long since promised to get. Running with the bottle out of our garden to the street, I suddenly discovered that perhaps more than anything else in myself I'm afraid of acquiring reflexes. While earlier in life, trying to imitate a grown man, I rejoiced at the habits, mannerisms and abilities I acquired, now I'm almost afraid of them because on attaining a different, adult, state, I found in the reflex a property that is inverse to the one I liked in childhood—the tendency toward old age of the spirit and death. That's what I noticed about myself as I was running out... When it rains, the gate in our fence swells up and becomes so wedged it its opening that it can only be moved by a good shove. On either side of the fence by this gate there are trees, and after the rain a large drop of water accumulates on each leaf. When, in trying to fling open the gate, I kick it forcefully, I shake the fence and with it the trees, and then a cold shower pours down on me made up of the drop on one leaf multiplied by the number of leaves. There is a certain aesthetic in this, but in general it's unpleasant, all the more so as a lot goes down the back of my neck. I always forget that having kicked the gate, I'll end up in an unexpected shower, and I had again forgotten about this today when I executed a whole series of sudden movements and hops with the aim of both opening the gate and not getting caught in the shower. I managed this successfully—the rain rustled past me—but, having skipped out of the way, I caught myself realizing that, independent of my conscious efforts, a brand new reflex had appeared, and I wondered what this might mean... I immediately associated this occurrence with the story by P. about the old man with the tea pot and also with the way I discovered that I sleep with my shirt next to me so I don't have to go after it in the morning, when the room has cooled almost to street temperature overnight. I also recalled that the image of the lulling of the consciousness, of the substitution of reflex for consciousness, the life of the intellectual without intellect is, for me, so very characteristic of our times—all this has been a theme of mine for a long time, as is evident in "Penelope" and in "The Garden" and in "Life in Windy Weather."

I took another look then at this autumn weather, so dear to my heart, as it surrounded me on my way to get the milk: the close, white sky, the tampled, limp pathway, the little yellow leaves flying down to my feet and marking my tracks, my path. And I felt sorry for myself.

October 11th

I'm in Toksovo again. For the third day. I'm softening up. Back to my notes. In that unusual satiety that possesses me here, I write my most emotional pages—the murk settles into sediment. There's no novelty to life here and it's a blessing. Actually, it's that everything is familiar, isn't happening for the first or even the second time, and therefore all the news is your own, within you, in its pure state. In front of me is the view described in the "Notes." I'm going for milk now and don't want to write a single thing. The relatives all showed up yesterday and it was just as described in "Life in Windy Weather." One neighbor had built a house, while another's had burned down. The Fyodorovs have had a fifth child but Glafira Borisovna died—and nothing has changed. All of it has been inspected, gone over, described—and is already invisible to me. Love is ending, remorse and gratitude for everything that surrounded me here is beginning.

I wanted to write of my war-time childhood in a spirit of calmness, omniscience and the quiet joy of recollections. But one sentence keeps me from writing, a sentence which appears in my window the moment I raise my eyes from the typewriter. Here in Toksovo, I have a more animated window than in Leningrad ....
....
....
....
....

....
....
....
....
....
....
....
....
....
....
....
....
....

there are trees in it and birds on the tress, one has a red breast, one has a green one, and a third is a magpie. And now, when it is already deep autumn and there are no leaves, through the intertwined, naked branches you can see farther, to our Lonely Street and the cottage opposite and the cross street there, Cheerful Street. There are few people or children now because the dacha season is long since over, but all the same sometimes a person will cross my view—one of the old local inhabitants. And the sentence in my window which has been keeping me from writing all day about my war-time childhood consisted in this: on one of the apple tress a single very red leaf remained, projecting itself onto the yellow, sandy pathway, and, in the tangle of black twigs which practically obscured this leaf, you can't tell at first that that little bit of red is a leaf—it trembles in the wind and I think that someone is coming along the yellow path to my house in a red kerchief and that in a moment, when she comes just a bit closer, I'll know who could be coming to see me. But it's the leaf. I realize this so quickly and instantly that it is only by an unnatural, reflexive action (as though by dipping my whole dirty paw into my consciousness) that I can extract it, just a bit disheveled, and admire it, by then without any satisfaction. And suddenly there really are two people going along the yellow road in red kerchiefs. The image is right, only they're not coming to see me. I went out with Anya to dig in the sand. I stand there and look around: beyond the fence are the branches, not yet green, through this cross-hatching I see the crooked antenna on our roof and behind the antenna is the sun, obscured as though seen through cheesecloth, which makes it indistinct, broad, and completely golden. It's all very beautiful and it means absolutely nothing. It could be a frame out of one of our talented films by a young director. Pretty, subtle, and pointless. Very contemporary, of course. Suddenly, from in back of me music started coming out of an open window and I felt like crying. There I stand with my mouth open, and the music is playing, and I'm looking at the antenna with the sun, and this doesn't add an ounce of meaning to it. A man on a bicycle rode by and also failed to add meaning. It's all beautiful, amazing, and pointless—there is no hidden significance or idea in any of this—it simply turned out this way. I had thought that the young director contrived his tableaux, manipulated them, and that they didn't really exist, only his desire to be artful existed. But you can find everything in our life, no matter what lies you make up. So I had thought and thought about what to do with man—where to place him and how to integrate him. First one thing seemed right, then the opposite. And suddenly I understood that no matter what you say about man—it will all be true. Because everything that exists is man. So you come out of the cinema where everything was untrue, just attempts, talented or not, you come out: here's the courtyard, the stack of logs, people in a crowd, the movie-goers of all sorts who have all seen the same film and cried; you go through the gateway, come out on the street, and everything's just as it was in the movies. In the theater, wincing, you thought: they've done this out of lack of talent, but then you come out and it turns out that life is like that, only in the theater you were scared to acknowledge it as your own, it's so poor. And it could be that the film is really terrific.

Yesterday my Papa came for the day. My theme. He couldn't hold out a single day without his granddaughter. Looking at him you begin to understand his trapped expression: his life consisted only in this. Really, he'll go on living and he won't die as long as his granddaughter is around. And his insane love for her clearly demonstrates how little life is left in him, if it is necessary for this love, as an essential purpose, to take on such hyperbolic forms. My father can imagine danger where it is impossible to imagine any. The fertility of his imagination is extraordinary in this respect. He came so he could build a little fence along our brook, so his granddaughter wouldn't fall in. He went around, not paying any attention to the mocking looks of the relatives who had come out on the scheduled Sunday to do a little work on the vegetable garden (he usually pays a lot, even too much, attention to what others think, but in this case his fears were stronger). He went around and trimmed the branches so they wouldn't poke his granddaugher in the eye. The abstractionism of this feeling amazed me. This is the materialist's theme—that the world is hostile towards him. You can poke out an eye, fall into a brook, pinch your fingers in a door—but to live constantly imagining these things and struggling with these as yet unrealized events seems to me to be so disconnected from life that it is precisely the materialists who are not realists in our life. And jousting with windmills is in this sense a symbol of the fate of the materialist. So Don Quixote is the founding father (like every founder, the most sincere and pure of his successors) of a new world view.

I'm going out for milk again. It's getting dark. The naked branches in the twilight seem as though something has happened to them but they don't know what it is. The road begins to fade and merge into the distance while somewhere on the mountain there is a bonfire and the smell of burnt leaves in the chilled air... I walk along, sucking milk out of the tea kettle as I go. We've decided to have milk for supper. For health reasons. These amusing attempts at health and order go on one's whole life. It used to bother me that they were never followed through or kept up. But now it's clear that it must be that way—regulations. These fluctuations between debauch and restriction produce the mean line of my life, close to the norm; the area of my life is like that of a trapezoid—half the sum of the bases times the height. It's all very simple: you economize on breakfast, don't take taxis, only subways, substitute sunflower oil for butter, while in the evening you drink a bottle of vodka which swallows up the saved kopeks in the seal of its own kopeks. We've decided to have milk for dinner instead of butter. I drank milk on the sly from the tea kettle spout on the way home. I got home to pour it into my proper glass, but there's snot in the glass, and I continue to drink out of the snout of the kettle.

October 27th (Prayer)

I have written of the cruel, fatal moment when the delusions and utilitarian ideas suddenly begin to peel off like a rind, when the world reveals itself to you in its unending and implacable equilibrium, when everything seems senseless and unnecessary to you, the relativity and transience of an idea freezes the heart, your hands fall like leaves, you stand naked in the autumn wind trying to hold on to the last of your withered leaves and you die in this moment of wisdom: the last leaf will blow away and you will no longer exist. For many years you support yourself with the hope of the coming spring until one day you can't hide from the thought that after spring, autumn will inevitably come and then despair, when it won't be the hope in the future spring, which you already know is no different from the others and won't settle in for eternity, but only the hope that will weakly comfort you. That is, you'll still be hoping that your wisdom will pass, that your stupidity, life, will be resurrected, and that, disregarding all your experience, you'll again believe in that very same spring. And you'll understand that this too is self-deception, and even embracing the deception, wanting to believe in it, you won't be able to convince yorself that you are again capable of believing it. So, okay, when even the relativity of relativity will have become clear to you, what will be left? Will it be wisdom, death, nonexistence? What meadows will open up just beyond this next and, apparently, final little bluff on your path? What will happen when you can no longer run back to retrace that part of the path again so as once again not to get all the way to the summit, fearing that there is the abyss, nonexistence, and the moment you step onto the peak the abyss will open on all sides? What comes after the final understanding of the system of things? And it's still frightening to take that last step, you still want to guess, you keep thinking it can't be that there is no way you can know ahead of time, before taking that last step, what lies beyond this bluff that blocks your view, so that once having found out, you could perhaps not take the step... It's terrifying and no one will tell you: will you fall or will you fly? And really, who could give you a clue? No one. They either have fallen or are flying, and there can be no exchange between you. You must decide; you must pick up your foot and put it on the peak. What meadows, what expanse, what mysterious landscapes will open before you, if they open at all?

Someone once said that everything of greatness is engendered by meditation on death. What is meditation, if not a drawing-near to the thing on which you meditate? This will all happen to you today, tomorrow, this second. You are in this and God is in this. You find God when you lose him. For a certain time I could not think of him: He was in me. I didn't even suspect it. Life killed him, social life killed him. No, it isn't that barbarous people fell upon an innocent soul and trampled it, they neither wanted to do that, nor did it happen. It was just that a great many of them happened along the path so that I developed a view of myself in place of a view into myself, and a comparison to them rather than a connection to them. Competition, a desire for a formal equality, a dissociation. And your god was lost, the one you hadn't noticed. And such a desert and death arose that only weakness was left, weakness that made social life into bookkeeping, love into lust, friendship into the desire for self-confirmation, and creativity into vanities. I couldn't even shoot myself except with my finger-gun.

For the last time I told myself today, and even this I said in a new sense, let whoever judges me choke on it. After that for the first time I prayed. It was in the metro, the new temple. I said: Lord, help me. I used to say this before, but then it was something like "goddamn it." This time I really meant it. And suddenly I felt better. In earlier times we would have said "god heard me." I heard myself and there was no more I. I suddenly felt I could hear my neighbor.

When the escalator was taking me down, I felt such death! It was physical, from my belly button to my heart everything was filled with it, my cells, my veins. The train came in, the doors opened, and I was surprised in a numb way that I was still able to take a step into the car. I thought, it's just some kind of constriction, it'll pass, but it didn't go away. There was no approximation in this feeling, this was not merely resemblance but rather an embodiment and a permanence. And the feeling was such that if death did pass, it would pass not in the way a disease passes and not in the way that feelings are forgotten, but only by a miracle, only if that of which I had not even an inkling were to help me. And I said: Help me, Lord.

Now it is possible to live. It turns out that it is possible to live in such a way that your love is love and creativity—creativity. And nothing will change in your life except the meaning of each step and action. So it will resemble the most ordinary life, with the most ordinary weakness and the ordinary sins. It's as though I could now do the same things that formerly were weakness and degradation but will be neither the one nor the other and will come from love. No longer can there be insults or calculation and judgment or the base shame for oneself and one's loved one just because people are watching. The dimensions are different.

And that path by which relization becomes tranquility and a mere symbol of the new, while really it is an internal permission to yourself for all those shameful things, a painless closing of the eyes, as though, having called a spade a spade, it ceased to be a spade, such a path also can also no longer exist—that's not salvation, it's a sort of salvationism. Salvation is a shore, salvation is a swim in the same old swamp. There are enough people, a handful, but enough, who understand everything and maintain their own former total incomprehension. God is not in them though they speak constantly of Him. What's more, they think the torturous chain of actions leads them to Him, but the last inch will always remain, and there they'll stop so as not to give themselves up in the end. This knowledge, this near-knowledge, is all the more heretical because it raises them in their own eyes, because they still keep comparing and measuring every one of their steps and how many centimeters behind they've left their neighbor with a ruler, and they just can't part with this pleasure. But if you plunge the final inch, knowledge will then truly raise you up, and not someone else, it will become reality and not a mirage of measuring up to your neighbors, not a self-aggrandizement, but an objective measure.

1963

The Lover

A Novel with Ellipses

"But I have this against you, that you have abandoned the love you had at first."

Revelations 2:4

The Door

The boy had gotten frozen through standing under the archway. A half hour had already gone by. Of course, since she was this late she wouldn't stop here. She would go right to the entranceway. Maybe she'd already gone in and up to the third floor, they had opened the door for her and she had entered the apartment... Maybe she was late and decided that he wouldn't wait so long for her in such cold and she was there already? And what about him...? But maybe she thought that he would stop by there. And is waiting for him there right now, on the third floor... But how can he stop by there if he had only been there once before and then all those peasants had made fun of him... and if, perhaps she hadn't gotten there yet at all.

The boy came out from under the archway and went up to the entranceway, looking around to see if she might not be coming to meet him, from behind him, or along the other side of the street. He went into the entranceway. Now I won't miss her.

It was warmer here. The main thing was that the wind wasn't blowing. He wiped his nose and cheeks and forehead. His face was burning. Suddenly it occurred to him that his face was now very red and that she would come in at this moment. The boy was ashamed of his red face and of his age. And he reddened even more at the thought that he was red-faced and just a little boy.

But she didn't come. At first it seemed to him that the door would open this very second. He watched the door, trembling. But either it had only seemed so, or else someone else had entered. Not her.

Then he thought that maybe she had gone past the entrance anyway and was waiting under the archway while he was getting warm here. He ran out to the archway—no one was there. Then he thought that at that moment she might be going into the entranceway. And they had just missed each other...He hurried back. There was no one in the entranceway. The boy stood in the hall behind the glass door and watched the street on the chance that she might pass by on her way to the arch. But at one moment, when he turned around to see who was coming down the stairs, it seemed to him that she might have passed the door and he just hadn't noticed. A fat old man was coming down the stairs. And something flickered by beyond the glass door— of course, it was her! The boy ran to the archway again. No one was there. And he came back.

I shouldn't be such a baby, thought the boy. You have to think everything over, not rush around and go crazy. Forty minutes had gone by and of course she would no longer come to the archway. Then it's one of two things: either she has already arrived and is sitting there in the room on the third floor while I rush around here below, or she hasn't arrived yet and then I have to wait for her here on the stairs. And not necessarily at the door, because she won't go to the archway anyhow now that she's this late. I can go up to the third floor and get warm at the radiator. All right.

The boy decisively mounted the stairs to the third floor. Warmed his hands over the radiator. Looked at himself in the window glass. Took off his cap, combed his hair, and put it back on. Adjusted his scarf. His face was no longer burning. He sat down on the radiator, unhurriedly took out a cigarette and lit it. His head began to whirl; everything swam a bit. The boy had begun to smoke quite recently. It was pleasant—like being seasick. He looked around at the smoke which he let out first from his mouth, then from his nose, then he tried to make a smoke ring...

Downstairs the entry door slammed. The boy trembled. Again he adjusted his scarf. Quite inopportunely his face began to burn again. And his heart started thumping. He knew already from the steps that it wasn't her. It was an old woman. She went by sideways somehow, looking him over from head to foot. She went upstairs like that, not taking her gaze off the boy, turning around her own axis in proportion to her ascent. She reached her door walking completely backwards. The door was next to the one the boy was watching. Looking around, the old woman barely opened her door, squeezed through this narrow slit with difficulty, hurriedly slammed it behind her, and then began to rattle keys and chains.

The boy looked at his watch; it was twenty minutes to ten. He had already been waiting an hour and twenty minutes. It was already late. He should have seen her and gone home already. Because Mama doesn't know where he has disappeared to for so long, just going to borrow a pair of compasses from a friend across the street. True, she had looked askance at his new shirt and shoes and said that he would drive her into her grave. However, she had long ago telephoned the friend and now they were talking, the two mothers. The boy went downstairs, called home and then his friend; just as he thought, the line was busy both places. The boy was glad the conversation hadn't taken place. After all, he would return soon and it really wasn't worth talking about it on the telephone...

But two hours had gone by. And the boy thought: she must be there already and they had somehow missed each other. He simply had to find out whether she was there or not. Maybe he was waiting for nothing?

He went up the stairs, slowing his steps more and more. But here was the door. He adjusted his cap and scarf again. He stretched out his finger to the bell. He hesitated: he remembered that handsome young man who had patted him on the cheek and laughed a careless chuckle. And she had laughed then too. At the same time the boy thought that he had to ring after all. Everything had to be explained. And when he did press the button after all, he felt bolder and more certain.

Behind the door, he heard another door open, out of which burst a confused noise; now steps approached and the lock clicked...

And now in front of him was that same girlfriend.

The noise was already distinct. The noise was of a very specific character, so that the boy heard not only the voices and the music, but even the tobacco smoke and the bottles on the table.

"Oh, it's you, kid," said the girlfriend, raising her eyebrows.

"It's me," said the boy.

"But she hasn't come yet," said the girlfriend.

He looked at the girlfriend steadily, trying to catch her glance, to understand whether or not she was lying. Because hadn't he heard her voice clearly among the others? And wasn't he hearing it now?

This girlfriend looked like a big, beautiful fish. And when the boy had clearly distinguished one voice among the many there in the noise, he disliked the girlfriend still more and she looked still more like a fish, only no longer a beautiful one. It was very hard to look this fish in its big, grey, slanting eyes—wherever you looked you always ended up between them, somewhere on the bridge of the nose. This fish was continually stroking its cloth-covered thighs, as though wiping off its continually damp hands.

The fish opens its mouth and the fish closes its mouth.

Then when the door was closed and it was as if the fish had disappeared into the wall, he understood the movement of its lips:

"She probably won't even come today."

"But I heard her voice," thought the boy, "there among the others! That means she doesn't want to see me. She is there with them, maybe even with him..." With the one who had taken the boy by the chin. And he was here, on the staircase... And she knows it. And she herself had told her girlfriend to "chase away that boy..."

"Snake," said the boy. "Snake," he said out loud. "Snake," he said, going down the stairs.

But what if she really weren't there, he argued. If it just seemed to me, a stupid jealous boy, that it was her voice... She couldn't lie like that.

"Stupid, jealous boy!" said the boy. "Stupid, jealous boy."

This calmed him somehow. And maybe the girlfriend had tricked both him and her? Maybe she didn't say that the boy had come.

"Bitch, bitch, bitch!" he said.

The boy stood downstairs and couldn't focus; he couldn't decide which of the three was guilty. But it had to be one of them. So everything would be clear.

He had to call her on the telephone. The boy was afraid to call her often. She said she had problems because of the telephone so that the boy wouldn't just call casually. The boy wasn't just calling casually: something had to be cleared up. Maybe she's at home and isn't coming here... Then all his doubts were useless and he must hurry home.

He put in a coin and dialed the number. His heart pounded. A rude voice. She isn't home. Yes, long ago. No, we don't know when.

In any case, thought the boy, he still had to wait. Maybe she's on her way and will arrive right away.

The boy went back upstairs to his radiator and lit a cigarette again.

He felt very calm and mature. He pressed his lips together, made a stern face, looked at himself in the window glass, thought various things about himself in the third person, and watched how he exhaled the smoke and shook off the ash.

But for some reason she didn't come.

The boy began to worry. He still had to buy butter, Mama told him to. Yes, and Mama...She's waiting. A disgrace. The stores would close soon.

How stupid...He should have bought the butter on the way over. Even if he'd been late to the archway, she wouldn't have been there anyway. That's stupid, how could I have known?...And now I'm going to miss her.

And she doesn't come.

But maybe he hadn't been wrong when he heard her voice and she was really there now and was really deceiving him...

Oh, it can't be! the boy said to himself. If I've already been waiting for two hours, then to rush into the store across the way for a minute, buy the butter and come back—it's a drop in the ocean. He wouldn't miss anything. According to the theory of probability. And one musn't think that she would come in that very second when the boy was absent. That would be delirium. One had to be a man. After all.

Making up his mind, he went out into the street decisively and ran to the store. He slipped past a woman getting ready to shut the door.

Everything was okay with the butter. He ran across the street, tore into the entranceway and rushed up the stairs...Maybe she had come in anyway just in that minute, maybe he would overtake her now. He ran up to the landing...No one.

He sat down on his radiator.

Of course, thought the boy, such a coincidence, that she should arrive just when I was away after the butter—such a coincidence couldn't happen. Especially since I returned amazingly fast.

It meant that she was already here and had deceived him. To approach her girlfriend now would be senseless. But maybe she'd gone out on some errand and hadn't been able to let the boy know. Maybe she hadn't even left home and they had simply lied to him that she wasn't there.

He had to go home. There was doubtless a great fuss at home. Yes, if she's gone out on some errand or if they'd lied to him, then he had to run home immediately.

Well, but if he weren't wrong—and it was her voice...There, in the room where there were bottles and smoke! Then how was he to convince himself and find out the truth? He had to wait until she came out. If she were there, she wouldn't disappear... If she came out, everything would be clear.

Downstairs someone clicked some latches. But no door slammed. No one came out. They weren't waiting for anyone else there... It was strange, suddenly all along the staircase people began banging latches and bolts, locking up for the night. Almost simultaneously the bits of metal began clattering on all the floors and this clatter was clearly audible along the whole stairway.

The boy remembers that Mama is also locking up for the night with the bolt and then he won't even make it home with the key. Also, he thinks, no one is getting ready to rob them... He flinches at each new click. He flinches before he understands that it isn't the door he's watching, but another.

Someone approached *his* door. The boy heard steps.

Now... the door will open—and she will come out...

The same way, only louder, latches clattered.

That means that they will all stay there for the night. Could it be that she too...

The boy wanted to throw himself at the door, break in—and see.

The steps went away from the door which was now locked for the night.

... He tears it open—she is there—he glances at her and says a few sharp proud words full of cruel truth. She sobs, she begs forgiveness. She crawls on her knees, embraces his legs. But he stands, pale, handsome, and nothing can move him to pity any more. He no longer believes in anything. And he leaves. And she sobs, weeps...

She weeps... The boy had seen her weep once. Then she had also been late and arrived in tears. She said that her brother had insulted her and that he, the boy, was the only one she had. The boy remembered and he began to pity her. His nose began to tickle.

He suppressed the pity and hesitated over what he had just imagined. He smiled ironically: childishness, stupidity... Because if you did break in... and she wasn't there... What would he say then to those astonished people? Where could he hide? The boy blushed, so vividly had he imagined the shame of such a moment...

Yes, and how could you break in?

Yes... but he had to decide somehow. He had to do something... It was already awkward to phone, it was late. But how could he find out? He went downstairs again, to the telephone. All right, he would call right now. If she answered—everything was okay, if not... well, he would hang up. The same rude voice answered. The boy hung up. And his heart pounded in some sort of emptiness as though tearing itself loose.

It was warm on the radiator. The fuss at home couldn't get any greater now. Maybe even less. He pitied Mama... The last thought flickered in his head like a small, grey, and frightened animal and disappeared at once. The boy was warm. Sweet shivers ran over his body. Everything was buzzing a little. He had no desire to move. You close your eyes—a bright green point starts leaping in the darkness—the trace of the staircase light...

Here he is lying sick and dying. Pale, thin. She finds him finally. She comes to him. She weeps: "Don't cry, I always loved you. You aren't to blame for anything." She cries and pleads: everything will be different. "No, there will be nothing any more for me..."

...The years go by. He comes to see her. His manly face bears the traces of adventures and difficulties he has endured. Thick curls falling on his forehead can't hide a deep scar. Grey curls. So young and already grey... "It's too late, it's all too late," he says. And leaves. She sobs. And he goes through hall after hall, opening door after door...

When the boy woke up he felt a chill. It was cold. Not cold, but chilly. The boy threw his arms out to the sides a few times and jumped a bit to speed up his circulation.

How stupidly everything had turned out, he thought. He should have told Mama beforehand. Or even better, he shouldn't have gone out in the evening at all and instead come here now: she wouldn't have been here anyway and he had been hanging around here all this time for nothing. He should have come now and begun to wait for her. And he would have said to Mama... he would have said something or other to Mama... Stupid. He had to go home right away. But now?... It was morning now, two or three o'clock. And he had to find out.

The boy sat on the radiator, drawing his head in between his shoulders, and breathed under his sweater.

And he no longer thought about anything.

Three o'clock.

Four.

The boy waited dully. Dozing off sometimes, waking up shivering. He already knew everything about this stairway: about the crack in the wall shaped like a bull and the other shaped like Maria Stepanovna, that Minka was a beetle and that Valya was a fool, and about the door, his door, what kind of buzzers were on it and how the thick felt stuck out at the right corner...

Steps. Voices. Two voices. The bolt clicked. It was his door.

The door opened.

It was she!

The boy leaped off the radiator. She glanced and recoiled. The door slammed. It was somehow all too fast: it flashed by and disappeared. The boy was at a loss. His heart pounded from the surprise and because he had jumped up so hurriedly after sitting immobile for so long. There were voices behind the door. The boy strained to make it out. And he heard voices there, a man's and a woman's, her voice. The boy was already certain that this noise, these two noises, were their voices. How clearly they were audible... How loud! The words spread, grew, and slid down over the boy...

The lock clattered again and the door opened.

A young man, the same, came out, turning back and saying something to someone. To her! The boy stood at the radiator and watched. The young man swung around and left. The door shut after him. The boy thought he saw her figure flicker there again. The bolt clicked. The young man came down the stairs. He came closer to the boy, closer. They were level. He glanced at the boy. What was in that glance! The boy grew cold; what wasn't there in it... The young man passed him; he went down and down. The boy looked after him. When the young man stopped on the last step he glanced up at the boy. There was curiosity in his glance.

The young man's steps died away in the silence.

The boy sat down again on the radiator. He bit his lip. Now he will wait. Now he knows she is there. He will wait and tell her everything.

"I'll kill her! Kill her!" the boy repeated.

The first door slammed at five-thirty. Someone rushed past on the stairway, fastening his buttons as he went. Then doors slammed more and more frequently. Above and below where the boy was standing. The doors slammed several times each.

At first the factory workers rushed out. They went past the boy in a business-like fashion, expressionlessly. And he was grateful to them.

Then the office workers. They flowed by, the women with purses, the men with briefcases. These stared, a few turned around. The boy recognized a few: the night before they had come upstairs and looked at him with curiosity. Now their glances exuded curiosity, burned with a question...

I'll kill her!

The boy shrank. He made his expression calm and indifferent with agonizing effort. But he stood manfully, biting his lips.

The doors slammed on time according to fixed laws. Like waves on the boundaries of the hour and half hour. The waves swelled and then dwindled to nothing with the last hurrying people, eating as they ran. Then there was a breathing space. The boy went limp and immediately felt exhausted.

His door slammed twice. But it was only the tenants, not her. The boy was afraid that they would recognize him. The first time he turned to the window and tried to whistle nonchalantly. The second time he pretended to be going down the stairs, as though from another apartment.

At ten of nine, the last wave subsided.

At nine-thirty, the housewives began to come down with bags, bottles and cans. But the boy was already tired of cringing at every passerby. He actually became indifferent to them.

When is she finally going to come out? he repeated dully to himself. He was no longer waiting in such sharp torment. He only wanted it to be over soon. But he was no longer able to go away.

The wave of housewives also subsided.

It occurred to him that if he had to wait another two hours, they would begin to come back upstairs.

And completely unexpectedly there was a noise at his door.

She came out.

Calm, beautiful... How beautiful!

She began to descend the stairs. She saw the boy. She recognized him. She smiled. How well she smiled! But no, you won't deceive him now...

"Oh, it's you, my young man!" she said. "So you were waiting for me the whole time, dear?"

"Yes," said the boy. His voice trembled and he gulped. "Yes. You were there all night. I waited for you under the archway—you didn't come. Then when I called here, you told them to say that you weren't here. You knew I was here... And in the morning at four o'clock you opened the door, saw me, and hid. And that man came out. I know everything!" the boy blurted out.

"Darling," she said softly and caressingly, "it wasn't that way at all. Not the way you said. I couldn't get to the archway on time—it just turned out that way and I couldn't do anything. I didn't know how to let you know. I came here much later. When you asked for me I hadn't arrived yet—I wasn't there. And then when I came up the stairway, you weren't here. I thought you hadn't waited."

"I was on the stairway the whole time!"

"No dear, not the whole time. No, darling."

"Don't call me that. You were there all night. With that man..."

"Stupid... I should get angry at you. Silly, it was simply late and I stayed the night at my girlfriend's, you understand? And that young man is her brother. We went to school together. He left this morning. He's going far away."

"No," said the boy.

"Dear, sweetheart, darling... Everything was as I said. Why are we standing here? Let's go. So you sat there all night? What must be going on at your house!..."

"Nonsense," said the boy.

She laughed.

They went out.

"Go on," she said. "Go on home, my young man. Tomorrow."

The boy went home. It wasn't very far. It was a warm, grey, foggy day. Everything was somehow wrong because of the fog. The houses, the cars and the people. Everything appeared suddenly and disappeared suddenly. Light, weightless. As if he were dreaming.

And his own body was also light, weightless. His thoughts too.

There was a pleasant buzzing inside him. Somewhere inside him nestled his dream.

So, thought the boy as he strode, so that was it. It was as she said. And I am a pig. I am to blame for everything. At home. And with her. A pig. Everything happened exactly like that.

1960

The Garden

The Twenty-Ninth of December

He didn't know when she would call. But she was going to call. She promised. She had to call. And Alexei kept on wandering around the apartment, pretending to leaf through the newspapers in the hall or to be going down the hall for a knife in the kitchen. When the telephone rang, Alexei leapt to pick it up but it wasn't Asya. His uncle, his aunt, his grandmother, and God knows who else were called to the phone, everyone except him. His mother too went up and down the hall and didn't say a word: she was hiding something. Nothing is worse than when she scrunches up her face like that. When she looks past him, as if he, her son Alexei, didn't exist. Alexei had grown tired of guessing and of paying attention to it: lately his mother had been making exactly that face at him all the time. And of course it makes her suspicious that he's hanging around here by the phone. So, when Mama appears in the hallway, Alexei comes up, picks up the receiver, and dials the time. The next time he dials some number at random but doesn't dial the last digit. "Is Vitya there?" he says. Vitya Koshenitsyn is a good one; Mama would like him to have a friend like that: the son of a colleague—everything's out in the open—who's doing well at school. Alexei waits long enough for someone to be called to the telephone. Then he starts talking about some solenoid, for laughs confusing it with a sinusoid, and does it so well that it even makes him feel better. Sometimes he's silent, as if listening to the person at the other end, or says uh-huh vaguely between the pauses or throws in some interjections. In the meantime he thinks up something and says: "Of course, the potential force of the constant of the block at the intersection of the magnetic curve of the system equals the hydraulic energy of the feeding of the electrode, alpha-omega-psi. That's just what I didn't understand," and hangs up. Mama would like that kind of conversation. But none of this really happened. It was only an idea, a daydream...

And then, of course, it happened. Suddenly he forgot about everything—what stupid thoughts had been going through his head?—and by the time he got to the telephone in a panic, his mother was already holding the receiver: "Alexei, it's for you." From the pursed lips, from her especially calm voice and look, it would be quite clear to anyone that this time it was Asya calling: Mama had recognized her voice. There's nothing to be done now—just don't blush, and come to the phone as calmly and indifferently as possible. Actually, there's no point in even putting on a good face: it's quite clear he hasn't been hanging around the phone for nothing. Everyone knows and understands everything—a bad game with a good face... Alexei takes the receiver. "Yes. Hello." He could also have said: "Asya." He'd missed the call anyhow and had been found out. But if he himself had answered or anyone else except Mama, he could have talked in the second person of the present tense and then nobody would be able to tell who he was talking to. But actually even that wouldn't help much: there'd be too much mumbling for Mama not to guess. Mama's very smart about these things. It's hard to see how she does it.

"Was that Mama who answered? What a beautiful voice!"

"And how did you know it was me?"

"From... the face."

"Mama's?"

"Yes."

She's laughing, for God's sake!

"But I wasn't the one who talked to her!"

Something immediately contracted in Alexei.

"Who did?" he says and is surprised himself how his voice drops.

"My husband."

"What does that guy want from you..." his words quiver, drag out and explode: as though one was like a stone, another like something liquid.

"Oh, Alyosha, don't be silly!" she says affectionately. "You know yourself..."

"Did you meet him by accident?" Alexei says spitefully and no longer remembers that he's not supposed to talk in the past tense: he betrays himself with the feminine endings "la," "ala," "yala," "ila". He doesn't realize that it's all the more senseless to betray himself since it was a man's voice that asked for him and now it turns out he's talking to a woman's voice. It's too obvious a lie. They don't like that kind of thing in the house.

"Now, Alyosha, why that tone!" Asya says, and her voice shows that she's not mad yet but may get mad, and what a little boy he, Alyosha, still is. "You know, I told you I was supposed to meet him..."

Well, let's say she never said that to him, but all of a sudden Alexei calms down anyway. And then it becomes obvious that jealousy isn't the point, as long as he's listening to HER, that perhaps he said the two sentences: "What does that guy want from you" and "Did you meet him by accident?" just because he got excited by her voice and not for any other reason. But you can't explain that on the phone. Anyway, what's the use of explaining. Anyway, that's not really it. Anyway, Alexei himself doesn't quite understand it all. And it turns out Mama pulled a long face not because she recognized Asya, but just the way she always does...

And now it's quite clear what the conversation is going to be about—

about seeing each other. Now, if he talks a little more and doesn't ask, she will ask. And if he can't hold out and he asks, she may well say that she can't today, that she's busy. And who knows what sort of busy she is there. And he says:

"So I'll come over."

"No Alyosha, I'm busy today." He knew it!

"Doing what?" as before, words are now liquid, then solid.

"My God, Alyosha...Doing the laundry. It's New Year's..."

"I won't bother you, I'll just sit there."

"Don't, Alyosha. Besides, everyone will be home today."

"I'll come anyway."

"And your mother..."

Now everything was clear. He'll come, of course. Although he's up to his neck in work. Finals. And Mama will give him dirty looks for going out again...

But the more Asya protests, the more likely it is that he'll come.

Asya lives at her friend Nina's; she rents a corner of a room for 15 rubles. Nina is a beautiful girl but no one likes her. Nina lives with her father, Sergei Vladimirovich, an unusual old man, one of the "old guard." And all three of them live in one room, extraordinarily empty and seemingly uninhabited. To get there, one must go up to the fourth floor, the highest in an old house. One goes up a wide staircase with steps that are comfortable the way they always are in old houses. On every landing there's a study bench set in by a window, for resting. And on the fourth floor to the right, there's a door...

And whenever Alexei pressed the bell, everything became tense inside him. Because here it was—a pause, a rustle, footsteps behind the door—anything could happen. Asya might not appear—And then try and guess where she's gone. Sit and wait on the comfortable bench made just for that. If Asya opens the door, everything's fine. But Nina may open the door or Sergei Vladimirovich, or if they aren't in and you ring again anyway—the neighbors, that's the worst thing. They make such faces when they open the door that he feels guilty, without knowing why, true, but that makes him the more guilty and dependent. And then again, if Asya doesn't open the door: either she's at home or she isn't. They can also open the door in various ways. Especially Sergei Vladimirovich. Opening the door is not so simple; there are a great many nuances here. For instances, what sort of expression will they have; will they be silent or will they say something; and what will they say; will they invite him in or leave him on the staircase...

Sergei Vladimirovich opened the door. He stood in the doorway as though not recognizing him; he was tall, almost pitifully grandiose; wooden, he stood, nothing changing in his immobility, and was silent. As though he were waiting for something. That's why Alexei couldn't say: "Hello, Sergei Vladimirovich," but said somewhat jerkily:

"Is Asya home?"

It seemed that the old man looked motionlessly at Alexei for a long while, but then, turning around briskly, he pushed the door open and went away, just as silent.

Alexei stood stupidly in front of the door.

Just then, as if to spite him, the next-door neighbor came up in back of him—two rings. She stood behind him, breathing down his neck. Alexei shuddered, turned around, and then she said with a friendly smile: "Have you rung yet?"

"Yes," Alexei answered firmly and moved away from the door.

"Ah, it's even open!"—with a bloated bag in one hand and a newspaper and a wallet in the other, she opened the door, went in sideways, bag first, and looked around with friendly curiosity. Then, having gone inside and pushed the door to behind her, just one of her fat eyes still visible, she said:

"Shouldn't I close it?"

"No," Alexei said in a voice breaking with anger.

She would have to show up at that very minute!

Her steps had not yet died away in the hall when the door opened, it was Asya, in a cotton robe. Her hands were wet, her face angry. Besides the old man who must have told her something, besides her laundry, now she bumped into her next-door neighbor—two rings.

"I told you not to come!"

Alexei needs nothing else. The living Asya's standing in the door—her cotton robe, her sharp shoulders under the robe, her wet hands, huge slippers, her voice, her eyes, her hair. And he's not just seeing things, it's real...

Asya looks at him and calms down.

"There's a war on, you see. Sergei Vladimirovich's pants got lost..." Now she's laughing. "Will you wait a half hour?"

My God, a half hour! An hour! Two!

A garden. A nook. A bench between a shed and the garden.

SHE: It can't go on like this any more. It's winter, don't you understand? But I want warmth. To have a place to go to. It's a must. And not always to eat on the money your mother gives you for lunch? And wait for you in the mornings, when I'm finally alone, wondering: will you come or not? You come, of course, you come... And kissing out here. And kissing on the staircase, too. It's cold, you know. You may be warm. But I'm cold...

HE: Don't talk like this... And you're wrong. It's true, of course... But I love you. And you... love me. And we're often alone. All alone. We're pretty lucky. Sometimes I'm surprised how lucky we are. And you know I do... all I can. But I can't do everything. But I know, just don't think... This much I know already: happiness is in each one of us, not in the circumstances. After all, we...

SHE: Darling... you're in love. I forgot. Let me look at you. How can one not love you! I'm evil. You're still a child. Why does it have to be like this?

Maybe I'm bad, probably spoiled... Although who knows? Everything is a shambles, absolute chaos... But I need everything you're ready to do without... After all, you live at home, right? Mother cooks for you? Right? You sleep in your own little bed? And you've got an overcoat? Why so quiet?

HE: I told you. I'll leave home if you insist...

SHE: Don't be silly! Now you're offended. What a child you are! All right, not a child... I don't mean it as an insult. But why does it bother you? Don't listen. Come on, let me kiss you... Here and here. And here too...

HE: Tomorrow I'll leave... I'll leave not because of you... I'll leave...

SHE: But where will you go, darling? And what for, anyway? For my sake? But what good is that to me? In fact, why would you leave? (She laughs) You... You can take me home with you, can't you? (She laughs more clearly and shrilly) Yes, to your place. You have a separate room, after all? It's small, true... (She bursts into abrupt laughter). You'll take me home with you and say: Mama, we've decided... (She laughs, rocking back and forth). I can imagine what a face she'll make! (She laughs, as if sniffling, then calms down). You're quiet? Why are you so quiet? What, you won't take me home with you? You feel weak, don't you? So take me home with you, all right? We'll start a new life. Separately, legally...

HE: Don't. Don't talk like that, please. You know very well...

SHE: What do you mean—you know? What am I supposed to know! That I can't go home with you? And if I want to?! Can't I go? W-why?

HE: Don't talk like that... You know yourself. It would be no life...

"Why—no life? After all, she's smart, reserved, doesn't say an unnecessary word. She's well-bred... Why no life?... (A pause) But sometimes I wish she were awful. That she were fat, sloppy, rude. That she counted each piece of sugar, for instance... How much simpler it would be! And I would be happy... (A pause) She's nice? How is she so nice? I know, I know! But don't you see it's not good to be so nice! It pays! Why, she's... Why couldn't I be like her? You're afraid of her! You are, right? You don't love her, you're afraid of her. (A pause) As if I were taking you away! That's all it is, if you think about it. You're not even part of it. Why are you so quiet? You are quiet, right? I know, your thoughts are just like hers now. You're alike. You don't know you're alike. But I know it."

"I'm not like her."

"Don't hide it. I wasn't talking about your looks. You understood perfectly."

"Yes."

"No, you're amazing. Only you can say "Yes" like that... (She laughs, as though screwing up her eyes). Yes? But nobody, nobody knows what you're actually like. You're still a baby—don't be insulted—you're still a baby. But what will you be like? My God! Everyone will go crazy. I'm the only one now who knows what you'll be like. Ninka asks me: what do you see in him? But I know... Only... I won't be with you."

"Of course you will."

"But you'd better not forget then. Let me see you once in a while. So I can take a look at you. You will let me see you, won't you? I'll already be an o-o-old woman."

"Don't talk like that. What nonsense!"

"Actually, I won't be all that old. A small dog is always a puppy. (She laughs dully). So you won't even have to be too ashamed to see me, don't worry. This kind of thing doesn't end..."

"But why do you talk like that...! It hasn't ended, has it? And it won't end."

"I don't like it when people talk like that. Even your voice is wooden. You don't believe what you're saying yourself. Even now you shake your head but you don't believe it. I don't like that. Why do I say that? I was at my husband's today... I know, you wanted to ask me about it the minute we left the house, but we were talking about something else, and you were embarrassed. But you didn't forget it, did you? Somewhere inside you there's still a question left. Hanging on a string... It's been hanging there all this time. Well, I'm 'that kind'... You believe me, but when there's a question, you don't believe me. Don't think that just because you have a 'noble feeling,' I'll change. I'll still be 'that kind.' If only because there's that question... That's not why, though. So, why don't you ask me why I went to see my husband?"

"It doesn't matter to me. That's not why I..."

"It matters, it matters a lot! It matters to everyone... I went to see him and we went to sleep... Yes, together. Why not, darling? Silly... After all, I'm his wife. And we aren't divorced yet. Why are you sulking? Shall I give you a kiss?"

"Don't."

"Come on... Silly... Don't pull away. I'll give you a kiss anyway. Yes, you are strong, strong... I see it. But we simply fell asleep. There was nothing between us. We fell asleep, and that was all. Believe me, believe me... I even gave you a kiss! So what's the matter? Oh, how funny you are sometimes! You still don't believe me?"

"I believe you."

"No, you don't... My God, how stupid of me! You're still wondering why I went to see him? And I talk as if you knew everything. But you don't know... Well, I went to see him because he stole my sewing machine."

(He's already laughing) "Your sewing machine?"

"Of course. You know, I thought I'd kill him. The sewing machine means everything to me, it's the last thing I have. It was my mother's. I thought I'd kill him... I come in, and he shows me a list. Everything that he still kept was on it; and my machine was there at the very bottom. And across from each thing was an amount. And everything was added up. Well, he shows me the list, blinks and says: 'But I've sold everything.' 'The sewing machine too?' I say. 'That too.' I say, well give me the money at least! And he says: 'But I don't have it...,' he says, 'I reserved four tables for New Year's at the Astoria. To say good-bye... Will you come?' He stands there blinking. And here I thought I'd kill him but all of a sudden I felt so sorry for him. I cried, but he was quiet... You see, he's been through hell too..."

"And you're going?"

"Where?"

"To the Astoria? To that..."

"He begged me so... 'You're so beautiful,' he says. Don't worry, I know his tricks. 'Are you really still seeing that infant?' (She takes his hand) Don't be angry, he meant you. You know, he saw us once. On the Anichkov Bridge, remember? I pointed him out... But I told him he's not worth your little finger. No, really, that's just what I said. And after all, we have nowhere to go? Don't worry, it's you I love, so nothing can happen... But it's New Year's! People, a holiday... And we have nowhere to go?"

"I told you... Everyone's going to Frish's..."

"I won't go to your Frish! I don't want to see them! The slobs. I know them through and through. They don't like this. I don't want them to look at me like that..."

"Then we'll go to a restaurant..."

"To a restaurant? But don't you know when New Year's is? The day-after-to-mor-row! So what restaurant can we go to now? It's even too late to go to some dive..."

"We'll find something. We won't be out on the street. That's impossible..."

"Exactly. Everything is so simple... But where will you get the money? You've already taken some for the holiday... There's no more. It was spent on me, to be sure, and I thank you... but there's no more. And what will I wear? What's the point of talking... I have nothing to wear. Either with you or with him..."

"And your green one?"

"Don't you know? But surely you know... It's at the pawnshop. And on the 31st the term is up. But it's the only dress I could possibly wear anywhere. You know that too... I'd love... but there's still this thing with the dress. And you can do nothing, nothing at all. You don't even remember and don't think about it for comfort's sake—that's how much you can do! I'd lo-ve... but I have to redeem my dress! That's life..."

"Don't talk like that! Just be quiet... I'll get it. You'll redeem it..."

"I'm sorry, darling... again I... I didn't mean to... But that's not the point anyway. You see, I don't want to go to a restaurant with you. That's not the thing to do with you... I want to be at home with you. At home, don't you understand? Darling... so that we could be together, just the two of us. And so that no one could barge in... no stranger. Where's that home?"

"I'll get it! (In despair) I'll get the money!"

"But where? Where will you get it, darling? You're so... There's nowhere you can get it... Don't you understand? 'Nowhere'—that doesn't mean just today. But that's not the point. Don't you see, it will be too little for me... All the same, it will be too little for me—that's the horror of it! For instance, I want so badly to go to the south with you in the summer. With *you*... That's no mere dress. Is that impossible...? But all the same, I'll go to the south."

"We'll go to the south too! (Almost with anger) My God, is this money really so... it's such nonsense! But if it's just the money... Then I'll go to work... Well... I'll get it in the end. I know where. And nothing will happen to me. Ten thousand, old style—I know where. And we'll go away. That's enough for us. It's enough even for a few months... It is enough, right? Is it enough?!!!"

"For a few...? And then what? No, darling, no! Forgive me! Don't pay any attention when I'm like that. Don't listen. You know, there's so much meanness inside me, you can't even imagine... It will go away. Don't listen... And of course, my dearest, we'll be together. What does the south matter to us? You'll finish the institute—I'll wait—so what if I'm five years older—it's nothing, sometimes the wife is even ten years older—and so what... Don't get upset, come now, my beautiful... is it worth it because of me... Why, I'm happy, happy that I have you! You see, I don't know what it was... I'm evil, forgive me... Everything will be fine. And we'll celebrate the New Year, the two of us will celebrate! I said it out of spite, but I've already arranged it: Nina will go off to a party, the old man will go to some friends of his too... and the two of us will be left alone... Just for an hour, for just one short hour I'll run over to the Astoria and then I'll come back... to you. So don't get angry, so, please, after all, I promised. I'll get everything ready at home for us beforehand. And then I'll come back at eleven..."

He was going home, smiling stupidly. He put his foot down confidently, and the snow crunched underneath it confidently. The streetlamps were lit here and there, and the passers-by appeared here and there, all engrossed and hurried. It was lighter on the Fontanka; ahead to the left the Engineering fortress loomed in heavy darkness. The lamps on the bridge were old and looked like signal houses, and Alexei felt as if he were in another age. No, not in another age; but as though he's been walking across this bridge for a thousand years, walking and walking. Ahead to the right the black trees of the Summer Garden showed white and he could just never reach them.

A bus with a single passenger braked, as if sitting down on its haunches, at a bus stop on the empty and half-dark Sadovaya Street. Alexei could have run and caught it, but he didn't run; he didn't try to catch it. He was walking slowly. He was smiling stupidly. Although he might have realized somewhere that it was probably the last bus and that he had a long way to walk to get home. But it was better to walk home and forget everything. It smelled of frost and of tangerine peels—of the New Year.

On the Kirov Bridge he got caught by the wind. And he stopped smiling. He swore at himself, he could have been home a long time ago and he wasn't home. And now there would be no more buses. No streetcars. And at that moment his Mama, the dress, Asya's husband, the finals—everything swirled above him, stirring up his soul—and Asya receded.

Suddenly a strange dog ran by; it was twice as long as an ordinary dog. It ran from street lamp to street lamp—the shadow of its legs—many of them; it ran purposefully from street lamp to street lamp and disappeared. Alexei burst out laughing.

And then he wondered how he could be so distracted and no longer feel so sharply what he was bound and obliged to feel. He was glad to be distracted by a dog. And in general, why did he have such indistinct and lazy feelings even when he thought they were distinct? And he seemed to think unwillingly, too. There was no passion in him...

And then he thought that half a year ago when it had all started with Asya, everything had been different. He'd suffered then and hadn't believed it. He'd had to find out something quickly that had been concealed from him and quickly understand and decide everything. In those days too, he'd waited for hours on staircases and in doorways, and seemed to see Asya walk away with someone else; and it all should have become clear very quickly—and then be over. Just one more proof—and be over. He had never lived so tensely and tremulously as at that time. He hadn't even suspected that it was possible to feel the same thing over and over and then once again, but always stronger and stronger; it had even seemed strange to him. And when indeed, some proof seemed to have appeared and it had become impossible to delude himself anymore, when at last everything had become clear and he'd had to decide, he suddenly stopped seeing, noticing, following. Even more than that, he'd begun *not* to see, *not* to notice, *not* to follow. Because, if before he'd kept telling himself that love needed trust, that is, truth and clarity, and couldn't endure deception, now love became higher than clarity. And ignorance, the renunciation of explanations, now contained trust and either the continuation or the destruction—who knows?—of his love.

So he walked, so he thought or didn't think, because how many times had these thoughts come to him already: there was no keen insight in them. And he never allowed himself to reach the logical conclusion, but began thinking about something else, not about this, as though smearing, rubbing out the sketch of his thought with an eraser, so as neither to understand nor to remember later... That's how it probably had to be, since he wanted to retain love and there was no way to do so. And thinking about the inevitability of any deed, action, or decision to act led only to a feeling of wild helplessness and dependence on everything, absolutely everything: his parents, the institute, living space, money, his own expenses and his childishness... That's what it all led to and to nothing else, and everything that was alive in his soul would die at that moment, yet this aliveness was what was more precious. And just to think about it meant beginning to fit his thoughts not only into the past when he'd wanted to find out and decide everything quickly, but also into the present—and that's where everything would fall apart. Because in all that time nothing had really changed... So he must not think that way; he discarded his thoughts in the middle—a pit, an abyss followed, he had no desire to step into it. The mechanism of those thoughts and the mechanism of evading them were already so habitual that it was no longer possible to say he was thinking that way.

He was freezing already. And then totally unexpectedly—a bus—he'd thought there weren't supposed to be any more—and Alexei jumped on.

The Thirtieth of December

First he grumbled and couldn't wake up. Then he grumbled and didn't want to wake up. Then he grumbled and made believe that he hadn't woken up. Mama was standing over him and gently but firmly with lots of experience and knowing all about it (how Alexei doesn't know how to get up and how he pretends so as not to have to get up, and that he's no longer asleep but merely pretending he is, and where he was yesterday)—Mama was standing over him and methodically, as if forestalling each possible trick or objection... Mama was standing over him and saying:

"Alexei, wake up. Yesterday you asked me to wake you up at six. Alexei, you're awake already. You have an exam today. Alexei, it's better to get up right away and torment neither yourself nor me. Get up as I've taught you: sit up and put your feet on the floor right away."

By now everything is hopeless.

"Right away, Mama... I'm awake already... I won't fall asleep again... I'll get up right away..."

"Alexei! Open your eyes!"

The least he must do is open his eyes... But they won't open. All the same, he opened them. And then he realized acutely how much he wanted to sleep. It was as if his eyelids were full of sand and now that he pulled them apart, the sand began to shift and bristle underneath them.

"There, you see... They're open... I'm not sleeping... I'll get up right away."

"Alexei, it's not my job to stand over you."

It was all over. And now he really was awake. And it was true, he had to rewrite the exam today—it was the deadline. He sat up in bed, cheerful at once, not sleepy, shivering barely noticeably. As a matter of fact, since he wasn't prepared, he at least had to write out some "cribs." An unconscious and horrendous student fear mixed with vanity arose in him, and at the same time the diligence of an honor student, although, to be sure, he had never been an honor student... Everything flashed by him—he had a daydream about how by some miracle he would be prepared and write an A exam, would be allowed to take his orals and get an A on them too—just imagine... He did everything very efficiently, yet at the same time somehow too carefully and minutely: he brushed his teeth, and washed his neck, and warmed his breakfast, and drank his tea. Down there, somewhere at the bottom where we have our motivations and justifications, it sounded like this: excess haste just messes things up; make haste slowly, the important thing is economy of motion and organization, and so on—the same honor student's game.

He came back to his room, sat down at the desk and took out the notes. He got the notes from Koshenitsyn who, of course, had already passed everything before anyone else. He had begged for it and got it for one night, yet had it for the third day already. But today he would certainly have to give it back.

He opened the notes, cursing himself for the lost three days; then he would really have known everything!—the sweet and deceitful feeling of the honor student captured him again, it was such a small vanity. He neatly tore out a clean sheet from a clean notebook—on which he felt like writing in a clean, clear hand, marking off margins with a pencil (it could even be a simple wooden one), numbering the pages and making up the table of contents after coming to the end of the notebook. It was soft and beautiful, and all used up—the delight and satisfaction, the labor and the fruit of the very same honor student. Of course, he had no such notebook, but he had that feeling, and so he cut off unusually neat strips for the cribs, many more than he could possibly write or even need.

A bed creaked behind the wall—Mama sat up, shuffled in her slippers to his door—Mama had come to check on that suspicious silence in her son's room, to see if he was sleeping. Her son managed to hide the strips and concentrate on the notes. The door opened, Mama saw her son's bent head (her son didn't turn around to her—it was a put-on, but neither he nor she noticed it). A sort of satisfaction appeared on Mama's tired face.

And Mama left.

At once everything relaxed inside Alexei. (He wasn't likely to be checked up on again.) His body suddenly began to warm up, it had become stiff down to the tips of his toes. He looked out the window... It was still so hopelessly, wintry dark there: only a street lamp sways back and forth, illuminating the white roof of a factory warehouse, and a watchman stamps his feet by the mushroom-shaped shelter. This picture is already eleven years old—and even now he sees it with the eyes of his distant childhood, which produces the feeling of a not-yet completely forgotten childhood nightmare that he still doesn't understand. Something strange begins to happen to his arms—they're growing, swelling, they are strange, not his own, and something horrible and irreparable, who knows what, will happen to him now. The background and location of the action of the nightmare is a winter morning, the school, getting there early, the cloak-room, the yellow purulent light which makes the walls a dirtyish pale blue, the same as light in the hallways and the classrooms, everyone's noiseless motion, and the teachers, like huge mice in the hallways...

Alexei looks at the alarm clock—he has just one hour left. He won't have enough time—something contracts from that same student fear. Feverishly he picks up a strip of the crib, neatly writes out the title of the theme and underlines it; of the sub-theme too—and underlines it. Now he'll have to copy cribs from the notes. The notebook grows thicker before his eyes. And then nausea, an uncontrolled despair, comes over him; he looks out the window again: the lamp, the mushroom and a clumsy cone-like watchman who resembles a black Jack Frost—the same warmth and stiffness steal up on Alexei—sleep.

Again he caught himself making a detour. He wasn't going the short way: through the central lobby, the picture gallery, the main staircase and the dean's hallway, but through the dining hall and the chemistry building, from the other end. Just so as not to meet any of the teachers or anyone from the dean's office. The thought that he was merely one of many who were in a similar mess before the beginning of the finals was irrelevant. Even so, he simply didn't want to run into anybody.

He observed with only slight surprise that at the beginning of the year he had walked boldly through the main hallways and didn't sneak by the dean's office—at that time everything was still ahead of him and he was going to start studying the next day. However, he didn't subject himself to any particular analysis while making the detour, it was no longer the first time, it had become a habit.

Almost everyone had assembled already in a dark little alley near the lecture-hall. They made quite a din. By the time he shook everyone's hand he too got excited, as if he'd been electrified. Everyone behaved differently. Bychenkov, of course, whined and asked everyone for something or made arrangements; he was, you might say, making provisions for himself with anyone he could. They were avoiding Bychenkov, but he would latch on to them; they would huddle together with him and finally consent. "And in the end he'll pass everything..." Alexei thought with hostility. Someone rustled a synopsis fussily, turned toward the wall—it was the last chance. It was Denisev. "But he won't pass," Alexei thought. Somebody else rustled exactly the same way, Frolenko-Khrolenko as they called him, but: "He'll pass," Alexei thought. Two others were still bolder than the rest; they were standing by the door itself, waiting to get in, they were, you might say, the center-forwards in everything, friendly kids, the nets, but they were successful everywhere—they'll pass. Suddenly Alexei felt something very degrading about being so afraid standing outside the door. He instantly tried to drive away that feeling; he began to bustle about with the others.

That is, he began to secure cribs from each person in turn—a hopeless enterprise. First of all, all of them had been "cleaned out" already. Second of all, all of them already had something for the exam—only he didn't. It made him feel bad: it seemed everyone would pass—only he wouldn't pass. Mishka was the only one left, his best friend, but he probably didn't have anything himself. Just to make sure, he approached him too. It turned out he also had them. Now there was nobody like him... And even now—how many times!—Bychenkov rushed up to him and whined: "I've already wiped out Mishka..." "I thought you wouldn't come," Mishka said. "Are you going to pickle them or what?" Alexei said maliciously to Bychenkov, but the door opened and there stood Instructor Vershinin; everyone rushed in. They crowded into the last three rows like herrings. "Childishness and stupidity," Alexei thought, pushing and shoving everyone and taking up the last edge of the last seat—"it doesn't matter, they'll move us apart anyhow."

"What is this kindergarten" assistant Bolshintsova said.

"She's here too... there are two of them," Alexei thought dejectedly, "and I didn't even notice."

"What is this kindergarten!" she said. "We chose a big lecture-hall on purpose. Just two persons at each desk."

All of them were choking with puppyish terror and weren't moving from their seats. It meant all of them but not each of them.

"This means all of you!" the assistant said. "Come on."

It looked stupid, the assistant was an interesting woman, and Alexei got embarrassed. "It's hopeless," he thought. "Why this weariness and depression...?" And he got up, almost the first one.

"Go up front, don't be shy" the assistant told him.

Vershinin finished sorting out cards and passed them around the room. Alexei sat alone, in front of everybody else, and twisted his card. He turned around: the "center-forwards" were seated in the best places, at the end by the wall; Bychenkov was also seated pretty well. Seriousness was already on everyone's faces—the fever of the exam—the faces looked unhealthy. Everyone fixed his eyes on his slip of paper and practically snatched it from Vershinin's hands. Vershinin was giving them out without haste, as though weighing them and not losing count. And now they were all distributed.

Alexei couldn't recognize the function drawn on his paper at all. He didn't even try to strain himself, it was so unfamiliar. He turned around to those sitting behind him. All, all of them were writing something—so it seemed. The center-forwards were cheating outrageously. The assistant walked down the aisle and met Alexei's eyes—he had to turn around so that she wouldn't ask: "Do you need something?" and anyway, there was no need to stick out. He drew a torus and another one inside it. The assistant sat down next to Vershinin; they began whispering. That's it, the right moment! His heart beats for the entire lecture-hall to hear. Terror-stricken, Alexei quietly takes Koshenitsyn's synopsis out from under his sweater. The synopsis has gotten warm there...And now his notebook is on his knees. Now he must... Alexei looks sideways out of one eye—nothing; Vershinin and Bolshintsova are talking, they're not looking. All he has to do is to find what he needs in the synopsis. But what does he need? Alexei turns the pages under the table—he can't recognize anything. The pages rattle. As if he were walking on a roof—that kind of feeling: a big clatter, and you might fall off, too. Alexei looks sideways at Bolshintsova: doesn't she hear that clatter? Bolshintsova looks sideways at Alexei, as though she had heard it. In fright he feverishly stuffs the synopsis as far into the desk as possible, so that now he can't even reach it. He sighs with relief. To hell with it.

Having rested, Alexei turned around: unimaginable activity was being carried on everywhere. "Is it possible *they* don't see it?" he wondered as usual. "After all, they're experienced people...They don't want to see," he thought. "But then why do they go after others anyway? Me, for instance, they'd catch me with pleasure...Victims," he answered to himself, "victims, as a warning. They can't get everyone. Who would study then?" There were already lots of toruses. "Just take it, draw out the function of the torus and hand it in...Hooligan, they'll say, but what abilities!" Vershinin was talking with the assistant; the assistant was smiling quietly and laughing melodiously. Alexei turned around: the same business-like bent heads, spastic grimaces giving clues, no one's looking at anyone else, the center-forwards are scribbling and Bychenkov is scribbling...Nobody cares about anyone else. Just then he caught a perplexed look from Denisev; he made him some sign, himself not understanding why or what it meant: Denisev makes a mournful face, in effect, I don't know a damn thing myself—everybody makes a face like that, even if he does know, in order to be left alone, in order not to take a risk for nothing...It's disgusting. "Everyone for himself, everyone for himself..." Alexei was drawing toruses. "Everybody's like Bychenkov to some extent..." Now if Bychenkov were sitting closer to him, Alexei would at least be able to amuse himself a little: he could turn toward him, scaring him, and see how he'd start hissing and waving him away and how Bychenkov's face would be half-mournful, half-hateful at that moment. This image diverted him a little. There's someone who'll never help anyone! And then Alexei had a daydream in which he suddenly knows every subject better than any teacher and at the exams turns all his teachers upside down, not all of them, but those he doesn't like; those he respects he simply answers so brilliantly, so brilliantly that they give him an A with five pluses and the eccentrics even give him an A^2... But already the first of his classmates is turning in his work and then a second. "Those bastards!" Alexei thinks. "What honor-student quickness. First or not, what's the difference! You've finished, help your neighbor! Before the exam they probably talked that way themselves, and now they're turning their papers in early. Such intelligence and seriousness on their faces..." Or: since they've finished and weren't caught, why be caught helping? They're afraid:

that's also why they're in a hurry to turn in their exams. The center-forwards, and Bychenkov... Even Denisev and Mishka are scribbling something quickly; it means they've come up with something. If just one of them would ask him: need some help, perhaps? Everybody passes by, turning in his work... True, one of the center-forwards did ask, but in such a whisper, almost purposely loud so he'd be sure to be noticed and sent out (and he'd turned his work in already, so it wouldn't have mattered to him anyway) and in doing so he had made such a scared face as if just waiting for the answer: "No, I don't need anything," that Alexei just waved his hand: no, go ahead... Still, the center-forwards are good guys, better than the others. Even the best guys are sinking fast now... Alexei folded up his sheet with the toruses inside, signed it and turned it in. He put it on the pile and went out.

"So how'd it go, Lyokha? So how'd it go?" the center-forwards fell upon him.

"Oh, don't ask," Alexei said nonchalantly.

"What's the matter, what's the matter?!" they whispered. "There were just four variants altogether, we decided. We've got answers to all of them. We would have passed them to you..."

"Uh-huh" Alexei said vaguely and began to walk away.

"You're leaving for good, huh?" he heard, but he wasn't there anymore. By the same circuitous route he went down to the basement cloakroom. The cloak-room was empty. When he entered it with his head bent down he always got the feeling that he was very tall, but it was only that the passage-way was simply very low. Two hat-check girls were talking with each other, bending out of their stalls. The radio was singing the song "When I'm at the Post Office..." that had been his favorite song when he was a child and he had still not completely stopped loving it. It was warm and cozy here. The electric bulbs burned dimly. Thick, shaggy, warm-looking pipes were stretched along the walls. He gave his number to a hat-check girl. She was young and not bad looking; there was also something curious in her face, almost lewd or something, or maybe it was just how she just looked at him, or maybe it was just the warm, dimly-lit basement. A very sweet feeling connected with school came over him, only now he was in school in a different capacity and knew what it was all about. He followed the girl with his eyes while she, swaying back and forth—everything on her was close fitting—walked in between the coat racks and came back, half looking, half not looking at him, not encouraging him and not really pushing him away. All this affected Alexei strongly. Particularly because her look and summons were not carried through—this affected him still more. He wanted to take her hand or pat her cheek or touch her breast as if accidentally, but he didn't do it and didn't say anything. He put on his coat and went out.

His eyes blinked from the brightness—it's light out already!—he took a deep breath and found himself free.

It wasn't twelve yet but he was home already. No one was there except Pelageya Pavlovna. Since his childhood he had liked it when there was no one home. He would wander around the rooms, poke his nose into closets and desks, make himself some tea and drink it with a macaroon, then read lying down. Then they would come home. It was good that classes ended earlier than work did. Two hours of freedom. On the daily schedule.

Pelageya Pavlovna was glad that Alexei had come home and that someone else besides her was in the apartment now; and gladdened, she left for the market. This was even better for Alexei. He bolted the door behind her so that now no one could get in with the key without ringing. This was done when someone was home alone. Pelageya Pavlovna had instituted this, because of her deafness.

Alexei got his aunt's fabulous paté out of the refrigerator, made himself a sandwich and dutifully put everything back in its proper place, just as Pelageya had had it. Having taken a bite from his sandwich he went into his aunt's room. The windows looked out on the courtyard and the room was gloomy. Even then Alexei still saw many things in it through the eyes of his childhood. Again he is seven years old when he goes in there. He goes in as if in spite of being forbidden to do so and chokes on his own daring. And he sees, it is always the first thing he sees, a yellow Venus, so naked and armless. And then the piano, the books. But now the effect of all this was very slight. Now the Venus was obviously made out of plaster and he himself was obviously indifferent to her.

Alexei looked over the pile of books on the piano, banged his finger on the keys. A sound spread around the room and melted away as though in the dusk. He finished eating his sandwich, wiped off his hands on the horse-cloth over the piano and opened the sideboard. He got out the open bottle of Cahors wine, measured its contents and took a sip, looked at the level intently, and took another sip. He put it back in its place. He topped off all this with a spoonful of jam. The jam was fresh and not crystallized—it flowed down straight away as if he weren't eating it at all. Again he put everything in its place as it had been before, and got out his aunt's prize from behind the pier-glass—an open pack of "Selects." He lit up. He sat down at his aunt's desk. The desk was antique and huge, with a great many drawers. He didn't start opening them right away but looked first at the desk itself, at its surface. There were many remarkable things there, and in all those little knives, glasses and calendars he recognized his old childhood friends. Some sheets of paper were lying around—mainly records of the proceedings of faculty meetings—they were of no interest to him. He read a rather recent letter from some rapturous Tussya, quite an old woman already; the letter was evidently intended for Kissya, his aunt. Does she remember how the two of them, etc. He became somewhat ashamed: it was such a long time ago—Alexei almost understood that he shouldn't have read it and said:

"Really, it's hard to remember...,"—grinned to give himself courage, but put the letter aside. All the keys to the desk were in one glass. He unlocked the drawers one by one. Little had changed there in the last few years, one might say, nothing. Everything remained in the same irreproachable order and in the same places. As before, memory was stored in the drawers and not much had been added to it over these years. He also recognized this pile of photographs, and that one, and bunches of letters—they were all the same. The life of these drawers had come to a stop too long ago. It was sad to see. Only one drawer seemed alive, the biggest one, in the center. Even then it had been alive. It was in use to this day. Current affairs were concentrated in it. Out of the eleven drawers in the desk they all fitted into a single one. But here too, old things could be found, his aunt was still using them. The book of expenses, for instance. And the address book with the telephone numbers. And again letters, but very few. Lists of friends. A card to the reading room. Something else. A few fountain pens and pencils in cases. A ball of yarn. A plump writing pad—Delegate—still completely unused. A note book. There, in between some other notes, Alexei ran across a list of bonds with a three percent (gold) credit. The list was very long. But in that drawer Alexei found just two bonds in all and no more. The two bonds were not marked on the list. That meant the other bonds were kept somewhere in another drawer. Alexei carefully looked through all the drawers once more, but—it had to be a thick pack—didn't find them. He clearly imagined what the pack had to look like, all wrapped up, tied with a ribbon, with a piece of cardboard underneath and written in his aunt's handwriting: 3% (gold)." Alexei imagined it so clearly that it even seemed to him that he had already seen that pack today and he tried to remember in which drawer he had seen it. But he soon realized that he was searching in vain, yet for the life of him, he couldn't imagine where else besides in the desk his aunt would keep them... He put everything back in its place, took those two bonds from the center drawer and stopped to think. They were smooth, straight, green, and somehow he didn't want to fold them. His eyes halted at the night table—a huge atlas of the world was lying there. Alexei put the bonds somewhere in Africa and went out of the room with the atlas.

    Having come out he went quickly but not hurriedly to Trefilov's room. He didn't inspect anything there but went straight to the desk. Although he didn't know where anything was, somehow, surprisingly quickly, he guessed the place where the bonds were, pulled one out from the middle of the pack and put it into the same atlas, with the first two.

    His heart was thumping—he noticed it suddenly when he was already out of Trefilov's room and going down the hall. He came to the entrance door and opened the bolt. For a while he stood dully in the entrance hall and then went into his mother's room.

    There was an unusual smell in the room and Alexei didn't recognize the room right away. A New Year's tree* was leaning against the wall. "Of course,

---

*In the USSR a New Year's tree is the equivalent of a Christmas tree.

a New Year's tree...," he realized, "it's the New Year." The tree was very nice. "Yesterday it wasn't here," Alexei remembered. "When did they have the time to bring it in?"

He sat down in an armchair on the other side, put the atlas on his knees and began to examine the New Year's tree, waiting for Pelageya.

"Where did they get such a beautiful New Year's tree?"

Things got more difficult for him at the savings bank. Basically, he had no idea how things worked there. Just to make sure, he took his passport. There weren't many people. There were two lines. For some reason he couldn't ask which line he was supposed to get in, so he got in the shorter one.

People came and went. The door would bang shut behind them.

And suddenly it was flung open with an unusual crash. Two men entered. They were unshaven, in quilted jackets and boots, carrying briefcases. Without looking at anyone, they silently went to a corner, pulled two armchairs over, put them together like a trough, pushed two chairs up to the armchairs, and sat down, as before quite strikingly apart from the others. They shook their briefcases over the armchairs—money began to fall out of them, crumpled into balls. It kept falling and falling—a whole mountain of it. Nevertheless, having let it all fall out, they looked carefully into their briefcases as if into telescopes, but there really wasn't anything left in them.

Then they began smoothing out the notes and puting them into packs: three ruble notes with three ruble notes, rubles with rubles.

Alexei liked these unusual men. All kinds of pictures flashed through his mind—each has a revolver at his side and suddenly they pull out these revolvers—everyone raises his hands, and the two of them clean out the cashbox...

The line was short enough but not the right one. Alexei got angry and went to the end of the longer one...There he noticed bonds in the hands of those standing in front of him and grew even angrier: how come he hadn't noticed right away!

The two men were still smoothing out and counting the money—watching them, Alexei calmed down again. So he was standing in the line calmly and was already at the window itself when the two men all of a sudden said something, he couldn't make out what, and began to put the money back into their briefcases.

They put it in and left. As before they bore no relationship to anything.

"I don't understand what's going on," Alexei thought, but an angry cashier knocked on the window pane. And of course it was Alexei's turn.

Blushing, he slipped the bonds through the window.

From then on everything took place as if automatically.

Some old woman gave him sixty rubles.

And no one asked for his passport.

...At home Alexei waited for a call. Asya wasn't calling. It's a hell of a nuisance, Alexei thought, when a person has no phone!

Asya finally called at eleven o'clock. She said that he should come tomorrow morning. But why wasn't she around today? She'd been running around all day long...

Before going to sleep he read *Moby Dick*.

The Thirty-First of December

Everything was just fine. Asya came to the door herself. She had on a coat which wasn't buttoned up yet, under the coat she had on her familiar robe. She was glad to see him and gave him a smacking kiss on the cheek.

"How nice, darling. Thanks for coming. You're always right on time—it's marvelous. Not like me. But you know, I've got a place in line at the hairdresser's..." She smiled. "It's just across the street. After all, I've got a date with you today." (She put a stress on "with you" and gave him a wonderful look. "I've got to be beautiful."

She was smiling. Alexei was blissful. Everything was brightening up and something soared inside him like a flock of birds. He took her hand and drew her toward him.

"No, Alyosha...don't tease...We're going to the hairdresser's now. All right?"

"And I got some money..."

"Yes?..." Asya said almost indifferently.

"Here."

"So much?" she said just as calmly.

Alexei was a little disappointed but grateful at the same time that she didn't cry out and start bothering him. "Where is it from?"

"I got it," Alexei said importantly.

Asya seemed far away.

"How nice," she said after a pause. "Give me some for the pawn shop. And ten rubles for our date. I'll buy everything. Ten is enough, isn't it?... Well, shall we go? Or I'll lose my place in line."

They went down into the street and Alexei was surprised at how wonderful the weather was. All around the snow was so uncommonly white and it seemed as if they were in the country. The houses were covered with frost. And even this old street with its small dark buildings was beautiful. The city didn't look the same, it was soft and smooth. It was a different city. "See," he thought to himself, "I always notice beauty when Asya is next to me, even if she doesn't notice it herself. Why, I can't even remember having seen the city, or the garden or the weather, or the sky by myself." The sky was remarkable too, it was white, close and soft, but very bright at the same time.

All this—just cross the street—and the hairdresser. Asya left him at the door and went in alone. In the second the door was opened he saw that the very narrow waiting room was packed, and that all the women were standing there with their coats unbuttoned; it was almost dark inside but behind the plywood divider there was a bright light. Asya at once jumped out the door in her unbuttoned coat and said:

"The line's moved a little but it's still long. There's no point in your waiting."

"That's all right," Alexei said. "I'll wait."

"You'd better buy some wine because I won't have time; I've got so many things to do."

"All right," Alexei said, "go inside or you'll freeze."

"And then come back here, you hear?"

It was impossible to breathe in the stores. He would go in, see the crowds, and despair. He tried several stores. Finally, he realized that he was merely wasting his time and that all the stores would be just as crowded. But he left the store he was in just the same. And then as he turned into some unlikely side street, he noticed a tavern and rushed in. Only peasants were in here, mostly drunk. They were drinking and wandering around with glasses in their hands. "Now, just wait your turn," they said, "wait your turn." There was a crowd but the line moved quickly, and Alexei was able to buy everything he wanted. "I guess you got your stuff, huh?" an unshaven old man said, giving him a smile. "Here's what I bought," Alexei answered, putting away the bottles. "Atta boy."—"Sure," Alexei got embarrassed. "Be nice to Pop," the old man said.

Everything was just fine. Alexei returned to the hairdresser's. He hesitated at the door but went in. He embarrassedly surveyed the crowd of women. They were all looking at him but Asya wasn't there. They all looked very simple, most wore robes and kerchiefs and weren't as mysterious as on the street. They were looking at Alexei but also kind of not looking at the same time. Alexei got embarrassed.

"Yours left already, she's gone," someone said piercingly, he couldn't quite make out which one, apparently the round one over there. Everyone laughed. Alexei too. And it was warm and cozy here, although crowded. And Alexei felt good from the words "yours," "yours left." It's cozy because it's a holiday, he thought. Suddenly he realized that he'd been standing there all that time and that he had to leave. He got even more embarrassed. He saw a pay phone.

"I've got to make a call..." he said.

A girl blocking the pay phone moved away. She was austere and beautiful and she moved away not changing the expression on her face for a moment; she remained aloof. He dialed a random number, looking at the girl. It's interesting; when she makes love she can't be so aloof? Perhaps she's the way she is so that people will wonder what she's like when she makes love? They cursed him on the phone, and he went out, trying not to catch anyone's glance for fear it might be mocking.

He expected Asya to answer the door, since she was home already, but Sergei Vladimirovich answered instead. He was unusually agreeable, sincere and fresh, he was smiling.

"Alyosha? Hello, come in. Happy New Year!"

And things were just fine. It's so pleasant when one can answer eagerly!

"To you too. Happy New Year!"

Alexei went into the room first. Both of them hesitated at the door but Sergei Vladimirovich was insistent, so Alexei went in first. Nobody was in the room. Alexei realized at once that Asya was in the kitchen. The room was the same but also kind of different. Alexei was always surprised how the same room could seem so different. Of course, even the arrangement of the things in a room means a lot. The same bow-legged table and the same three metal beds, the same bureau, once mahogany, and the same already indistinguishable wallpaper—all this seemed in its place as never before, and the fact that the room was on the whole quite empty was also somehow significant. It was even somehow brighter, more proper, as though the semi-darkness were cleaner and warmer; and it was in fact warmer, the stove was heated unsparingly. Sergei Vladimirovich also seemed well-suited to the situation today. "Probably because it's a holiday," Alexei thought, "and it's spread everywhere..."

"Sit down," Sergei Vladimirovich said, taking some shoes off the table, and smiling confusedly at this.

"But where's Asya?" Alexei asked.

"She hasn't come home yet. But she'll come any minute now, don't worry. If not now, then soon."

"Of course, she was probably in the dressing room," Alexei said to himself, "and I didn't look there."

Sometimes Sergei Vladimirovich was a really great old man. At such moments his odd appearance would become particularly striking. "As a type," he would say, "I look very much like Bunin, don't you think?" The shabbiness of his clothes accentuated all that in him. He wore a black field jacket with black buttons that he'd had made for himself. The jacket was thick as an overcoat. Apparently, it had once in fact been an overcoat. It was convenient: he needed neither a shirt nor a tie. When Sergei Vladimirovich became aloof the jacket looked pitiful. Today Sergei Vladimirovich was not aloof. Rolling his remarkable "r," he was telling about how he'd been a corporal or a cadet or something like that, that is, he'd been studying to be an officer, and how as a group of bachelors they would set off in troikas to gypsy women, how wonderful it had all been: the snow and the champagne. Then he took out a yellowed photograph of a villa in the Crimea and another of his first wife, a perfect beauty; and it was already all so familiar to Alexei that it even seemed strange that Sergei Vladimirovich didn't remember anything else... Always the same thing and he always says it as if he didn't even believe it himself: but did it really happen?—and that's why he tells it over and over, as if insisting.

"But did it really happen?"—he suddenly knits his brow bewildered, as if answering himself: "So what? Maybe it happened. And maybe it didn't. Could be either..." And suddenly he grows silent, although not for long, and his face becomes distressed. "Like out of a play," Alexei thought. "He's like out of a play..."

Then they drank some tea. Sergei Vladimirovich got out some stinking Roquefort. "It smells like car-r-p!" he said and laughed—they drank tea with Roquefort. And then Sergei Vladimirovich even brought Alexei a glass of liqueur. The liqueur was terrible, peppermint or something. And Asya still hadn't come.

Sergei Vladimirovch was already telling him the price of each item.

Asya still hadn't come. Alexei was already thinking this: she told me to come to the hairdressers's... and then she came out and he wasn't there. He huddled up, it was getting hard for him to listen, and Sergei Vladimirovich got his chess set out—Alexei couldn't stand the game. It seemed to Alexei that it had gotten very dark, although it was still early to get dark; the room grew strange.

Then the door opened, they turned around... The room was long, the windows and the door were at opposite ends, and the light from the window was so faint, it hardly reached the door—so you couldn't see what went on by the door. A big pine tree was entering the room. Then Alexei saw Asya behind the tree; he jumped up to help. The pine tree was pricking him, a branch brushed against his eye, he laughed, relieved, with the New Year's tree in his arms. And Asya laughed too.

Sergei Vladimirovich found a dusty stand for the New Year's tree. Alexei set up the tree, then the three of them together carried it to all four corners till they found the one they liked. Alexei stepped away from the tree, unusually excited and constantly clasping and unclasping his resinous palms which became glued and unglued.

"We've got to run, we've got to run," Asya said.

"Where to?"

"To the pawnshop, we have very little time."

Alexei was surprised for some reason, the pawnshop seemed to have disappeared by itself.

"Will you go with me?" Asya said. Her face wore a distracted expression. "Or maybe you'd rather wait here?"

"Of course," Alexei said, "I'll go with you."

"Whatever you want. I can go alone..."

Alexei was already getting dressed.

"Stay, Alyosha," Sergei Vladimirovich begged, "We'll finish the game."

"We'll finish later," Alexei said.

It was three or four stops to the pawnshop and they were there. Asya was preoccupied and once in a while nodded to Alexei.

A square appeared in front of them. A church and a garden in front of the church. The subway. A market place in back of it. One couldn't see it but one felt it somehow. The side they were standing on was dark, because of the apartment buildings, and the pawnshop was right there. It was somehow hidden, concealed. Asya said they had to go through the courtyard and then up the stairs but now, when Asya stopped in front of the building for some reason, Alexei could feel the pawnshop just as he had felt the market place in back of the church.

"You wait here, I'll go alone," Asya said.

It seemed to Alexei that there was no reason to be shy, they could just as well go together, but by nature he didn't interfere when he wasn't asked and so he stayed standing there; Asya went through the entranceway. For some reason he got very upset seeing her go away.

She was gone a long time. The place where he waited was uncomfortable, right in the midst of the flow of people. He'd picked a spot right in between the trolley stop and the bus stop, in between two lines—and there he stood. Fifteen, twenty minutes, a half hour went by. Then Alexei too went through the gate. Going up the stairs, guided by the blurred arrows on the peeling walls, he imagined what the pawnshop looked like (he'd never been to a pawnshop before) and he saw something like the hairdresser's he had seen that day. He had opened a door—it slammed behind him with a rusty squeak—and he found himself in a curving hallway. He still couldn't see anything from the door except a light at the end of the hall. He went farther and when the turn around the bend opened up to him completely, he saw a line. The pawnshop didn't look like the hairdresser's after all, but more like a laundry. Alexei looked around for Asya and couldn't find her. Then suddenly someone behind him touched his elbow.

"Let's go over there," Asya whispered.

They moved away from the crowd and Asya said,

"It will be a while yet. Maybe you should go home? Really, it's not worth waiting for me. Go now and come at eleven, all right?"

Her look was absent-minded. People were waiting, it seemed, in silence. The light was unpleasant: dim, lifeless. But mainly, the hallway which wasn't at right angles but curving around, that hose, dark at the entrance and bright at the other end... Alexei felt a little queasy. The air too...

"All right, I'll wait on the street," he said.

Asya seemed to shake something off, her look focused on Alexei, it grew warm:

"Silly, you go right home, don't wait," and she gave him a smacking kiss on the cheek.

Going down, Alexei ran into a man on the dark stairway who gave him a somewhat strange look and who, because of it, immediately looked familiar to him. Alexei was still thinking about him as he went farther down the stairs and out into the courtyard and onto the street, but he couldn't quite remember. It even began to seem to him that it was Asya's husband, but he wasn't sure because he hadn't seen him clearly the one time he'd seen him, and he hadn't really seen him on the staircase. Nonetheless, he grew more and more uneasy; so he didn't go away—he waited, although he didn't go up to the pawnshop to check: it would look as though he were following him and that wasn't true. After a half hour, he couldn't stand it and slowly but surely, he began to move through the courtyard and go up the stairs. He opened the door and went through the curved hallway but absolutely nobody was left there, only a woman locking up something.

"It's closed, it's closed," she said. "Happy New Year!"

"To you too" Alexei mumbled and began to go down. He was on his way down— and suddenly someone sprang, laughing, from behind—it was Asya!

"This is it!" she said "This is it!—She took out the dress from her bag and showed it to him. "The same one. Do you know how much everyone liked it there! Even the appraisal-lady asked me to sell it to her... Darling, were you waiting all this time...?

Alexei was no longer upset, he tried to forget everything that was incomprehensible and he asked no questions. As soon as they saw each other, everything was normal...

"But now I'll put you on a bus," Asya said when they were on the street, "and you'll go home." The street was quite dark already. "It gets dark early," Alexei thought. "These are the longest nights of the year."

I'll put you on a bus and you'll go. I still have to buy everything and prepare and then get ready myself. You'd just be in my way. Go put on your grey suit. I want you to be handsome."

The bus was going away. Asya stayed at the bus stop with her arm raised. Alexei kept looking through the rear window, Asya was moving away and he saw some dark figure, a shadow, next to her. "The church," he thought, "or someone getting into line." The shadow upset him.

Then the bus got closer to his house and something kept stiffening and tightening up inside Alexei. It got still stronger after he got off at his stop, and the closer he came to his house, the harder it became to walk and he walked slower and slower. It was like something out of a child's nightmare; it was frightening, but he wasn't sure exactly what was frightening, and so it became even more frightening. Lately, it was difficult for him to go home, or rather, the very first moment was difficult; opening the door, enduring the first looks and greeting, not knowing whether they would start asking questions and whether he'd have to tell lies... it had been like that ever since Asya had come along. But today there was also... today it was more unpleasant than usual, and Alexei couldn't understand why. He even knew what it was, he even remembered, seeing the New Year's tree in Mama's room... Yesterday... it was easier for him not to understand what was bothering him than to think about it. He tried not to recognize his foreboding, and he succeeded. But the fact that his fear was somehow stronger this time, that it was already a foreboding and not a mere feeling, was important. It was the foreboding of something irreparable.

The Garden

It was busy at home and warm too. The New Year's tree in Mama's room was already trimmed and didn't look as mysterious in the electric light as when he'd seen it the first time. The thirty-first really was a special date because the cold and austere faces Alexei had been seeing for some time weren't there. Mama said nothing to him and asked nothing, she was cheerful and somehow carefree. She kissed Alexei on his forehead and handed him a little box: "Although you don't deserve it," she said, smiling. Alexei was so happy with the absence of coldness in the house, with not having to hide and shrink, that suddenly he felt half a year younger, that is, very much younger: younger by a whole life, younger by an Asya. He realized how much he loved Mama and the house, he hugged Mama, covered her with kisses; Mama seemed to soften in his arms; he suddenly became aware of how small and tiny she was and yet something else struck him in this surge of tenderness. Suddenly he realized it was half a year since he'd come to Mama in this way, hugging and kissing her, it had somehow fallen off, vanished—and Asya was part of that too. His hands felt awkward just now as he hugged Mama. He was also surprised that he hadn't noticed it sooner, after all, until Asya there was such love between him and Mama! And his tenderness with Mama must have been broken off too abruptly, so Mama could not have failed to notice it ... But he never once felt that she had noticed it. He also thought that in this whole half-a-year he could remember nothing from his home life, everything was Asya, and that was surely cruel and unjust on his part. He felt awkward, perhaps even ashamed, in front of Mama, but above all, in all that surge of emotion, the feeling of awkwardness in his hands hugging Mama wouldn't leave him; they were simply wooden, with no warmth in them, so his hug seemed false, somehow shameful, and even base. He felt even more awkward because he sensed that Mama had no such feeling. For Mama, everything was as before, and probably, even more strong, as with someone who misses you. That's the way things were, and so Alexei was the first one to move away and at that moment he noticed such happy sad eyes that he felt like crying. He suddenly felt so helpless that he hurried off to his room.

He thought that he and Mama would of course never really become strangers to one another, things would be set right and return to normal, but ... He became very, very sad, but it wasn't unpleasant. All of a sudden he really felt that his childhood was gone. And he thought how strangely little man accommodates inside himself; but he didn't think that this was so for everyone, but that HE himself accommodated so little inside him, and he blamed himself for it. Something comes along—and there's no room left for something else. The cruelty of such a discovery didn't startle him though. It was as though he felt that it was part of the inevitable nature of things.

And Alexei began to think about something else. "I want you to be handsome," Asya had said. He got undressed and started warming up. He had given up athletics lately, even though before it had been almost his main activity every day. His body resisted exercise now. But in that coercion—as though remembering with his body—he felt joy. When he'd gotten warmed up, he opened the vent window. The smell of snow came sharply inside.

He exercised according to a full system that he'd carefully made up at one time, one exercise after another. There were also exercises which were quite complicated, acrobatic, and the fact that he was able to perform them just as before gave him an earnest satisfaction. A feeling of the strength and obedience of each muscle awoke within him, a feeling which not so long ago had been almost the chief evidence of his full value and equality and perhaps even of his superiority in this world. The triumph of his body, so habitual before, was particularly pleasant now.

The next exercise was supposed to be a run, so Alexei began to put on his sweat suit and sneakers. Having dressed, he looked at himself in the mirror: he liked his drawn and darkened face. His legs seemed to be running already—they felt so light and strong.

He didn't run though, but for some reason went down the hall to the kitchen. Pelageya was taking a goose out of the oven, his aunt was preparing her extraordinary New Year's charlotte, Mama, squinting weak-sightedly, was peeling cucumbers, and Trefilov was standing with his back turned toward everyone and smoking as he looked out the dark window. Everybody turned around to Alexei, only Trefilov didn't turn around.

"Are you really going to run?" his aunt said, and her tone was friendly even though up until this very day she seemed never to even notice him: that's how angry she had been that he had brought grief to Mama. "It's the thirty-first..." Alexei thought again. Pelageya, who never cared about these things except perhaps out of curiosity, was now simply angry with the goose and looked disapproving. Hearing aunt's voice, Trefilov turned his head, gave a sidelong look at Alexei, let out a puff of smoke and ehemmed.

"Yes, I think I'll take a little run," Alexei said. After his exercises and the open vent window, the kitchen smoke was particularly unpleasant—and he ran off.

He breathed the frosty air with delight. He ran along the bank of Karpovka up to the Botanical Gardens and then he ran along the fence. He felt as though he were looking at himself from the side, at how lightly and beautifully he was running. If only some girls were here to see him. But the place was deserted. It was always deserted here, but now there wasn't even an occassional passer-by. "Everyone's getting ready," Alexei thought. It was amazingly quiet, and the lamps weren't burning. There was a slight frost but the snow was crunching under his sneakers—the only sound aside from the noise of his breathing. It was very beautiful—but Alexei no longer saw anything, because being out of shape was telling now—he felt sick. First he got out of breath, then his legs grew heavy and strange. At that moment, totally inappropriately, two girls appeared and began giggling: he's running into the New Year... And Alexei slowed to a walk. His spittle was like glue... His chest was burning somewhere high up as if about to crack. His heart throbbed all over.

At home he carefully brushed his teeth and shaved. Then came the shower. Hot at first, then cooler and cooler and finally, moaning, Alexei turned off the warm water and splattered ice-cold water all over himself. Steam came from his body. Having rubbed himself down, he put on a robe and hurried to get dressed. He did everything thoroughly and with feeling.

When everything was finished he went into his mother's room and looked into the big mirror. He stood up straight and was satisfied with himself. After such a complex of tortures he always found himself handsome.

Then he went into the kitchen again where they fed him a holiday dinner almost by force. He didn't want to eat, but Mama wouldn't let him go out without dinner anyway.

Finally he was all ready and there was just enough time left to get there.

"Well, I'm going," he said to Mama. Now he was supposed to add "Best wishes for the coming year" or "Happy New Year," but to say that was awkward, false somehow, since he was forsaking his house, and he didn't say anything.

"Well, Happy New Year to you," Mama said and standing on tiptoes, kissed him on his forehead.

"You aren't staying with us?" his aunt asked. As before, there was nothing metallic in her voice but it emphasized something anyway. She knew very well that he was going out.

"No, I've got to go with the kids..." Alexei said. And just the same he forced out: "Happy New Year to you all!"

Everyone smiled and waved but there was an effort and a strain in it by now.

Alexei went out of the house with a heavy heart feeling guilty but resisting awareness of it: there is no guilt, so what's the matter?

But on the packed and noisy bus it went away.

Going up the stairs, he realized that he was very nervous. Because of the Astoria... Did Asya go, or didn't she after all? And if she did go, has she come back already, or not? It's unlikely she's back yet... He was going up slower and slower, and felt more and more ill at ease. He also thought that almost up to Asya's very door, up to eleven o'clock, he had tried not to think about it at all, the whole day, no, two, he wouldn't let himself think about the Astoria. Ringing the bell, he was already very nervous. As a matter of fact, it was always that way—is she home or isn't she?—but now it was as if he had never really been nervous standing in front of Asya's door until today.

And Asya opened the door for him.

She looked as he'd never seen her look before. She was sparkling. She was laughing and saying something quickly, he couldn't remember what. She was obviously glad to see him. She held up her cheek.

"Carefully," she said. She didn't let him hug her: so as not to crumple her dress. But even without her warning, Alexei felt that he should neither touch nor breathe on such beauty. He even kissed her just as one probably kisses an icon... His cheek was cold, from being outside. Something seemed to prevent him from seeing, he looked around like a near-sighted man without glasses, he saw nothing around him, as if Asya and he were in a bead of light and everything else was dark. And the feeling of pride split him open: say what you like, but this woman here all the same belongs to him! But he also felt a sense of non-participation, fortuitousness in all this beauty, as though such things could only happen in dreams and not to him—no, he didn't deserve it.

Asya made him sit down on a chair so that he wouldn't get in her way; she still had the salad to finish. At that moment he noticed the salad in front of him and a still-unopened container of mayonnaise next to it on the table... And it turned out that Asya loved him, because if she didn't go to the Astoria then everything was clear, and if she had gone and still came back so soon, then even better. It astounded him. Asya tied an apron around her and mixed the salad. She dropped her hands into it and stirred the mass, and in that too there was frightening beauty. "You look handsome today," Asya said. His blood rushed to his head. "How come you haven't said anything about my New Year's tree?" Asya said. At that moment he saw the tree. It was decked with all of Asya's familiar pins and beads; the tree was basically green and it was great that it was all green. As soon as he saw the tree, its smell spread all around. That also astounded him.

The salad was ready and suddenly Alexei noticed all the other things on the window sill already prepared. Asya came up next to him without her spoon, her hands cleaned of the salad. "You're still sitting here? How obedient you are, its marvelous!" she gave him a smacking kiss on the cheek. "We'll set the table now. You'll help me." Then she ran to the wall and turned on the radio. Immediately someone began to sing. Asya pulled Alexei off the chair, began to turn him around, pull at him, laugh. "You're so funny... and handsome," she said.

And suddenly Alexei saw Asya's face changing.

Her eyes went past his cheek about one millimeter, she was almost looking at *him*, that's why the change was particularly unpleasant. So he didn't want to turn around: a cat the size of a tiger could be standing there, or a gorilla the size of a house, or... in short, like in a dream. He turned: Nina was there with two or three other girls whom he'd seen before, Nina's girlfriends. They were her friends from some hobby group, athletics-drama-cars-chorus. They came in without saying hello and hung their coats on the hooks near the door. Right under the radio. The radio was singing a song about them: "Many lads are bachelors." Alexei looked at his watch; it was quarter to twelve. He began to look around for Asya, Asya wasn't there. And Nina wasn't there either. "Hello," Alexei said. The girls answered, each one separately, quite politely, with attention, examining him. Asya and Nina entered as though together. But they also entered quite separately somehow, their walk, their bodies expressed irritation at sharing the space around them. And as if they were shoved away from one another at the door, Nina went to her friends,

Asya—where else?—to Alexei—they didn't even look at each other. "Tam-tam-tam-tam," Nina began talking with the girls under the coat hooks. "Well, what's up?" Alexei asked. "To hell with them!" Asya said with hatred. "Tam-tam-tam," came from the corner. Two groups in one room which have nothing in common with each other, not looking at one another. As though one didn't exist for the other. "Are they staying or what?" Alexei asked. They were thrown out, thrown out of the party," Asya said furiously. "The beauties...No wonder." It was very strange to watch how Nina and the girls didn't seem to notice Asya and himself. They were spread around the room already. But they existed without each other and in each other, like the world and the anti-world, or something.

It was really disappointing—it destroyed the holiday. And not just any holiday, but New Year's. And this one in particular. This New Year's was a mystery for Alexei, a miracle, a tangible happiness. But the fact that Asya was so upset scared him more in the end, and he said: "Well what can you do...since that's how it is. You can't throw them out...The house isn't ours. In any case you couldn't throw them out. We've got to celebrate somehow at least, make it human. So don't get upset...It's not the last time." Asya was upset. "Let's invite them to our table too" Alexei said "and we'll celebrate together. Of course, it would be better just the two of us, but we've got to salvage a little something." Shyly, he touched her shoulder, he was afraid: she could burst into a rage and take it out on him, Alexei, but he isn't guilty! "We'll invite them, O.K.? Of course, they're fools, carrying on like this... it's not even them...it's Ninka. The girls don't really matter. Well?" Asya's face calmed down or rather, sank down. "Well, all right," she said. "It's time to clink glasses anyway, there's no point going on about it."

"Girls," she said "come join us, since things have turned out this way." The girls looked at Nina. But Nina wasn't looking at anyone. "Thank you," she said in an impossible tone. "We're not in the habit of inviting ourselves." "But really, girls," Alexei said, "it makes no sense to spoil each other's holiday, Nina. Don't you see, we mean it. We can't celebrate with you in the same room..." "We're not going anywhere!" Nina screamed. "You're out of your mind..." Asya said with mocking pity. "No insults, no insults, do you hear!" Nina yelled. "Be glad we put up with you! And anyway...found your mama's boy!" "Leave him alone! Leave him alone!" Asya darted into the middle. "He's not yours. You've never even seen anyone like him! They were right when they threw you out, you deserve it!!!" With her hands on her hips, sideways, with short dance steps, Nina came out into the middle. She was the spitting image of Lolita Torres, or so everyone said. "Whore!" she shouted "Whore!" "Don't you dare!" Alexei jumped in. "And what are you butting in for? Dunce..." said Nina, emphasizing each word. "What do you mean, dunce?" Alexei got upset. "Go away" Asya said somewhat unkindly. "Tam-tam-tam-tam-baram" came from the girls. "You're jealous?!" shouted Asya. "Thrown out?...Jealous!" "Teaching children?!" "Jealous! Jealous!" "Enough! Enough!"

... Alexei. "Tatatam-baram-tamtam!"—the girlfriends. "Old maids!"—Asya. "Trata-ta-tam, oo-oo"—the girlfriends. "The clock is striking!" Alexei shouted "It's twelve o'clock!"

Everyone shut up. Froze. True. The clock was striking. Tram-tamtam-ram-baramtam-tamtam!—wonderfully, melodically. Bamm! Pause. Bamm!...

"Well, to hell with them! To hell with them!" Asya jumped up and drew Alexei away. "Here!" she shoved him the champagne. "Hurry!" She moved a stool over to her bed and threw a towel over it. Oddly, a lot of food could fit on it. And she did it all so quickly, it was hard to see how. The champagne popped. "Bamm!" was heard on the radio. And a pause. Not just a pause—it was longer: a silence. "Happy New Year, darling!" Asya said. "Happy New Year!" "Tam-tam-tam-tam-tam-tam," the radio played the anthem. They downed their drinks. Asya sat down on her bed with her back to Nina and her girlfriends. "Sit down," Asya said. "Don't pay any attention to them." "I'm not," Alexei said. "Everything's fine. Everything's fine!..." Asya sobbed. "But what's the matter! What's the matter!" Alexei got upset. "Nothing... But just now," Asya said. "Don't listen to what she said..." she smiled through her tears so pitifully and unhappily that Alexei almost began to cry. "But do I... do I ever listen to her?" Alexei said with fervor. "Eat some of my salad... Let's eat it without the plates, OK? Eat it right out of the bowl... It's good, isn't it?... It is, right?"—"Very!"—"Is it darling? No, really, is it good?!" Asya's voice trembled, she was going to cry. Alexei too could hardly restrain himself and his eyes blinked; he couldn't see well. Suddenly such tenderness came over the two of them that you could start crying just from that. "It doesn't matter, doesn't matter," he said. "We'll have fun anyway, right?" Asya said. "We're happy!" Alexei said. "Yes, yes, exactly! We are happy," Asya said. "Don't pay any attention to them." Not paying attention was difficult... Although up till now, starting with the chimes, there really wasn't anyone in the room for him besides Asya and himself. But still, he was sitting facing them and they were too conspicuous, especially Nina. She paced from one side of the room to the other like a tigress. Her eyes were, so to speak, burning. She walked around, smoking nervously. "She doesn't even know how to smoke," Asya said all of a sudden. "Give me that." They were all smoking. Asya was sitting with her back toward them, but Alexei felt that with her back she could see them better than he and that she was suffering. Nina kept on pacing. Her girlfriends were standing there like a sorrowful portrait. The three graces.

"That's strange, too," Alexei thought suddenly. "Now they probably all feel bad, feel bad about themselves. But if you tried to do something, make peace or say you're sorry, it would be even worse. And then everyone would feel even worse about themselves..."

Everybody calmed down a little. But that didn't make things more pleasant. Just the other way around. Everyone had kept something back from one another, hadn't finished swearing, and because of that, tension was hanging in the air like a powerful force field, telepathy, field-psi, Alexei said to

The Garden

himself. And he also thought: "Both the quarrel and the shouting had dragged on because no matter how low each one had fallen and no matter what each had said, still, no one could say the worst insult that was on the tip of her tongue, nor commit the worst act. And Nina, it's amazing how badly she'd wanted to say: "Get out of my house!" but no matter how enraged she'd gotten, she couldn't say it.

Something got stuck in his throat. Alexei looked at things from a distance all of a sudden. He even saw Asya from a distance and she moved away immediately. Quite literally, he somehow saw her from far away, although she was sitting right next to him. It was a bad feeling. Although it calmed him. But there was coldness, indifference in this—a slippery snake. It seemed he didn't know why this woman was next to him, or why they were sitting on the same bed or how that came to be? What is this room with all these totally unfamiliar people in it? What were they talking about, shouting, suffering, quarreling, why? Complete nonsense. Alexei felt ill at ease, even scared, he didn't want to see things that way. It was like an optical illusion in a popular magazine: now you see black—and one shape, then you see white—and the shape is completely different. You're looking first one way—then the other, as if there were some switch in the eye, a knob like on a T.V. set: click-click. It was the first time that he'd looked at Asya from a distance—and he got frightened, although he didn't quite realize it: suddenly from now on he would start switching—first this way, then that way. He didn't want that vision for himself, dissonant with his feelings. Perhaps it's more intelligent, but happiness is destroyed by it—it's already knowledge of a sort—he didn't want that knowledge. It made everything strange.

Asya got up and went over to Nina. They stood aside and whispered something. Their whisper became louder, it expanded. "Tamtam-tam" could already be heard from their corner. But suddenly something stopped them, the noise broke off unexpectedly, and didn't come to what Alexei had expected—the repetition of the scene, and they separated. Asya came up to him boiling with rage. A whisper, vicious and incomprehensible, almost a hiss—that was what Asya would have wanted to tell Nina, but had restrained herself. Alexei again saw only Asya, not from a distance now—it was a relief that it wasn't from a distance, and he was saying: why take it to heart so, you mustn't, just forget it... "If we were just on the staircase!" Asya said (the words were for him, their malice for Nina). "Or even on the street!" It fluttered in Alexei's throat, he was choking, he couldn't have said a word now. Asya flung herself to the door, grabbing her everlasting robe from the back of the bed... Alexei just about managed to look over embarrassedly at the rest of the participants, when Asya, as if instantly, had her robe on. She carefully hung her green dress on the back of the bed and covered it with a towel. She was whispering something furious but at the same time carefully smoothing out the creases in her green dress. For some reason Alexei noticed this incongruity and at that moment thought that the fact that he'd noticed it was also incongruous with his own upset state, in essence, the same incongruity as Asya and her dress. But she already had her coat on and was tossing her arms around so, that it was hard to make them out; her high-heels were neatly put way in a box, and on her feet she was wearing her street shoes, the ones without heels. "Put your coat on" she commanded Alexei, and put some wine, candies and pastries into her bag... She straightened up. At that moment Alexei saw her face had gotten somewhat flushed because she'd bent down before, furious and unhappy. He wanted to say something right away to help her, but he couldn't think of anything. He felt the words that came to him might make Asya still angrier. That wasn't what he wanted, of course, and he felt unhappy about his clumsiness and stupidity: he can't even say anything right. Asya looked at Alexei, the blood drained from her face and her face became whiter. And as though along with her blood, while she was looking at Alexei, her irritation and fury also went away; her face got calm, kind and sad: "I didn't behave well...?" Asya said. "I was rude? Forgive me, I wouldn't want to be ugly in front of you... Don't look and don't listen when I'm like that... I always feel very bad later that you've seen me that way..." "What do you mean, Asya! Don't be silly!" Alexei said. "You're right... and it's all understandable."—"All right, but forget it, darling, you didn't see anything... here!" She slipped him the bag of food. "Let them choke!" And, without turning around, they went out of the room.

The stairway was empty, dark and deserted; the bench they were sitting on, the unique bench on Asya's stairway, was under an enormous lancet window. The reflection of the moon or something, or of the snow in the courtyard or of the windows where people were celebrating, barely reached where they were. It was barely a reflection (was it, wasn't it?), it was some slightly quivering, elusive geometry of the window frame on the floor, on the wall, on Asya's wonderful and unusual face. "Oh you, my sweet little deer! My precious eyes... What eyes," whispered Asya and he melted and was falling; it wasn't terrifying, it was sweet and very terrifying, wild, Asya's face was moving toward him, inside him, about him, and he, Alexei, didn't exist at all, he vanished, dissolved... Suddenly, it seemed, this stairway was full of resounding steps and voices. His heart fluttered away like a frightened bird and sank down slowly, fell back to its place; there were people there, many of them all along the stairway, coming up toward them, after them. "Here they are!" the leader shouted; they took their hands and led them some place, to their execution, to Golgotha, but they were happy all the same... The stairway, it was full of rustle and absence; there was no place to run to, he was chained to it, and Asya's face was above him, below him, everywhere.

He was empty, he literally felt he was a shell, as if they had taken his brain out, and he seemed to be spreading out, crawling away and yet not budging... he was drunk, wasn't drunk... The snow was falling from somewhere in weightless, disintegrating wisps, there was no moon and the lamps weren't burning; but the light—there wasn't any, yet it was coming quietly from everywhere, like the snow, along with the snow; it was very quiet and they were silent—they were walking in their garden.

...Suddenly he realized that he was already walking alone. It was dark, the snow was flying from all sides; the sensation of time and space vanished. Where is he? Where is he going? Why? It's the Field of Mars. He is going home. Because Asya and he had parted to go home. He felt that the blind mask of joy that had stiffened on his face began to fall to pieces now. It was as if he had regained consciousness. He couldn't remember... Asya said; "Let's part now so that it will remain as good as it really was." For some reason he suddenly remembered how Asya and Nina had run out of room, how they had whispered several times in the room... Was it possible they had just played a trick on him and now they were all together, and... he seemed to have become transfixed over an abyss, with one foot in the void already. He became terrified. He drove the feeling away.

He tried to remember something else. There was a beautiful garden and they were there, the two of them. They were sitting on a bench, and the even surface of snow, almost strange without any tracks on it, was in front of them. It wasn't strange however, because they had come to the bench not by the path, but from behind, falling through the snow. The snow was lying on the path so evenly that its surface was imperceptible; as if it had sprouted up from the ground like some white grass: it was delicate and weightless like mould. But the most important thing in the garden of course, were the trees. And looking at the dark, almost warm trunks and higher up—at the branches, the twigs and the sprigs,—they saw that the trees weren't simply covered with hoarfrost or snow, that the snow wasn't simply lying on the twigs,—the twigs themselves seemed to be made out of snow, thick to the point of strangeness, like white coral. The snow on the branches repeated all their curves and lines, all their most intricate abstractions; and the trees seemed repeated by the snow. They didn't resemble trees any more, but were like enormous uprecedented crystals, crystaline lattices. No, not even like that: the crystals were the usual size, it was just that they, these two, were unusually small, tiny, dissolved, they didn't exist. The beautiful bottom of the sea... And they were sitting there—a path was in front of them, as though overgrown with snow that had sprouted up, it seemed, before their very eyes, And they had always been sitting there, just as the enormous, already very old trees with their dark, warm trunks and branches, repeated by the snow, had always been standing there.

Later, when the silence began going out of them, they drank and ate and talked endlessly, it wasn't important what about nor could he remember—the feeling was beautiful. It contained the realization that this garden would appear in a dream in ten, in twenty, in a thousand years. It might even appear in someone else's dream. The garden somehow became a thing of the past before their very eyes. Finally the garden didn't really exist, it simply happened to them—it was luck, of course, but it was better not to think about it.

Actually, they didn't sit in their garden a very long time. Alexei realized it now, having looked at his watch. It was nothing at all, in fact. And then somehow they parted, he didn't remember how. Asya ran off all of a sudden. And he didn't see her home... Again an abyss opened up. He wasn't about to think about it.

He was walking home slowly, without thinking. Having remembered the garden and forgotten the abyss, alone once more, he again became intangible to himself, dissolved—was he walking, floating, soaring or what? And so without thinking, identical with the snow slowly flying now upwards, then downwards, then in all directions, he found himself on his street. On the right was his house, on the left—the Botanical Gardens. He felt tenderness toward the garden, he didn't feel like going home, the same foreboding of something irreparable moved in on him, made him shrink and not feel like going—and besides, it was still early. He walked along the fence, went down the Karpovka toward the Nevka, he had just taken a run down that way, only a few hours ago, hundreds of years, thousands... everything had been different.

"And what happened at home?" he thought. "In those thousands of years?"

Nothing had changed... The old men had drunk two glasses each, turned pink, talked about the past, had almost gotten lively. And had gotten tired. They had gotten tired and said goodnight. And now they were sleeping.

And the holiday passed just like last year and like ten years ago. The holiday was in the past. Principles...

"And what if they've found out...?" he thought again and quickly drove the thought away.

He pictured his aunt sleepy, or Trefilov sleepless, or Mama, opening the door to him with a reproachfull look... And he couldn't stand even imagining this look.

"It's better to sleep outside!... he thought angrily and joyously. And he climbed over the fence—he remembered the spot from childhood: a tree bowed low to the ground and gradually falling and breaking down the fence year after year. It didn't take much effort to climb the fence.

He wasn't afraid to trample the snow in the garden, and he went along as if on skis, leaving a long unbroken trail behind him—two tracks. He scraped the snow off down to the ground here and there, and the trail turned black. Something big, tall and round at the top loomed black in front of him. He thought of all sorts of things, he even imagined that it was an enormous head, although he realized already that it was a rick, or a haystack, or a haycock—as they called it there. He tried to climb up, got short of breath, the snow thawed in his sleeves and under his collar—it was silly even trying to climb up the steep hay. He walked around and discovered a kind of protruberance, a platform, at one spot—the hay had slipped down from one side there. The platform wasn't high up and he could climb onto it. There was a lot of snow there, and by the time he spread it around he felt that his legs and sleeves were soaked, but it was warm, as long as the snow didn't melt. Having turned the snow upside down, he cleaned himself off and began burying himself in the hay. That unusual smell of the hay that he had stirred and woken up in the middle of winter, and the smell of snow, and the smell of his wet mittens...! He remembered this smell, although he had never in his life even been in a village and had never slept on hay. He remembered or rather, felt—and the feeling was indisputable and precise,—that all this had already happened before: the haystack and the winter and the same trees, and he had been a little boy with an unfamiliar face... It seemed to have been in his childhood, but not in this one, in another one—in one of his former lives. He hadn't been his current self then but someone different, a completely different person. And that's when it had happened to him, this smell... in that other life.

He lay down at last, pulled some hay over himself, taking out wisps on each side and already falling asleep... For a while he lay on his back and looked up: there were branches of a tree and branches of another tree, all white, and between them, there was a space. Then he took out a handkerchief. Taking it out was awkward, his "blanket" kept falling apart, he even got angry, but he did get the handkerchief, covered his face with it and gropingly threw some more hay on himself.

It seemed to him that as soon as he closed his eyes he immediately fell through to some place which made him wake up in fright; he had just opened and closed his eyes, as if he had blinked. He didn't see or understand anything, he was suffocating, wet, something had fallen on him while he had his eyes closed, and now, when he opened them, it didn't disappear, fall away, as a dream is supposed to. He couldn't feel his body, face, arms. He shrieked, it came out weak, not loud—he shot his arm up spasmodically, as if uncertain whether it would obey him, and he whisked from his face the thing that was choking and terrifying him... the handkerchief. He saw the white sky in front of him, all covered with the branches of the big trees. And in that white sky right above him a huge black crow was flying, replacing the white sky with itself. It was flying and screaming as though repeating his own cry, it was flying, always flying, and screaming sharply, piercingly and anxiously.

The First of January

Asya had said in the garden then that they would go out to the country the next day. Looking at the trees, she had felt so much like going out to the country. And they would go to Sestroretsk, her girlfriend lives there, a girlfriend who is much older but a beautiful person. How many times had she invited Asya to come but she could somehow never get around to it. But tomorrow they'd go for sure. They'd ski or just take a walk and then spend a little time with her girlfriend again in the evening. She has a whole apartment...

Alexei woke up late. It wasn't clear whether it was just a generally dark day or whether it was so late that it was already getting dark. He didn't feel like moving and kept lying there just the way he had woken up. The beautiful thing that had happened yesterday came to his mind but it had somehow lost its sharpness, it seemed to have happened a long time ago. It's as difficult to remember as a dream, Alexei thought. He wanted to remember it just as sharply as it had happened but he couldn't. He just kept getting more awake. Lying in the half-dark room he felt suddenly how fast time flies; here he's lying, not even moving, and it flies by, it doesn't stop. A feeling like this wasn't terrible—it was simply a dull inevitability, the order of things, so it goes. But the fact that the very same time had taken away yesterday was ridiculous. And suddenly he remembered that then, in the garden, there had grown within him, even distracted him, the feeling (but he'd driven it away then) that he not only lived the fullest life that anyone had ever lived but also that the time keeps taking this life away from him. That's not exactly how he had thought, but he'd had some similar feeling. And he'd been right, he thought, to have driven it away. That's no life, with such a feeling...

And as he was recollecting this he also remembered that they were supposed to go out to the country today. But it's so late already, it's as dark as the evening... Maybe Asya had called already? Maybe she'd gone alone? Then he remembered in a remarkably vivid way, as though he'd just seen it...

He heard the cry of the crow in his memory, and saw as if from its flight the tops of the trees and himself lying in the haystack, motionless, face upwards, his arms spread, deep at the bottom somewhere, with a white handkerchief in one hand. This woke him completely.

He at once sat up in bed and pain reverberated throughout his whole body. Absolutely everything ached.

First he had to find out what time it was. He shuffled around the room—it was absolutely amazing how everything ached!—the clock showed half past six, it had stopped. Dressing hurriedly, he imagined that everyone had already gotten up long ago and now was wandering around the hall, from the rooms to the kitchen. But he didn't see anyone in the hall and actually, it was suspiciously quiet. He dialed the time on the telephone—and cursed: it wasn't too late but too early; it was all of half past nine, that was why it was so dark. But the fact that Asya was still sleeping and, of course, hadn't called, set him at ease.

"How come I'm up so early?" he wondered.

Nonetheless he didn't feel like sleeping. He tried to loosen up his wooden aching body a little: he took a shower. It was all of ten o'clock and the same silence and darkness hung over the entire apartment. He dived back into his bed and settled down with *Moby Dick*. It was a remarkable book. Everything he read in it was so tangible, simple and exact; and yet so painless, so easy and sensible; but he'd read no more than a hundred pages from the beginning. It went so slowly but it wasn't unfolding tediously, as a matter of fact nothing had unfolded yet—he was delighted with the book. He'd just been reading about how two friends who had suddenly found each other were lying in one bed at night, not sleeping but having a heart-to-heart talk; and he read further:

"We felt very nice and snug, the more so since it was so chilly out of doors; indeed out of bed-clothes too, seeing that there was no fire in the room. The more so, I say, because truly to enjoy bodily warmth, some small part of you must be cold, for there is no quality in this world that is not what it is merely by contrast. Nothing exists in itself. If you flatter yourself that you are all over comfortable and have been so a long time, then you cannot be said to be comfortable any more. But if, like Queequeg and me in the bed, the tip of your nose or the crown of your head be slightly chilled, why then, indeed, in general consciousness you feel most delightfully and unmistakably warm. For this reason a sleeping apartment should never be furnished with a fire, which is one of the luxurious discomforts of the rich.... For the height of this sort of deliciousness is to have nothing but the blanket between you and your snugness and the cold of the outer air. Then there you lie, like the one warm spark in the heart of an arctic crystal."

At this point, Alexei jumped up, opened the window, and dived back into his bed, and sat himself up, pulling his knees up to his nose. So he sat there, not reading *Moby Dick* any more.

Then he began smoking in that position and to complete the picture ought to have been thinking about something intelligent; it turned out he wasn't able to think about anything just now, but he felt good just the same.

Then a sort of drowsiness came over him, he closed his eyes and then opened them, he felt how warm he was all over, but his nose was cold, and all this together was really not so bad and he closed his eyes again.

"What the devil is this!" Mama slammed the window. "What trick have you thought up now?"

"The one warm spark in the heart of an arctic crystal," Alexei said. It had been a long time since he'd opened his eyes this easily, it was a pleasure to open them and see the world clearly right away. It was vacation childhood, it was clearly a holiday.

"Haven't you caught a cold?" Mama said, having already coped with the window. "What did you do that for? You've chilled the entire apartment..."

"A warm bed" Alexei said "is one of the luxurious discomforts of the rich."

"What's this nonsense, Alyosha..."

"It's all right, Mama. Happy New Year!"

The apartment was coming to life. His aunt and Trefilov, both grown very quiet after the holiday, appeared in the kitchen. They had luxurious left-overs for breakfast. "Left-overs are sweet," they kept saying. By some general consensus they didn't turn on any lights and so they were moving slowly and sleepily in the dusk; the day was dark and imperceptibly turning into evening. Asya wasn't calling. "She must have gotten up already," Alexei thought. But she wasn't calling. He'd already heard all his relatives' stories about last night's celebration and had talked himself about how his had been: oh, he said, it was fun and good. On Mama's insistence he enumerated the names of all the kids that had been with him, spoke about the sort of girlfriends they had, what they'd eaten and drunk. The difficulty lay in one thing: in remembering what he'd said so as not to get confused later. He thought he'd remember. As always, he was already cursing himself for not having gone to Asya's even before she called, but soon he realized that it would be awkward to go: who knows what's going on there after last night.

Asya called at four o' clock. "Of course we can't go anywhere so late," Alexei thought.

"So are we going or not?" Asya said. She was cheerful, excited and wanted to go very much.

They met at the train platform. Asya was wrapped up, rolled up and new, somehow.

"Look, I swiped Nina's pants!" she said and laughed. "Do they look good?"

"They do," Alexei said and also laughed. "And what's going on there?"

"It's all right. But do you know that they left right after we did?"

"No-o."

"We could have come back."

Then they began recalling and picturing everyone's faces. Ninka's, her girlfriends' and even their own. And they laughed a lot.

Then they got on the train. It was quite dark outside the window. You could see your reflection in it already. And they, Alexei and Asya, were still in the city, they could see the lights of the street lamps and the windows of the houses and also some small dark blue and red mysterious and cheerful lights along the tracks. The radio played some insipid waltz. And the car, brightly lit from the inside, was carrying the reflection of itself—its benches, ceilings and passengers—in its windowpanes, as if outside the panes, so that there was another, illusory car on each side, the left and the right, and the reflection of Alexei and Asya also lived its separate life in the illusory car on one side of the train. The waltz played, the train made a turn, the city lights turned around and flew by and it seemed to Alexei that their car and they themselves, and the illusory cars with his and Asya's reflections, and the street lamps and the windows of the houses—all this was dancing to that slow insipid waltz: it was turning around, rocking, moving away.

But then they left the city, nothing remained in the windows except the reflection,—it was dark right up to the next station where there was light, a platform, one or two people waiting—and it was dark again. Yesterday made itself felt, everything ached sweetly, they dozed off, Asya on his shoulder, they spoke little. But they felt good, and could ride this way for a long time.

When they arrived, they didn't even feel like getting off and losing their drowsy warmth. But they got off and the frost that had set in toward evening clasped them and they breathed in the pure non-city air, they felt happy. All their inertia went away; what fine fellows they were after all for having gone out, and how could they live for months without the country anyway!

But her girlfriend wasn't in, she'd gone to the city. But today they couldn't care less and so they weren't even disappointed and went—it was Alexei's idea—to Fox Nose, a friend of Alexei's lived there. But his friend wasn't in either. But again they weren't disappointed and they wandered around and drunk up their bottle on a bench by the bay under a big pine tree. They couldn't see the bay at night, it all fell away steeply there, but they breathed the bay and then moved quietly toward the train. They felt completely worn out in the car and they slept all the way to Leningrad. And they parted, Alexei didn't even walk her home—it was late, and he had to get up early the next morning.

Right by his house Alexei hesitated again, it suddenly became absolutely clear that something had happened at home while he had been away; that they already knew; what they knew—he didn't even allow himself to think about.

At home it turned out that his father had arrived.

The Second of January

That day was lucky. It could have been because his worries which had dissappeared on New Year's still hadn't come back. He almost didn't care whether this or that schoolwork would come out well; and everything took shape sort of by itself and yet, in the best way possible. Even his institute wasn't busy today, hardly anyone there, half-dark. No one was in a hurry; and those who were forced to show up, seemed not to have lost their holiday yet, they kept to themselves. It turned out right from the beginning that he'd come in the nick of time; they were just starting to write their exams over again. Very few kids were there and just one teacher, the same Bolshintsova, a beautiful woman. Things weren't as solemn, Bolshintsova kept on going out; and Alexei, without haste and seemingly effortlessly, not even noticing how, neither copying it all nor solving it by himself, took the exam. It came out neatly.

After this, everything worked out well for him. That is, wherever he went, just the person he wanted was there; all the student obstructions and hindrances were quickly solved, almost by themselves. He smoothed things out and got some notes he badly needed. Things were working out like this, and when something suddenly fell through, something completely trivial, someone wasn't there or had just gone out, he realized it was a sin to try his luck any further, that was enough for today. After the first misfortune the next one may follow, as always, and then the next one and the next one, and a wretched chain would start; and that's a fact, its not worth spoiling the day... And so without suffering a defeat, still preserving in himself today's startling ease of success, he left the institute.

And everything else went as if the law that makes bread fall butter-side down didn't exist at all. This was rare for Alexei; he had always felt that the devil in charge of that law had a particular predilection for him; he couldn't get out, so to speak, from under the shadow of his black wing. But now some buses were approaching and he too was approaching just then, and the bus turned out to be exactly the right one. And five kopeks turned up in his pocket, and he didn't have to suffer with the fare box and the change, and he found a seat by the window. "Once things start moving, they kept on going!..." Alexei thought gloriously. "One must simply sense things all the time and not cut oneself off." What it is one must sense and not cut oneself off from, you ask him, and he couldn't tell you.

Just in case, he went to Asya's but she wasn't home, just as she'd warned him yesterday: She had to go to the Forestry Institute about a job. So he only made sure she wasn't in but didn't get upset, that is, he didn't lose his mood but, on the contrary, with unusual success he got into the movies right away and they started on time and the picture didn't disappoint him.

It was already dark when he was going up the stairs, he felt light at heart coming home. Judging from the coat rack, everyone had already come back from work, but that didn't depress him either. Today was one of those rare days when he could count on warmth and equality, he had only to tell Mama about his successes and add some lively details in that cheerful voice that he was going to use today without the shadow of a lie. He wouldn't have to see the stony, strained faces and the stern silences—everything would be natural at last—a patriarchal picture.

And so, at Mama's usual, neutral "well, how did it go?" he should immediately give an account of everything and then she'd thaw out.

Having taken off his coat, he went straight to Mama's room. It was dark there, only the television screen glowed green.

> And the land of arid heat
> Forgot about growing...

a green, austere man was reading with feeling.

Two dark shadows, Papa and Mama, were sitting by the television set, and Alexei said to them in the voice of a hard-working man:

"Hello!"

"Hello, Alexei" his parents answered quietly.

He sat down on an empty chair. It would be unnatural to start talking about the institute right away, he must hold back now because he always talks about the institute reluctantly, forcedly, because as a rule he needs to hide things and that's unpleasant no matter what. So today too he must show that it's just his manner, that it doesn't depend on his successes—he just doesn't like talking about the institute, that's all. But the question he would answer so eagerly today didn't come. His parents were watching television silently and very attentively.

> Muttering, vegetating
> And an absurd hole...

"What's he reading?" Alexei asked in a still cheerful voice.

Mama turned the knob but didn't switch it off completely; the sound disappeared but the picture remained.

"We have to talk to you, Alyosha," she said in an even and quiet voice. Papa dropped his eyes.

"That's it. This is the end," Alexei said to himself, realizing what was coming now. The nightmare had begun. Nothing could be more dreadful.

Mama talked. A false, dissolving feeling settled on Alexei. It seemed to him: this isn't happening to him and about him—this isn't happening, he's dreaming—he isn't dreaming. Everything was blurring before him like a damp blotter... And that undefined rip, its fibres, confused his reason; Mama's face grew incomprehensibly white, it was turned away from the television set, her mouth kept speaking and then not speaking but just kept moving all the same, as though they'd turned Mama's sound off but not her picture. Then her face moved away somewhere into infinity, it became tiny, indiscernible,—and from over there, far away, Mama was telling him something. His father was sitting quiet as a mouse. Some other man, also green, was swimming on the screen as if in an aquarium. Alexei turned his head aside, the screen got crooked and the man got short, distorted, and started swimming like a frog. The bubbles on the screen enlarged and toyed with the green edges. Mama's face drew near again—he could already perform this like a trick—and moved away. Deformed men-fish were swimming in the aquarium. They silently opened their mouths just as they were supposed to. Everything in the room was lightly tinged with a greenish aquatic light... To Alexei it seemed they were all some weird family that had plunged into liquid and there they moved and lived, at the bottom of the room-jar. In the aquarium on the screen the water-plants started swimming, everything broke into a run and kept running. Suddenly, it stopped: some creature began sinking slowly to the bottom and disappeared there. Immediately another one, just like the other, detached itself from the upper rim and with its mouth open, making swimming motions with its arms, began sinking quietly to the bottom—there it disappeared. And yet another one, just like the other, its legs first and then its head, swam out and plunged into the center of the aquarium. Alexei changed the position of his head: the creatures began grimacing, grew disfigured, broke up... Something flashed and a ripple broke into a run. Mama's face returned to its initial position, her sound was suddenly switched on. "Do you understand?" Alexei heard. "You'll go immediately and do as I said. Do you understand?" "Yes," he wanted to say, and as if it were a terrible dream, he somehow couldn't: he just opened his mouth, it unglued itself with difficulty, it was dry and something squeaked in it. Mama made a sign to his father, and his father, lightly and not looking in Alexei's direction, as if not really walking, slowly sailed through the room; there, in the darkness, he rummaged as if in silt and swam back, holding three green notes.

Alexei could no longer recognize things. He seemed to be switched off, dead. His head was ringing lightly and thinly. He felt as if he weren't walking but flying. And that all that is, in fact, is not. He even felt some odd lightness.

...His aunt's room seemed about the size of a television set. The white light from beneath a green china shade reached just to the center of the desk that disappeared into the darkness, and fell on some papers. His aunt turned her face toward Alexei and somehow rode away from the desk into the shadow along with her armchair. Alexei heard no sound from the movement of the armchair, as though his aunt sitting on the armchair was a closet door and the door had opened. His aunt's face was bright green from the lampshade, it was frightened and she herself was somehow compressed.

"Here, I stole this from you" Alexei said in a measured voice.

He put two green notes on her desk. Aunt's face became distorted, a ripple ran across it and she said plaintively and thinly:

"But what's the matter...what's the matter! Well, sit down!...Sit down for a while..."

...In Trefilov's room absolutely all the lamps were lit, even the night lamp, but he himself was standing facing the black window and smoking.

"Here..."Alexei began.

"Put in on the desk, "Trefilov interrupted, without turning around. Alexei saw that Trefilov's ears and neck became thick with blood, and now both his ears and neck disappeared in frantic puffs of smoke.

He didn't turn the light on in his room. He had to close the door as tightly as possible. Trying to do it inaudibly, he grabbed the handle with both his hands and pulled, first lightly and then more and more strongly and finally with all his strength; he even rested his foot against the doorpost, till the handle began to creak. For there were no locks in the apartment...

He undressed slowly in the darkness, laying out his clothes carefully on the chair, something he didn't usually do. Now, standing barefoot on the floor, he brought his pants up to his eyes—found the crease and hung them out neatly on the back of the chair. He put his shoes—heels together, toes apart— slightly nearer to the legs of the bed and not in the middle. And then he lay down.

He was lying huddled as in a somersault, he breathed into his knees trying to warm himself. And suddenly, not just the room, which wasn't really so big, but even the bed appeared huge to him. "How small we all are," he repeated to himself. "How small we all are ... " "It's so funny the way you say small," Asya laughed. "Small ... My darling!"—"Here! Here!!!!"—Alexei said and tossed the money in packs of notes, in p-packs!!! They scattered in a fan like a flock of penduli, every leaf flying back and forth, they sank slowly and with a shudder lay down on the floor. And he kept flinging them, flinging them to *their* feet. To *their* feet ... They were standing there, miserable, dejected, so old ... Suddenly he began to feel sorry for them, painfully, to the point of tears—and he forgave them, HE forgave them.

He imagined an enormous performance being put on, requiring the efforts of the entire world, with him as the main character. He's a prince, in fact, the future ruler of the entire land. Everyone knows that about him and yet everyone is silent and goes on performing this show for him. It's as though he must be brought up in ignorance and then told at some moment who he really is. This remote denouement is a silent scene—and everyone turns out to be your servant, your subordinate ... And their servitude and obedience to him, to their ruler, went so far that they did the impossible—they didn't betray themselves in any way, they endured this monstrous performance all their lives. The way they endured it surprised him more than anything else in the whole performance. After all, both the passers-by and the strangers walk by and recognize him but they don't whisper to one another, don't show any sign, as though they really didn't know who he was.

The unnaturalness and cumbersomeness of this artificial performance in which whole continents, countries and peoples exist only as sets at such a far corner of the stage that none of the main characters even sees them, and only so that at some point in the years-long performance, in one line spoken by the one thousand and first character, it can be casually mentioned that they *do* exist and go on living somewhere—seemed strange and awful to him. The upsidedownness of a life where he, the ruler, was the most powerless of all, and everyone could humiliate him, not fearing sanction, for their only law was to follow their roles ... such upsidedownness where even loyalty to him had to be expressed by inexorably played cruelty to him, seemed absurd, almost funny. And the fact that the actors knew another life besides the performance, and only he, he all alone, had to exist in that performance as if it were life, was unfair. Because after all he had figured out the deception ... A mad loneliness, deceivedness, uniqueness in the world ached sweetly in Alexei. And he already pitied everyone ...

And his parents, the poor things, had simply been given the main roles; they were the most appropriate to play the play already written by someone, they were merely instruments. It was hardest for them, they had to work harder than the others, they didn't even have time to live a little in the real, non-theatrical world ... Such was the monstrous reality attained by this production in which they had to suffer, to get sick, to go hungry, and actually die, only because their future ruler had to know and experience all this. What a diabolic labor! They are probably gradually going crazy and behind the curtain already take the performance for real life; they love the theater and don't want to part with it as if it were the real world and real life.

But the play's ending is harsh; it's impossible to violate it, the end comes and they let him know everything that they were hiding earlier, he becomes a ruler, and they, his parents, who have entered into their roles to the point of madness, don't know what to do when their role is finished. He feels sorry for them, even loves them and brings them closer to himself; after all they were only cruel out of necessity and in reality they loved him, carefully hiding it, afraid of the anger of the director, unknown to him, and yet sometimes they even violated the script... As for Asya. a punishment is probably awaiting her, because she betrays the real life that's beyond the show... That's why she breaks away so abruptly and painfully at times, because her cruel role in the play never comes easily to her, she always forgets her role and brings the real life in with her that is forbidden for him to see. Perhaps, she has to pay for it at the rehearsals. They put up with her only because they can't replace her with anyone else. But maybe she doesn't even digress from her role, maybe that's the sort of role she has, the last one before the end and before all the secrets of the other life are revealed to him; the sort of role that's somehow preparatory to the final scene...?

But maybe he's no prince at all, but the most unfortunate man—the subject of a huge experiment? Maybe they want to see what happens with a man (the main character) when he lives his whole life in an absurd performance in which everyone knows their role by heart and never makes mistakes, and only he is without a role; he lives accepting the performance as real life and he lives for himself, "really and truly," and doesn't know that he's performing for someone, who coordinates his acts with an already written role. And the entire play is written, everything is thought out with an inhuman cleverness in order to always obtain from him the one possible reaction and no other, no matter how complex it is to contrive.

But if that is the case, then the experiment has already failed. Because he, the unfortunate experimental rabbit, has nonetheless understood, no matter how hard they tried to deceive him... he has understood that besides the performance there is another life, the most important, the most alive...

... That's what Alexei was imagining. He had warmed up already and stretched out calmly. The terrible lump under his heart seemed to have melted away and so Alexei could draw himself up. He was recovering little by little, imagining other things as well. Then that too went away. His head felt free, but he couldn't fall asleep.

He took a few barefoot steps, the floor was cool, it felt nice. He went to the window and opened it. The air and the snow fell on his chest and face—Alexei shifted by the window from one foot to the other. He saw the familiar street lamp dangling under the roof of the warehouse, but there was no watchman. Alexei stood there a little while, breathing and looking, but he wasn't forcing himself: he stood there as long as it felt nice and when he got cold, he closed the window. Next he switched on the lamp and stood in front of his books, not knowing which to choose. He needed a book now, and he felt along their backs, which one? Suddenly he remembered a book that he had read when he was nine or ten and hadn't read since. All these years he hadn't thought of it but now he remembered the strange feeling he got from the book... He was suddenly convinced that the feeling was indispensable to him now. Surprised that he'd forgotten about it for so many years and remembered it precisely today, he rummaged behind the books—the book could only be there, because he hadn't seen it in the first row. He was rummaging and thinking about the book. What was in it, what it was about, he couldn't remember although he already saw it in memory, its binding, its pages, its print. He remembered that he'd taken it out of the bathroom, someone had thrown it out there, and he'd read it with some mysterious fondness, carefully, word by word, although he hadn't understood anything in it. But his incomprehension was, and this he still remembered, of some special magnetic quality. And so, rummaging behind the books, he suddenly found it, blew the dust off, and clapped its sides making a ball of dust fly out of it. He realized he was freezing, ran to his bed, climbed fussily under his blanket, delightfully, his sheets felt still colder, he was warmimg up slowly.

Having thawed out, he opened the book with curiosity, but its outer inspection didn't satisfy him in any way. The first eighteen pages weren't there at all, the last one was the nine hundred and fifth, but it wasn't the end of the book because there was a comma at the end of the page. He remembered that sometimes, after a certain number of pages, the name of the author or the title of the work is given at the bottom. He didn't find it here either, but he found that pages 33 and 34, 49 and 50, 65 and 66, 81 and 82 were also torn out. The only thing he understood was that the book was printed without the letter "yat"*, therefore it wasn't old although it had seen its day. After this inspection, with almost scientific interest, he started reading.

But he understood little of it. That is, he caught himself having read, let's say, three pages and not remembering anything he'd read. His eyes slipped over each word that looked familiar by itself but what they said all together slipped away from him. So, having started with page 19 he remembered the very first line: "... that never explain anything to us in life." And after three more pages another sentence stopped him: "And if we start speaking again about God we won't understand each other,"—it stopped him only because it was the last sentence of these three pages, it was followed by a blank space and the heading: "Second Letter." He became angry at himself for reading without catching the meaning. That could happen with a textbook when you get lost in thought or imagine things while continuing to read at the same time, but now

---

*"Yat" was dropped out of the Russian alphabet after the Revolution.

he wasn't thinking about anything and was reading with ease, almost with enthusiasm...

He went back to the beginning but understood little more. "I am an old man and do not have the right to the weakness of youth..."—just a bit of a sentence stuck in his head but no more than some information about the author, that is, that he was old. His excitement with his find and childhood memories began to diminish and his persistence to wane. The idea which was so pleasing to him at the outset, that he'd not understood anything then, but now, having lived, so to speak, and grown wiser he would understand everything, turned into a disappointment: it seemed he had understood more when he was a child.

The "Second Letter" was endless and after the sentence "Thus what shall we dwell on in making the selection?" he started scanning, reading easily, almost merely turning over the pages, and he didn't even notice that he went from page 32 directly to page 35 without detecting any loss of continuity in it. He grew impatient: when does this endless letter end?

Therefore he read the "Fourth Letter" almost with some enthusiasm. "But if you really do not believe it, I am ready to prove it simply and clearly" it began.

Even simply and clearly, here again Alexei didn't understand everything. It was like this: first everything was a fog, then a break and a little piece of sky. It wasn't contemporary language. But he could already feel something in it and remembered the feeling. Something like a translation into his, Alexei's, language was coming out, a translation and adaptation. Excluding the completely incomprehensible blanks, this chapter was talking about how love is in us and above us, and if you are still alive you can still love too and if you can love then what sort of thing is it and where is it from? Alexei understood everything about desire and passion—it really was "simple and clear"—they were separate from love. The part about pity was already rather obscure. Pity turned out to be almost above love but then below love, too, in any case, love and pity also turned out to be different things. The discourse about jealousy interested Alexei most of all.

Jealousy turned out to have nothing to do with anything and was even the opposite of love. Now it seems to me I love, the strange author said. Now I follow on the heels, I chase, I adore, I hate, it's hot one moment, cold, the next, I pry, I demand, I call, I dream, what else? I'm jealous, I ask questions, I lay claims... And once I lose face like that then what do I expect if I come to know the particulars? A lie only. Because of a lie—that's exactly what I want at the moment I lose my life and my face. But no matter how jealous I am, there's always one last question that I'll never ask. People always come to be afraid of the destruction of their faith and by their nature never seek that destruction. And here—"love abides even in disbelief, like faith." "That's true," Alexei thought. "With me it was that way too, at the beginning of my friendship with Asya. But later on I understood that I shouldn't ask questions. I understood by myself. Or else, we'd have nothing left now." He went on reading—everything got confused: on and on about God! And suddenly the connection was restored. "What is ruin and destruction in love for such people?" the author asked. "Suicide and murder?" This was, after all, the tragedy of the last question asked; no matter how man avoided it, it cropped up inexorably and had been asked now—and everything collapsed; man couldn't cope with it. And to ask that question was senseless: man knew everything anyway, but he didn't allow himself that knowledge. And he was right. Does love have any rights? Is the person we love guilty? Why that violence? Do we want to crush the loved one and our love with them ...? It began to talk about God again and Alexei skipped over the entire page. And suddenly: "My God! How small we all are!" the strange author exclaimed. "That's it!" Alexei was full of joy. We can't accommodate anything inside us, the author said. And when love comes, even that nothing doesn't remain. There are those who love and there are those who are loved. They aren't castes. It's just that everybody is loved by someone and loves someone. And then—everyone is noble for some one and base for someone else, gentle for someone cruel to someone else, great for someone and worthless for someone else, everyone lies to someone and tells the truth to someone else, etc. And all that comes "from the small amount our souls can accommodate." It all happens to the man who "does not believe yet miraculously is still not dead but alive." And to him I say: where did this love come from that's inside you who are so tiny? Where did you get it from? Why, it's not from the loved one, she's still smaller, there's no such exclusiveness and singularity in her, no—you introduced it. And if you agree that it's not from her, that you were simply ready for love—and it arose, it was inevitable, love, but the one you fell in love with was accidental, if such a train of thought is clear to you, then let us understand: does it come from you? But it doesn't come from you. You too are tiny: look how nothing remained inside you when love came ... You become base and cruel to many who'd been around you till your love came, although perhaps you don't even notice it. The enormous thing that is love doesn't leave a dot in your tiny space and it even tears you apart and goes far beyond you. You grow bigger than you could ever have grown without it; but in what you were without love you grow still smaller. Therefore, how could something big arise from within you? Therefore, it is not from within you.

Next, everything grew confused, got twisted ... It turned out that what was under discussion was not love after all. It was just to explain all this to people with no faith, in a language comprehensible to them, clearly and simply. And if one is to speak seriously then.........................
....
....
it all was beside the point, beside the point.

Suddenly, as though a propos of nothing, there followed a description of a beautiful garden, but it broke off just as suddenly, because right here a page had been torn out.

...Alexei closed the book. He felt strange. He understood some things and didn't understand others; he skipped the part about God, but the discourse about where love is from: not from the loved one who's so accidental and tiny, and not from him who's also extremely small, and if not from her and not from him, then from where?—affected him strongly.

1960-1963

The Third Story
(The Image)

Whenever Monakhov was reminded, by friends, relatives, or by people who happened to hear of it, that he would soon be a father, he saw and heard them as if from a distance, and was only somewhat surprised by the expressions on their faces—either earnest or sympathetic, but uncontrollable, always with a trace of a tick or a wink. However, what it was they were winking at was not, apparently, entirely clear to them, it happened involuntarily, so that a dignified face would then succeed these expressions. Whether they themselves were fathers or not, these dignified faces confirmed their initiation into the mystery: yes, they knew what was there behind that door that Monakhov still had to open. It was as if the door led into Christmassy childhood; behind the door was the tree with burning lights, under the tree a pile of presents, and in the pile one of them is yours or mine. And it's awkward to suggest to the child which one is yours, but you still want to take him aside later and tell him that this was the present you gave him—though it is embarrassing... Well, thought Monakhov, the kid, after all, is mine and no one else's.

And he liked it much better (though "like" is not the word) when, instead of a dignified face, a more vulgar and honest one would appear. When, giggling, some fingers would make a goat with horns, poking his stomach with it, cootchie-cootchie-coo, honestly letting you know that they know what and where children come from. Oh you naughty so-and-so! This approach was, at least, more direct and proper, and somehow seemed less indifferent.

Monakhov would in turn explain, as if justifying himself, that though his wife had been taken to the hospital, it was not to give birth but to lower her blood pressure, that her time was not near yet, that his wife still had to give birth, but noticing expressions of boredom and impatience several times, he stopped doing this. Besides, he, too, got bored: repetition dulls experience and then it is lost. It was as if he were accepting an invitation to some short ritual, and he would recreate on his face the same expression as that performed by his interlocutor, be he a relative or an acquaintance: it was either the dignified one, or the giggling one with the corresponding but weak half-goat—and he felt no anxiety or shock, no sudden realization, no dimness, no elation—no emotion at all from these reminders. He only felt a certain impatience from each of these meetings and even without any special antipathy to the questioner: his look, though not exactly fleeting or fixed in the infinite, would become simply indifferent; impatience would be wound up inside him in a spiral, and then he felt as if he could perform some pirouette or turn and fly up lightly along this spiral, moving off, taking off and breaking into flight, singing and dancing along with the light-headedness of a crazed Ophelia, while a whistling swarm of shiny bluish disks would fly out of him.

His strange expression did not embarrass anyone, however. Everyone understood that, naturally, he was worried.

But he would part with his acquaintances and walk on, slightly surprised at his own lack of emotion on the verge of such a significant event in his life.

Actually, the realization that neither the thought, nor the reminders of his imminent fatherhood elicited any emotion from him, was in itself his only feeling on this score. He meditated on the strange role of the father in this whole business: once, and that's it—he doesn't continue further, he is left rejected and abandoned. His feeling, arrested, grew in a void. How do I fit in?—he would ask himself paradoxically.

It was simply too much for the brain, he once thought cleverly of his lack of feeling, which somewhat disturbed him.

He visited his wife daily, brought her things and wrote her letters, reporting on the state of his various affairs, which, just at this time, were also at the end of a term, to be born at any moment. His work meant a lot to him and, consequently, to his wife, who shared and knew all about his concerns, and, consequently, to his future son or daughter.

He would write the letter, put it in her package, and go to the street that passed under her windows. He didn't even know how to whistle and would try to attract someone's attention with signs, so that they would call his wife to the window. This made Monakhov feel awkward and slightly humiliated each time, and he inwardly fought these feelings. His wife would finally appear and they would communicate with gestures, smiling and nodding, not quite hearing or understanding each other, while the passers-by would smile kindly, observing this touching little vignette, for which Monakhov, of course, disliked them. Then his wife, frightened by a doctor or a nurse, would disappear from her window. This haste and this fright seemed somehow improbable to Monakhov. He would remain standing for some time underneath the empty window, while other wives from other windows would look at him and he at them, and then he would go home, or wherever, with something like a clear conscience or a sense of relief... His wife still had to give birth.

On one of these days, Monakhov's affairs did finally take a new turn, and everything was crowned with success. It must be noted that Monakhov's affair was a complicated and a significant one, and his success both great and deserved.

This success was sealed by a certain important paper received by

Monakhov which confirmed that he was connected with the affair in which he was involved even without the paper. But it was as if before the paper had been signed, neither the affair, nor his work, nor even Monakhov himself, had existed. Now, however, on the basis of this paper, he was beginning to receive a significant amount of money and various signs of respect. It was this very paper that he now held rolled up in his hand and tapped against the director's desk. And then he folded it as if carelessly and shoved it in his pocket.

On the stairway he thought he had slipped it outside of his pocket and he broke into a sweat. But no, it was in place. He unfolded it, looked tenderly at the seal and the signature, and read his name on it with surprise and satisfaction. The last name was all written out in capital letters, and the surname and patronymic in normal ones; he was even surprised at having such a name, as if it were not even his. He decided to go to his wife's hospital immediately and share the happy news, and the bus arrived right away. "Not bad, not bad," no longer hearing the words, Monakhov repeated them in rhythm with something while getting on the bus and feeling his paper again, for reassurance.

"Well, all right, well, all right...," he repeated, looking out the window. If he were asked why all right, he couldn't say—the weather was good.

"Good lord, Alexei!" he heard, recognizing the voice immediately but not believing it, and at the same moment feeling the chair next to him sinking, and the fragrance of the perfume "Queen of Spades" was still the same—all this in the one moment when, starting from the unexpectedness, he quickly turned to the speaker. And what amazed him most of all was that it was really she, that he so immediately recognized her even before seeing her. During all these years he had not met her even once, nor even thought about her, when suddenly...how deep her imprint was on him...

"Well, hello," she said, giving him her cheek with such a familiar motion (of course, in order not to smear anything!). At this moment the bus veered and he, unwittingly or not, with or without pleasure, had already touched it, in the process looking at the passengers out of the corner of his eye: how might others view all this and weren't there some acquaintances there.

"And you are still just as awkward," she laughed. "Now do it properly..." and she gave him her cheek again with that same familiar motion. And he, aware of a complete loss of sensation in his lips, carefully, this time without looking at the passengers, as if giving up, but not closing his eyes so that he saw, too closely, a wrinkle filled with face cream that hadn't been there before, kissed her cheek.

"How can this be..." he muttered, moving away with relief, already in the habit of taking advantage of the fact that every movement can be interpreted in any way, if you just give it a little direction: so, unable to cover his embarrassment and even his distaste at what was happening, he managed to lend a shape of natural agitation and confusion to his embarrassment. "How can this be..." he muttered. "Can this really be...Asya..."

And they began to talk animatedly. He talked, too, but only began to hear what it was about two bus stops later, in the meantime trying to master his surprise and disbelief: who could imagine that this woman sitting next to him was Asya? And it was not that she had aged or deteriorated, although there was that, too, but that the voice and face were really hers, and that the faces of strangers would now have seemed less distant to Monakhov. And somehow he began to understand that if that previous Asya were by some miracle to appear next to him now, the effect would have been the same. Because the Asya that he remembered never really existed. There was the image to which he clung year in year out, the image which survived even the suffering of the break and was preserved in memory. Now it was as if he were holding a portrait, comparing it to the original, and nothing matched. Asya, the older Asya sitting next to him, was but an awkward amateur forgery and he even felt strange talking to her as if she were Asya. And this movement, so familiar, with which she offered him her cheek, seemed false and unnatural to him, and that same voice and that same giggle were also ersatz, chemistry, physics, anything but the truth, and even the eyes which he always thought the most beautiful he had ever seen in his life, though blue as Asya's were, appeared shallow and empty, and he had to admit that even his wife's eyes were more beautiful. But, as he was gradually becoming convinced that this, indeed, was Asya and there was no doubt about it, a reverse reaction took place—in this process of matching with the original—he began to distrust the image. The image began to crumble, to disappear, and suddenly flew off like a little cloud and, though Monakhov did not yet grasp this, it flew off forever, leaving for the future only a mechanical recording of events, retained in memory, which he could now reproduce as if by a push of a button, replaying the automatic and the constant chain of words now deprived of meaning, which he himself could no longer assimilate. This crumbling of the image, occurring probably for the first time in his life, so clearly that he could see the lines tear and the colors disappear, was unconsciously painful. And when the image finally evaporated and dispersed, melting like a little cloud, he felt a sense of relief and a returning of liveliness—and he became interested. Because the sensation which came over him now was really curiosity: that is precisely what is involved in matching old mechanical recordings with new ones still unknown.

It was just at this point, having passed two stops, that he heard what it was they were talking about, and experienced a slight difficulty, because now being curious but not remembering the beginning of the conversation, he was in danger of repeating himself. This would seem inattentive and he did not want that, feeling curiosity not only about the conversation but also about the new woman sitting next to him. He quickly realized, however, that this, too, could be accounted for by a quite proper agitation and that he could rely on that.

"So did you just get back?" he asked.
"Goodness, no, I haven't been away."

"How is it we haven't met even once?" Monakhov asked with genuine surprise. "Before, we used to meet every day without even planning to, how many times would we just run into each other on the street, besides our dates, but since we broke up—not once. I was convinced you had left."

"And you're still so rational..." she laughed, tenderly. Again Monakhov noted the unnaturalness of her intonation, but now it suited him fine, because it seemed to suggest some possibility which was attractive to him but did not hold him responsible for any consequences. Then he realized that all these vague possibilities should be clarified and checked out right now, for it was so tempting to construct a precious "memory" like that, but he after all knew nothing about her and should check it out.

"And where are you going now, if it isn't a secret?" he asked.

"To work," she answered.

"No kidding!" Monakhov inquired again quite sincerely, "So you actually take this bus every day?"

"Of course," she said.

"But I take it to work, too," Monakhov said. "How strange, this is the first time we've met..."

"It's very simple, we just take different buses," she said.

"Yes..." Monakhov intoned and gave her a puzzled look.

"Why are you looking at me like that?" she laughed. "As if I were dumb. We simply take opposite buses: you work where I live, and I—the other way around—so we're always crossing paths."

"Well, that's something!" Monakhov said with feigned admiration. "Your head is still just as clear. I would never have figured it out."

"What do you think," Asya laughed coquettishly, "that I must naturally be senile? Do I really seem so old to you?"

"Oh no," Monakhov said, not quite sincerely, "you look marvelous," and in order to lend verisimilitude to his words, he said this somewhat crudely, but so that any woman would easily forgive him, and this fully confirmed his sincerity. "Remember, you yourself used to say: a small dog is always a puppy. So..."

"Right, right," Asya cheered up. "A small dog..."

Suddenly looking at her face once more, Monakhov discovered that it really had not aged, but was even more youthful. After all, he was just a boy then, and she five years older, and now he had sort of caught up with her. This really was a strange feeling, because recently he had suddenly begun to notice when meeting people after a few years and remembering how they used to seem much older before, that he now found them to have grown younger, because he no longer felt that they were that much older than he. He especially noticed this with his English teacher from school, whom he met on the street occasionally, and she was getting younger before his very eyes, and was even beginning to seem more attractive as a woman, so that he even walked her home once, having met her at an exhibit, and they actually were aware of themselves as man and woman then, but something still stopped her at the last moment, and they parted.

"You too haven't changed a bit," Asya said, "although I see you're beginning to get grey," Monakhov caught and recognized this tenacious look of hers, the kind she always had when she dragged him about to shops, the kind with which she looked at passing men; he hadn't like it then but now it flattered him. "Girls must like that: a young face and grey temples."

Monakhov, though again aware of her unnatural intonation, was still terribly flattered; she had hit his soft spot, so to speak.

"I'm even missing teeth now," he boasted stupidly in the same vein. "I have to have them put in."

"Your suit is nice, too," she said, her eye gliding down his jacket with that same tenacious look.

And suddenly Monakhov felt liberated, relieved, as if the heavy weights of self-oppression had fallen off, so that he became a man with certain rare qualities—he simply felt desire, augmented by all the details that went against his taste, his intelligence and his morals, that struck him in his old love after so many years. This was not remembrance-recognition, but something quite contrary and paradoxical—the reverse side, the negative of his past emotions. The likeness seemed all the stranger, all the more distant, unclear... Because, by the same token, the old feelings themselves were the print of that same negative.

This was partially the beginning of what is now called, since no one is up to choosing a better word or to figuring it out, a "starter." Something false and contrary to all feelings and thoughts, but at the same time most truthful to the present moment, was coming out, breaking through the shell. Something that had been pushed away in the constant fear of oneself and of one's weakness to cope, something carefully kept from others and even more from oneself, something that was oppressed by the solidity of what was generally acceptable in this or that circle and never decided by the individual at all, and because of this was constantly sticking out, crawling out—and there was a sweetness in that. And arranging to have a drink together, as if with nothing in mind—but all for that. And there is a necessity for this and a sort of a regulating organization which even has an order and a sequence. And no one would ask himself "why?"—it would sound indecent, tawdry, even unfair. Just for fun, a drink among friends, a "starter"... Here one would shrug his shoulders, as it were, close his eyes—and go. "So what, so what?"—one would repeat senselessly. And a princely feeling of "everything-is-possible" would suddenly start flowing from one to the other, enveloping everyone, and the morning after everyone would part quietly, but with scurrying eyes.

This whole mechanism of "starting" held so little mystery for Monakhov that it was becoming an even greater mystery. The current was already established, it was mutual—both he and Asya felt this immediately, immediately allowing themselves to, and the current grew and intensified from the exchange. And suddenly they fell silent, as if everything had been agreed on. They were silent for a while as if resting—the way one inhales a cigarette, and then continued the conversation without looking at each other, in that tone of new intimacy and distance after intimacy which they could not have allowed themselves right away.

"And how is your doctoral candidate?" Monakhov asked with that eternally stupid satisfaction in his voice born of an imagined superiority over another man, if his woman happens to be next to you.

"We're separating," Asya said lightly.

Somewhere, like distant shadows, the memory of the past still remained in Monakhov: of the hatred toward this man and of the pain. The feeling of satisfaction that any moment now everything will happen, and that he will be taking a woman from "the other" as at a different time the other had taken her from him, would have been all the stronger—but this piece of news had two sides. First of all, he found out that Asya had been with "that guy" all this time, and that bothered something that had been in him in the past, it still seemed to matter to him, and it would have been better if it had been someone else who had not appeared during his, Monakhov's time, but during the other's. Second of all, if she was still with him after all this time, perhaps it would be better if she didn't leave him, but stayed—he loved her so. And then all this would happen—a minor victory, like writing in a back date, or like forging a signature.

"So you've been with him all this time?" unable to hide his disappointment, he looked out the window: he had already missed his stop.

"And you're still jealous?" Asya laughed again, and her laughter now seemed lifeless and clinking to Monakhov, though the crude exactness of the question surprised him. As a person who was so far beyond the primary source of his thought that he no longer saw its goal, nor its point of departure, just the eternal middle, the desert, the straightforward flight over that whole sea of reason and the outright naming of the thing he could no longer discern beneath the detail surprised him...

Monakhov was silent in surprise. Asya said:

"Our daughter will already be going to school next year."

"Imagine that," said Monakhov, repeating her sentence to himself and senselessly moving the word "already" around in it which calmly fitted anywhere in the phrase, finally making it collapse. "So you managed to marry him anyway? I thought he would never agree to that..."

"What do you mean! He begged me to..." Asya said.

"So he convinced you," said Monakhov.

"Well, no, I actually wanted to myself," she said.

"Yes," said Monakhov.

"And you," Asya asked, her eye taking aim again, "any children?..."

Monakhov started slightly and became thoughtful.

"No..." he smiled uncertainly.

Asya smiled.

"But are you married?"

"Yes, I am," he said, still thinking. For some reason it seemed that although her being married was quite all right with him, he himself ought to have been free somehow.

"So you're lost to women, then. It's a shame," Asya said.

"How should I put it..." Monakhov straightened out, puffed up and fussed in his chair. "Depends for whom...For you, no..." he finally said, exhaling noisily.

"You blushed! You blushed!" Asya laughed. "Still the same baby!"

"I am a young colt, high strung and proud..." Monakhov sang. And they both laughed and begun to talk animatedly, though Monakhov still could not remember what about. "Why is it" he wondered uncomfortably, "that the moment I begin to behave in a way that in my estimation is not at all childish, women say that I am a child?" and he slightly turned his grey temple to Asya. They kept laughing and talking animatedly, interrupting each other and retaining nothing; the blurred spots of faces swam and jumped—he was no longer embarrassed by the bus—and he floated weightlessly above everyone.

"We have to get off," Asya said suddenly. "We," Monakhov thought.

They were already on the islands... On both sides of the street the old trees stood free, without fences, already almost naked. A run-down yellow house appeared somewhere behind them—they were walking down the street which curved, connecting one bridge with another. And Asya asked:

"Well, and your wife, what is she like?"

"What do you mean, what is she like?" Monakhov was somewhat dumbfounded.

"Beautiful?"

"Yes, probably," Monakhov replied, unwillingly.

"Does she look like me?" Asya asked and made a face. It did not suit her.

Monakhov turned away from the face thinking of an answer, trying to remember what she was like, his wife, in a couple of words, and suddenly got excited by an unexpected discovery, which had never occurred to him before.

"Imagine," he exclaimed, "how strange... She is the complete opposite of you. As if chosen on purpose," he laughed and caught himself. "Imagine a woman, as beautiful as you," he said diplomatically, "but the complete opposite of you: in height, in body, in voice and type..."

"The impression is of something very large?" Asya said, and this time her intonation really worked, and Monakhov laughed and suddenly remembered the Asya he loved: before, too, not often, she would come up with a good phrase. He suddenly remembered Asya's closeness; desire, almost desperately, arose in him.

"And in temperament," he added, depressed, again surprised that everything was opposite, even bed, and that there was something to this, it was not just without rhyme or reason. "How is it that everything is inevitably connected, in order to be whole..." he thought. "So as not to fall apart."

"And you live with your Mama, of course?" Here Monakhov again remembered the whole Asya, the way she said "m-mama," the Asya whom he had feared at one time, and perhaps did not even love, but wanted even more than the Asya he loved.

"This feeling hasn't weakened in you with years, I see," he added.

"Oh, yes! And how does she get along with her?"

Monakhov noted this "she with her" as an unwillingness to name either one, catching in this and in the tone some jealousy, which flattered him.

"Very well," he said, convinced, though he had no basis to be, and glanced at Asya sideways to see how she would take it.

Asya took it with extreme indifference and seemed to be thinking about something else.

"So we can't go to your place," she said.

Monakhov missed a breath.

Asya glanced at him and burst out laughing.

"You're still the same!"

Monakhov made an undecided motion with his hands.

They reached a red church and Asya stopped.

"Don't walk me any further."

"Why not?" Monakhov said, hurt.

"Simply because someone's waiting for me at the bus stop." She looked at Monakhov's miserable face and laughed happily. "Yes, waiting."

"Your husband?"

"No, my fiancé."

"Listen, aren't you tired yet? Are you getting married again?"

"What can I do..." Asya sighed, sincerely.

"How much energy you have!" Monakhov said, almost with admiration.

"I get tired..." she said simply.

"You have a room, a good salary... You should have a rest..."

"Oh, with pleasure!" Asya smiled tiredly and winked to Monakhov. Her wink did not come out right. Monakhov felt uncomfortable.

"Is he a nice guy at least?" he asked.

"Want to see?" Asya said. "I'll go ahead. You follow me, as if you were a stranger. In the evening you can tell me how you liked him. O.K.?" Asya asked, excited and insistent.

"All right," said Monakhov. This "you'll tell me in the evening" cheered him up a lot. He didn't really expect that everything would turn out quite so easy.

Asya went ahead. He waited and then followed her. Coming up to the bus stop Asya stole up behind a tall man standing at the end of the line and, jumping up, grabbed him from behind, and hung on him. Her rippling laughter, and the way she jumped up from behind and embraced the stranger was so exactly familiar to Monakhov and hadn't changed a bit. She, short, stood on her toes, he, tall, bent down giving her his cheek, and they began an animated conversation, still holding hands. Monakhov felt a strange shift in his brain, he so clearly remembered himself as this tall man now. "Who is he? Who is Asya? Who am I?" he thought strangely and looked at them somehow sideways, slightly tilting his head, like a chicken. There was a light ringing in his head. "She shouldn't..." he thought, but this was not about the tall one, but about himself, it was himself he felt sorry for, not yet knowing why. "I shouldn't have known this..." he thought. "One shouldn't know anything about anyone," he thought with irritation, suddenly imagining his wife, who could have come up to him just like that, leaving a tall one, let's say, around the corner. "Damn it!" Monakhov said through his teeth, but had already come up to them, looking over the face of the tall one carefully. Monakhov liked his face and felt sorry for him. There was, however, some vanity in this. The tall one suddenly picked up his face from Asya and looked into Monakhov's eyes, carefully and kindly, and Asya had a chance to wink to Monakhov at that moment. The tall man bent down to Asya again and Monakhov was already past them, trying not to look back, feeling his skin tighten on his back into a restless, shivering fold. He walked on, feeling the paper with a phone number on it in his pocket, he was supposed to call her in two hours, and felt a mixture of satisfaction and unpleasantness. "Here you are..." he thought, self-satisfied and sad. "The roles are reversed... No, that was no role then!... There's a lot to think about in all this..."

"And do you remember? And remember when...?" fragments of the bus conversation caught up with him. He didn't remember. Rather, everything that he remembered was exactly what she didn't remember. He wandered aimlessly now along the street, not seeing anything, in consternation going over pieces of their conversation. This is what shook him: it turned out all these years Asya had kept (hiding them from her husband?) and reread his, Alyosha's, letters. "You wrote wonderful letters!..." Monakhov flushed, uncomfortable that the childishness of his words remained on paper. He didn't remember them. She knew them by heart. "Don't be silly, I didn't know how to put two words together in those days..." "You did, you did!"

But in this embarrassment it wasn't altogether clear who was ashamed of whom. This Monakhov of that one—or that Alyosha of this one? Was Monakhov uncomfortable because of Asya's excessive sentimentality (which he hadn't expected) or because of his own failing? After all, he was the one who had loved her, she didn't love him, and what happened...? He had been sure at the time that he wouldn't survive it—but his death passed, like a disease, as if it had never been. But for her, it turned out, all this had actually been part of her life. Almost the only thing in it. Of course, that was an exaggeration, a trap... but with all her insincerity, Monakhov for some reason believed in his letters. She was the one who had betrayed him, yet he was the one who turned out to be unfaithful now. He was amazed by the faithfulness of his betrayer.

"Isn't that something! Never met once in ten years—how people disappear! Perhaps it's the ten years that have disappeared?" Monakhov was thinking when he suddenly came to the hospital. He checked up on his wife's health: everything was all right, her blood pressure was down and she would be released soon, so that she could spend the rest of her term at home. He wrote his wife a letter; the words did not come to him, and he could not remember anything to write about. When already quite far from the hospital, he remembered that he had been rushing to his wife to share the happy news of his morning success.

Mother was baking a cake and circulating through the corridor, from the room to the kitchen and the kitchen to the room, constantly forgetting and then remembering something. It was impossible for Monakhov to be alone with the telephone. Suddenly, to his surprise, he discovered that he was nervous. He felt just as he had ten years ago, perhaps as bit duller, but the same. His feelings turned into a sidepath, overgrown but amazingly familiar. In this sense he seemed to become ten years younger. What was worse was that, unable to feel anything for long, he recognized this almost immediately. In any case, he buttoned his coat, mumbling inaudibly about cigarettes that had run out, and, experiencing a satisfaction mixed with agitation, he ran out on the street.

In the phone booth, having dialed the number and waiting for the ring, he became really agitated, without observing himself: what if she was not there or if the number was wrong... time stopped for a moment and he started, hearing an unexpected voice and, already surmising that it was Asya, asked just in case: "Is Agnessa Mikhailovna there?"

"It's me, silly. Come over," said Asya.

The kindergarten which Asya ran was situated on the outskirts of the city, in a new part of town. Monakhov was standing up straighter and his step was becoming progressively more sprightly as he approached his destination. He asked for directions with assurance, easily understood the explanations, and found the way readily. At some moment he caught himself and felt unintelligent. "Does the victor have to be stupid?" he thought, but at the same time was happy with this stupidity, almost congratulating himself for it: "But how much more assured I feel," he said to himself with a half-smile.

There was a yellowish house in a park surrounded by a fence. The park was empty. Monakhov crossed a trampled-down lawn in front of the house, passing by the little mound and the mushroom and the empty swan decisively, as if he were walking in a crowd, not looking at anyone, but everyone was stopping and turning around to look at him with admiration. He felt taller than he was. He was growing very fast as he approached the door; the hall and the stairway were already small for him—this seemed natural for a kindergarten—a kind smile appeared on Monakhov's face as he was going up the stairs, ready to pause on the way to pat the head of a kid who would run up to him, but all was quiet and empty. All the noise was only the noise of

Monakhov's blood. Opening the door with the plaque "Administrator," Monakhov was already so tall that he bent slightly so as not to hit the doorway.

Asya met him in a very businesslike manner, hardly looking at him. Monakhov immediately went back to his proper height, which happened somewhat abruptly, so that he felt humiliated, and the low chair was unexpectedly deep and Asya towered over him at the table—his rejuvenation receded. Asya was carefully copying from a notebook. Monakhov read the heading: "Work Plan." Asya underlined it in red pencil with a ruler... Monakhov wanted to make a joke about a kindergarten work plan but didn't. He just kept sitting quietly. The chair was uncomfortable.

The phone rang. "Dearie," Asya laughed. Monakhov sat back, pressing himself into the chair, looking at Asya from a distance, feeling estranged. Asya was arranging to go for a fitting: "Don't offer it to anyone else. We'll come over." Asya laughed her ringing laugh, as if the laughter were separated from herself: "No, no, you don't know who!"—and winked to Monakhov.

She hung up, ran out from behind the table and sat on Monakhov's knees. Kissed him. Laughed. He tried to kiss her, in turn, but she slipped away.

"Just a second, Alyosha. One more phone call," she said, feeling harrassed.

It was a business call. Monakhov listened to Asya and was a bit surprised. "This is shocking!" she said. "But the children are freezing!" She began unbuttoning her uniform. Under the uniform was a slip. Monakhov did not expect this. Asya caught his eye, looked at her breast and suddenly looked at Monakhov so frankly and honestly that Monakhov skipped a breath. "What do I care!" she yelled at the same time. "You want trouble? You'll get it tomorrow," and she threw down the receiver.

The tone in which she spoke on the telephone, and the look she threw him flattered Monakhov immensely, although he couldn't have told himself why.

Asya went to the cupboard, throwing her uniform off on the way, putting on her blouse, saying "do me up," offering her back. Monakhov carefully pulled up the zipper. A teacher came in. Monakhov remained sitting in the same chair, but it was already as if something mysterious had happened in this room: his position was the same, but while earlier it was uncomfortable, now it was nonchalant. He listened to the conversation condescendingly. The teacher, a whitish girl, was saying something fast with an accent, looking up at Monakhov absentmindedly with either curiosity or lust, which also flattered him. Suddenly noticing that Asya was looking at him knowingly, he got embarrassed and turned away. The teacher got confused. "All right, Nastya, you may go," Asya said.

When they came out of the kindergarten into the park, they saw two men carefully sitting on a bench, eating and drinking. Monakhov was moved by this peaceful picture and said to Asya:

"Shall we have a drink somewhere?"

"I'm not supposed to drink."

Once again Monakhov had the sinking feeling of a presentiment of defeat.

And as time went on, Monakhov at times had no understanding at all of what was going on. He pushed his way behind Asya through stores, banging strangers' legs with her bag. Asya would become so distant in the store that he was reminded of the ten-year-old feeling of accompanying her just like this, and although now he was not suffering and was independent of her, he felt disconcerted seeing such a complete absence of himself in her. There was on her face one of the few expressions she could not control, when she was touching things—steady, tenacious, completely absorbed. It was so strange and unlike her that not only the Monakhov in love, but the present one felt uncomfortable. It was as if all of her were exposed, her head included, as if her wig had been torn off, and this face she didn't control had to be, with fear, acknowledged as the true one. And when, leaving a counter, she would turn to Monakhov trying on her previous face, putting on a hurried half-smile, carelessly, her two faces would not quite match for some split second, and the eyebrow of one would get the eye of the other, and the lips would be on one cheek. Then Monakhov felt as if she were holding a mask on a stick in each hand and was a bit confused as to which one to put on, but then she was already hurrying to another department, for shoes.

They bought shoes, which Asya put on immediately.

She was happy, cuddling up to Monakhov, looking him in the eyes, laughing and chirping: he began to feel warm, pleasantly embarrassed, and it felt as if it was he who had bought her the shoes.

He visited someone on business with her. A thin, dark-faced woman with grey unkempt hair in an unclean dressing gown embroidered with crysanthemums gave her rough hand, introducing herself as "Tosya." Asya would begin from a vague point. At first Monakhov did not understand, and then got tired of trying to. The woman smoked nervously but it was simply her habit, because she was not at all nervous—it was Asya who was nervous. They shifted to a half-whisper, and later disappeared altogether into the next room. Monakhov leafed through the magazine "The Bulgarian Woman." Asya's voice was becoming excitedly loud through the wall, but the words could not be distinguished. Monakhov closed the journal. On the cover there was a famous woman tobacco picker, and so it occurred to him to smoke.

Asya came out, obviously after an argument.

"Let's go," she snapped at Monakhov.

"Give me a light," she said, stopping on the landing on the floor below. She took a greedy puff.

"What happened?" Monakhov asked in a thick voice and was startled that he didn't care at all what had happened there and moreover that he didn't even want to know.

Asya looked at him attentively as if shaking it all off, and smiled bravely.

"It's all right. Let's go," she said. "Let's go to my friend's, remember, the one I talked to on the phone."

They went on, silent. Monakhov submitted himself dumbly and passively to being led. He didn't care where to and did not notice the route. He was waiting apathetically for someting he did not want to name to himself concretely, i.e., it was quite obvious, he was waiting, understanding with certainty, though he didn't know where or when, that all this could not end simply. But Asya had definitely taken the initiative at some point, and he retreated into parasitism, leaving all the arrangements of how, when, and where to her, and only thought that it used to be reversed... "If someone has to grab the heavy end, the one who grabs it first gets it," he thought metaphorically, thinking suddenly becoming difficult.

On the stairs Asya stopped him. Quickly and in a businesslike way she gave him a wet smack on the cheek...

"You wait here," she said. "I'll arrange it with her first, explain everything, and then come get you."

Monakhov remained, thinking over the "arrange" and "explain." Asya had disappeared with happy exclamations.

He sat down on the radiator. It was cold. "Of course, the heat isn't on yet..." he thought slowly. "It isn't winter yet..." He was chilly and it suddenly seemed that he had been waiting for a very long time. For years. People would come up the stairs, looking him over, and disappear into their burrows. Monakhov was not bothered or embarrassed by these glances, or by their thinking he was waiting for someone like a young boy. "That's the trouble, I'm not a boy any more..." he thought, feeling neither quite serious, nor sad. Before he always thought that everyone knew everything about him and that they all wanted nothing more than to read his soul. Now these looks no longer bothered him. These weren't the same looks as before. In the end it was perhaps because he had simply got used to peoples' looks, for now he knew how little they cared whether he existed, or didn't—and in peoples' looks he saw mainly indifference to him, Monakhov. "And what's there to be interested in..." he thought.

He began to smoke. He suddenly felt dizzy. This sensation was exactly the same as when he first began to smoke. For a second he felt very young. "That must be from hunger," he realized immediately. "I haven't eaten since morning," he thought with boredom. "Yes, everything repeats itself..." he thought sadly. "All situations are identical. Like prints. On the dot. Just paler. Or like when the record gets stuck. Everything is the same, only the sound gets worse with every turn. The scratches, the cracks... Everything is the same, only we are different..."

He sadly looked at the door behind which Asya had disappeared. When will she finally come get him? He didn't want anything any longer, just to warm up, to be given some tea at least... "And anyway, did I really want it?..." Monakhov thought suddenly. "Perhaps I should just leave?" But he kept waiting.

And he kept thinking how everything was the same... That there she was making him wait again, arranging complicated meetings, dragging him along after her on a complicated itinerary and schedule—all the same, but not the same. He did not suffer from it, not a bit, not like before. "I accept her independent existence, separate from mine, I agree with it. I am simply... indifferent..."

Monakhov dozed off. He dreamed of the hospital. He shook his head and saw Asya before him. She laughed a staccato laugh.

"Well, let's go," she said decisively.

Monakhov stood up, his feet, asleep, felt like someone else's. Asya took his arm, but instead of taking him upstairs, she led him downstairs. He looked at Asya's friend's door questioningly.

"Can't go to her place today," she said.

Here time again disappeared.

He heard a long inhuman cry, but for some reason it was not frightening. Strangely distant and close at the same time. Somehow he was not surprised at the cry and came to by the candy factory. He could tell this by the nauseating sweet smell which brought him back to reality. The street was deserted, the street lights were burning and it was already nighttime. They walked on and the soles of his feet burned. This was a distant suburban neighborhood, and then Monakhov understood that they had crossed the whole city on foot. They stopped every other minute and kissed long and passionately. Monakhov's hand was embracing Asya's neck, and the other one surprised him very much: it was under Asya's coat, under her dress, under her slip. He was touching her breast which had changed a lot over these years, it was too soft. He wasn't comfortable walking this way but he could not suddenly pull back his hand which he so strangely and suddenly discovered, right on the street just like that. He couldn't understand anything. A street cleaner looked out from a doorway. Asya jumped away from him and laughed like a girl. Monakhov shook his freed hand and laughed idiotically. They started running.

"Let's go this way," she said.

Along the park's central walk the lights were still on and there were still some people around. Monakhov realized that it was not that late yet. And only then it occurred to him to look at his watch—it wasn't even eleven yet, he put it to his ear—no, it was running. There were some couples on the walk, a few—they seemed to slip out from the dark little paths, squinting at the light and disappearing again; the other people, careworn and rushed, had but one goal—the train; the shortcut went through the park. One of them, dark, as if made only of shadows, asked Monakhov for a smoke, and then Monakhov realized that he hadn't smoked for a long time and looking at his lady with pleasure, certainty and self-satisfaction, he, too, lit a cigarette. Today he understood everything only with the help of others: the time, the place and his own desires—he could no longer figure it out by himself.

The path continued downhill and a cool breeze appeared. The air seemed fresh to Monakhov. He inhaled it too deeply and became sentimental.

"It's as if nothing has changed... I haven't walked like this for ten years. As if no time had passed..."

"Yes, we still have no place to go," Asya said.

Monakhov, overflowing, tried to pull Asya towards him again, but she evaded him.

"Let's sit down and have a smoke instead," she said.

Here, by the pond, it was completely dark. Monakhov sat silently and as if separately for some time, wooden from his interrupted motion. The darkness and the quiet which surrounded him when they sat down was now filled with rustle and splashing; something large and awkward was tossing and turning in the bushes not in one place, but as if jumping about, getting comfortable, and flying up again, it seemed like an inflated mattress cover to Monakhov.

"I didn't tell you," said Asya "there are muggers here... It's dangerous at night... Not long ago an eleven-year-old girl was raped and killed here..." Asya giggled again and Monakhov thought that she moved away; he heaved forward, falling on Asya awkwardly and heavily.

"Don't," she said and got up, deftly slipping out of his empty hands. She stood over him as he remained half-lying, propped on his elbow, watching her pull down her hitched-up skirt. Her knee, on his eye level, seemed like a little face to him; he looked at the vague spot of Asya's face and was amazed at the similarity.

"Get up, get up," Asya said.

Monakhov got up dumbly. Asya walked ahead, he followed, feeling awkward.

"This is the shortest way," said Asya.

Monakhov no longer asked himself, the shortest way to what.

"Here we are," said Asya.

Monakhov was standing in front of a two-story house. There were no lights in the windows. The park around the house was dark, and in front of the house a strong light was burning on a lonely lampost. Its light fell in a broad cone and lit the little hill and the empty swan which seemed black; the edge of the light lit the half-window below the first floor.

"Whence they departed, thither have they returned," Monakhov said with an intonation he himself did not understand.

"You wait here," said Asya. She bent her leg, took off her shoe as if shaking out a stone, and handed it to Monakhov. He took it mechanically. She was standing on one foot, but he didn't understand. Then she handed him the other shoe. Monakhov stood there holding the shoes out in front of him, one in each hand. Asya now became shorter than he and, because of this, somehow more defenseless and closer. She was the old Asya to him now, the one he knew once—of course, they didn't wear high heels then...

"Stay here," she said.

He watched her cross the lit-up spot and approach the house. She was walking in stockinged feet across the rough sand in front of the house and Monakhov's toes curled under in his shoes: at her every step he felt the sand piercing her. Her legs became sort of short and fat, he now recognized them as she walked awkwardly, and caught her skirt on the swan's beak. Monakhov felt pounding in his throat and his eyes clouded over. "She doesn't even mind ruining her stockings..." he thought. Asya came up to the door, put her ear to it. And only then did Monakhov realize that she could have taken her shoes off at the door, that there was no reason for her to have walked barefoot across the whole front yard. He made an involuntary gesture, as if handing her shoes over and even opened his mouth, attempting to say something, but remained standing just as he was. Asya pulled at the door, tried some key. It was, apparently, the wrong one. Monakhov saw Asya bend over to pass under the windows, stealthily move along the wall and stop at the iron fire-escape ladder, brush off one foot with her hand, and place it on the iron rod, the first step, then brush off her other foot and slowly climb up. Her feet bent at every step, almost embracing the rod, and just as he felt the sand piercing her before, Monakhov now felt the cold iron under her feet. Asya crossed the line of light and was now in the dark. Monakhov perceived the now slow and heavy dark spot. A sharp and tearful feeling overtook him. "Yes," he thought in admiration and amazement. "A director... Not for nothing... It wasn't for nothing that I felt that way then... It was just this that I loved in her...," he thought, following the dark spot, guessing Asya in it and swallowing the nervous lump in his throat. He discerned her standing on the windowsill, pulling on the window frame which would not give. Monakhov held his breath, a boyish anxiety and fear were bursting inside him. Suddenly he heard the crackling and ringing of falling glass. Asya swore out loud. Three windows below lit up at once. Monakhov stood still, neither dead nor alive. When he raised his eyes again to where Asya had just been standing on the windowsill, she was no longer there. He heard voices in the quiet house, as if cheering themselves up, the light went on on the second floor as well. Then the voices became muffled and the light went out upstairs.

    Monakhov stood under the bush, tensely observing the house, holding Asya's shoes awkwardly in front of him. But in this quiet he discerned only the rustle of the pine behind his back, and he suddenly shrank and wilted and began to shiver, again remembering that he hadn't eaten the whole day, and shivered again.

    It suddenly seemed to be dawn to him, he realized that time had passed but did not know how much, though he felt that he had been standing under the bush with the shoes in his hands for an eternity. The house again was blind and dumb.

    Breathless with courage, he stepped out of the bushes. He stood for a moment, looking around. In small steps, holding the hand with the shoes in front of him, as if following them, he tottered across the front lawn and stood under the mushroom, staring intently at the dark windows. He stood for a long time under the mushroom before he decided—and here again, a childish and joyful feeling of danger and fear overtook him—to run over to the door. He put his ear to it but heard nothing. Just something ticking inside. The "inside" seemed dark and thick as a brew to him, ticking like a mine. Something squeaked loudly, Monakhov's heart jumped up loudly and stopped somewhere without beating. He jumped away from the door and pressed himself to the wall. But it was nothing—he just imagined it, it was quiet again. No longer aware of what he was doing, as Asya had before, he stole over to the fire-escape ladder and had already raised his foot to the step... "Alyosha..." he heard the hissing whisper, started, caught, and saw Asya on the threshold of the open doorway—she was motioning him in. Awkwardly and almost guiltily, he went back, and Asya grabbed his hand, hard and painfully, pulling him inside, into the dark. In the dark he kept shoving her shoes to her for some reason, while she kept impatiently and brusquely nudging him forward; one shoe he dropped and that seemed to him to fill the whole house with a terrible crash. Asya shushed him fiercely. "Don't trip," she said, "there's a step here." And he tripped. "Agnessa Mikhaylovna, is that you?" a distant voice asked. "Yes, it's me!" Asya answered angrily, rushing abruptly down the corridor and somewhat upward, dragging Monakhov behind her and roughly squeezing his hand. She pushed him into some room. "Sit quietly and wait," she said and closed the door on him. A light went on behind the door and came in through the crack. Someone called Asya, she answered cheerfully and brightly, and both voices, talking animatedly, hurried off.

Monakhov looked around. It was a large room with many windows. The windows looked out on two sides, and some light was coming through them. The diagonal and ghost-like shadows of the transoms fell on the floor. Large rubber plants darkened the corners. Small chairs lined the walls in rows. In the center there was a large ship with little flags, and two rocking horses stood nose to nose with one another. On the whole, the room was somehow very empty and tidy. This was, as Monakhov gathered, the playroom.

Trying not to make any noise, even a squeak, Monakhov took three heavy steps and lowered himself weightily onto a small chair by the wall. He stared at the small crack of light under the door and listened. Having sat down, he felt his fatigue. He stared dumbly at the ghostly, flickering windows for some time and thought of nothing. His eyes could now see well in the dark. He even saw a portrait on the wall and made out Lenin in it, when the door opened a bit, the light came in seeking out Monakhov, and Asya slipped into the room. She was wearing a smock. "You're alive?" she said, laughing. Her face was somewhat wild and beautiful. "Alive," he said. Asya embraced him impulsively, youthfully, awkwardly pressing his head to her breast and stood still for a second in this awkward pose. Monakhov's neck was uncomfortable and he had trouble breathing. He was getting stiff in her embrace and felt nothing. Asya suddenly moved away and crouched in front of him. "What's the matter?" she said, holding his head in her hands, as if turning it and looking it over. "What's the matter with you?" Monakhov was silent. "All right," she said, "Sit here a little longer. I'll be right back." She stood up sharply. "Here," she shoved something into his hand and went out. It was two small, wormy apples, with rough black dots on them. Monakhov, puzzled, turned them in his hands. "Eve," he said. "Adam..." He bit into an apple—he thought the crunch must have echoed all over this dead house. Somewhere below him, above him, on all sides, there were children sleeping, like larvae. Monakhov placed these children in the space beyond his shoulders, but for him they were inanimate. "They had these little apples for desert today..." he thought. He felt that he did not want or expect anything, and he felt disgusted with himself. He somehow understood Asya and thought her beautiful, but he did not like himself at all, because he thought he should now be in a stormy state of emotions and desire, otherwise why should he be here, in the middle of the night, in a sleeping nursery school, in the playroom? What else could have brought him here, a mature, respectable man, with a family and position? He thought all this was some nightmarish trick, a counterfeit of all desires, feelings, thoughts, because the moment we realize that we want something, we no longer want it, but only want it as long as we do not understand what is going on. That desire is not desire in the sense that it can be told about and explained, but something quite different. That desire gets lost somewhere on the way, if not at the first step... And what lies have been told about the power of desire and emotion, based on deeds accompanying them, though they bear witness to something quite different, to our inability to cope with them... and the irrationality itself—it's not from strength, but from the vagueness and opaqueness of our sensations... The truth of any generalization frightened him.

With a shaken glance, Monakhov took in the volume of the room he was in, and it seemed surprisingly fitting for him, both deserved and justified in its improbability. Only the unlikely should happen to me now, because I am not real. I don't even have dreams any more, only fragments of objects and faces flash by before falling asleep—that's all. Because why do I need the unreality of dream, when I myself am so unreal already. Not in time, nor in space, nor in relation to any one body in this world... He thought then that that which we usually mean by real or unreal should change places.

When, in childhood, feelings were real—people were unreal: they were vehicles, objects, they were—images. When experience lent reality to the people in our eyes: there they are before us, objective as they are, having volume, unjudgeable—then feelings became unreal. Now feeling became an image, the image of feeling. There is no feeling, only the image of feeling, no love—but the image of love, no betrayal—but the image of betrayal, of friendship, of labor, or work, etc. And a person with experience could make even less sense out of this world than a child, he became even more confused in it because of the unreality of his own emotions. He began to have a choice where before the feeling allowed none: to like—not to like, to do—not to do, to act—not to act... And both variants, with experience, suddenly became identical, equivalent: equally good, or equally bad, or equally indifferent—to leave, or to stay, they'll come or they won't, to sleep with someone or not... Realization threatens emptiness and disillusionment, and then all that did not take place, that did not happen, or did not exist brings almost a satisfaction, hardly justified by the conservation of energy and of other possibilities—those last resources.

As in a snowstorm.

You have been wandering for a long time, you're tired, it is suddenly getting dark. Neither time nor direction exists. Where did you come from and where are you going? You can no longer see the womb-stove, and can not see the goal yet either. The middle. It is howling. Swirling. The maelstrom. Sleep is taking over. And the fear suddenly disappears. You feel warm and indifferent. Into the snow drift—and to sleep...

The same sudden shriek woke Monakhov. It was incomprehensibly near and distant at the same time. As if Monakhov were screaming to himself from afar... Again, Monakhov was not surprised by the scream, but continued his thoughts, now more concretely and more lazily, as if he were riding somewhere and feeling queasy...

How painful is experience, not its acquisition, nor its birth, no—experience itself, its presence. What a mess! We all fell apart at some point, when we began to relate ourselves to the world... This, indeed, was experience.

Thus he thought, crunching the apple, and it resounded as he chewed on it, resounded in his head, like a rockfall, and only gradually, through auto-suggestion, did he convince himself that this was not a general crash which makes everyone wake up and jump out of bed running with screams of terror and amazement, but his own small inner crash, in a total, dense silence.

> And in the silence of near-collapse.
> On little chairs we sit all night...

He remembered the lines which always moved him and which he had always liked for their incomprehensibility. And suddenly a cold rapture of understanding, of complete understanding of these lines struck him. Wasn't that something! No matter how distant, strange and unusual the image, it was always absolutely concrete, not only exact but actually extraordinarily related to objects. Here he is, Monakhov, sitting on a little chair, in just this kind of silence, in the silence of near-collapse... A-ma-zing! It's about him, exactly, just like him—he thought with an obliterating enthusiasm, and tears came to his eyes, he was afraid to blink them off, they were few, they filled his eyes and stopped there, although he so much wanted to cry uncontrollably, sobbing, but no longer could, it was already interrupted, and he could only prolong them in his eyes, two large sweet tears, afraid to blink...

A child cried upstairs. Monakhov even looked up at the ceiling, and the tears rolled down. Voices resounded again, excited, they augmented, approaching. One of them was Asya's, reassuring, another, suspicious, was unpleasantly simple. Monakhov was no longer frightened, he did not freeze, his heart did not skip—his heart was beating evenly and even if he were arrested and led away handcuffed now, he probably wouldn't protest.

But Asya persuaded the foot steps, and the voices began to move away, and something evaporated and disappeared in Monakhov, like a cloud. He looked out the windows calmly—they seemed brighter, perhaps—the chairs and horses emerged from the corners, losing in mysteriousness, becoming simply dull, worn out. He felt expectant, as if he were feverish, in the clinic, waiting to get a leave of absence, waiting with that emptiness and apathy of a coming flu in order to leave after all the unnecesary checkups and reports to go lie down quietly and try to fall asleep. For the first time, probably, during the day, that fear of home, of a late return and explanations, arose in him. True, his wife was in the hospital, but then he ought to feel all the more distressed and ashamed—but he chased away this flutter of conscience. He also pushed away the foreboding of having to pay for this, and even thought: what for, and what sort of payment could there be? He could not simply explain any of this truthfully to anyone... Well, he can make up something: his wife was in the hospital, and his mother won't betray him... He winced at such considerations, but his disquiet grew, and the worry of how all this would end and settle down circled above him, coming lower and lower.

And when Asya came in again, they looked at each other, in this pre-dawn institutional and unmysterious room, as if from afar, as strangers. And only for a second did Monakhov mind that for Asya too it was all over, but he immediately agreed with her in his mind and it was even more comfortable and quicker this way.

"You know," Asya said apathetically, "one bitch there suspected something... You'll have to leave now. She'll get it from me!" Suddenly, emotion appeared in Asya's voice. "I've been wanting to fire her for a long time... So come on, we have to get out quickly, before she sticks her head out again. I stuck her in the pantry..."

"What do you mean?" Monakhov asked with indifference.

"Just sent her in there... Well, go on..."

So they went, and the way seemed much shorter than before. At the door Asya said indifferently:

"Well, will you call?"

Monakhov hesitated to answer.

Then, for a second, Asya's gaze became deep and attentive, a sad flicker of fatigued expectation flashed in it and died.

"I'll call," Monakhov mumbled.

"Do call, O.K.?" she suddenly whispered clearly and desperately. "Be sure to call! Do you hear? We'll go to my girlfriend's..."

"I'll call for sure..." Monakhov said.

Then the door closed behind him, and he went across the front lawn with dignity, controlling the inner urge to run, and when he turned at the bush, where for a second he saw himself standing with the shoes in his hands, he took a deep breath and began to run. He ran through the park, whose dark trees were already getting lighter, ran as if someone were chasing him, and he even really thought he saw bandits and muggers who were about to stop and murder him. "They'd be right, they'd be right," he kept saying to himself as he ran. And only when he ran out of the park, bumping into a sleepless policeman, who looked at him uncertainly: should he stop him or not?—only then, as if stumbling, he began to walk, breathing heavily. From around the corner, screeching, a service street car appeared which was going his way, and surprising himself by his nerve and quickness, Monakhov smiled and winked at the policeman and jumped on the step. The policeman just shook his fist at him—that was all.

Monakhov was going home, and he felt better. He was shaking on the bridge, emerging from the steam at dawn, and he looked at the world with pleasure. And what could have seemed like an unfortunate adventure suddenly pleased and even cheered him, almost filling him with satisfaction. "What luck," he thought, "that nothing happened." He was so pleased that he had not attained the goal that had so possessed him today, that this accidental continence and unexpected purity almost began to seem like a personal achievement, a conquered temptation and a confirmation of his high moral qualities. "Nothing happened, nothing happened," he kept repeating to himself, and only for a moment it flashed through him that this "nothing" contained something hopeless and final, and that there was nothing to be proud of...but he quickly went on to the consideration of what to tell his mother, and nothing came to mind. "I am tired of lying, I don't want to any more," he thought almost smugly, adding this inability to come up with an excuse to the continence he had managed today. "How would I go to the hospital, how would I look her in the eye..." he thought with satisfaction. And he was filled with satisfaction with himself, with his wife, with the life that didn't really work and disintegrated every day, but somehow worked in the sum of these days. Still, he really should think up something, he remembered, jumping off the street car. He was quite near the house now, and it suddenly dawned on him that he didn't have to make anything up, that he could tell it all as it had happened. Almost all. And if it had happened..."I couldn't have," he thought.

"Well, maybe I will call her yet..." he thought, feeling quite at ease now, and putting on a cheerful and brazen air as he went up the stairs. "Maybe we'll meet again..."

While he fidgeted at the door, getting out the key, looking for the keyhole, the door suddenly opened and on the threshold stood his mother, disheveled and sleepless.

"It's you?" she said coldly.

"It's me," Monakhov said, looking down, and his cheerfulness deserted him.

His mother, walking backwards, retreated into the hallway, and Monakhov followed her timidly, carefully closing the door behind him, trying not to make any noise. He was afraid to raise his eyes, knowing the look now directed at him, its coldness and the pursed lips.

His mother stopped backing up and Monakhov stood still before her.

"Where in the world were you?" she said.

Monakhov was silent, feeling a coldness and ruthlessness growing in him.

"A boy..." Mother suddenly sobbed, and Monakhov, amazed and frightened, began to raise his eyes slowly, "A boy..." she sobbed, embracing him with her hands, light as dried petals. "Let me kiss you... You have a boy!"

Monakhov looked at her in terror.

"Well," she cried, kissing him on the numb cheek that kept moving away. "You have a son!"

"Why a son?" Monakhov said.

1971

The Forest

> The days of man are but as grass:
> for he flourisheth as a flower of the field.
> *Psalms*

1

"No, there's no need to see me off," said Monakhov, again lightly hugging his mother who had settled against his chest like a piece of fluff, and, after a momentary hesitation, he added for the sake of finality, "Someone's seeing me off."

His mother gave in.

His father, fully-dressed, with head thrown back and mouth slightly open, was sleeping his usual oblivious sleep; his nose had grown sharp, the skin of his sunken cheeks whiter than his long grey stubble... Monakhov bent over this landscape of cheek. Life's forces bubbled somehow spaciously in his father, as though they were too freely contained and were begging to emerge from the frail body which lay on top of the blanket and already seemed not to weigh down the bed. Monakhov bent down to his father with a cautious kiss and managed not to think about—that.

Then, after dashing about in all directions, he was off, with a heavy briefcase in one hand and basket of fruit in the other, the flaps of his raincoat winding around them. He kept getting entangled and stumbling, yet didn't fall; he seemed instead to be about to take off. In the hall he bumped into the tub and the pitcher fell from the shelf into the water: "Don't worry, it's all right," said his mother. "Kiss your wife for me," she said a little uncertainly.

That didn't call for a response.

He gave his mother another peck on the forehead since he couldn't embrace her as his hands were full, and he kicked the door open and was gone with the same speed with which he had hastened here a week ago. At the end of the side-street he looked back for the last time—his mother was on the porch... Suddenly the side-street became rounded and shortened, as in a lens—a momentary trick caused by tears: the foliage, unusually glossy and separated into individual leaves, peered out from behind the small fences; as in a postcard the sky was very blue at the end of the street, as though it were the edge of the earth and broke off where his mother was standing on the porch...

This picture froze and then disappeared around the corner; Monakhov emerged into another dimension and gave a sigh of relief, a bit embarrassed at his own sincerity and surprised at the strength of the love which had welled up in him.

Around the corner it was a different city: the streetcar was rattling along, taxis were moving forward slowly and dully, twenty-story boxes—the pride of the city—were going up: the supermarket, the self-service, the university. And here Monakhov had a stroke of luck—contrary to Tashkent rules, a taxi let out its passengers right in front of him. Pulling himself together and becoming self-important, he flopped into it.

"The airport?" asked the driver, who had put away the basket in the trunk.

"Right," said Monakhov.

The car gave a jerk. The delicate thread which had bound him to his parental home stretched and snapped.

* * *

Monakhov had started out for Tashkent totally unexpectedly. What was unexpected was not only that he had started out but that he had actually gone. That is, he had intended to go there for so long and had not gone for so long, that not to go again and again didn't upset anyone. So he could have never gone. His mother would probably have come up at some point for a week. He hadn't seen his father for three years.

What, was it really three years? You'd never think it was three... It was as if it were yesterday, or if not yesterday, then at least ten years ago, but not three. How strange. Those years passed like a drum roll, from the outside, from on top. Someone was walking on the roof, rummaging about, lighting a lamp. Monakhov kept tossing from one side to the other in an uneasy sleep. Divorce, the dissertation, a car accident, his young wife. Neither of them died... An insignificant episode. The middle way. Turning grey.

And it turned out that while his life continued, his parents' life had passed—an uncomplicated story called "a whole life." The entire family spent the war—Monakhov's late infancy and early childhood—in Tashkent, but even after the war his father continued building something in Asia, some cumbersome permanent structures... And it was there that he retired. There was some vague talk about his getting his own house, about a secret family (to this day Monakhov didn't know for sure—both his parents succeeded in maintaining dead silence about this throughout his youth). So there his father remained, on the pretext of having gotten used to the climate. But suddenly (and it was precisely these twenty years that Monakhov hadn't noticed), he aged, fell sick, was left alone, the house was almost taken away from him... He didn't ask anything of his wife, but their son, almost the present-day Monakhov, had moved from the Petrograd side to the capital by this time and she, the old woman, without having forgiven him, suddenly took off and went to the father, not the son.

That was the last time she visited her son...

That was why Monakhov could tell his new wife that he was making the business trip solely for the sake of his parents; he told his parents that he'd managed to arrange the business trip to visit them; he told his chief that he'd never have gone had he not grasped the full complexity and importance of the job; the only person to whom there was nothing to say was himself: he was leaving with pleasure, but didn't want to go.

Yet turning into his parents' street he suddenly felt a great lump in his throat that he could neither swallow nor eject; but he didn't choke or start to cry. Only his mother shed a few tears, very quickly and briskly; his father had a coughing fit, using up whatever strength for caresses he had in the weak embrace he gave, and then lay down, indifferent, as though his son had never been away. His mother started feeding him—she had no time to cry or express her feelings. How they'd aged!

And it turned out that he, Monakhov, had been so right to realize his intention and come. This spirit of sacrifice with which he permitted himself to be loved was notorious. It gave rise to a feeling in him that was so keen it was almost equal to love. He wanted to cry all the time. He didn't even recognize Tashkent—his semi-homeland. Not even for a second could Monakhov manage to become the barefooted and flaxen-haired child that he'd been here. That Tashkent no longer existed. A recent earthquake, like a revolt of time, had buried his childhood for good, letting him understand finally that the location of his motherland wasn't yet or wasn't any longer a homeland. That Tashkent no longer existed—it couldn't be otherwise!—his parents lived on a side-street which had been preserved by a miracle. It was as though they were his homeland. With their aged powers they retained memories around them so solidly that everything was preserved right up to the turn in the street... Still, the old man was in a bad way. The side-street would melt away if they weren't there. And it was this that Monakhov thought, more or less distinctly and with surprise, as he looked at the old couple. And he felt like crying (at the loss of his own love, had he but known it). He saw this, however, as his still loving them, with there being nothing to be done with them, nothing one could do; what a deep and undemanding despair love was. Because of this, his despair seemed wonderful to him. God, how stale I've become!—he grumbled to himself at this.

And their separation ended right away; he quickly had enough to eat and fell asleep, falling onto his mother's bed and letting her admire him as he slept—a classic scene!—and transfer her gaze to her husband, or rather, now only the father of her son...

...His father awoke first, having relived his son's arrival in his brief sleep. Through his nap the son heard the father's creaking and groaning and realized he was home at last and didn't want to wake up. It was as though he still had a chance of waking up a few years earlier, when the Monakhov that existed now didn't yet exist. But it was impossible not to wake up: his father purposely clattered his shaving gear and rattled the bureau as he took out his underwear... Yes, it wasn't as unusual for Monakhov to wake up in his parents' home as it was to wake up as himself: he was getting used to it. "He's trying to make me see him in the best light..."—without opening his eyes Monakhov could see everything, knew each of his father's steps: there was the broom rustling, which meant that his father had gotten tired of the washing he was going to do and had switched to a "useful" task—sweeping the clean floor... But father was the same as ever; it was the son feigning sleep who wasn't... His mother, of course, was refraining from breathing in the kitchen so as not to awaken her son; she'll find her husband with his broom and there'll be a scene... Monakhov could picture his mother distinctly, as if he were seeing her through the wall: she was sitting there, having thought of a noiseless task, weaksightedly sifting through the groats which she hadn't had time to go through for a month—and now there was time; his mother sighed... The rustling of the broom subsided—this meant his father had gotten tired. The TV clicked and hummed as it warmed up. Father's TV wouldn't come on immediately—he was ready to discuss this topic with his son, but the latter was still feigning sleep. Silence. There was nothing else he could amuse himself with. "He won't be able to hold out now—he'll start talking," his son smirked, "in his sleep."

"Alyosha!" his father called, fairly loudly.

His son opened his eyes.

"Were you sleeping?" his father was dumbfounded. He stood in the middle of the room leaning on the broom, "Sorry... I thought you'd woken up."

Monakhov Jr. was touched by this childish cunning and smiled at the feeling of closeness.

"It's O.K., I was dozing," the son said in a velvety voice.

The screen lit up and a fragmented sharp picture flickered on.

"And that's the way it'll stay until it warms up," his father said mournfully. And while the set was warming up, his father elaborated upon its treachery: "If it's an agricultural program, the picture's fine. As soon as it's skating or a ballet competition, it stops working completely..."

All the repairmen were swindlers and hacks... The talk got onto how people weren't what they used to be...

His son willingly agreed with him.

But this didn't suit his father; he began to defend the very times he'd just railed against. No, the times had nothing to do with it; what about the universe, he said heatedly, and progress?

His son got angry: what the devil did the universe have to do with it when...

His mother found them arguing. She came in at their loud voices.

"You woke him up, of course," she said angrily to her husband, "and he's had no rest at all."

"No, really, mother, I've slept enough," her son the peacemaker said hypocritically, looking at his father, who was ready to bristle.

"He's only had half an hour's sleep..." His mother was annoyed to find them acting just as though the son had never gone anywhere, as though the three years that his father had not seen him had never been. His father had forgotten that he hadn't seen his son for three years.

"All right," controlling herself in her turn, his mother said in a brisk voice, "Go and take a shower and then dinner will be ready."

"Good heavens, Mama," Monakhov Jr. exclaimed with falsely cheerful horror, "I've already eaten enough for two days and that was less than an hour ago."

"It's pancakes... you used to like them so much!" his mother tempted him.

When he heard about the shower, Monakhov Sr. resolutely threw his towel over his shoulder.

"That's right—you have to take a shower now, when Alyosha is ready to wash!" his mother exploded again.

"It's O.K.," sighed Monakhov Jr., "I'll take a shower later."

Monakhov Jr. chewed the pancakes, trying to recall when he had liked them. He couldn't.

Monakhov Sr. came in and as a reward for the violence he had committed on himself, for the feat of shaving and washing, he looked magnificent, and like an eagle and splendid fellow he glanced at his son.

"I wouldn't mind some of those things either," he said with playful condescension to his wife who, propping up her cheek in the classic fashion, was watching her son chew.

She got up without concealing a sigh.

"You've never eaten them in your life!"

The picture was finally in focus. The son glanced at the TV from time to time while his father told him about what he'd seen the night before and so didn't see what was on now—that same ballet competition he'd been so eager to see.

The mother kept darting dark hostile looks at the father.

Father, of course, ate off his knife "on purpose"; the pancake would slide off and he'd manage to catch it from below and chew it whole, still continuing, however, his narrative about yesterday's TV program.

"At least let your son watch TV..." his mother said angrily.

And suddenly at this family argument which had scarcely warmed up but which also wasn't dying down, their son began to feel as warm as though he were at a campfire, as though it had worn him out; he stretched luxuriously and yawned. His mother was already plumping up the pillow...

And so he slept and ate the whole day. His mother would pass like a girl, a silent shadow, from the room to the kitchen, from the kitchen to the room, throwing a cold glance at Monakhov Sr., who continued telling his son about all he'd seen and read, and she invited Monakhov Jr. to help her in the kitchen.

"He knows we need to talk..." she complained to her son when he came in to join her.

"What can I do to help?" asked her exemplary son.

"Everything's done, don't bother. Sit here a bit. Tell me about yourself. Shall I pour you some tea?"

Her son drank tea and had to tell her about his other life—about the capital, his career, his new wife and his young apartment. And it all became as distant to Monakhov Jr. as it really was. It was as though these three years were being taken out of him bodily like a drawer. And then he was as though he'd never left and parted from them, except for a small dark rectangular void inside (where the drawer had been). "How are they?"—the question kept whirling round and round inside him. (His mother maintained her own independent relations with his former family...) But he didn't ask. Just as his mother didn't ask: "So how are you? Satisfied? Happy? Otherwise why undertake..." "I named you after my husband's father, but I wanted to call you Mitya..." sighed his mother. "Perhaps Mitya would have been a happier choice"—her son smiled to himself. So they continued talking not about the thing for the sake of which they'd drawn each other aside, but about what they knew together: again they talked about father. How he'd gotten weaker, how he'd lost weight, how he didn't sleep at night, how he didn't eat anything, how his character, which had always been like that, had become totally unbearable. Nothing had changed, and again time hadn't passed... Monakhov peered out into the yard: holding on to the fence, the blue shadow of his aunt who had died of cancer a year ago passed by—he saw her distinctly: she hadn't changed at all; the last time he'd seen her she had looked exactly like that. "She didn't suffer at all, she went in her sleep," said his mother. "Distance is really something!" thought her son inwardly, "Three thousand kilometers is equivalent to the last three years... I turned off the road but it turns out I'm back where I started from..."

And then his father came into the kitchen to "bother" them.

"Come on, Alyosha—it's an interesting program about animals..."

And he started retelling what he'd just seen. His mother sighed as Alyosha went and watched TV while his father continued telling him about the beginning of the program as it went on and ended, without interesting him at all.

"Imagine it," said his father (he was already talking about something else which he'd switched to), "a forest!" and his eyes flashed inappropriately with a great and abstract feeling, "A forest, it turns out, isn't simply a lot of trees, but a forest is an association."

"It's clearly not simply..." his son grinned.

"No, really," his father continued, letting the irony pass, "They're all connected by their roots, which are entangled, and they comprise a single system. That's precisely what it is—a system."

"So what?" said his son.

"For example, a tree can be dying slowly, but as soon as it dies, it dries out the next day. Scientists think it's a riddle. But it turns out that as soon as it dies the forest immediately withdraws all its juices into its system. That's why it dries out immediately... It turns out," said his father, hearing his son's silence, "that a forest is not a multitude of trees, but a collective, a society, and each tree doesn't stand independently, but only together with all the others, and needs them all...."

"Humans always have to project their own notions onto everything in the world," his son said through his teeth and lay down flat on his back against his mother's pillow and closed his eyes to be more convincing, "I'm tired of humanity."

So he slept and ate, ate and slept, and by the end of the day had become so relaxed that it seemed to him that not one but several days had passed, that he'd been there a long time, as though he'd never left... And in one day he aged together with the old couple by three of their years.

That's why in the morning he swallowed his mother's breakfast with a youthful appetite (at his own place he didn't eat that much even at dinner), planted a smacking kiss on his mother's forehead, smiled for her sake at his sleeping father, and even with a certain joy burst out onto the street as though into freedom, readily and excitedly rushing to take care of his business which had seemed so unpleasant and uninteresting in the capital.

2

"Now turn right, and then a little to the right again..."

"What's the name of the street?" the cabdriver asked with displeasure.

"That's exactly what I don't know," said Monakhov, getting excited, "I can show you."

They drove on in a roundabout way while Monakhov recalled his parents with increasing and incomprehensible sorrow. The magnitude of Monakhov's betrayal kept growing: God! every extra hour with him was as precious and essential to his mother as though it were the last, and here he was driving about God knows where instead of making his way urgently to the airport. It was as though he were on a hook. As long as he doubted, as long as he thought it unlikely that this enterprise would come off, he erected a facile, cunning, rickety construction, a real piece of espionage: he called his wife to say that he wasn't certain but that perhaps he'd be delayed two days or so: "Don't come to meet me"; he told his mother that it was a pity, but it was likely that he'd be called away urgently two days earlier: "Don't see me off"; and he told *her*, for whose sake all of this had been set up, that it was extremely unlikely, but he'd try to come for a day and might be able to stay, but he wouldn't be able to stay for her birthday in any case—what difference did it make if they celebrated it together a day earlier? At a single even fleeting suggestion of any thought about what a web he'd spun, he felt dizzily empty, and then, strange as it seemed, he would spin it with greater energy and finality. as though at last he'd made his decision—consolidating both variants: that perhaps he'd have to leave sooner, and that probably he'd manage to stay on. The chink between the two possibilities became more and more distant, it gaped wide. The more doubts he had, the more certain he was that it wasn't worth it, the sooner he knew somewhere in the back of his mind that it would take place despite of everything.

So that only at the very last moment, perhaps when he was already seated in the cab and the cabdriver asked "The airport?"—precisely at that moment he leaped over the chink and found himself on the other side, when he decisively told him to go in the opposite direction. Like all weak people he was bold precisely when it came to rash actions; he was stubborn where they were concerned, afraid of getting a reputation for indecisiveness precisely where any decisive person would reconsider the situation and then easily change his mind. What Monakhov would forget was that at these responsible moments no one was observing him, no one was leaning over him from above with a trump card in his hand: so will our Monakhov be a coward or not? He didn't understand that if it came down to a question of cowardice, then both decisions would be made not through boldness—only a third alternative would demand boldness, which no one would ever remember, and any choice was cowardly. It was bolder simply to see what would happen. And it was on account of this that there was always indecisiveness up to the last moment, so that this leap would look as though it were involuntary, governed by fate.

Now he wouldn't tell the driver to turn around even at the point of a gun. There was only remorse, a surge of guilt, the shadow of a retribution, hazy in form, but it was on account of the present moment; that is, fear gripped him. And he wouldn't show it. (All the same, at that moment when we permit ourselves something, we know perfectly well what the consequences will be, we know that we won't escape and evade them, and it's only when we must pay that we forget completely, so as to be able to say "What for?") Remorse swelled—and the old folk's faces rose before him as though they were real...

He hadn't even looked properly at his father, hadn't said goodbye to him... The skin at the base of his grey bristles which was whiter than the bristles themselves appeared solidly before his mind's eye; it was like river silt between sedge. For some reason it was specifically a river bank, a fishing rod, an overcast sky, and his father fishing—the complete evenness of whitish silt between the stalks of grey sedge. Monakhov blinked away the picture of this lake. And now his mother's gaze was fixed upon him, girlish in its reproach... How can one pretend to oneself that others don't see anything, don't think or notice anything, just because they give no sign? It's precisely when they don't give a sign that they know everything. She's been around, mother has—hasn't she? It's not as though he's not her son and not his! She knows and sees father. Maybe she doesn't love her husband so as to continue loving her son?...

He'd been there for only three days. On the fourth... What did she feel as she wrapped each fruit in paper and placed it carefully like an egg in the basket, when she said: "Don't forget to unpack them as soon as your car gets there" (not plane, but car...) Ah! Driver, rush back! But he didn't say that. The wail was only inside him—outwardly he was as smooth as a stove. And a stove doesn't warm firewood, but burns it up.

And even during those three days what did he do besides graciously eat and not argue too much with his father...? Only now in the car did he finally experience those three days in their full force: he saw everything, understood everything, and felt everything. In these ten minutes the last three days seared him, just as during those three days his unexpected departure from home, which he'd not been able to feel back there, in Moscow, had seared him in its turn; the sharper and more recent the moment, the more stupid and self-satisfied the fleeing Monakhov felt. Right up to the take-off—that was when it hurt, when it began to torment him. "What is this?" Monakhov thought now in exasperation. "Tomorrow I'll be living today, but where am I right now?"

And with this sensible thought he drove up to the house whose address he didn't remember but could only "show."

Irreparability fanned his face when, looking insensibly about him, he glanced at the sky as though retribution were already gathering there, and pulled the basket of fruit out of the trunk—a heavy reproach.

"Monakhov! Oh, Monakhov! So you *did* come, after all! Monakhov, Monakhov..." However many times in a row she might pronounce the word "Monakhov," it was new every time, as though there were a language consisting of one word in which one could nonetheless express everything, even the subtlest ideas...

It was a gratifying moment: it hadn't been for nothing, after all... here was the person who really needed to have him come... here was real irreproachability...

"Monakhov... Monakhov!" She kept repeating in a sing-song voice, taking the basket from his as though he were a girl.

Not for nothing, no-o-o-o-...

* * *

Still, all this had turned out strangely. He hadn't expected it...

He'd probably eaten and slept his fill at his mother's the first day—he got down to the business at hand with great energy. Two feelings had coexisted in him as he rode here, two expectations: one, that he was coming to people who, though they did it poorly, did what they had to on home territory, that he'd be getting in their way, sermonizing and advising them, he would cause unpleasantness for someone, would give someone a dressing down, whereas they would have to maintain a respectful demeanor, nod without understanding what he was explaining and instructing them to do, he'd get angry that they weren't concerned for their own good, and they'd sigh with relief when he'd leave; everything would tighten up as never before, new methods would not be adopted, and the old ones would continue to operate, but ineffectively; the second variant was that he was from Moscow, a specialist, a Ph.D., his company would penetrate the problem like a knife going through butter and everyone would finally come to himself, get into motion, come to life, if only for a time: there'd be a ray of light, something would be set in motion and suddenly—anything can happen—things would finally be off to a start.

His business trip experiences suggested and justified both such outcomes. But which of the two would occur could only become apparent once he was on the threshold, as he crossed it, entering the office... the first phrase, the first glance... and from that point only one of these two was possible, irreversibly: either, or.

And he apparently had slept and eaten well—energy was bubbling up in him and successfully pushing through the coolness and disillusionment in such a way that the warning which accompanies any clash with an alien world and business couldn't occur in Monakhov himself. Everyone had already taken this into consideration—rumors followed somewhere behind him and outdistanced him—and everyone would almost jump up when he came in.

He didn't care about it personally, he wasn't involved in it, but the prestige of his company had to be protected, and for those Monakhov was visiting it was a very serious thing.

In Tashkent they were building an important structure that had been designed by the institute in which Monakhov had developed and got ahead. In one of the shops a new kind of ceiling which hitherto had not been used domestically had been designed. Then the ceiling collapsed, cutting short two workmens' lives. And this was even a "blessing" because it had happened during the lunch break—otherwise it could have been many more. Can you imagine if it had happened when the shop was already crowded while the workers were changing shifts?! The tone of the superiors' reprimand was particularly sincere because the superiors would catch it indiscriminately, by department.

What made it so convenient for Monakhov was that he had no involvement in this affair, but understood it adequately, better than the others. He felt a pleasant freedom in that everything was clear to him right away, whereas all the others were frightened and tense, involved—it was as though he were moving about in spring water, and the others in glue. That he and they were as though in different elements within one dimension was an especially important feeling. Even the heat was nothing to him; he felt dry and sharp, quick—whereas the locals perspired under the weight, swaddled in the tightness of the mutual bonds between their work and their personal life. The satisfaction of personal knowledge, a confidence in one's work, a certainty that one is right, which stem only from a difference in qualifications—these vouchsafed Monakhov elbowroom and freedom, so he didn't perspire and understood everything before it was explained to him, saw through everything and even further, even noticing the independent behavior and traits of the "involved" and dependent people who surrounded him; he even managed to see himself from the side, not to his detriment, but in the interests of the resoluteness of his insight and understanding. With a clean, dry (long-fingered) hand he lightly, with a touch of contempt, laid out a solitaire game of drafts and reports while they with their short fingers kept senselessly shoving the same piece of paper at him and offering explanations. ("I understand that, I understand"—he would move it aside again). And having laid out his patience, he would shuffle once again, and making a mark (not with his nail, but with the blunt point of a pencil) would say: "And what's this?" And—ha!—it became clear to him that that was precisely what they didn't want to show him, what they were hoping he wouldn't notice, although they already knew that someone would notice, of course, but maybe not right away. "And this here," he made a second mark. That one they hadn't even known themselves. They didn't even understand right away. Only the short-fingered one, the culprit—he understood right away. A shadow of pity even flitted through Monakhov, who at that moment had become hardened from power (not administrative, but intellectual power, which is sweeter)—the fellow caught at himself, almost at his heart. This short-fingered square-set fellow in a bishop-like hat with totally gold teeth was the chief engineer, and his "Volga," which he offered to Monakhov, was waiting for him at the entrance; but Monakhov refused, and also refused to visit his two-story private residence—there was to be no reception. (Monakhov himself didn't have a Volga or a private residence—he had only his head).

And so it turned out that it wasn't his company's fault because everything had been calculated correctly, but the fault lay in these people, the gold-toothed one and the others, who, due to ignorance or even criminal neglect, had ignored these correct calculations. And who should turn up but the irreproachable and honorable Monakhov..."No, it's not his business to mitigate the error—by an oversight due to negligence or aggravating circumstances. That was someone else's task." Gold teeth flashed guiltily in the culprit's mouth like children. "No," said Monakhov, "and did the workmen who died have any children?"

And he really said this quite simply; there were no dead or live people in his mind at that moment. This was only the unavoidable conclusion of the judicial (not the judicious) mind, and that was all. And here you have a specific instance of correctness breeding amazing callousness in people. Or brilliance in one's field. Or let's call it power.

He felt great, however, as he came out of the entry gate, magnanimous, precise, thorough... The final bureaucratic formalities (he'd registered the business trip), the final cool handshakes; no, he'd write the report in Moscow, they'd send them a copy, of course: no, he was very touched, he understood the customs and traditions of eastern hospitality, but must decline (regarding the reception at the country residence); no, he wanted to walk about a bit (refusing the "Volga")... At this point he couldn't hold back a discreet half-smile (he too was human); to take a walk—after all, this was the city of his childhood where he hadn't been for so long... He felt wonderful.

"This is some business—it really is some business," he kept muttering with satisfaction in rhythm with his light springy step. He screwed up his eyes, lifting his face to the pleasant heat. And then:

"Monakhov! My God, Monakhov..."

Talk of someone he hadn't thought of once. This struck him in a flash, but he didn't have the time to think...

"Is it you, Monakhov?" And immediately she answered herself happily in the affirmative, "Yes, it's you."

Monakhov gazed with pleasure; this eastern Russian girl appealed to him now just as easily and irresistibly as she had before. It was as though they'd parted yesterday—three years merged into one day without a trace. She stood stockstill as though about to break into a run, as though she were on a threshold, and stood like that undecidedly, unsteadily, clumsily—Monakhov saw all of her in this pose. He wouldn't have believed it, but what he felt was actually joy.

But he didn't have time to get a word out. It was as though the wind had swept them away. And what can you say on the run...? She breathed the word "Monakhov" about ten more times, while he said "Natasha" perhaps once. She ran a little ahead, pulling him by the hand, one could almost say dragged him, were Monakhov not following her so willingly. And he wasn't the least embarrassed that all this was in the open, that almost all the passersby were stopping and standing stockstill, thunderstruck, gazing after them... First of all, he knew that it might only seem that way to him, and secondly, let them be envious!... And how could he help but rejoice that such a beautiful, strong, bright creature loved him just as she had formerly, loved him for three years and not only had forgiven his cruelty at that time, but hadn't even registered it... It was splendid! He actually wanted to ask as they ran, "What on earth do you see in me? What's special about me?" As though she'd finally tell him, since he was the one she loved so much, how he, with all his acquired trash, nonetheless inwardly stood out from everyone else. What was so wonderful about him? Without doubt he'd receive the reply: "You're Monakhov! You're a fool, Monakhov..." "Well, well... Monakhov was puffing and panting. But they'd already dashed in. The courtyard, the entrance, the stairs, the door... Monakhov didn't see anything around him. Here, gasping for breath, she managed to utter "Monakhov" one more time. But that was all.

That's how it happened. "It's that kind of day," thought Monakhov, becoming firmly convinced of the freshness of existence. He examined the room, which was narrow as a cot: a branch in a milk bottle on the windowsill, a hanger with a long dress on the wall like a picture, he himself on the mattress on the floor... there, also on the floor, stood a radio-gramophone—a sign of well-being—he was again touched by this girlish poverty.

Natalya was enjoying herself as if she were in heaven. She showed him her girlfriend's letters, her album, her diploma—as though all this testified to the reality of her existence more than she, tall and lively, did herself. "Don't look at that photograph; this one's not so bad..." Monakhov looked at her in person and laughed, pleased. She lived at such a rapid pace—she didn't have much of anything and all of it was displayed. She had lived life without him from their parting to this moment just as impetuously. So that it would work out. So that she could be entirely with him.

Monakhov was half-listening and half-looking: all these things were confirmations of one and the same thing—she loved him... He liked Natalya. Now he had an extraordinary opportunity to be convinced of it: perhaps he'd always liked her. Specifically her. Monakhov was struck by this discovery; why, if he were free (no, not simply unmarried—that wasn't what he meant), if he were himself and not the person he'd become, not as everyone saw him, but as he himself perceived himself, Monakhov, not as everyone wanted to and did see him, and even convinced him he was... No, if Monakhov were indisputable, solid, then Natalya would be precisely the woman who was destined for him, whom he'd accept without question as belonging to him, one to one... Why was he letting the chance slip by? Didn't he trust himself? Didn't he know that he was exactly that—himself? He liked everything about Natalya, and nothing was contradictory, everything was just right: the Mongolian heaviness of her face, and the clumsiness, even the vulgarity... He imagined what would be said by the undisputed beauties in his life whose opinions (mainly of themselves) he accepted so absolutely that it never occurred to him even once to take into consideration his own taste, which therefore remained undeveloped... he easily imagined the grimace, and the venom of the feminine criticism, a milligram of which sufficed to destroy what he liked for him... It seemed to him that if then were now and now were then, he'd have enough strength this time to take his own view into account.

But it was irrevocably late. Catching his tender elegiac glance, Natalya was transported by her own life: she had a life of her own too, after all—that is, something she could tell about... Monakhov tried to figure out, to explain her attraction to him, but it was so indisputable for him that he couldn't explain it. The more assiduously he disassembled her features, the more incomprehensible the whole remained: he didn't find a single symmetrical, a single beautiful feature, except perhaps for her complexion... Of course, her complexion. He sighed. Yes, nothing exceptional—it was uniquely combined! As though the behavior and the look came from different people... Separately everything was commonplace, it could belong to others, Monakhov had even encountered it separately before; together, in such contrast—her face and the vivacity of her face, the voice and the sense of the words it expressed, the strong beautiful body and the ruggedness which didn't belong to it, the seeming randomness of its movements—all this disintegrated, contrary to theory, but in itself it was so simple, natural, and convincing, that it was right just as it was. The looks of one person and the soul of another... It was as though all his life Monakhov had been wrong, attributing these features separately to people, and now, belatedly, he finally saw who they belonged to originally. It was as though all his life he'd encountered exceptions and erroneously generalized from them and only now, reversing his useless experience, he had run into their primary source.

Natalya stumbled, repeating herself: her life ended with this latest meeting with Monakhov. And she felt complete and nothing more. Monakhov alone dominated the desert of her life.

"And Lenechka gave me this..."

"Who's Lenechka?"

"Oh, Good Lord, Monakhov," Natalya exclaimed impatiently, even angrily, "That's how you listen! There's only one Lenechka. The one who looks like a duckling, you saw him..."

"What do you mean I saw him?" Monakhov was amazed.

"In a photograph. You also saw him in person."

"No, I didn't."

"He was hanging around the entrance when we arrived... Well?"

"I don't remember. What does he want from you?" Monakhov suddenly said rather strangely, not in his usual voice, and got angry at himself. Natalya was pleased:

"He'll kill me," she said looking hopefully at Monakhov.

"So... it's serious between you?"

"Of course it's serious," she said scornfully, "He's simply madly in love with me."

"Why do you torment the boy?" said Monakhov with self-satisfaction.

"Me torment?!" Natalya became indignant, "But I'm his mother and he's my son."

"So that's how it is," smirked Monakhov, "So why is he going to kill you...? What a bloodthirsty fellow."

"Oh no, he's good-natured. He's very good-natured. Pathologically so."

"And he'll forgive you for coming home and going right past him with another guy?"

"You're a fool, Monakhov," Natalya got angry, "It's none of your business. If you must know, I never lied to him. I told him right away that I had a man."

"What man?"

"The one I love."

"Who's that?"

"You."

Monakhov believed her. How did she have him?—he thought to himself in amazement. When she'd never had him completely and forever...

"And what did he say?"

"He didn't believe me. When you speak frankly no one ever believes you. People lie so as to be believed. It's funny, he follows me about and is jealous. He's extraordinarily suspicious. But tell him frankly: 'I don't love you, I'm going to someone else, I love someone else, I've just come from someone else,' and he'll laugh happily, as though I'm joking and he'll start trying to kiss me."

"That's understandable," nodded Monakhov.

"Understandable? You understand it? How can you understand it? Were you ever not loved?"

"Well, no...not loved is not the right word—" Monakhov responded slowly.

"Not loved! Monakhov was not loved!"

"What are you so happy about?" Monakhov was upset.

"Just because. Perhaps you're human...Perhaps you're human, eh, Monakhov? Perhaps I don't love you for nothing. Maybe I'll still be able to fall out of love with you?"

Drawing her to him, Monakhov said, "No, you won't," in a voice so unnaturally thick that for a second he felt ashamed. But she could no longer see that...

Natalya was frankly content as she looked at the ceiling with a wandering gaze. It was now the exhausted Monakhov's turn to say something. He had nothing to brag about—such as today's victories at the factory—and he played down his role. Natalya wasn't listening and was laughing; one moment it seemed to her that his lips weren't smacking right somehow, the next that his ear wasn't in the same place as most people's... Monakhov was trying hard not to get offended. She did hear the part about the workmen who were killed, however:

"Did they have any children?"

And though Monakhov had used this argument that morning himself, that had been demagogy which he'd not experienced in a heartfelt way, and here was Natalya... Natalya delighted Monakhov. She seemed to be a little girl, a fool... And suddenly such a change! Monakhov was deeply moved. But the victims were again incidental to his consciousness—they went to the credit of his beloved.

She also heard the part about the gold-toothed fellow:

"Ismailov? I know him."

"You do?"

"I worked as his secretary. Come on, what kind of crook is he..." (Monakhov quickly got indignant with ready warmth.) "He has an enormous family—seven daughters..."

"And has to marry all of them off?"

"Precisely," said Natalya, "And what about you, are you happy?"

He hadn't thought she'd ask that question. He'd thought she was somehow above it, free of everything of which he himself wasn't free... He got a little upset—a little cloud ran across the ceiling, even a rain cloud. She's a woman all the same... He determinedly complained about his dissatisfactions: yes, to be sure, life wasn't working out. For some reason he thought that his misery would please her. She listened, bored.

"Now that's a misfortune," she teased, "What kind of misfortune is that! Having old parents—that's misfortune!"

And again he was struck by her perceptiveness. She didn't have a father, and her mother had died just at the time that Monakhov was suffering in his personal life, during the last three years. He still wondered how Natalya had grown so much bolder. But he didn't remember his own parents.

Natalya went over to the window—dusk was quickly gathering there, and it was already totally dark in the room. For a long time she too peered out at something in the lighter shadows.

"Lenechka?" guessed Monakhov.

"No," she said and started dressing with determination, "And don't you dare talk about him."

"And why not?" scowled Monakhov.

"Because... He's a very good and intelligent boy."

"Really."

"You know, he writes such poetry!" said Natasha vehemently.

"Now, isn't she a little girl?" thought Monakhov, "A child."

"Great," he drawled, "Does he dedicate it to you?"

"He does!" said Natasha challengingly.

"Do you remember any by heart?"

"I do."

"Recite some," Monakhov tried to embrace her.

"All right... Move over."

Come quickly and depart!
By five—dawn has set its muzzle,
The mist has thinned, and the thieving night
Has followed you around the corner.

A clock without hands is the best coat of arms.
I fall into cotton embraces.
With the repulsive word "love"
I rhyme the void of measure.

Don't worry! for this life I won't pay more
Than you. No change necessary...

Monakhov burst out laughing:
"How old is he?"
"Eighteen."
Monakhov gave a still more artificial and hearty laugh.
Natalya was hurt:
"You don't understand anything. What does age matter? If you must know, I'm only four years older than he is. It's you who's the old man, you engineer's soul. But we like it."
"Aha!" said Monakhov, "I'm an old man?"
"A dirty old man!"
He suddenly felt sad, nauseated—the brevity of existence overtook him: something had already been, as if word for word, moment for moment, the same world... something of this inimitable element had already been. Monakhov didn't feel anything, neither brief pain nor offense, as he became mortally offended. He rose determinedly, pursing his mouth and with a chiseled profile started pulling on his slacks.
"What are you doing?" Natalya roused herself, "Where are you going? Are you angry? You're not really angry—What are you doing, pretending?" observed Natalya correctly.
There was no answer Monakhov could make to her perceptiveness. He finished dressing in still greater silence. He had already gotten into his role, and the more sincere he was, the more he faked it.
"Monakhov, dear, forgive me! I didn't mean to. I didn't say anything. The poetry's bad, Monakhov! Wait, where are you going? I won't any more. I don't know what... Monakhov! Monakhov, I beg you!"
Monakhov graciously allowed her to embrace him. Cold, proud.
"Monakhov, don't leave! Please don't leave!"
Monakhov, of course, had nowhere to go to. He stopped pretending—and broke into a happy smile.
"You didn't leave! You didn't! Why on earth do you have those clothes on? Take them off! Monakhov..."

Toward nightfall they went out into the deserted dark street and Monakhov felt he was in the south. He knew and loved this feeling like the first cucumber of the season. It was a feeling as though he'd just had a steam bath and then gone out: it was light, warm, and it was already evening. After a steam bath even if he went out when there was frost Monakhov always recalled the south. It wasn't exactly that now he recalled the steam bath and compared the two.

"The south—this is the south," he said, heaving a deep sigh.

The sky was studded with stars and the street lamps were aleady out, yet it was light, somehow, in this dead of night. There was the smell of a campfire and of the first dry flowering. Mimosa from the market had shed its blossoms here; a chestnut was preparing its candles...

> A chestnut was blocked by a bird-cherry tree,
> The French Boulevard was in bloom,
> Our Kostya, it seems, fell in love...

sang Monakhov and burst out laughing.

"Imagine 'a chestnut by a bird-cherry tree'... I sang that when I was a child. I was here when I was a child."

"And you fell in love with it?" Natalya happily planted a smacking kiss on his cheek.

The holiday didn't end. A girl beside him, and specifically Natasha. Monakhov felt so youthful! He regretted that he'd long ago forgotten this and not experienced it. Life... He felt exactly as he had some time ago on a field trip in some village, after a dance... It wasn't that he felt he was young, he felt *like* a young man. There's a difference. This was a vague thought; like someone stirring, a rustling; something took wing, flew off, brakes squeaked. "Like a young man," sighed Monakhov, listening intently, but as with the bathhouse not thinking the thought, not comparing, not recalling. He suddenly said:

"Listen, are there steam baths here in Tashkent? Do people steam themselves here?"

That was all that he needed for it to be complete...

Such an empty, full night! And what an abundance of life, a life which runs right up to you, breathless. For some reason he had faith in it right away; he believed that this was life, and not just city noises: a branch swung, a bird took off, a thought rustled and remained behind, unacknowledged and ungrasped. He'd never know what he'd just thought about: that filled him with joy; he inhaled this warmed gasoline-permeated air with its traces of the smells of perfumed flowering... He saw nothing, and this quivering "nothing" was alive. And the main thing was that it was empty...

"Natalya!" a voice rang out from this emptiness, and right there, like an apparition, a white shirt appeared directly in front of him. Another separated itself from a tree trunk, and a third loomed in the dark without showing itself.

"Lord! Now they'll give it to me!" thought Monakhov without any fear. More precisely, this youthful fear leaped up and subsided in him in a kind of surge. There was still more of that scattered light of total night—it was so light!—the silence became even more complete and the rustling clearer.

"What's going on?" said Monakhov sternly and confidently, but his voice came out so constrained, as though it weren't coming from him. No one heard him.

The infinity of this instant finally ended.

"Is that you, Zyablikov?" Natasha answered openly and easily, and stepped forward towards him. Monakhov tactfully hung back a little.

When they stopped, they suddenly became visible to Monakhov, as though they were under a street lamp. The first one was mumbling something to her with restrained sternness. She answered easily, deliberately lighthearted. Monakhov watched all this, mentally replaying a youthful series of never-realized blows (it was a long time since he'd fought like that!). But what surprised Monakhov was Lenechka's age—he was a man of his own age. Stocky, puffy, unshaven, almost as if he had a beard, in a crumpled dirty shirt and sandals on bare feet. Monakhov was watchful, bountifully endowing his first impression with sympathy for the unsuccessful lover: there's something in him that appeals to me...Lenechka's non-competing appearance (that means Zyablikov is his surname, which in Monakhov's consciousness suddenly started to suit Lenechka very well, just as his looks and even his unexpected age started to increase his appeal*)...calmed Monakhov down somewhat. The hopelessness of a rival's claims...Catching himself at this point (all the same, everything in Monakhov was accelerated now and made keener): "How much of the feminine, even of the old womanish, there is in men"—Monakhov smiled with satisfaction.

Natasha waved her hand in farewell and returned to Monakhov. Lenechka turned to the friend lurking behind his back, who was as stocky as he, but hard to see, and they both joined the third; they merged with the tree trunks again and vanished.

"Well?" asked Monakhov.

Apparently he didn't ask it right; he gave something away.

"Were you frightened?" Natasha gave a laugh. "He's as good-natured as a pillow. Isn't he really like a pillow?"

"Without a case," said Monakhov angrily, "What does he want?"

"That's Zyablikov! Zyablikov always wants one thing. He asked whether I had something to drink."

"And you said?"

"I said he'd had enough. He's already tight."

---

*Zyabnut' means to shiver, to freeze. [Ed.]

"Tight? And why did the two of you talk so long?" asked Monakhov jealously.

"He was asking about you."

"What was he asking?"

"If you had something to drink. Why you're like this, as though you'd been sandbagged; if you were drunk yourself. He asked if you wanted to drink. I said no, you don't and you won't..." Natasha suddenly got upset. "He asked whether you were a decent man. Why are you nagging me?"

"And what did you say?"

"Me...I said you were wonderful."

"And he said?"

"That's when he said it; why are you nagging me? What do you care?"

"Just asking. Your fellow's strange..."

"Why?"

"Another in his place..."

"And why mine?" flared Natalya.

"Your Lenechka..."

"That's not Lenechka. Lenechka was standing in the back. It was Zyablikov, he writes children's books about nature...!"

"And I thought it was your Lenechka..." For some reason Monakhov became cheerful, "I was even surprised that he's so old..." he spoke quickly.

"What difference does it make to you?" Natalya was surprised. "No, tell me, isn't it all the same to you? Isn't it?"

Monakhov smiled.

This peaceful, tender combativeness awakened in him some memory from childhood, when it also turned out that he'd been frightened for nothing, when things were the opposite of what he'd feared.

"And Zyablikov—does he also write well?" smiled Monakhov.

Natalya didn't answer.

"Lenechka took a telegram out of my mailbox," she finally said in a dead voice.

Monakhov didn't understand.

"My aunt's coming to visit me tomorrow."

The next morning Monakhov discovered that his life had become unusually complicated.

His mother wasn't talking to him. Her jealousy seemed amusing to him; she treated all daughters-in-law dubiously, yet always took their side in these cases. In her jealousy the wife would become irrelevant and his possible betrayal would not satisfy her as a form of vengeance, but upset her with fresh jealousy. That's what he thought, and he was wrong. He had to smooth things over, however. To do that he exaggerated his success at work, which had detained him so long. His father willingly listened and nodded: he'd encountered similar cases in his own work. His mother calmed down and said: "That means you've taken care of all your business?"

Her observation was to the point. It meant that her son could spend the remaining days without stirring out of the house: he could eat and sleep, talk his fill with Mama and perk up the old man. Monakhov was touched : he really liked women very much once more. And his mother was a woman. By definition.

"Oh, Mama," Monakhov was so affectionate this morning; tender, moved, he embraced his mother, "My Mama."

"Yours, yours! Who else's?" his mother replied gaily, speaking rapidly.

"What a fool! What mistakes!" exclaimed Monakhov inwardly, not watching the soccer game which his mother had switched on for her son despite his father's grumbling, even though Monakhov hadn't even much insisted on watching, "Pass your own by—and you pass your life by..." A goal! Monakhov started: missed. He smiled. In revenge for the change of program, his father was talking about aliens from outer space—his mother's most hated topic. Their son glued himself to the screen without seeing it and nodded to his father without hearing him. His mother was happy at her son's affection.

And suddenly he realized that he was already late for his date... And he further realized that he'd got caught—he'd overdone it in his stories about work.

He made up something unexpected, no longer caring about its probability, and when he got there at a run Natalya was no longer there. Dashing around in vexation, he left.

The next day it turned out that she'd been late and he'd missed her by no more than five or ten minutes. Her aunt had taken over Natasha's place, so they roamed about the streets. Natalya was silent. Monakhov had dried up. He suddenly remembered that he'd forgotten the call to his wife—they'd been strolling at the arranged time. He got totally out of sorts: where had his holiday disappeared to? And so quickly!

They had an argument. Natalya lied about something and he got exasperated. She said he had no rights over her. And, she said, she wasn't to blame that they had no place to meet. Monakhov had nothing to suggest.

Then she proposed that perfidious plan for her birthday.

Monakhov agreed, but after calling his wife and visiting his old parents, he realized it was impossible.

So up to the end of his business trip, until the day of departure, Monakhov retained all three possibilities; with a superstructure of conditions and stipulations he erected three rickety buildings without pulling down a single one of them. To return to his wife on time, to stay for another day or two so as to spend a bit more time with his parents, or, presenting these pretexts in the proper quarters, to spend two days at Natasha's celebrating her birthday. These possibilities remained until the last day without toppling, for they leaned against each other and developed in parallel lines. It was costly to choose one and extract it—then the remaining ones would topple to their foundations. So was it worth developing them so skillfully and so long? Why not settle on one right away? This lack of economy dispirited Monakhov. "To count upon impunity is uneconomical," he formulated with an ironical smile. Yet, as before, he simultaneously wanted and didn't want everything: to go unpunished; to spend time with his parents; to be exposed; to return soon to his wife and be commended for his selflessness; and to enjoy himself at Natasha's and at the end of it to be completely unmasked.

The nearer the deadline drew, the more these possibilities acquired a tormenting power that was more or less equal to passion. He thought he hadn't expected such strength of feeling from himself anymore.

He assumed, nevertheless, that were he to choose the option of staying with his parents, it would be unlikely that he'd really spend the time with them, because in that case a further possibility still remained. And to remain with them as a pretext and yet not spend time with them was revoltingly ugly. It was for this reason perhaps that he chose the third option—it at least destroyed the two remaining ones. He immediately and decisively got ready to go to Moscow. In order to cut off these two options it was necessary only to call Moscow and to warn his wife about his unexpected arrival—and he delayed doing that. For a start he called Natasha at work: until the very last he had thought he'd be able to stay and come to her birthday party, and now— definitely—he was going away, yes, tomorrow, anything else was out of the question, impossible to talk about on the phone. Although what he could say off the phone he hadn't thought up yet. "Why don't you say something?" Monakhov shouted at her into the receiver as though he were angry, "I'm listening, what are you silent for?" When people don't understand you it's impossible to understand, which was what irritated Monakhov. He already believed in the inevitability of the decision he'd made and its independence of him—to leave. And here he was unjustly, silently, accused of having a choice and a will. But he couldn't do otherwise. It wasn't at all because he wanted it that way. But he couldn't. "Why don't you say something?" If she were to say why she was silent, what would he answer? But she remained silent, and after each slammed down their receivers angrily, Monakhov realized that all three options were still open.

But as far as Mama was concerned, he was already leaving. The departing Monakhov differed from the one who was staying in the special courtesy and the indulgent arrogance of all his movements, a masculine way of being affectionate. He helped his mother go to the bazaar to buy fruit for his trip, easily carried the heavy basket for her, pleasantly towering a head above the crowd at the bazaar.

And there he ran into Natasha, which for some reason he found especially unexpected after the telephone conversation that for some reason precluded meeting her right here at this bazaar. There was a boy with her

(Monakhov immediately thought of him as a "boy"), of draft age, short, stocky, with wide sloping shoulders and clumsily long arms ("The Duckling," Monakhov suddenly remembered). He kept fluttering around Natalya, who sailed proudly along (she was a bit taller than he or seemed taller); he'd jump back so as to see her, to discover her beside him—then he'd laugh (an enormous mouth, thick lips) and he really was exactly like a duckling. It was also understood that he was "ugly," but they were tactful... And yet in all this obvious ugliness, Monakhov noted, there was a certain something... A very nice boy, he thought without any basis whatsoever, which was the case... His mother turned aside to examine some almonds, and at that moment the "duckling" made a face at someone to amuse Natalya, and Monakhov modestly and respectfully nodded to her. Natalya jerked her head still higher, perhaps in a nod or perhaps, on the contrary, in a refusal to nod... And she rushed off.

"Lenechka! Follow me!" she said imperiously to Lenechka, who, like a child, had lagged behind and gotten upset (because he'd pulled a face to no purpose—it turned out she hadn't seen him). And Lenechka rushed after her joyfully, almost skipping along.

"What a little girl she is, after all!" Monakhov smiled affectionately and sadly. But he felt a heat in his chest; easy as it had been not to imagine her at separating, now that he saw her it seemed that he hadn't been separated from her.

"Oh, damn!" he muttered, his gaze following the rushing "duckling."

He was a fine boy...

And following her with his gaze, Monakhov experienced a twinge of melancholy; a life which had long lost its bloom awaited him. Perhaps the last color was vanishing from its canvas. For the last time the impossible scarlet skirt flashed by—it raised the dust, then disappeared... How could he let it slip by again? Again he forgot what he'd just realized... And what had he realized? "How could I not see her for three whole days!" he realized clearly.

And she—she'd understood him perfectly. "How can it be, Monakhov? We won't even say goodbye..." she'd said the last time.

"What do you mean, we won't say goodbye?" the satiated Monakhov had not understood then. "My aunt will come. You won't be with me then..." Only now did he understand her frank, simple homespun "say goodbye" and "you won't be with me." He felt choked: he could have seen her both yesterday and the day before... and tomorrow—would he really never see her again? He wanted so badly to run, to catch up with her and stop her. It would be so simple...

He stood there, his face expressionless.

His mother, who'd gone ahead of him, was squinting near-sightedly, looking for him in the crowd and not daring to call him loudly. And his mother's nearsighted, slightly frightened and even irritated face was what Monakhov saw right after Natasha's. "Damn it!" he muttered, gently taking her by the arm. And the old woman's face lit up like a girl's, full of tiny tremors of love and happiness. And suddenly it was easy for Monakhov to imagine what his mama had been like as a girl.

"What is this?" he thought lovingly, "Even in the life of a one-woman man there are so many women: a mother, a grandmother, a daughter..."

This strange thought existed independently.

If anything could help Monakhov with the problem of choice, could arouse initiative in him, it was that strange call...

Virtuoso that Monakhov had been at his job, smoothly as he had manipulated his business trip, he was nevertheslss punished for his professional distortion; a messenger was sent after him (his parents had no telephone) from that very SMU where he'd settled affairs with such finality. And this time it was not Ismailov himself who servilely flashed his gold teeth, but a miniature boy of about thirty in an embroidered skullcap like Ismailov's, with a Youth League pin on his modest little jacket, who smiled with exaggerated respect, showing teeth black from chewing tobacco. And precisely because Monakhov couldn't imagine anything of the kind—there couldn't be any mistake on his part—the phrase "in your interests" which was skillfully tossed off by this boy who was immeasurably beneath him in position (although the boy had a small house on the outskirts of town and a "Moskvich" car, which Monakhov sometimes dreamed of having) unnerved him; that phrase made Monakhov so indignant (but also frightened) that—he went. (Furthermore, not in a company "Volga," but by tram, which in some strange way confirmed the appropriateness of that phrase).

It turned out... But after all the things Monakhov imagined (there can't be anything wrong, but what if...) it turned out to be nothing so terrible, just because there was no logical basis for fear. It turned out to be partly politics, partly boorishness, at which Monakhov was not so good and clever as he was at engineering but which, as he became convinced, was a subject no less complex than science and more essential. In its own way this whole maneuver was no less enthralling than a detective novel, but it should have been in a particular style, not this one. In a short summary for the uninitiated all this wouldn't be effective... A paragraph of the agreement was found, existing formally in all contracts, but until now not considered by anybody to be particularly unbusinesslike or aggressive. Some violations in the degree of the author's surveillance were also discovered. Some arrangements which had existed in oral form but which were unconfirmed on paper were, shall we say, interpreted in a special way... In short, the harmony of Monakhov's conclusions was, if not destroyed, then shaken—a qualified legal mind had pored over all this. Besides all this, a small error was revealed in his, Monakhov's, calculations, not a major one, not one that overturned his conclusions in their entirety, but the brilliance of his expertise lost some of its luster. Monakhov couldn't imagine that Ismailov himself had caught him in this error—there was an engineering style and method of inquiry here, a higher level of qualifications which Monakhov hadn't expected to encounter here at all. His vanity was wounded above all precisely by this trifle, which in itself in no way jeopardized the whole business (the whole affair was threatened rather by the adroitness of the legal aspect which did not upset Monakhov at all: it was a reason for reflecting upon how much we care about the success of a business *per se*, and not merely our own success in it...). "Who is this Einstein?" wondered Monakhov, irritated and intrigued. There was no Einstein, only Ismailov (the youth in the skullcap was smiling somewhere in the background). All in all, they had "shown" Monakhov. And moreover, in so doing, they'd shown him that they weren't threatening him with anything, they weren't as merciless about his omission as he had been about theirs. So he was given to understand. They thanked him, shook his hand, invited him to come again. In brief, Monakhov clearly understood that neither he nor his conclusions altered the state of affairs, which rested solidly on foundations that were far from theoretical. He'd not accomplished what was wanted of him, and that was all. They'd find others... And the most depressing thing, perhaps, was that they'd be no worse at understanding the business than Monakhov, if not better. And another thing: they could have done without sending for him. And what was more, he may as well not have come. He'd come. And in doing so it was as though he'd put himself in his place. "The East," thought Monakhov.

Then came that strange call. The secretary, an overripe Russian woman, came in and whispered something to Ismailov, glancing at Monakhov with compassionate curiosity (interesting to know in what way she was privy to my failure?). Hearing her out, also looking briefly at Monakhov in a new way, Ismailov picked up his multi-line receiver and extended it to him.

"You've probably made a mistake," Monakhov was at a loss, "It's impossible that someone would—No one knows that I—" He stopped short.

"It's for you," said Ismailov.

"For Monakhov!" trilled the secretary, tuning in, "I said, who's Monakhov?" Meanwhile Monakhov, with eyebrow and shoulders raised to indicate the extreme degree of his perplexity, his potential sternness in the event of a misunderstanding, came around the table and took the receiver from Ismailov, "And they said to me—the executive from Moscow," chirped the secretary.

"Monakhov here," said Monakhov in a manner that was alien to him; he felt absolutely dreadful: "The executive from Moscow."

"You don't know me," a low and at the same time strangely youthful voice came over the line, "but that's not important..."

"Hello? Who's speaking?" said Monakhov, for some reason blowing into the receiver.

"An acquaintance of yours—"

"What's this nonsense?" thought Monakhov.

"Natalya... she asked me to give you a message, that you must come see her. She has something to tell you that's extremely important to you. It could threaten your life..."

"What rubbish!" exclaimed Monakhov, his gaze following the secretary, who was running towards a receiver parallel to him, "Who's speaking? Isn't there any other way of passing on a message?"

"She's very sick," the voice sounded more remote, as though the receiver were being pulled away.

"I can't talk any more," and short beeps sounded.

"Hello!" a red-faced Monakhov blew into the receiver. And he didn't grasp right away why Ismailov had wordlessly stretched out his short-fingered hand to him. Ismailov took the receiver from him and placed it on the hook as he would a precious object.

It was absurd, but as a result Monakhov left Ismailov's feeling humiliated. The secretary's wide-eyed stare followed him out.

"Just wait!" Monakhov was seething; he was striding towards the house with swift, vicious strides; he went to the top and exposed Ismailov; he reprimanded Natalya as one would a schoolgirl; he apostrophized himself with cruel irony: you fool, for instance. Chuckling over his other suppositions, he could not, however, altogether dismiss them from consideration: that Natalya really was sick, or that her admirers had set a trap for him—that Lenechka or that Natalya through her own methods had found out about some danger that actually was threatening him; to be killed, but by whom? Here he laughed out loud at himself, ignoring the passersby,—you're a kid, too many movies! If all this was Natalya's trick to make him come see her, then he should see through it and punish her by not coming. But even in that event there was something flattering to Monakhov in this persistence, a confirmation of his appeal... But if this was a threat... his heart contracted with boyish fear, then Monakhov became cheerful, imagining how he would scatter this cowardly ambush, and if he got beaten up, then that too would somehow suit him... In any case, he wouldn't chicken out, he'd go, like a fool (from their point of view), he would crawl headfirst into the mousetrap, without getting mixed up with the police or notifying anyone. The more frightful the picture he drew for himself, the more daring he became. And what if Natalya had set this up to test his nerve? This was a possibility he hadn't considered, yet it was the most likely: a test for lousiness... Satisfaction for slighted female vanity: as if to show he wasn't worth getting so upset about.

And for the sake of this last possibility, which somehow contained both of the first ones, Monakhov remained in Tashkent for another day so as to pass such a test honorably, so that all the others wouldn't pass it.

It should be mentioned in Monakhov's defense that to the end there remained the courtly view, however improbable it might have been: that she was sick, that she herself could be under some threat...

3

"So here I am..." Monakhov smiled to himself, following Natasha, who was strong and easily carried the heavy basket. For a second he fancied that this was where he had been going in the first place: arriving from somewhere else, not from his mother's or his wife's. He perceived the apartment anew, as if he'd never been in it. He squeezed through the dark entrance hall between Natasha, the basket, and the door, whence the kitchen was totally visible: a dry grey-haired disheveled woman with a cigarette in her mouth was washing the dishes.

"Aunt, this is Monakhov," said Natasha, putting down the basket.

The aunt moved back, squinting nearsightedly in the darkness of the entrance hall without seeing anything, and nodded welcomingly, as though the smoke were getting into her eyes, as if to say, sorry, my hands are wet. Monakhov shuffled his feet in courteous embarrassment in the darkness.

"Come on, come on. You've just got here. You need to take a shower," she said loudly for the aunt's benefit and dragged him farther down the corridor which was just as dark, "Don't pay any attention." And Monakhov followed her, gallantly dancing about in front of the aunt, as though someone else were between them, some animal he had to avoid stepping on... "What story has she told her?" thought Monakhov sourly. This family consisting of him and the aunt, just formed in a second in the corridor, didn't suit him. The misgivings which were turning out not to have deceived him emerged in real earnest. Concern about his own deception, which had been fading, seized him. "I'll ask her firmly right now why she set up this call to Ismailov. And then..." But he didn't get to ask her.

He didn't recognize the room either. Formerly conspicuously empty, it now contained a ridiculous number of new objects: a dining-room table trimmed with an aluminum stripe, and as part of the set, a matching chair; an antique wooden angel's head, a genuine piece with its nose broken off and wings behind its ears, was hanging on a new nail; a large foreign photograph—a naked white girl beside a giant white insulating cleat; a large skin of an animal unknown to Monakhov lay on the floor, and on the skin, hugging his scruffy knees, was a very unshaven, disheveled man of Monakhov's age, certainly not Lenechka...

Monakhov was at a loss.

"How funny you are, Monakhov!" Natasha was delighted, "What's the matter with you? This is Zyablikov, you've already seen him."

Monakhov approached him with hand outstretched.

Making a purely formal motion to rise, Zyablikov extended a tiny unwashed hand.

"Monakhov," said Monakhov.

Zyablikov, however, did not say "Zyablikov," but merely looked attentively at him. This gaze bothered Monakhov a little, although it didn't contain displeasure or a challenge—it was as though he could see through Monakhov. This impression of Zyablikov's wit, as yet not confirmed by anything, aroused in Monakhov a mixed feeling of respect and hostility.

"You've cluttered it up," said Monakhov for something to say.

"This," Natalya pointed to the table, laughing, "he and Lenechka brought yesterday from the café on the corner."

"What do you mean?" Monakhov didn't understand.

"Just like that, they took it by the corners and carried it off."

Zyablikov seemed to be listening with interest himself.

"And this—angel," Monakhov poked a finger at the cherub, "Is it real?" he asked, guarded where his knowledge of art was concerned.

"That's not an angel, it's a cherub," said Natalya proudly. "What's the difference," thought Monakhov irritatedly. "Lenechka wouldn't give me anything but a real one." Monakhov remained silent. "And this is Zyablikov's skin."

"Not mine, of course, but a yak's," said Zyablikov. And this joke, unworthy of the impression of wit which he'd created on Monakhov, was really nothing but courtesy. Monakhov laughed most readily: Zyablikov's sense of democracy had won him over. It turned out, however, that he alone had come without a gift. He thought of the basket of fruit, but at once rejected the idea as too cynical. He was almost surprised at himself for not having thought of a gift, convinced, apparently, that he himself was a gift. Monakhov smiled ironically. Zyablikov opened a box of some amazingly long cigarettes in front of him.

"I roll them myself," he said.

From a false feeling Monakhov readily took one, sat next to him on the skin and now kept twirling the cigarette in his fingers, spilling the tobacco.

"I've given up smoking," he said.

Without a word Zyablikov took the cigarette from his fingers and replaced it in the box. Monakhov smiled helplessly.

Natasha went out to the kitchen—Zyablikov was silent, and Monakhov was silent too, depressed by his thoughts. As if he only now understood. When he was inwardly flailing about, choosing one out of three paths, why did each of the three keep becoming the only one? Why was that? Why was it that if he were to choose Natasha, then once past the threshold they would enter a bed as broad as a public square, and be alone together, without interruption apparently, until it would be time for Monakhov in his turn to leave? This whirlwind from the threshold, as a reward for his decisiveness, this apportioned space of a private birthday—this alone could tip the balance in the choice. That is, various choices break with reality, while a choice, in multiplying, attempts to reflect it... The evolution of the variants: he conquers who is clever enough to appear the most seductive. And here are Zyablikov, the aunt, the cherub,—all of which would have been so easy to imagine from the outset. "Choice distorts the goal," Monakhov held this notion in his thoughts for a bit, the way you hold a finished form in your hands, a spare part whose place and function are unknown to us—such an appealing thing, but useless—and put it aside, forget it because of its uselessness.

Natasha beckoned him out into the corridor.

"What's the matter with you, Monakhov... You're a little fool, Monakhov," she kept saying, embracing him like a pillar, "Why are you sulking at Zyablikov? What's he got to do with anything?"

Monakhov was surprised at this assumption. He was thinking all sorts of things, but he wasn't thinking he had a rival. Because he considered himself outside any competition. Such a thought couldn't even enter his head.

"So, is your Lenechka coming too?" he asked.

"They'll leave, they will!" said Natasha vehemently, embracing him and loving him even more, "I couldn't not invite them," she pleaded.

Monakhov was satisfied with the preference accorded him and he kissed her. He returned from the dark corridor to the illuminated Zyablikov, and tried by his whole demeanor not to compromise Natasha; that is, he somehow indicated that nothing had passed between them in the corridor. Although how can one show that? And how could anything have happened in the corridor? Zyablikov glanced at him again, once more giving the impression of wit. It was as though he too wasn't saying anything about what Monakhov didn't show.

"Well, should I go?" asked Zyablikov.

"Of course not, don't be silly" Monakhov started dissuading him, blushing in delight, "There's no reason for you to go," he said uncertainly.

"I have a ruble," said Zyablikov, giving him another look.

"Oh—" Monakhov was extremely embarrassed by his slip, and with hurried readiness he busily started taking out five rubles, ten, all his money. Zyablikov's hand lingered for a second and decisively took only five rubles.

"What *are* you doing, Monakhov?" said Natasha, "Why did you give him money? You'll drink too much, you won't last until the evening. You're a fool, Monakhov. Zyablikov is simply my friend. He's nothing to me. What are you doing, Monakhov...! He'll be coming any minute...Monakhov...Auntie!"

She fled.

Zyablikov turned out to be a really entertaining fellow. Monakhov hadn't met anyone like him. He was a great traveler. He'd sailed down Siberian rivers from their sources to the ocean; he'd hiked across deserts and the taiga, and all this, apparently, was true. He could live half a year alone in the company of mosquitoes and pine needles and he wouldn't drink, not only because there was nothing to drink but because there was no reason to. The rest of life, including himself, he knew no worse, it seemed, than the forest, and he despised it, apparently, so profoundly that it left him calm and contemptuous.

Stupidity, of course, irritated him because it was difficult not to notice it both when there was little of it and when there was a lot. In general he appealed strongly to Monakhov, and Monakhov tried to please him and show his intelligence, repeatedly slipping on his inaccuracies. But it wasn't Zyablikov who turned off his lame words with a glance; Monakhov himself would immediately catch himself up on them, correct himself and steer on course—what a pleasure it was to talk to an intelligent man. In short, they were really drinking.

Natasha would run in from her kitchen chores.

"So, are you ready?" she'd say affectionately, fingering Monakhov's hair. Monakhov would freeze under her caress, not knowing whether it was flattering to him or excessive in Zyablikov's eyes. He'd pretend that nothing much was going on. Natasha's hand would stop, losing its tremor. Monakhov would sense her arrested gaze behind him. Suddenly she'd leave the room.

And at that moment Monakhov would start telling some of the incredible things that his father had told him, the ones he'd listened to so scornfully. Now, editing them slightly, he discovered in them an increasingly greater and ever penetrating significance. Tortoises crawled to the sea and cried...birds took the azimuth along the plane of the earth...some last surviving monster lived on alone in no less ancient England...

Zyablikov could find similar incidents in his own experience.

Monakhov was delighted. He laughed sincerely and a little longer than sincerity demanded, rocking exaggeratedly. What if Zyablikov was more intelligent, Monakhov was loved, so his pride wasn't wounded, and he was even happy that he felt younger, as though he'd fallen into childhood, making himself comfortable in the shade of an older friend. Zyablikov leaned down, confidentially breathing in his ear:

"There's some loot, you get it?"

Monakhov nodded in agreement without understanding. He accepted the "loot" with the same readiness with which he swallowed the "red"—the worst wine, of which Zyablikov had managed to buy an incredible quantity for Monakhov's five rubles. "It's a totally straight deal," Zyablikov whispered. He knew where the treasure lay. All he needed was a partner. It wasn't simple to find a partner. You need a serious person. And it turned out Monakhov was just the one.

"The one thing I don't like about you," Monakhov pricked up his ears, for some reason immediately ready to take offense, "is your mania for work." Monakhov laughed with relief. "So you're a brilliant engineer, what next?"

Monakhov had difficulty knowing what next. What next was what would come next, that's what Zyablikov said. But he could get a million right there.

Well, sure, Monakhov probably agreed.

"It's a bargain!"

Natasha came in. Monakhov was deep in conversation.

"It's funny," she said, "What a child you really are."

Monakhov pricked up his ears: was that good or bad? Was she flattering him or making a dig?

"An absolute child," added Natasha.

She was making a dig at him. But that was only because she was hurt.

"Listen here," Zyablikov swayed as he sat, "There's more loot..."

"Don't you listen to him!" Natasha burst out laughing, "Is he inviting you to dig up a burial mound?"

Zyablikov looked at her devotedly and latched onto her hand, trying to kiss it.

"Get away!" Natasha shook him off without any anger.

Zyablikov smoothly tumbled over sideways and was already asleep. A childlike smile illuminated his face.

"He's dead to the world," said Natasha, "And how about you, Monakhov?"

"What?" Monakhov was more or less smiling.

"You're a traitor, Monakhov."

After quarreling a little with Natasha, taking a shower, and sobering up, Monakhov grew gloomy. Zyablikov was still lying in the same position on his skin, and was indeed dead to the world. What was the point of all this? It smacked of puncturing, of defeat, of his own mediocrity. It wasn't worth resisting all that. He'd piled it up... Monakhov sat on the edge of a chair, hardened, renunciatory, as though not even touching the air of this alien, superfluous apartment. He was clean and fastidious after his shower.

Natasha moved back and forth, setting the table, and he didn't look at Natasha.

"Don't be mad," Natasha tried to embrace him.

"I'm not mad," replied Monakhov, bored.

"You don't love me, Monakhov."

"Why do you say that...?"

"Don't worry, you never once told me you love me. You don't owe me anything."

"Did I really never tell you?"

"Spare me, Monakhov! Get with it! This is me!" Natasha pulled him about, "I love you. You came to me. My name's Natasha. Dearest..."

And she buried herself in his knees. Monakhov took a last look at the unconscious Zyablikov and closed his eyes tight, encouragingly stroking her head. He sat perfectly still, moaning slightly from time to time.

And then the bell rang, tearing his skull apart.

"Damn!" groaned Natasha, jumping up.

The entrance door banged, a bass voice began to drone, the aunt burst out laughing, and someone flew along the corridor, brushing against the walls with the rustling of a bird.

An inconceivable bouquet of tulips that couldn't get through the doorway entered the room, and when at last it squeezed through, behind it appeared the absurd, thick-lipped, flushed face of a boy. He could barely hold the bouquet which was falling apart, and in addition, a fat book was slipping out from under his arm.

An expression of malice lingered helplessly on Natasha's face, as though there was nothing that the malice could hold on to.

"You can't imagine how I ran!" the boy breathed with rapture, and, finally dropping the book, bent down to retrieve it, and the flowers scattered. The aunt appeared above him, melting into a smile.

"Lenechka's arrived," she announced, as though it were news.

And of course he was the one Monakhov had seen at the bazaar that time...

Natasha flushed, pressed her hands, or the back of her palms, to her face—to cool her cheeks, and stumbling against a flower, she shot out of the room.

"What's the matter with her?" asked Lenechka in fright, looking around the room, searching for the cause, and completely oblivious to Monakhov, as though he weren't sitting in front of him still in the same chair. Lenechka's prominent eyes, the color of the emptiest sky, gazed at the place where Natasha had just stood, and didn't see her. This heavenly perplexity gave Monakhov the opportunity to come to his senses and he rose to meet the newcomer. Lenechka, still not seeing Monakhov right before his eyes, finally realized that Natasha wasn't there, and disappointedly throwing aside the few flowers that remained in his arms, dashed out in pursuit, almost knocking over the aunt.

"Listen! Listen!" he shouted as he ran, "Wait..."

The aunt started gathering up the flowers, pursing her mouth and not looking at Monakhov. Zyablikov was sitting on the skin like a pane of glass, and watched her with a wide-awake gaze as she bent down.

Lenechka furiously banged on the bathroom door:

"Open up! Come on, open up! I have to tell you—" he was whining.

And Monakhov didn't quite understand everything.

The room, filled with tulips, was transformed again; the table was set, the candles lit. It seemed to Monakhov that he had been there for several days in a row, and each of these days was unlike the preceding one: just as his notions about this day differed from the way it had begun, so did the evening of the day differ from its beginning. It seemed that everything was going in reverse sequence, as though this day's film were being shown backwards. They were sitting around the table now as though it were yesterday the way it might have been at the beginning, but not later. Everything suddenly became clean, festive, and decorous so unexpectedly. Zyablikov, completely sober, was pleasant and attentive to the aunt; Monakhov liked everyone, but Lenechka more than anyone; everyone liked Natasha, but she wanted to be liked most by Monakhov, who liked her less than she wished; Lenechka didn't see anyone besides Natasha. They toasted with champagne in the aunt's glasses and ate last year's marvelously preserved watermelon. And the watermelon, which especially captured Monakhov's imagination (he wasn't from Tashkent), this watermelon, which couldn't exist in the present, further strengthened Monakhov's impression that all of them now were only a memory of the party that had already taken place.

Natasha was festively pretty. Whatever else there was, what had happened in this "memory" of Monakhov's had happened above all with her and for her, and not simply in his memory, but right *now,* in her life. This was *her* birthday, that was the whole point. Next year she'd already be twenty-four! She was scared and cheerful. Monakhov filled her with love and horror. Lenechka's rapture flattered her and plunged her into despair. The combination of the two of them aroused her fear and curiosity. And it was fear and burning curiosity which for the most part illuminated her face and colored it in such a way as to seem to the first one to be the light of her love, and to the second, the reflection of the first one's love. Natasha willingly glowed in this little fire. Incidentally, Lenechka was so in love with her that he wasn't even jealous. It was rather Monakhov who got jealous, "There's someone who loves her! There's the one to whom she's everything!" he thought with envy, glancing at Lenechka's face, into that heavenly puddle in which Natasha was reflected. Oh, how it lived and breathed! As though his face were flying on him, like a rider on horseback! Forward! To her, to her!—joyfully succumbing to this speed. He was on his way to her all the time; he'd be on his way, would arrive, would finally see her, and then would set out again. He would set out to her across the table, across this distance of two meters, as through infinity, which neither frightened nor stopped him. And Monakhov was happy to look at Natasha, flattered to read her glance, but he had only to see this flight of Lenechka's face—he couldn't not follow this endless and joyful fall with a heart that would fall in turn—and then it was hard for him to look at Natasha, who wasn't looking at Lenechka, but was waiting for his, Monakhov's glance. Her wide eyes glimmered so nakedly, so openly, focused on what would happen; soon—not now, but in a minute, in an hour, nearer and nearer—would come the decision! Not hers, but someone else's, and it was clear whose. She had done everything, had wound everything up, had produced the inevitability and now she could only wait. And waiting was joyful—she wasn't counting on anything or harboring any illusions, but she could still hope a thousand times with no basis, just as Lenechka could hope a hundred thousand times, as Monakhov would hope just once more in his life...

Lenechka moved about ceaselessly and smiled blindingly with his fat, sparsely-toothed mouth, cried unembarrassedly with joy at seeing her with his empty eyes, like clouds in a tall sky, and whatever indifferent nonsense he spouted, he only declared his love, only once again a touch differently told how he loved her, how everything that happened on earth was for her sake, or how everything that happened was connected to her. Natasha never heard him, but how protected she was by him! Oh Lord! What a hollow gloomy silence would descend if Lenechka, whom she didn't hear, were to fall silent. Lenechka didn't give a damn that he was ugly, clumsy, unloved, didn't say the right thing! Monakhov admired him with envy. It was impossible not to love him!—thought Monakhov, feeling an unexpected (because so unaccustomed) warmth beneath his heart. "Really, woman is a miracle," he mused further, inadvertently catching Natasha's burning glance and quickly avoiding whatever assurance there may have been in his own—"What does she want me for? Oh, it's no good!"

The aunt, who had once even sung on the stage and whose former husband had once worked in a circus, smoking, squinted at the smoke that was held in her hand, as though it were getting in her eyes, and her air of significance, her provisional nature, as if she were in exile in distant Tashkent, were, though excusable, so borrowed and recognizable that Monakhov avoided looking in her direction. Only a wise person like Zyablikov could endure such a thing (it was rare when cynicism successfully masqueraded as humaneness). Natasha knew what kind of person her aunt was, playing the role of mother today—this was part of her repertoire. Monakhov avoided looking at the aunt anyway, more because he wanted to avoid the least suggestion of a guarantee.

"Perhaps you'll recite for us, Lenechka?" said the aunt in an indulgent chesty voice.

"Yes, yes, do!" Monakhov seconded her with interest.

"Natasha knows the poem, she won't be interested," said Lenechka.

"Do recite," said Natasha. Monakhov's unexpected interest pleased her. "I tried to recite it for him but forgot."

For the first time Lenechka glanced briefly at Monakhov as though at an object.

"I've reworked it," Lenechka was upset about something.

"Recite, don't put on airs," commanded Natasha.

"O.K.," said Lenechka, and closed his eyes, "Just a minute. O.K. 'Dawn.' That's the title. So, 'Dawn.' "

> The world stood, as though I'd died...
> I was absent from it, and gradually
> It cleansed itself of that which I
> Had made my own, attributing it to God.
>
> Everything in everything was alien and transparent,
> And the last contour melts before one's eyes.

We'll take with us an incidental detail for remembrance:
On the horizon the yardkeeper rises like the sun.

How kind and hackneyed is the sweep of
His broom! A toy... How disappointing
Matter appears in the dark:
We can be seen through, though I can't see myself.

An end to the end—the beginning of all beginnings:
The world is so wonderful, as though I'd not been in it;
Transparent meanings I'd not collated
With the word, and in the beginning was the sky.

And as though I'd never been in it...
...A farewell line lies in an envelope—
What nonsense!—as if one could live on
After death for two days by mail.

    At first Monakhov couldn't rid himself of a feeling of awkwardness at Lenechka's singsong voice and his swaying. But he believed almost right away that Lenechka was not putting it on—he already knew that. He kept looking at Natasha because it was the first time he had the chance: she wasn't looking at him now, anxious as she was for Lenechka. "She's his sort of person!" thought Monakhov with jealousy and surprise, "How can she not know that?" The aunt was screwing up her eyes. Zyablikov was rolling an enormous cigarette in his fingers, tidily catching the tobacco spilling from it in a newspaper.
    And now something appealed to Monakhov. Either he had got accustomed to and overcome his embarrassment at the reading, or he'd stopped worrying about Lenechka, now that he wouldn't humiliate himself too badly. He listened with increasing attention and surprise, whereas Natasha completely stopped listening in her agitation: she was watching Monakhov listening...
    "It's almost over," said Lenechka.

Run faster. They're taking aim at us.
We're surrounded by false concepts!...
Resist to the last man. For now not alive, but whole.
You won't break through their cotton embraces.

There's a formula! "For now not alive, but whole,"
Anaesthesia, ether, compressed ozone...
You were late, I didn't come in time.
You never used to wake up early...

> Dream of yourself. Open the door barefooted
> When I ring my ring...It's me. Aren't you glad?...
> Don't open. Look into the door's peephole—
> You'll see the open garden cell.
>
> And I'm not there. And there seems to be
> A steep precipice below. Empty mist swirls up
> Like milk being spilled...
> Your house has floated away, has cast off, my lass!
>
> And you've remained on board
> And are gazing into the void with swollen eyes...
> And there's a taste of metal in your mouth...
> And on your face, slight irritation.
>
> You didn't even know there was a precipice in the garden...
> The cock's crow froze there so high!—
> Don't look down...Closing the gate,
> Go home. We'll part ahead of time.

Everyone was silent.

"It was better before," said Natasha jealously.

"Really?" responded Lenechka readily, "I didn't like it just now either. The hell with it!" He lightly waved the poem aside.

Monakhov dutifully thought it necessary to say something about it. For some reason he blushed.

"Really?" Natalya responded with the same readiness as Lenechka, "Good for you, Monakhov! I didn't expect it. What did I tell you?" she said triumphantly, "Now you can see for yourself..."

Monakhov, without looking at her, apologized and, blushing again, even asked to have the poem copied.

"I'll write it down for you right now," agreed Lenechka.

"Here, have a smoke," said Zyablikov, who hadn't raised his eyes all this time. And he offered Lenechka an unexpectedly long "double," a "cigar."

Lenechka broke into a blissful smile and took the mysterious cigarette.

"Don't you dare smoke!" said Natasha angrily.

"All right," Lenechka at once agreed and put the cigarette behind his ear. "Then let's drink."

Apparently he felt awkward after his poetry recital.

"To our poet!" proclaimed the aunt.

Monakhov raised his glass with particular alacrity. To his own surprise, the poetry turned out to have made a great impression on him. This impression seemed to be emerging by degrees. He kept looking sideways at Lenechka and dropping his gaze. All the absurdity and childishness of

Lenechka's appearance now bore for Monakhov a certain mark of significance. In acknowledging, in "getting to respect" Lenechka, it was as though Monakhov were searching in him for changes that were the direct consequences of this recognition—and he didn't find them. It was still the same Lenechka who with pleasure washed down his recital and rapidly forgot about it. "And Natasha, it appears, is his Muse..." Monakhov thought slowly and looked at her with that glance. She was looking intently at him, as though trying to make him out from a distant perspective.

"Monakhov..." she said, "Oh, never mind..."

"What?" he responded.

"Nothing."

Zyablikov was manufacturing another cigarette. His movements were measured and exact (but it was as if his impatience lapped at this deliberation all the more keenly): the closer to completion he got, the slower they became, exhausting themselves. He was finally satisfied with its neatness and compactness, and reverently struck a match. Having lit up in the most careful manner possible, he began to behave even more strangely: letting out a bit of smoke, he would immediately convulsively draw up behind it, grabbing it back with his greedy mouth, and driving in the stream of smoke which was escaping from the end of the cigarette with his little palm—he resembled a fish just pulled out of the water. He was extraordinarily preoccupied, and Monakhov didn't dare ask him why he was doing this, but it didn't surprise anyone else. He completed a series of these furtive little inhalations, then leaned back, went limp, and closed his eyes: a careful, blind smile barely touched his lips. "A strange guy..." thought Monakhov. The aunt, having lost Zyablikov, squinted at Monakhov. It turned out Monakhov had been wrong to suppose that she had something against him—she probably just felt self-conscious before she'd had a drink. She looked at Monakhov and began quietly, but somehow professionally, to hum: "I will keep silent, I won't say a word." "An alcoholic," thought Monakhov. "What do they want from me?" he exclaimed almost hostilely, meaning his irresistibility. He shifted his gaze to Lenechka—he was still looking at Natasha, every bit as undaunted, with the same mute rapture, as though that alone would be enough for him forever. "What a high...," murmured Zyablikov blissfully.

"I shouldn't have come... I should have left for Moscow... I've really made a mess of it: who knows what to do," fretted Monakhov. "How can he not notice anything!" Now he got angry at Lenechka. "I'm here—he knows why and what for. In your place I'd... I don't know... I'd have killed me long ago! How does he stand all this...?" Monakhov sternly pulled the bottle toward himself and drank a full glass in resolute solitude and became ostentatiously gloomy. "Good God! What is this? Have I died, or what? Why don't I love anybody...? Neither her nor my wife. I don't even love myself. Or even my mother!" he thought this in words and became really horrified. But he did love! How he loved... Here's how he, just like Lenechka, had loved!—

he realized, and closed his eyes tight: everything from the depths of his past years unexpectedly welled up, as though it had always been right beside him, as though it were yesterday, and the main thing was that it wasn't consecutive, wasn't in sequence, but all at once, together, as though on a single canvas, as though time didn't exist and everything was happening all at once: today, and yesterday, and tomorrow—all in one dimension. This welled up dazzlingly, but as soon as he started recalling the sequence it receded immediately and there remained the feeling that for a second he'd been Lenechka, had sat on his chair, and had stared at Natalya and nothing had existed except... Yet something had gained a foothold, had stuck in his mind out of this amalgamated clump: something he never remembered any more, and to which then, twenty years later, he realized what he hadn't even noticed then, hadn't seen, hadn't understood, didn't want to, in fact couldn't understand, and wouldn't have accepted then at any price...

... Asya worked at an optical plant... Monakhov distinctly remembered those lenses now, she'd bring them home sometimes—such pretty little things. She worked on two shifts, and the evening one was convenient for young Alyosha Monakhov; he could come to Asya in the morning, when there wasn't anybody in her apartment and his parents thought he was at the institute. And that's how he lived every other week. But one time he got two weeks in a row: Asya was on sick leave. And so he rushed over a little earlier, happy, dreaming of finding her still sleepy... but he found her far from sleepy. She was sitting in her faded robe, which was his favorite, with a wide-awake expression, and across the table from her was sitting some guy with a bottle of port. Now Monakhov was surprised that he hadn't been upset or surprised, but only annoyed at the obstacle. From the appearance alone of this guy young Alyosha was sure he wasn't anyone he should be jealous of. The guy was different from Alyosha—he was ugly. Unfashionably dressed and middleaged. Now when Monakhov examined him through the prism of time it was obvious that the guy was shaven and well-dressed for the occasion, and wasn't at all old, but was even very strong and fresh-looking. They weren't at all embarrassed at his arrival. "This is... (Monakhov had forgotten the name), my colleague, I've told you about him, he's come to visit me," said Asya. "And this is my Alyosha." Monakhov remembered his firm, smooth handshake and glance. Yes, she had actually mentioned once or twice before that there was some fellow who kept paying her compliments and inviting her out. Alyosha hadn't paid attention; everything connected with her work bored him. Nowadays Monakhov himself knew men like that, came across them. Now he saw that his glance was not stupid or grasping (work superintendents are like that), that he conducted himself with a dignity that was, moreover, habitual to him, that he was decent and reasonable not only in relation to himself, but to other people too—a solid fellow. Except for this first legitimate glance, he didn't once behave nastily, neither dropping any hints nor being overly observant or superior. Yes, he was a good guy... Oh yes, now Monakhov heard much better her occasional casual references to him! Although what Asya's story was worth—about the fact that he'd had a fiancée after the war, a Lithuanian or a Latvian, where he'd been fighting, and they loved each other very much, and she'd perished tragically: she was straightening her skirt, which had got caught (talk about a realistic moment in a romance!) while they were amorously swinging on a swing and she fell straight onto the spikes of a garden railing... When does one tell a tale like that, eh? And that meant he still hadn't got married—Asya also mentioned that. And he made a good salary. Mmm—ye-es. The fellow conducted himself well: he didn't try to pull the wool over anyone's eyes with a flow of words, he didn't talk nonsense—probably all he said was to offer the port, but he didn't insist on that either. He simply sat solidly in his chair, and it was as though the chair beneath him became more solid. Monakhov now saw him as though he were right at his side, this fellow whom he hadn't remembered once in his whole life: his durable grey suit ironed, in the naval manner (oh yes, Asya also mentioned that he'd served in the navy...), a dark blue shirt, a bony face with a youthful complexion, and for some reason he remembered especially clearly his hair, extraordinarily straight and unyielding even now, and he would comb it from time to time in front of Asya... Monakhov brought his face still closer into focus: that stubby neck with its protruding little tuft of hair, those intelligent elephant eyes, that crooked bony nose, long and jagged... "Ooooh!" moaned Monakhov now, but his fist did not penetrate through the thickness of years. That's O.K.—he comforted himself, let it be... It's difficult to suspect your first love with such an unromantic rival... But later, what happened then! It was awful, positively awful. The fellow finally got up (had she asked him to leave or not?—I don't recall) and left, but not for good, he was supposed to return soon, he'd left his port... Asya sat on the bed, Alyosha on his knees, kissing her hands. Asya said he shouldn't, the fellow would return soon. She actually explained suspiciously much, why he'd come, how she was obliged to him, that he'd been angling for an invitation for a long time, that finally she couldn't refuse, that he'd leave soon, and Alyosha could return, but that right now Alyosha should leave. But Alyosha for some reason wasn't interested in her explanations: who wanted to hear about some person who didn't matter to him in any case... and now look at what happened right before Monakhov's very eyes—oh God! Even now he couldn't believe it. It seemed Asya gave in to Alyosha after all. "Okay, get a move on," she said and was somehow either distracted or indifferent and cold. But Alyosha was happy and rose from his knees with triumph, with which he glanced at the "colleague" who had come in almost instantly. After this he quickly said goodbye, and obedient to Asya's will, went away without giving it a thought so as never to remember it again. And the "colleague" stayed... "Oh-ho-ho! Such are the sufferings of the young Werther," wailed Monakhov inwardly. "Is this what happens with the story of his purity and the sufferings caused him? oh-ho-ho! Why be surprised at Lenechka then?"... At this point Monakhov became just distracted enough to remember where he was. He raised his eyes to Lenechka to confirm his discovery. But in the meantime Lenechka had gone. And Natasha wasn't there either. Zyablikov was asleep. And just at that moment, yawning and emphasizing her boredom, the aunt rose from her seat and with her glass in her hand went to her room without saying "good night," probably having taken offense. It was probably these yawns of the aunt's that had awakened Monakhov from his reveries—how long, then, had he been reminiscing? A second or an hour? If an hour, where had the two of them gone for so long...? he wondered, without suspicion.

The door closed behind the aunt and Monakhov returned to his story... Really, what kind of tricks were these! he was indignant. "How did I dare not see how terribly she lived! Poor penniliess girl! That's what 'love is blind' means! Blind or not blind, but how convenient! Blind even about oneself. One sees only what one wants to see... Whatever one wants to, one sees. So does that mean I didn't love then either?"

Natalya came in noisily and animatedly, and Lenechka came slowly behind her, like a blind man, with his head thrown back, his face stiff, carrying splashing light and pain as though afraid of spilling them. She went directly to Monakhov, ruffling his hair.

"Monakhov dear, I abandoned you, forgive me. Did you miss me?"

Monakhov gave her an unfriendly glance.

"Don't be angry, Monakhov... I had to tell him," she added in an undertone.

"Tell him what?"

In the meantime, Lenechka, like lightly tinkling glass, went by them to the window, stopped, and leaned against it.

"That I love you, that I want to be with you right now..."

"You said you'd already told him!" Monakhov whistled in a whisper.

"No," frowned Natalya, "I told him just now."

"Then why did you tell me then that you had?" Monakhov didn't understand.

"I wanted to see what you'd say."

"And what did I say?"

"Don't worry, you didn't say anything."

"So maybe you didn't say anything now either, but you're only claiming you did...?"

"Oh, Monakhov! I told him. How sad, Monakhov... You have no heart."

"And do you, to tell him such things?"

"How could I not tell him" Natalya was genuinely surprised. "I want to be together with you..."

Monakhov digested this response.

"So what did you tell him?" he finally came up with. "Only that you love me and want to stay with me? Or that you've already... as you call it... 'been together with me'?"

"Good God!" Natalya flared, "What's the difference! As though it's not clear! What am I, a little girl? Whatever happened, ... I said I love you, and that's enough."

"So then there's... Then it's O.K.," said Monakhov with a grin, "He'll cope with it..."

"What are you talking about?" Natalya was puzzled.

"He'll cope with it consciously. Worse things than that have been coped with," he gave another grin, "I'm playing..." he thought, "playing a role. And my role is incredibly badly written!"

"You're really dishing it out, Monakhov!"

"Should I go," said Lenechka inaudibly, finally realizing that he was leaning against something, and turning away from the window. He hadn't heard what they were saying.

Natalya didn't hear him.

"I'm dishing it out... *You're* dishing it out! To hit a man with something like that right between the eyes!" Monakhov whispered loudly.

"That's O.K. It's not so awful. It's awful until you're told. You, for example, haven't yet told me you love me... And I'll never feel more awful than right now..." Monakhov didn't say it even then. Natalya sighed. "And even if you say it I won't believe you. You yourself said he'll cope with it. He'll write a poem..."

"Should I go?" said Lenechka more clearly.

"A poem?" Monakhov gave a start.

"Are you still here?" Natalya was surprised.

Lenechka submissively took a step toward the door.

"Wait," said Monakhov resolutely, "there's still some left..." He went to the table, poured the wine into glasses and gallantly handed them around to the cast of characters. Lenechka clutched at his glass as if at a straw. Natalya turned away. "You promised me you'd copy out the poem..." said Monakhov, clinking glasses with Lenechka.

"I'll do it right now... I—" he glanced at Natalya with fear and hope, "I'll do it in a second. I'll copy it quickly." While Natalya kept silent he hurried over to the corner, sat on the skin, and settled down with a little book.

"You're a bastard, Monakhov," Natalya whispered calmly, went to her corner, and lay down on the mattress.

Monakhov also settled down on the skin and now observed the scene with doleful satisfaction: as before, Zyablikov was sleeping like the dead, Natalya was lying with her face to the wall (were her eyes open or closed?), Lenechka, bent into three, was writing shortsightedly and rapidly in the book on his knee... "So childlike..." sighed Monakhov, taking in his pose.

He closed his eyes wearily (just in case Natalya should turn around)... "You didn't even know there was a precipice in the garden..." How do you like that! He'd memorized it instantly. That meant it was good. Or rather, maybe it was. He should ask Zyablikov what he thought, he hadn't expressed his opinion... But Natalya says he's a wonderful writer. Think of it—he is published all over the world... in Paris... Monakhov easily visualized Paris, where he'd never been, but had trouble visualizing Zyablikov, who was sleeping opposite him. And what if Lenechka is a great poet. Funny. Can't be. What do I know about these things? But what if he is?... Who am I then? d'Anthès, Martynov? What nonsense... Strange people. I didn't think Natalya moved in such circles. In Tashkent especially. Different people. A Bohemian, his mother... There are all sorts of people—that's what I forgot... And how alike they all are! Identical. Me, him... (Lenechka continued scratching away on his knee). He's not me, after all, there's a twenty-year difference! He suddenly realized that he and Asya could have a son that age. Horrors! No—no, he was wrong. Lenechka was different, not at all like him... Did I know even a hundredth part of what he already understands in his poetry?... It's strange, though: in his poetry he's clearsighted, but here he's blind. It's funny he can't apply it... Didn't I use to write poetry? But God, better not remember what the poetry was like. Maybe he really had talent?... What's that to me! Monakhov got angry, "So he's got talent, does that mean I should be afraid of history? Or else they won't study me in school. Even if I've been given the same role as d'Anthès—did the tsar secretly set me against him? Or a society inimical to his talents? It's ridiculous. Perhaps it's actually very disrespectful to treat talented poets not as people but as property, as clowns; to give up one's women to them, not to duel with them, to regard them as a divine breed, as though they weren't the ones who had spat in your face... No, I'm an ignorant engineer, a blind instrument of fate. It's more honest that way. I want to sleep with Natalya, and that was why I set this all up and disregarded my wife and parents, and she wants the same thing. Isn't that enough? And if I deny myself for his sake, won't I be playing precisely the same role as far as he's concerned, if not worse? Natalya is mad at me, so how is he going to make out? He's a good boy, I've gotten to like him. But do I love anyone? I was a good boy too. So that fellow of Asya's, seeing my apparently holy simplicity, should he have crossed himself and run? As it was, he acted fairly, in a brotherly way... Horrors! And what's also a horror is if Asya then... Perhaps he came back and she got out of it somehow and nothing happened between them? You won't get at it, you won't get an answer, you'll absolutely never know. And even if nothing happened then, who am I that understand everything now? Even if it did happen it's a lost cause anyway once I find out and know what the heart shouldn't know with its intelligence, and not with its damned brain. What's to be done with Lenechka? Why did I meddle, idiot that I am! Oh, I was so moved, I felt an affection that didn't exist. How many more times am I going to fool myself that I exist, when I don't? But how long have I not existed? Oh, a long time. God, what torture to be without love! You keep on fooling yourself, you keep on hoping, but— nothing! A brush on the lips and that's all. It's passed by. You see, if you have a heart, you feel, but without a heart, you don't. And the fact that you don't have a heart—isn't that a feeling! That is hell on earth, and for an unknown sin besides. But if you have a heart, you can sin and rejoice. Who knows who's worse off. And maybe I have an enormous, kind, generous heart? But I don't even know that—whether I have one or not. Something there beats and quivers, but what is it? So one wonders, if I loved Asya more than anything in the world, did I love her at all? I don't remember anything—it's an enormous dark bag. With a happiness that was over, it seemed, but I thrust my hand inside at random—and pulled out such rubbish that I won't thrust it in any more and won't reminisce. It'll be truer, more sincere...I don't remember anything. I don't remember her face. I don't remember her love. Really—I don't remember. It seemed that to part with her was death, yet I don't remember the break, or the pain, or tragedy—nothing. I simply had to die, each second doom threatened me, yet the second passed and I didn't even notice. Asya simply disappeared—that was all. I don't remember. Yet something of the sort must have taken place, some drama, there couldn't not have been one. No, I don't remember...I remember that Asya was there and then wasn't and for some reason I was at the beach..."

"I've finished," Lenechka whispered in his ear.

"Ah..." Monakhov came to.

"Only I wrote down another one. Not what I recited."

Monakhov took the piece of paper. Lenechka squeezed himself into a quiet ball. Monakhov ran his eye over it, a shiver ran down his back, his eyes stung, the text swam. Monakhov brought it into focus again—in a large provincial hand was written the following:

> This woman is not completely drawn,
> This woman is not completely patched up,
> To this woman...

The lines swayed, running lightly into Monakhov's mental ear; with pleasure he allowed himself not to understand all of them:

> There she sits unconcerned,
> Uncombed—there is no need.
> And her hand has no watch,
> And her face...

Suddenly the slander became comprehensible to Monakhov and he understood all of it.

> What should I, who am going off to see other women,
> Do with her, whom I've stopped loving...

"Well, well!" Monakhov, stirred, smiled tenderly.

Give her unnecessary beads to wear on her breast?

"Ah!" sighed Monakhov and from pleasure missed the following lines:

> Nothing in her is remorseful
> Nothing in her will awaken.
> She'll turn her face away, press her fingers together
> And will powder herself in a frighteningly unfamiliar way.

Monakhov *saw* it, and total ecstasy gripped him.

> I'll come to her somewhat drunk
> I'll tumble into the yard, start breaking glass...

Monakhov was almost crying, the last lines swam blurredly in his eyes and suddenly ended.

"Stupendous!" he said.

Lenechka was more embarrassed than flattered.

"Do you publish?" Monakhov asked abashedly.

"No, they'll never print me. I only write about love."

"Hmm—yes," said Monakhov, "Don't we have anything left?"

"Shhh!" said Lenechka, glancing sideways at Natalya, who was lying face to the wall, and he put a finger to his lips with a roguish air. He stole past on all fours, rummaged behind the cupboard under the skin and crawled back with a bottle of "red" in his hand and a giant cigarette behind his ear.

"Here we are," he said in a whisper, "Zyablikov's hoard."

Monakhov glanced at Lenechka, then at the "great writer," and grew cheerful; one condition of greatness was satisfied—the latter was still as though dead: he was deathly pale. He glanced at Natalya's back and again shifted his gaze to Lenechka—the latter was completely content. "Well, enough of that," thought Monakhov, "did she really tell Lenechka anything at all? Maybe she only told me she had? Maybe she simply told him to go away without going into explanations? That's an order, she said—obey it..."

Lenechka uncorked the bottle, wiped the mouth, and passed it to Monakhov.

"Only there's nothing to eat," he said, "What I'd give to stuff my face! I could polish off a loaf of bread in one bite without water."

"What a kid he is!" Monakhov was delighted.

They sat on the skin with shoulders touching, taking sips of wine, passing it to each other—and they felt good. Monakhov realized this clearly—that not only he, but Lenechka too, felt good. Lenechka was now looking at Monakhov with almost the same eyes as he looked at Natalya with. Monakhov hadn't expected Lenechka to be drawn to him as a friend so sincerely, so suddenly, so totally. "He's simply like that," thought Monakhov. "Completely." Maybe he likes me because Natalya loves me—he thought suddenly. And so he's drawn to me as a brother..." As a father..." thought Monakhov tearfully. But that thought slipped by and receded—it wasn't appropriate: after all, he had a son already. "A schoolboy..." Monakhov winced.

"You want some?" Lenechka held out a smoking cigarette to him.

Monakhov nodded gratefully and inhaled greedily.

"Did you finish school?" he asked thoughtfully.

Lenechka had left school.

Monakhov tried to set him on the right path. Lenechka listened respectfully, but without hope, glancing at Monakhov and waiting for him to finish... And Monakhov dropped the topic.

They started an argument about poetry, about which Monakhov unexpectedly began to understand a lot.

"No," said Lenechka, "I'm no poet! I haven't written anything yet comparable to that—" he nodded at the pages in Monakhov's hand.

"In my opinion, this one's good too," Monakhov insisted, "At least from the middle on."

"Oh, it's all hogwash..."

Both of them suddenly found that awfully funny. Monakhov imagined "washing hogs" so vividly that he almost wept with laughter. Lenechka roared helplessly, looking at him.

"Ha-ha-ha!" he laughed.

"Ssh!" Moankhov kept putting his finger to his lips, pointing at Natalya. They tried to laugh in a whisper, choked, pushed one another—acted like schoolboys.

Monakhov was happy at acting like Lenechka's peer.

Their laughter and mutual prodding suddenly developed into a fight during school recess. They rolled about on the skin, romping and snorting. It was fun! Monakhov got out of breath—after all, he was twice as old, he wanted to take a rest, but from it!—Lenechka rushed at him with excitement and puppy-like playfulness. Laughing, Monakhov surrendered, trying to get his breath back as he lay under Lenechka. But Lenechka got carried away—the child!—he pressed, puffed, and suddenly it seemed to Monakhov that his eyes were furious. Monakhov came to his senses and easily tossed him off. Lenechka immediately calmed down.

Something ended.

Monakhov got his breath back, cooled down, froze in the same position, leaning against the wall, looking at Natalya's back. He didn't want to move or talk. He couldn't even shift his gaze. "I'm drunk," he thought.

So he looked in front of him at the same spot and easily imagined that he wasn't there, that he'd died.

A kind of invincible transparency lay between him and Natalya. Natalya floated up and seemed to hang suspended above the mattress. It was as though Monakhov was no longer sitting, but standing, shuddering lightly, and some fine line obstructed his path. The wall disappeared—there the moon and lamp post were sitting on one another, and this double light brought everything on earth to a stop, as if everything—they and he too, had the most transparent substance poured over them, and were like flies in amber. "The past looks like that," thought Monakhov.

Strange as it may seem, he really didn't recall how he and Asya had finally split up. There was no pain there. The plot had no denouement. He distinctly remembered some beach, but he was already without Asya. That was his first memory after Asya, and by that time they had not been seeing each other for a year. What kind of year had that been? What had filled it? Nothing but a flight, with the first stop a beach in Petropavlovsk, where everything froze in that second as in a photograph. At first he didn't think about this peculiarity of his memory at all, accepting it as necessary, as a blessing, and then he began to be curious—what had happened, where had it gone?... And with a great effort he managed to pick out some dim memory, moreover, of something that had happened exactly a year later: the interception of some letter, when they were no longer together, some humiliating trip to the kindergarten summer house (Asya was working again at her first profession) under the pretense of getting a magnifying glass. He couldn't find this summer house, then did find it, and to his surprise, Asya turned out to be there. But further it was flat again: he was making his way back through the same woods with the same offensive magnifying glass in his hand. And there was something or other too about the magnifying glass... wasn't it a fantasy?—later it turned out that he didn't have the magnifying glass at home, and if he really had gone in order to get it and had taken it, then where had it got to later? All this, I repeat, was vague, indefinite: as though there had been no quarrel, no drama, no trauma, and a year passed afterwards—it didn't exist either, but then, how did the break begin?

His last memory of Asya, with which everything ended, was a dream. He had several awful dreams in a row, more alarming, dangerous, and frightening with each day. But this, the last one, was the most frightening, and afterwards, as if they had been cut off by a razor, his dreams stopped completely, and he didn't dream again until that time which he could pinpoint conditionally, that is, with the word "beach." It was then that for the first time before sleep something flashed by him: a set of angle bars, a clock and castors, debris, the leg of a celluloid doll, gear wheels. And the first coherent dream he had was when he met his future first wife. He awoke beside her in a sweat, all from that same frightening dream, and for a long time he examined her beside him, unfamiliar and sleeping, like a variation of the same dream. And soon he married her.

He remembered this dream as the last thing in his life with Asya, but again he didn't recall what this dream came after, what it was connected to, what events preceded it, so that he couldn't establish any link with the incidents of his life.

And suddenly he either finally remembered the dream twenty years later or he fell asleep and dreamed it again.

... He was in an endless city or house, a city under a roof, like a theater,— a backstage life was in motion everywhere. He knew that Asya was there and he asked those he met for directions. They directed him farther and farther— shadows thickened, darkened, it became stuffy in this backstage world, and people's faces became more and more dead and made up until they became openly crude masks of papier-mache. He knew that something awful was happening, that Asya must be saved, that she was there, that these corpses were leading him astray on purpose, and guided by instinct alone, without asking them the way, he rushed forward—to where Asya was. He ran, and it seemed to get more spacious and light—he could breathe. And the corpses cropped up in his path less and less frequently, leaping aside and squeezing into the walls in fright... And there ahead finally appeared light, air, freedom! The ceiling was high, as in a temple, and the buildings became vast in dimension. He saw an immensely wide staircase in front of him. It led below as if in cascades: at the end of it, in the very depths, he barely made out a wall—the staircase was leaning against this wall. This wall was far in front of him, and he raised his gaze up along it until he began looking directly above him: there the wall ended, receding into a high vaulted ceiling. He realized that he had to run down the staircase, and he ran with surprising ease. He flew over several steps at a time with long imperceptible strides, running faster and faster. He heard a shout behind him, and a lot of voices at the same time. He glanced over his shoulder: the staircase led far above there, at the very top of the landing, where he had only just stood, he saw a crowd with dead faces: behind the ones up front more and more kept arriving constantly, others ran up, piled up, and kept heaping up; standing over the staircase as over a precipice, they shouted in horror. He suddenly felt happy and he ran down faster and faster, and at the same time he saw himself running, as though from the side: his body was flying downward, his head, like a clown's, was turned around 180 degrees and looked upward at the crowd. They were pointing below with their hands, they were piling up on top of one another, nightmarish yellow faces, and were shouting in fear, "He'll crash into the wall!" He became more and more happy because of this shouting, he understood he'd get there, crash—and everything would disintegrate, none of *this* would remain. He flew. The wall was already right in front of him, he was raising his hand gaily, when suddenly at the very wall his speed evaporated, as though he'd run into an invisible and elastic pneumatic-like barrier; he hung frozen at the wall, and his hand stopped in its vigorous swing a millimeter from the wall and impotently slid down, and, completely wilted, he too slid down and saw only the wall high above him, so high that he couldn't see it any more...

He opened his eyes, but the unpleasant sensation that he hadn't the strength to move, that he couldn't feel his hands or legs, didn't pass. As though he were dead. It wasn't as if something had gone to sleep. The ability to move and feel his body returned unexpectedly without the pins and needles or the stitch that accompanies the return of one's circulation. He had to remember something, but his poor head just couldn't make the effort. It wasn't as though, as is usually said in such cases, everything depended on it: it was simply that he had to remember. But it was as though he had a tight tape on his brain, it was curved, behind this tape was precisely what he had to recall, but there was no way to break through the tape.

"Monakhov!" he heard, "Monakhov!"

He desparately wanted to sleep. He didn't feel his body and lay as though in the air, in cotton. Beside him lay warm Natasha, he recognized her voice, but hadn't the strength to raise his lids. He only embraced her more firmly, moved his lips and floated off, his weightless body slipping into a pit of sleep.

"Monakhov!" The voice, strangely, did not come from his side where Natasha was, but fell on him from above. This strangeness pulled him out of his sleep, he half opened an eye and saw a bare foot, or more accurately, its big toe. It was Natasha's foot, but he'd never seen its toe so close up. And he was embracing and pressing not against Natasha, he quickly realized, but Lenechka, who was sleeping beside him. Monakhov found this touching.

"Monakhov!"

He closed his eyes and feigned sleep, decidedly not wishing to awaken again in this life. "One would have to love this toe to see..." he thought through this unwillingness.

"You're not sleeping, Monakhov!" The voice above him said entreatingly, "Come to me, Monakhov!" Monakhov shut his eyes in fear, "You're a bastard, Monakhov. I could kill you right now..."

"Please do..." thought Monakhov. But Natalya didn't kill him, she just went away heavily in her bare feet.

He didn't know whether he had his dream again or whether he fell asleep with recollections of it, but that was the most distinct thing with which he again tumbled into non-existence. "So I did die when I didn't die," he managed to think tranquilly, "I perished at that moment when I didn't perish..."

And endless nuances of what he hadn't thought too.

He slept.

***

He woke up unmistakably, fully, completely, but didn't open his eyes. He felt chilled and shivery, lying dressed and stiff on the floor. And someone was pressing close to him, curled up, warming his side, rubbing against him and smacking his lips.

Monakhov opened his eyes and saw Lenechka beside him. It was getting light in the room. There was no one there besides the two of them. Monakhov remembered everything immediately—the whole evening, as though everything that had occurred during it had happened not in sequence, but simultaneously on one plane. He remembered and moved away from Lenechka almost in disgust. Lenechka, also apparently getting cold toward morning, had squeezed himself into an even more pathetic fetus and was whimpering like a little animal.

In the morning light, with his cold extremities creaking angrily, Monakhov surveyed all the events of the last days, and said to himself: everything is simple in this world, but we—we complicate it. He went through the apartment, but didn't find a trace either of Natasha or of Zyablikov. Crude thoughts came in contrast to those of yesterday: how could he have failed to understand Zyablikov's role right away?—it was more than strange...Who could have played Monakhov's role prior to Monakhov—Lenechka? And Lenechka...Where had they gone off to alone then? Just what he needed, for things to be distorted. Monakhov recalled all of yesterday's thoughts and feelings. A fine thing, to have all the recollection of that optical expert have such an effect on him. For whose sake had he denied himself Natasha, detained Lenechka—could it really have been for Zyablikov's sake? He was filled with irritation. People...thought Monakhov, glancing at Lenechka, who had rolled up like an animal in a burrow—"What are people?" All this—their constructions and systems, accusations and torments—all this is such a wedding ritual, a dance, ruffled feathers, it's all a lie, disguises, adventures, calculations, one has to circle about so complicatedly in order to perform an act that is so simple and mundane that it's even extraordinarily accessible. A moth at a lamp.

Everything was painful, annoying, and clear to Monakhov. Finding his basket and briefcase in the passageway, he slipped outside into the street.

The morning came at him in a wave of cleanliness and freshness as he walked away with large angry strides. It was getting rosy, the dust was softly subsiding and the air was thick and transparent. Monakhov walked, sliding the morning apart, and it had been a long time since he'd returned home so early, so tremblingly, in such a light desert. He covered distance easily and now was walking in a wholly different town, from another meeting which also was somewhat unsuccessful, and his soul was strangely coming to life, surprised at itself, and rejoicing.

> Here am I going home as though in a lake...
> I'm going like a fish out of water.
> We've thrown over
> As many women
> As don't need us.

It was, of course, childish nonsense, but the first line...

The first line hung in the air like a morning mist over the earth.
"Lord!" exclaimed Monakhov, "That's exactly it!"
Here am I going home as though in a lake...

Lenechka's line was like that morning and contained it. And that morning was contained in that line in its entirety. They were equal. They were one and the same thing.

He now knew clearly that neither Natalya nor Zyablikov nor Lenechka was the point—only he, Monakhov, was. He cursed himself now as he faced the morning—everyone except him was worthy of the dawn...He knew everything now, how it had been, how it was—there was no secret there. There was something, however, which he still didn't know: for example, that Lenechka had written out for him not his own poem, but one by another poet*—Lenechka simply had liked it more than his own—but this wasn't that important.

"Oh, why am I doing this!" Monakhov started grinding his teeth. But he didn't stop, didn't turn back, but even quickened his pace along the empty roseate road. Away from the empty place beside Lenechka and away too from the empty place beside Natasha.

4

Monakhov spent the day at the airport in a haze. He endured everything that comfortless reality had to offer: the heat, the crowdedness, and the time...He thought himself undeserving even of that. He conceived of the life of the innocent passengers as simple and understandable, and the fact that they naively didn't suspect his, Monakhov's, abysses, that they didn't mark him out as a leper from their common body of expectancy, was undeserved by him as were all the good deeds that life had granted him. He understood his humiliation in these elevated terms. He humiliated himself in this way in order to grow a little in his own eyes, collecting the alms of indifferent glances. "There still is a way out...Everything isn't lost while there's still that! To lose oneself among people, to melt in them.., to blend, to disappear...to become like them, on a level with them..." The more he found humility in a verb, the more it suited him. These verbs rigidified in Monakhov's body and the pain subsided. He sighed as it left him. The more generously he let this surrounding life, so indifferent to him, enter him, the more readily he accepted all those who had never needed his affection and would not encroach upon his readiness, even if they were to notice it—the more tolerable those close to him became, those who surrounded him so tightly: his wife, and Natasha, and Lenechka, and his mother, who'd turned into a basket of fruit—a heavy reproach at the bottom of which Monakhov already suspected a fruit stew. So far it wasn't dripping.

Flights were being delayed, but this didn't affect him yet: the same

---

*L. Gubanov (A.B.).

number of unbearable hungover hours remained until the flight—the hands were suspended in time, as if time itself were standing still, and it was because of this that the airplanes couldn't fly, and the people, always the same ones, didn't budge from the same seats. But Monakhov did have a ticket—a guaranteed return in his pocket—Monakhov was prepared to wait it out: they were waiting for him where he was going, nothing was spoiled there by yesterday, once there his whole business trip could easily be erased; his past wasn't there and his wife was. "Yes," Monakhov smiled ironically, "My wife isn't the past—my wife is the most immediate thing there is..." There was no past in his thoughts, none of their experience, not a single one of their daily quarrels rose in his memory—what he did think was how had she put up with him for so long, so long that now he had the possibility of returning to her, otherwise he'd have nowhere to return to.

For a second his wife flashed before him, as though in a corridor; he saw her belt. He wanted to see her face—something weighed down his eyes, and she managed to disappear into her room, closing the door. Monakhov remained staring at the rug in their miniscule passageway, the worn slippers beside the rug—but couldn't for the life of him remember his wife's face. This seemed important and the difficulty was absurd. Natasha's face, on the other hand, emerged easily, filled the whole screen, his whole brain: "What are you doing, Monakhov?" precisely this glance and turn of phrase. He tried to push aside this image by imagining Lenechka—again, no: this grinning bit of soap would slip away. Yet suddenly—a pose captured in a single stroke—Natasha's aunt was squinting... To hell with them! Monakhov looked at his watch for the umpteenth time—it really had stopped! That's why time wasn't moving! He'd forgotten to wind it in all the confusion, which wasn't surprising. Perhaps it had even stopped yesterday...

And Monakhov felt relieved. He felt so much better now that in one second almost two hours had flown by: now how long, now it's almost no time, I can wait—with that positive attitude he wound his watch, adjusted the hands as though he were doing something useful. He came to life—what other useful thing could he do?—he gave his place up to a gypsy with a baby. She didn't bat an eye—she immediately sat down and took out her breast. Monakhov became cheerful: the people... He bought a book by Zyablikov about penguins. What else? Now he roamed along the halls, his knee knocking against the basket, smiling indulgently at his own foolishness: there wasn't a single place left. And yet one still couldn't compare his present condition to the one that had just passed: there was no comparison. "It's a good thing I didn't take the hair of the dog this morning," thought Monakhov, "It's a good thing I didn't call Natasha..." And it turns out that he'll get home even earlier than expected. They'll only begin to expect him tomorrow, but he'll get there today, God willing... It will seem that he rushed, was dying to get there... Monakhov wasn't at all embarrassed by the unpleasantness of such calculations: it was convenient for him, it made him comfortable... He mentally settled into his former life in anticipation, and now it pleased and satisfied him—it was as though he were wiggling to get completely comfortable. The routine and ordinariness of his everyday life suited him as a prospect to the same degree that they did not suit him as life. Now he had no greater joy than to nestle in his own niche. "And what if he were deprived of that?" thought Monakhov, "Of that standard, small-sized... And where is he? What will he have left? What does he have! Well, his title... You can't go wrong with that, they say. But what is he without his title? Well, he knows his business! But who would know that without the title...?" It seemed strange to him: he'd struggled, made it, his life had consisted only of successes: he'd finished school, he'd graduated from the institute, he'd completed graduate school, he'd even defended a dissertation, and so what? He'd surrounded himself with invisible lines: his family, work... But without them who was he? Is there a Monakhov or only a job registration? "What nonsense comes into one's head in the morning!" Monakhov scoffed. "Maybe I should have a drink after all?" He threw a glance around the room—planes still weren't taking off. "And how about them?" he thought suddenly in awful illumination, glancing over the room. "How many of them are there?" There were many people gathered beneath this endless roof (Monakhov glanced at the concrete sky of the airport and identified the type of ceiling). This airbreak had sucked them all in, and Monakhov wasn't more important than they. Each one of them was granted as much life as he was. Each was bound by the same invisible and unbreakable threads of belonging to it, and none of them, even when cursing his fate, would exchange it for anyone else's. Monakhov got lost in this generalization—it was reminiscent of this endless waiting room packed with people that was before his eyes in any case.

Time, however, moved and passed. God's will is known to the airport alone. In the general pause, someone's time of departure was announced, and the lucky fate of those individuals inspired everyone with hope. And imagine how Monakhov felt, having estimated the general delay and already firmly counting on taking off no later than... suddenly to realize that it was his flight that was being called first—his! And knocking against his basket, just like eveyone else in all this confusion, he didn't understand where the check-in was and whether it was precisely the right flight; he was surprised at Aeroflot's decision to send him, Monakhov, off on time instead of letting the delayed flights go first. But we don't analyze the reasons for our own luck for long, accepting them on faith or as deserved. Monakhov calmed down, finding himself in the right check-in line. Here he was convinced finally that his ticket was all right, and he began to separate himself from the crowd, which was so bustling and senseless—he really didn't understand them: why are they pushing, why the crush? One figure caught his attention—all in black: evidently a widow. Monakhov saw a thin leg in a thick stocking and crude shoe, the stocking wound around like a screw... then a sweaty neck, workworn like a hand... red blotches of excitement stood out on it: under the kerchief her eyes burned with the passion of the line. The widow had gotten oriented even later than Monakhov—now she was shoving her suitcases against him. Two old lady relatives egged her on with gutteral clucks. There seemed to be something familiar to Monakhov in her wild face. As though he'd already seen her somewhere... He couldn't know anyone here—that was definite. Monakhov let her go ahead of him. "How old can she be?" he thought. "She could be sixty, thirty..." He was alone again, so clever, understanding everything before it was said to him: he didn't push, he knew how to behave—an educated and experienced passenger. He was the only one like that here and when he caught the inviting glance of another one of his kind, a glance which invited him to share a skeptical smile of initiation, one must give Monakhov his due—he didn't start winking in response, but was embarrassed. He caught himself, coldly averted his gaze—and separated himself from this comrade.

And everything kept going more smoothly for Monakhov: they allowed him not to check his basket, he got a seat by the window and not over the wing, and what was most incredible, the airplane was not only leaving on schedule, but those usual half-hour delays which all his life had plunged him into bewilderment as to what should be considered the time of departure—boarding, the start of the engines, or the take off—even this half-hour was not anticipated. "Really? It can't be..." rejoiced Monakhov—the airplane had already been moved aside and was rotating its propellers. "So it really is the take-off," Monakhov decided (there were fifteen minutes left). "We'll take off exactly on schedule down to the last minute..." That meant that he'd be home and now it was definite... He'd still get home very early. They wouldn't be expecting him. Won't she be surprised!

Monakhov turned away to the window, a diffuse smile straying across his face. Ahead he saw the lights of the restaurant and the baggage claim—they were lit, it was rapidly growing dark. "Yet when they announced boarding, it was still completely light..." On the side, a propeller was rotating, first more quickly, then slowly, as if in one, then in another, direction. All this was a guarantee, and Monakhov's heart was filled with a peace he hadn't known for a long time. No, what had watched over him was not what he hadn't expected yet, what it would have been so easy to expect—the husband's unexpected return from a business trip—even before that happy moment something had watched over him, the thing that no one—neither you nor I—could have assumed... Chance.

The whole plane was quivering now from pre-start agitation, the propellers had dissolved in the air from the rapid rotation, when headlong towards the plane Chance ran out in the shape of Lenechka. Let's clarify it right away: it wasn't Lenechka. But the fellow was young, and his wide face was lit up by such a simple-hearted and open smile that for a second it definitely seemed to Monakhov to be none other than Lenechka... The fellow was well illuminated by some floodlights that shone at an angle, one couldn't see from where, but night was approaching, and Monakhov could have made a mistake. He could have made the offer or Natalya could have sent him, and Lenechka would have agreed to any commission of hers... He might be running now worrying only about failing to execute Natasha's command... One could see the fellow run out of the restaurant, waving a suitcase as he ran as though he were stopping a taxi. He didn't look like someone who'd had a lot to drink—he was only an awkward kind of guy, like Lenechka... Monakhov sympathized with him; who could have expected that they'd be boarding so soon! He'd almost gone into town himself... But the fellow was also something of a fool: who would let him board? The boarding steps were already put away, and the hatchway was pulled up. And there he was, running, waving his arms, shouting as he ran—you couldn't hear him; what on earth can you hear with the motors going? And the pilots most likely didn't hear; they were laughing and shaking their heads... The most appealing thing about this fellow was that he smiled even as he ran, as though he was jubilant at having made it all the same, and had no doubts that they'd let him on. And there he was, running right up to the plane, from Monakhov's side, as it happened, both arms raised, as though he were tearing the finish ribbon, waving his suitcase above his head—with his arms opened wide, he soared like a bird. His legs flew up—Monakhov could see all of this as clearly as if he'd been seated especially to watch it—and he fell flat on his back to the ground, directly under the airplane wing. Monakhov didn't understand anything yet, he only caught the general "Oh!"—he wasn't the only one watching. The fellow lay under the wing; it was dark there. Someone leaned with all his weight against Monakhov, breathing the odor of cheese and dried apricots into his face with sensual curiosity—Monakhov didn't turn aside, he was looking beneath the wing, mesmerized, and didn't hear his own whisper of "Lenechka..." And then a bright shaft of light picked the fellow's body out of the night—it wasn't Lenechka, of course. A fuel truck drove up and lit up "not Lenechka" with its headlights. He could have been a soldier, a serviceman on leave or even ("a real shame," someone would say) demobilized: the field-shirt he wore didn't have shoulder straps. In his hand he still gripped the suitcase which had been chopped in half: crumpled underwear spilled out of it like innards. Monakhov saw all of this, but didn't take in everything: for the moment it was just the suitcase. And then, shuddering for the last time, the propeller stopped, black against the light, with its lower blade pointing in the direction of the fellow, and everything became clear and Monakhov saw everything: the fellow's forehead had been cut obliquely by this propeller, and under his head slowly—so slowly!—widened and froze, widened and froze a puddle black and thick as the night. He was still alive but there was no doubt about his death. His mouth was still stretched into a smile and his lips barely quivered; his eyes were closed. It was as though he were sleeping and smiling in his sleep, and his dream was pleasant. His smile melted, but didn't disappear entirely; it had the same form but a different meaning: an elevated tranquillity, and something like a thought which was at first surprising and unusual, and then finally comprehended by the same mind in which it had been born...this thought struck Monakhov. It grew like the pale spot in proportion to which the puddle widened like a black nimbus—and this was his brow...Death approached in waves; life poured out in waves. This nongradualness struck Monakhov's stunned consciousness. Just as the congealed terrible puddle under his head seemed unchanging, and suddenly one could see how it had spread more, so did this pallor which was already the last, to the last drop, suddenly become even whiter. "He's dead," said Monakhov to himself finally and he was convinced of it—and suddenly again (it would have been impossible to notice if one hadn't been watching as fixedly as Monakhov), his lips moved in that imperturbable smile—he was still alive. Monakhov waited for the agony he'd heard and read about, but there wasn't any. But there was an elevated thought that increasingly illuminated this great brow. Monakhov wasn't a poet and so one can vouch for the veracity of his observations: for the first time a human being was dying before his eyes. And each time that he said to himself, "He's dead," it turned out not to be the essential significance of that great thought that illuminated and calmed the soldier's face; but Monakhov didn't ascend with him; he wasn't up there, he was alive. One set of boots, then another stamped around the young man. Once Monakhov looked up: a thick-set fellow in a peaked cap who had emerged from a car had a very proper expression on his face: stupid, and angry at life. His face didn't express anything except this superior annoyance—that was his tribute. Realizing that those inside the plane could see him, the man went off into the night.

When at last the "first aid" van came, the fellow was dead. The doctor didn't take his pulse.

A casual orderly dragged out the stretcher. It occurred to them to extinguish the headlights. How dark it became! And that was all. They drove off...

The interior of the plane became visible, and the hubbub reached Monakhov's ears: "It was the airstream..." "You have to watch out..." "So young..." And—what else?—The airplane literally swarmed with live people. Like peas in a monstrous pod... Everyone was drunk on this death. They discussed whether the propeller had been bent—that was unlikely. Then we'll take off? It was strange to take off just like that, but on the other hand, why not... Sobs strangled Monakhov. An absurd death... The incident was absurd, but not the death.

Quite a long time elapsed before the crew emerged from the cabin with suitcases which were very reminiscent of the soldier's. People stared indecently at them—they didn't look at anyone. They weren't guilty of anything. Embarrassed, red, as if they had been caught at something indecent, they hurriedly went down the aisle. That's right, the crew was traumatized, reasoned the passengers, a change of crew... Some more time elapsed, it became unbearably stuffy in the airplane. There was no longer any death, the hubbub grew: all sorts of things happen, it was time to take off. And then, to general consternation, they were taken off the plane.

With a sigh of relief, Monakhov separated himself from the crowd. The street lamps in the foliage, the urns for trash, the dusty smell of some first pods, the stale little pools of warmth, the shadow of the leaves on the asphalt, the spit, the cigarette butts—all this partly pacified him. But how could one continue living now? After a being had departed before his very eyes, Monakhov couldn't. Monakhov couldn't, and here he executed a finite series of logically unsound actions called Life. Running away from himself with rapid strides, he went straight to the restaurant, where they'd stopped serving vodka a minute before. Yes, in accordance with the established city ordinance, after seven... "It's only seven to seven!" fumed Monakhov. Five to, he was corrected, and at a quarter to we... Monakhov described colorfully how a human being had just perished. People started listening to him. They went into details, sympathized with him. Once the waitress learned that the man who'd died was not related to Monakhov, she lost all interest in the death, but did bring the vodka. Monakhov drank it with great revulsion and difficulty. It was as warm as Tashkent. In the booth it smelled of urine—Monakhov was calling Natalya. He babbled triumphantly about death.

"What's the matter with you, Monakhov?" Natalya got frightened, "What did you think? You haven't left yet, Monakhov dear..? Come to me. Nobody's here. I slept in my aunt's room, silly!" cried Natalya in a low voice. "How dare you... Zyablikov left by himself. I sent Lenechka away. For good, until tomorrow, he'll show up soon. Do come, Monakhov..."

"A person died," said Monakhov.

"What person? What are you saying?! Do you want me to come..?"

Monakhov was silent. What could he say?

"I'll come. Where are you?"

"No," said Monakhov sternly.

He came out into the same air. Monakhov was weak, weak, but not that weak—he didn't experience any shame now, and that felt funny somehow. According to Monakhov's formula, life abided in him—in him alone, not in them. The vodka went through him as though it had never been; you can't buy a second vodka for the same death. Now it occurred to Monakhov that he was probably making a mistake. To the railroad station! That's the way to do it, let's take the railroad, the way it used to be...

The street lamp in the leaves, the urn, the butts, the dusty warm gasoline-colored fumes—there was no need to turn around; all of this was the airplane. New, shiney, belonging to some foreign airline—Monakhov hadn't ever seen one like it up close. Bah, all the faces were familiar. At the turnstile in front of the exit to the landing field the passengers who had got to know each other from his flight stood in a united group. The fellow in black, the sophisticated one, who had picked him out at the check-in as one of his own kind, now approached Monakhov directly as one of his own. "They'll announce boarding any minute now. They've given us a TU-154 which they cancelled for the flight to Delhi. It gets there in an hour less. We'll be in Moscow at almost the same time we'd have got there on the other one...Can you imagine?" he informed Monakhov excitedly. "Yes," said Monakhov blandly and moved off to one side. What was he so proud of?

Before five minutes had passed everything turned out precisely like that. The collective from their flight, not a whit daunted, but solidly united by the common death, threw itself into the assault on the fantastic airplane. Two sets of stairs were attached to the airplane and boarding took place in two lines simultaneously. Monakhov hadn't ever come across such a practice either (he'd seen something like it in a movie...). You'd think it would be twice as fast—far from it! The stewardesses were swept off the steps, the teeming crowd hung over the rails in clusters. Cries and moans. Monakhov had never seen anything like this either. He hadn't seen a lot of what he was seeing today. "How do you like that!" he was surprised. "We all just had a maximally vivid demonstration of what it can do: it's a meat-grinder, death... And not a single person handed in his ticket, not one dashed to a train! We saw what it can do—and everyone dashed to it with even greater excitement..! No, people don't learn. People aren't machines, but animals." Monakhov couldn't recall such a crush since his infancy, since the war. "Everyone will get to go! Where are you going?" the last squeak of the stewardess was drowned. Where are we going... Above the heads Monakhov saw the widow astride her suitcase and suddenly recalled where he'd seen her. She was the widow of the shift foreman Nurimanov, who'd perished in the accident which he, Monakhov, had uncovered so cleverly. At the time they'd pointed her out to him briefly in the director's office. Monakhov hadn't noticed her then—now he examined her as she had been then: her Nurimanov had perished exactly like this soldier right now... Did I have any understanding of what had happened, of what had occurred, besides the incorrect coefficients? An expert... No, you won't surprise people with death, or with a jet either. So many wars, deaths, transports..! Pretty recently, during his, Monakhov's, life. Yesterday and today it was accidental death—the day before yesterday, though, it wasn't accidental. Monakhov looked differently now at the assault on the plane: how was a jet different from a transport train?

A lofty thought! So what about you, Monakhov? He didn't even need to turn to sense Natalya's presence behind the turnstile. She was tearing onto the landing field, and for the moment, in the night, Monakhov could still act as though he hadn't seen her. He dived into the thick of the crowd. And emerged triumphant in the battle for the steps. Before diving finally into the belly of the plane, he looked over his shoulder to see Natalya, who'd torn through every obstacle, running along the landing field. She didn't see him.

...Monakhov flew without smoking, with his seat belt fastened. Announcements were made on the radio in English and Hindi—the Uzbeks twisted their heads and laughed. The stewardesses, of superior height and quality, were polite, almost to excess. There was something insulting in this—it seemed as though they were too lazy to adjust to the circumstances. "Our plane is making the flight from Moscow to Delhi," said the radio in English before it occurred to them to turn it off.

"It's clever, though, clever..." thought Monakhov, beginning to doze, "We'll be in Moscow practically at the same time..." his eyes sought out the fellow in black, but didn't find him. "You've got to hand it to Aeroflot: the whole incident was handled with maximum speed and tact. The same crew couldn't fly just like that. After all, there was a murder... How cleverly the factor of death is taken out of it all. At the same time!! What a triumph. All you need is the next model. Progress eliminates death... If you constantly have first caviar, then a new airplane pushed on you, then it's no wonder you don't notice death, or life either. They've privileged us... Why not a verb? And there was no death. There was something . But there was no death."

And Monakhov thought about how he'd probably never thought about death until that day... We go on living and it's so close, it walks noiselessly behind our backs... it keeps on flapping about... You go along, there's a rustling. You think there's something there. You turn around and there's no one. Nothing.

Monakhov thought about death, about how he'd never thought about it...

He slept.

In his dreams he couldn't get his things together—the usual story... He was late, he was already too late. And he only had three things: in one room he'd left his jacket, in another, his tie... He floundered about the rooms, the galleries, the flights of stairs cluttered up with scenery and props—the film studios of dreams—and everywhere he managed to meet someone he knew, to get into a relationship, to commit himself to something... And his jacket was—there it was, he had only to stretch out his hand...

5

Their embrace disintegrated right away. His wife quickly stiffened in his arms and moved away.

"What's the matter with you?" said Monakhov as though he didn't understand. In fact he understood everything perfectly, everything was going by the notes: he'd been handed a score. Each had begun his part.

And Monakhov was preparing again for another role... But in the same play he hung the same raincoat on the same hook. His wife's belt flashed by—she disappeared. Monakhov examined the rug and a worn slipper. He'd already seen this. Moreover, literally—yesterday.

Monakhov sighed, seized the basket and headed for the kitchen after his wife.

"Fruit," he said, "It should be unpacked right away."
"Who did you buy it with?" his wife attacked him.
"What do you mean, who with?" Monakhov was hurt.

The joyful uniting task for two—unpacking and putting away the fruit—Monakhov now had to do by himself: his wife pointedly avoided the basket. This was an absurd pretext for jealousy—it was too weighty. It was precisely for this reason that Monakhov didn't answer in a hurry: the injustice here was so patent that she herself should see it. He took out each fruit one by one—examined it, turned it around. He kept needing a new plate or bowl; his wife would hand him one without looking, getting irritated at each of his slow, clumsy movements. An argument was brewing in the kitchen, filling the few empty corners in the six square meters—it hung suspended. Monakhov examined each fruit and admired it. These were touches equivalent to his mother's—a reciprocal relationship. "Who with—" he muttered inaudibly under his nose. "Some nerve, who with. . ? Suddenly, however, he saw Natalya, her red skirt sweeping along the bazar stall. "Obviously with... It could be any number of people..." His wife's question didn't exclude this possibility: who with—not these fruits, but perhaps others, though at the same time... Monakhov smiled ironically and shook his head: logic... His wife was a very logical woman, he gave way in the face of her inflexible consistency. He never held out in an argument—he would begin shouting, stamping his feet, shaking a fist at himself—and he'd prove to be in the wrong. "Why are you shouting? What have I said that should make you shout?" And he couldn't distinctly recall what; as it turned out—nothing. What had set him off? "That's what," Monakhov's thought boiled in pursuit of the argument that hadn't gotten going yet. "There's life, and there's the idea of life, the abstraction. And life, as distinct from one's idea of it, is not obliged to fit into an ideal scheme..." It seemed to him that his wife suffered precisely from this lack of reciprocity and not from life. She demanded of him that his spirit be constructed like her idea of it. "And she, she herself!" Monakhov would immediately fly into a rage; the well-nourished little injuries readily lined up in a level row. And yet this peculiarity of hers was unique; her thoughts in relation to life delighted Monakhov with their conformity, while on the other hand he was distressed by the attempt to apply them to yesterday, and to him, Monakhov. For instance, now she could say: "What do you want? A separation is in itself an argument." You have to know how to think such a thought. "But we're alive—we're not shooting an Antonioni film!" roared Monakhov inwardly in response. Or: "How can someone whom I don't know exist for me? I don't know your mother, how can I take an attitude towards her? To simper because she's yours—that's not what you want. If someone's not there, they're not there. There are no strangers in nature." Monakhov wouldn't have disagreed with her if they had been analyzing a book and not him. She could also say the following: "You weren't here, how can I know that you exist the way you did before? You were here, and then you started not being here..." And then: "And where did you get the idea that the me you've come home to is me? Maybe it's not me anymore. You didn't switch me off when you left..." "But I went on a business trip!..! Not to play around, not to have a good time. On a bu-si-ness trip!" Monakhov mentally defended himself. "How do I know why you went! Perhaps you went to see her..." his wife would descend two levels and become more comprehensible and lovable to Monakhov: all these abstractions were everyday, live jealousy to which the highest mind is not alien. This was the appropriate moment to try and embrace her again, to draw her to him. But she would bristle implacably—and Monakhov would fly into a complete rage. And it would begin!

Everything was going peacefully so far. Monakhov was arranging the fruit—it was stacked up neatly to the very bottom. There was none of the pulp which he'd worried about for nothing, as it turned out. The kitchen was flooded with light that streamed from the plates which were piled up on everything: both the refrigerator and the window ledge. "The sun and mother—these are the two sources..." thought Monakhov sentimentally. He would never have said that aloud: oh, for a pronouncement like that his wife would have really let him have it! And he'd never prove to her that it was precisely for that... Monakhov sighed, sadly admiring his own handiwork. Yes, he'd never before encountered such a demanding relationship towards reality—that everything should correspond to the level of ideas formulated to date...of course he hadn't encountered it... Had he encountered it—he wouldn't have gotten married—that was the point. He'd married when he'd been exhausted and tired out by everything that wasn't yet his wife... How he'd suffered without her in his former life! Now it turned out that he'd suffered in the past scarcely more than now. What was unendurable now was precisely what earlier had attracted him to her, and what had become attractive was what once he'd not been able to endure. How strangely we love..! His wife suddenly nestled against him when he wasn't expecting it, and he melted. His wife bit a fruit and half-closed her eyes with pleasure. She admired the fruit. "It's all so sunny!" she said. He'd been afraid for nothing... She said just that. "How pretty she is!" realized Monakhov suddenly. "She's a girl. She's just a girl." "You simply love her"—he heard Natalya's voice.

Did his wife hear it too..? This really was madness... Suddenly she pouted, turned around, and went off to her room, leaving the half-bitten fruit behind. "What is going on!" Monakhov finally got angry. "What torture! All the troubles and miseries I've gone through—and that's what I get!" This was only a phrase: he didn't clearly remember any individual thing he'd endured, not any of it... His whole unremembered stay in Tashkent was now perceived by him as his one overall merit, one general suffering which he'd endured just for the sake of this return. He'd avoided all temptations and reefs, he'd made his escape, and here he was! He wallowed in grief. Out the window the night was black. The window gazed blindly into the kitchen, reflecting the ugly fruit...

"And what is this?" said his wife in a voice trembling with torment.

He realized that she'd "found" something. She'd already rummaged about in his briefcase. Although there was nothing she could find there: Monakhov was particularly careful on this count. Yet she'd found something.

She stood behind him, her face white, holding out Lenechka's poem. In her other hand she held Zyablikov's book as secondary evidence.

"What kind of scribbling is this?"

Monakhov was upset—he remained impassive, frowning.

"But I like this poem," he said, getting insulted on Lenechka's behalf.

"You know very well that's not the point," said his wife, "Whose is it?"

Monakhov looked at his wife with cautious amazement and lowered his gaze. There was something mind-boggling in this liquidation of logic, the boundaries of common sense didn't exist; and anyway there wasn't any such thing—*common* sense, there was only sense.

"A...boy wrote this," explained Monakhov calmly. "The son of a woman neighbor," he added, surprised himself at how unconvincing this was.

"A woman neighbor?" His wife got off the track so readily that she astounded Monakhov again.

"Spoon, fork, plate! I'll try to avoid words of feminine gender," he said venomously.

"That wouldn't be a bad thing," said his wife, undisturbed.

"It's mine! It's my poem!" Monakhov let go, "I wrote it. I dedicated it to a young girl in Tashkent."

"Go on lying," said his wife with satisfaction, "It's inscribed to you. And the handwriting isn't yours."

No, Monakhov refused to understand... "And yet I practically told the truth," he smiled ironically. He wanted to say: "What are we doing?!" and didn't say it, he wanted to call her by name—and didn't. They avoided calling each other by name. They both considered it hypocrisy. They rejoiced that they had so much in common when they saw eye to eye on this. "When someone calls you by name, it means he's lying," his wife would say.

"And how about in the forest?" thought Monakhov now.

"Hey," he said peaceably, and shuddered: a plane flew by overhead.

(Their house was on the edge of Moscow, near the airport, and planes would land over it. They'd gotten used to this noise and didn't notice it.)

"Yes," said Monakhov, following the noise with his gaze, "It's interesting. I just remembered. My father was telling me. He's always reading something and telling everyone about it. All kinds of popular scientific nonsense. But one thing he told me was remarkable... Imagine, a forest..."

His wife was looking calmly out the black window through which nothing was visible and—it was all right—for the time being she wasn't about to interrupt him.

"A forest, it turns out," continued Monakhov hopefully, "isn't simply a lot of trees, but it is something like an association, even a collective. The trees grow not in isolation, but as an entire forest. We can't see it, so we hadn't realized it, but all the trees are tied together by their roots into a single system. And they aren't single trees, but the forest in its entirety exists as a single organism..." Monakhov got excited because suddenly he himself understood the thought he was expounding; and the thought kept turning, and until now Monakhov had not seen or suspected *that* side of it. "And so it turns out," Monakhov lost the thread and couldn't find the words for this new thought. "It's strange that people didn't know that until now... The hydrogen bomb, cybernetics, you name it—and yet such an obvious thing gets discovered later..! Of course it's one whole!" his voice shook. "And how did they discover it? It was considered a riddle why a dead tree dries out. It gets dry right away, it doesn't dry out with time... And it turns out that in dying it gives back all its juices to the forest. The forest sucks them in with its common roots. And so it stands dry..."

"How awful!" said his wife.

He didn't notice any irony. And perhaps there wasn't any.

"And it turns out," said Monakhov, "that the life of one tree is needed by the whole forest," he broke off and got upset. Some other thought like an enormous beast stirred outside the window in the night. He didn't catch it.

His wife stroked his head with a barely perceptible motion and immediately removed her hand.

"It's already late," she said, "You're tired."

Monakhov felt a surge of joy, tried to embrace her, and again she twisted out of his empty arms.

...Monakhov lay in bed and felt insulted by life. Life in this instance lay beside him in a new nightgown bought for his return. There were clean sheets on the bed. They were husband and wife. It was night. They were alone. Neither of them was asleep. Both lay on their backs, trying to avoid touching. Between them lay a nonexistent white border. Apparently they loved each other: this border was impassable. Both wanted one and the same thing, but there wasn't a power on earth that was capable of overcoming this invisible obstacle of the unarticulated. And there were no words which were capable of taking this wall apart brick by brick—of translating it into words.

He knew that she was waiting for a confession from him and almost with malice he realized that he would never (ne-ver) release her from this waiting. She, you see, would like to know the whole truth... Who wouldn't! Only it doesn't exist. The whole truth—that's everything: that night, and that chair, and the shadow of the thermometer on the window sill, and the moon which had hidden behind the cloud... So did the moon not exist if it had slipped behind a cloud? ...To tell her *everything* one had to begin like this: "In the beginning was the word, and the word was..." Monakhov smiled ironically and, invisible in the darkness, his face felt separate, as though it belonged to someone else. Could he tell her about Lenechka? He couldn't, because then he'd have to tell her about the birthday. Could he tell her about the birthday? He couldn't, because then he'd have to tell her about Natalya too. Could he tell her about Natalya? He couldn't, because then he'd also have to tell her about... he'd have to tell her about exactly what she, bypassing the *whole* truth, wanted to know. And if he told her that there'd been nothing, that he'd slept only with Lenechka (at that moment Monakhov sincerely remembered only that)—she wouldn't believe him. Fairy tales... That's precisely the point, that he can't tell her *anything*. He had nothing to justify! But whatever he'd start spinning to her now beside him, it would come out as self-justification. Well, how could he explain to her that she had nothing and no one to be jealous of? Was it likely she'd appreciate his zeal and sacrifices? (Again he meant that he'd resisted Natalya...) Monakhov felt that life (his wife) was unjust to him. He felt mistreated.

Separation was life lived separately. In other words, he'd lived *life* this week, and it was *his* life, not hers. There was something to be jealous about! Not about Natalya... He had had an experience which she hadn't, their life was separating now over this experience, and in a certain sense couldn't ever converge again because Monakhov had no way of sharing this experience with her...

And anyway, would she want to know? Perhaps she wanted nothing less. Perhaps this was more awful for her than death—to find out what she wanted to. Perhaps she really didn't want to find out, but was pressing as one does on an aching tooth... No investigator would have caught the scent as she had with Lenechka's poem, and then what? She was satisfied with the first, the most unreasonable, explanation. It was exactly that—unreasonable—and she was satisfied: had it been reasonable, she would have tried further. She hadn't brought Zyablikov to light at all... Monakhov felt a blend of hatred and rapture when he understood how close his wife had drawn all at once to his reality, only from the other side; it was as though they were touching glass from two sides and fingers were touching fingers, but through glass... What an impetuous touch! With the help of what signposts did she find such a direct route in complete darkness!? Love? What the hell kind of love was it—this rush to destruction..? Monakhov couldn't, no, he couldn't live in such a fixed world. Life isn't built so that one can know more about someone else than about oneself.

Monakhov tried to push his hand through this divide—and couldn't; he was afraid of bumping into something, he was afraid of remaining with his hand outstretched, he was afraid of caressing emptiness.

And so he puzzled and reflected, examining the shadow etched from the dry bouquet below the ceiling. It seemed he must confess something. Monakhov thought about the extent of the confession, about its percentage, what percent both he and she could stand, but then it wouldn't be a confession. Something had to replace it, but what? There was nothing which was equivalent to the whole truth yet different. Again Monakhov recalled his father, that he was weak and sick—he saw his sleeping face, with its sudden swamp of bristles... he examined it more closely now than he had at the time. Perhaps his father was worse than sick, perhaps... That's it! That's what he could tell her which was equivalent to what she was waiting for. She couldn't shrug this off... You couldn't say that Monakhov reasoned cynically to quite that degree, but he did it consciously enough, nevertheless.

"You know," he said with feeling, "My old man is really in a bad way..."

The shadow of the bouquet trembled and shuddered as though from his wife's sigh. And then a hum followed this light trembling of the dead flower's shadow: a new airplane flew over them extremely close. "With a force of five," thought Monakhov, and for a second his entire being was back in Tashkent. An inexplicable childish horror seized him. He pressed against his wife.

"What's the matter with you? Calm down..." said his wife anxiously, and stroked him tenderly like a child. She didn't ask, "What's the matter, my little one?"

"How is it we don't understand," said Monakhov brokenly, in a child's trembling voice, "that others understand and feel the same things we do! As though we alone were like that... How did I decide that I understand better what people tell me than those who tell me what I understand so well already. You know, my father told me about the forest—that means he felt and understood exactly that, since he was telling me about it. I was the one who didn't understand what he was saying, not he. I only understood today. But at the time I listened to him condescendingly, with half an ear, and was sure that I understood everything, whatever he might be saying, better than he did himself. He doesn't understand what he's saying, in other words, but I understand—what nonsense! God..." Monakhov felt cold. "And I'll never be able to tell him that I've finally understood him. Never!"

Tears filled Monakhov's eyes pleasantly. He lay on his back, and his eyes became like two little lakes. He looked through his two fat tears as though from the bottom, and didn't see anything. He blinked, and the little lakes spilled over.

"Don't love, don't..." his wife kept saying, kissing his wet temple.

"How could I not understand!" Monakhov tortured himself. "I won't see him again. He's..." Monakhov couldn't say it out loud.

"Don't die! Just don't die! Anything you want, but not that!" he prayed to himself. And he remembered his father's saying that his whole life he couldn't forgive himself for his father's death. Grandfather Monakhov was sick and summoned his son, but he was in love and was with her when his father died. "But what if suddenly..?" thought Monakhov, growing cold. "While he was at Natalya's. After all, his parents thought he'd left... Suddenly there was a ring at the door: a telegram..!"

And if the forest is one, then he and his father are simply one tree... The stream of life had flowed for the last time from his father to him, almost with the same force with which it had flowed when this instant was beginning.

Monakhov experienced a headlong expansion of his being—it opened—it was as though he were hanging in air over the bed. This live flow of his powerless father's last strength washed son-Monakhov's enlightened soul, and, transparent again, let into itself all the pain around it. It was as though Monakhov had flown up in pursuit of his father's soul, and the icy clean wind whistled in the cleaned carcass of his soul: stars were visible between the ribs. Monakhov Jr. felt alone, way up there. For the first time, the days and experiences emerged not separately, but all together as they had been—they were all together always; both yesterday and tomorrow, as now, in a single dimension, in one soul, containing in it all souls, just as one tree contains in it the whole forest, which contains the tree... His mother and his father, and Natalya, and Lenechka, and the wife and the child who already existed, and this wife and the child who was yet to come...

All of them were in him, and there was no one beside him except his wife. He suddenly clung to her with a strong, desperate, and lonely feeling that couldn't even be called love. This loneliness leaped out of him like a wild beast, like a howl, and the more tangibly it did, the more feverishly and profoundly he pressed against his wife, the more dreadful and unappeasable became his isolation. Through the window an airplane roared by again, very low, as though falling on the house, making the glass tremble and hum—it chopped up the black forehead of the night. Death, which Monakhov had forgotten so stubbornly, so completely and well, death in the form of a soldier fell like a star out the window, giving back to Monakhov the last drop of life he needed—Monakhov cried out, a faint light spread, strangely illuminating the night's objects—chairs, curtains, and walls... And in that instant an eternal particle of death went through Monakhov, in order to continue his father's life outside his son.

1965, 1972

The Taste

"And onward I continued—
And fear enveloped me..."

Pushkin

She's not my sister, my daughter, or my mother...she's more like a relative than they are, a stranger. Such arrogant, useless embarrassment: knowing each other, we don't want to know about each other. Now we'll go our separate ways. Superfluous...What's superfluous? Everything that came afterwards was superfluous. And now these minutes before departure, this hypocritical platform, they're superfluous. Platforms always make you hypocritical. After all, you're waiting to leave...The most passionate partings, the most bitter separations—each time he only wanted to get it over with as fast as possible...Let the train leave, let them stop looking into each other's faces in front of everyone. What more can be squeezed out of this minute after the night, the day, the suitcase, the washing of socks and underpants and the apple for the road, after reminiscing about last time, the uncomfortable position, was it in the hallway...? No, they seem to have managed to leave that for next time...He wondered, during those genuine moments, was that feeling of hypocrisy mutual? Or was it only he who was so unfeeling...Some unfeeling—he was biting his nails...But he always, always, wanted everything to disappear as soon as possible under the wheels, out of sight—into the heart. And right now, he didn't want this. It was unnecessary, there was nothing to say, and no regrets...he didn't want it. But it was a shame. They were nervous. Embarrassed. It wasn't that he was restraining himself, he was just too lazy to say: I've betrayed you. The unknown expanse of her life which didn't exist for him lay between them like a level field full of yellow flowers...It was almost as if he were dreaming her just now, the way you dream of people who have been dead a long time, who haven't kept up on things...But just think of all that's happened after them...An empty space, two words are too little, ten—too much, we'll get by in silence...A kind of comfortable awkwardness. Almost coquetry: only a little, because she hadn't gotten any younger over the last ten years, or any prettier, but nonetheless—the same face, the partial smile, the unfinished gesture...Unfinished—this whole life is one nightmarish lack of finality! As expressed by this basket here which I'm supposed to deliver...God knows what's in it! Who really needs it—me, her, the one who's getting it, it doesn't even need itself. And we need each other like a fifth wheel. It reminded me: a fifth wheel... That's part of the coquetry—that it was just for fun, unnecessary, beside the point... He got annoyed, surprised by the limp remnant of jealousy which had nonetheless rustled under a ten-year thick accumulation. Now it was time to go...! He imagined her going back home as if she were going to a hut beyond the yellow field; she had the same face as had just flashed past across the field, just as indefinite, evasive, addressed to no one in particular, not to him or to the other... A dream, death. Had they kissed or hadn't they? They had. They kissed the air over each other's shoulders. A weak cheek, soft, soon it would be like grandmother's... That must mean he remembered that cheek. By comparison... Now looking out the window: the last face, suddenly something in her awoke, trembled—or did it only seem to? Or can't a woman ever do anything just for the hell of it? Or... Oh no! What a hat the silly woman's put on...! It stands up like a straw bag... what a woman, Lord forgive me! He almost cried. And then she was finally carried away, he didn't need to lean out the window with a benevolent-tender-indifferent-seductive-independent-warm-humane-masculine-smile... Whew! A completely different person stood up in the corridor looking for a seat: freed, tall and slender, unusual... Strange, after all, he's been free for ten years already—what had he just been freed from? Not just from his discomfort on the platform? That was the point, not just from that...

Monakhov moved along the corridor, half excusing himself, not bumping into anyone... he raised his eyes—from the other end of the car, coming toward him was SHE! Monakhov of course instantly smiled at his unwarranted motion—stared at the girl walking toward him along the corridor: there could be no doubt: it was she! He almost made another unwarranted motion, he almost rubbed his eyes and shook his head. He opened his eyes—it was she.

She was dressed in the same dress, only she'd taken off the hat... The same hair, the same hairdo, the same modest gesture as if she were being watched, a challenging modesty... It was as if ten years hadn't passed... Monakhov straightened himself up to meet her. She surely couldn't help seeing him now! She'll raise her eyes... In about three and a half seconds time hummed through a thousand revolutions and froze hanging with Monakhov above the same abyss: he saw his wife at this moment exactly as he had seen her then, when she no longer belonged to him. His heart ached. She was exactly ten years younger than the one who had just disappeared with the platform. That feeling that all these ten years, albeit without great regret, without mourning, were in vain was suddenly confirmed in the flesh: these ten years hadn't existed, and she—where was she going? Who was she going to see? Why didn't he know anything about it? She'd gotten on the train, light and free, ignorant of the sly coincidence by which Monakhov turned out to be in the same car... "I'm *not* following you!" Monakhov was already preparing his answer. One consideration which hadn't yet surfaced bothered him; the image began to struggle, shattered, was covered in ripples... With an effort Monakhov dredged it up struggling from some whirlpool: ten years ago *she* couldn't have been dressed like that—there weren't any maxis then, heels were different, they didn't wear that kind of hairdo, ten years ago the passengers were dressed differently... The resemblance was after all reinforced by the fact that his former wife who had just flashed by on the platform and the young one coming toward him were dressed identically. And that was the sole condition for recognition: if she were to appear now dressed as she was then, as she should have been ten years ago, then perhaps he wouldn't have recognized her and would have walked right past her... His image shattered and disintegrated entirely. She raised her eyes and didn't recognize him. As was to be expected. The glance of a completely different person. Colorless.

Monakhov sat down, thinking about the striking resemblance. Forgetting the unpleasant glance, he was amazed all over again. He should have asked her casually about something to hear her voice... The voice is such a peculiar thing! thought Monakhov. It was still Moscow out the window, they hadn't even passed the store for the blind called "Dawn." There were six hours of exhausting travel ahead. Maybe they should get acquainted anyway... No, they shouldn't. Really. But it certainly was an amazing resemblance! And the coincidence was even more amazing! And she hadn't gotten married... Monakhov thought about his first wife, that she was the only one. And where had these ten years gone, he also thought. There didn't turn out to be anything new in these thoughts. And then he thought about that. A strange idea! And it was gone. About these ten years, how before, everything continued uninterrupted, and then it all disappeared... that only the one and only endures, but the rest simply disappears. That nature was responsible for every first time, but man himself for everything secondary. But he isn't responsible. And then all sorts of things... in flashes. Just try to remember what's out the window... that meadow, village, woods—they're unrepeatable, right? One could love them more than life itself... They can be your motherland! But no, however much you force yourself—it's gone by, disappeared... Had he loved? Had he been loved? Could he have not changed his life or should he have changed it even sooner and more radically? And had he actually changed it or had it changed itself? Had he chosen anything at all or had he been chosen? And didn't it seem that he used to live and feel differently in some way?

Monakhov was thinking, but no thoughts were formed. And it wasn't that he'd already heard something like it or read it or said it himself or already thought it, no, there was nothing externally recognizable about these thoughts—they were really *his,* current, immediate... but nonetheless they were erased like the landscape in the window. They came to his mind for the first time but had all somehow *already been thought.* For the thousandth time this crow was passing through his head and thoughts hung around familiarly like a colleague you see every day but never once greet ... And still worse, they had already been thought *by someone*. What's the matter with you today, Sidorov, are you missing a leg? You don't say! I didn't know ... That's how he suddenly saw his thought, missing its head ... There it is! Gone again. And it was as if he were watching its disgustingly fleeting back. So, when it all broke up ... (and again he didn't say to himself either what had broken up or when ...) from that time on not one thought had been thought out, but had only *come to mind*. It would come to mind over and over and he already recognized it as the thought he had never thought out. He would recognize it like a chance passer-by in a crowd, like a fellow passenger in a tram, but the passer-by passes by and the passenger gets off ... until the next time. So that's what "nothing's new" means! Monakhov realized. Not that it's already happened, but that it never will for you. "All that was, All that's dear ... " Long ago has disappeared! That line everyone, himself included, has heard a thousand times suddenly hummed inside him, *it* was still there. Alive. What's so special about it? What does it mean! Monakhov was indignant. It's a feeling, he answered himself. And sighed with relief.

About absence, emptiness ... about death! That thought is never equivalent to itself ... And it was already gone.

There was a taste in his mouth. That horribly enduring taste of a pie from the station buffet. There it was, spreading and growing, disgustingly insistently and evenly. Stalwartly. Yes, a stalwart taste! That's permissible in the "truthful and free" Russian language ... The taste had settled in his mouth like a lump, carefully measuring the cavity of this empty temple. It kept being there, unlike his thoughts or the landscape in the window which kept rushing past. Why do they rush off? Where do they go? And again: the thoughts and the woods. Well, try remembering that little barrel with the branch ... No! Ridiculous. They don't exist, as they didn't before. But the taste does, no matter how much you swallow.

In irritation Monakhov turned from the window to look at the passenger. In fact he'd been meaning to look at her for as long as he'd been meaning to get up to go out to smoke and maybe at the same time rinse out his mouth ... The passenger was looking out the window with a particularly aloof independent look. Bitch! Monakhov flared up. Why do they have such an independent look, bitches in particular? Only women sitting on line for the venerologist have such inaccessibility on their faces ...

In the smoking compartment, blowing smoke out the window, Monakhov rediscovered space for a while: the trash basket, the fire extinguisher, some directions under glass, the door to the toilet, a gob of spit—everything in its place. He should have gotten up to smoke long ago ... he let out the smoke emphatically and felt better. Why was everything depressing him? He caressed the fire extinguisher with a benevolent gaze: You're in place, friend! Do you work? And the fact that on the fire extinguisher there was a picture of a man (who had manged to change into a jumpsuit) correctly holding exactly the same fire extinguisher on which, in turn, was a picture on which... this childhood infinite regression which immediately multiplies a thousand times in your brain for some reason was not repellent to him, on the contrary: he smiled to himself tenderly, as if winking to the past. As in the past the black lens of the field flew off, or rather flew away from the window, like the flap of a wing, in a sudden burst, then, having flown away to one side and described an arc, returned to its place before smoothly disappearing completely. This winged pulsing of the landscape out the window with the starlings fluttering up from the furrows in imitation of the landscape, flying up in order to settle back in the same place over and over again, as if while they were in the air, the earth had manged to catch up with them... Yes! He remembered!... Monakhov thought triumphantly. The wing sank. It's only fair, thought Monakhov, and didn't get upset: you can't keep getting high over and over again.

Children these days don't wave at passing trains... When did that happen? How much time must have passed, including his own, for those groups of them to become so rare, for some of them to stop waving, for it to be embarrassing to wave when the others didn't...

There weren't any more starlings, but a little smoke-blue forest appeared beyond the field. It did a trick that had always delighted him as a child: it would keep running ahead of the train while the embankment with its white stones and stumps would rush backwards in grey clumps, and between the forest which had run ahead and the embankment which had flown off jerkily under the wheels, an immovable point hung suspended, an axis, as if a peg had been driven in for the field of vision to revolve around. There it was, an instant center of revolution! The mathematical abstraction revived with the graphic clarity of his schooldays. "She'll come out now," he suddenly decided.

The door to the smoking car opened; he steadfastly did not turn away from the window.

Now she'll ask for a cigarette...

And, oh wonderful, there was a little girl on the embankment like when they still waved... just like them in a polka dot kerchief, with little knees... she was standing and waving, like a ghost.

Now the only thing missing was that the double should have the same name, that she should be her namesake besides... Of course she had a different name, just as she had to be dressed differently. She was probably called Sveta.

Monakhov guesed everything about her, her name, where she was studying... She was going to take her last semester's exams, it's hard to reach her by phone in the dormitory, they don't call up to the rooms, but she could come down to the phone at an agreed time. Monakhov didn't hide the fact that he was married, but the way he looked away with a slow gaze did a good job of conveying difficulties he didn't wish to speak about... Sveta was a good, simple, intelligent girl whom Monakhov would not want to deceive...

He gave her a cigarette in the most gallant manner—but the realization that he knew every step discouraged him, and he didn't strike up a conversation.

The landscape was about to be reanimated, then died again. And it got dark, so it couldn't be seen. So he couldn't think anymore about how you can't see it. But about what it was in himself that Monakhov couldn't come to terms with. What was so surprising? That he just couldn't get used to a change that had taken place so long ago? Or even admit it? These thoughts too (erased by someone, maybe himself) had already been thought... Age! Is that how it spread its wing over him? Maybe Monakhov just couldn't get used to the fact that he wasn't twenty-five. But why, really? He wasn't in pain, or short of breath, he looked good, he hadn't aged. None of us would suspect how long, even having adopted current attitudes we have been under the influence of ideas we assimilated and forgot in our school days. Where, for example, did we get the idea that aging is purely a physical process? Age! thought Monakhov. That is the great law that governs man! Monakhov couldn't admit its effect on him, while its effect on those around him was objective. The application of this law to himself meant that his life was essentially lived and not in the future at all. In that case he had lived it either the wrong way, or without having noticed, or in the wrong sense. His prospects, which had always been open, suddenly slammed shut. Lord! I'm not ready... On the other hand, he was no worse off than anyone: his mother was alive, his children healthy, his wives were unhappy but also healthy and had everything they needed... and when were they ever happy, I'd like to know! Monakhov flared up automatically. If the reason for his bad state of mind was only that he hadn't made them happy in their opinion, that was nonsense, that could be ignored. And although he nonetheless couldn't ignore it, something vexing connected with them remained on his conscience, it was clearly not the most important thing. That was just the point, that Monakhov *himself* was discontent with himself, not that others were and —knock on wood!—he even had his health. What was so painful about the absence of pain? Unbearable. Was everything really over...? What's "everything"!? How can he keep on not answering a single question... These questions multiply simply by dividing. Where did he get the idea, where did they all get the idea—his wives, his children—that life was supposed to be going on all the time, every second? And not even by itself, but according to our ideas about it! Reject the social system—and yet reflect it in every way so fully... No, it's *ours,* this system, and yours too. Go on, go on! It was a mistake to have scraped life to the very bottom long ago. How can I be surprised now by being unfeeling? How is our Sveta getting on...?

She's insulted. Not looking at me. Well, thank God. But, Comrade Monakhov, you'll have to begin your life all over. You can't relive the old one—just straighten its tail a bit. So it won't hurt too badly... Oh, it hurts! And you're no picnic with your guilt and duty! Why do you go to such lengths, to the surprise and disrespect of your loved ones? Who needs your humility and sacrifice! They need *you,* and where are you? Come out, come out wherever you are... Why are you shoving this life, like a piano to the seventh floor! No, that's enough.

Lord! Can't one thought come to mind which I haven't already thought? I've already thought them all...

Svetochka was sleeping with her mouth open. Monakhov imagined her looking that way early in the morning... on someone else's pillow... her poor rags strewn carelessly around the floor... the birds are chirping, the window's growing light... and she, after all this storm, is sleeping soundly with her mouth half open... Monakhov looks at her with distaste and stealthily, trying not to wake her up, slides off the bed, barefoot on someone else's floor, his shoes in his hand, damn it, where's my other sock?... Monakhov wanted to go out but the floor was shaking under him... The train roared in the night, careening by the signal more and more gaily, as if no longer following the track... No, it was a good thing he hadn't struck up an acquaintance... Monakhov dozed himself, for a while trying not to forget about his mouth, profiting from another's experience... until he fell asleep with all the unaffectedness of sleep.

...It's not so scary. One object can be similar to another object... and here are two similar people... And this similar object serves its purpose as the object it resembles serves *its* purpose. And this person who resembles that one lives her life as the person she resembles lives *hers.* What's so remarkable about that?

Resemblance or similarity had never particularly interested Monakhov, at least he had never encountered anything frightening in the phenomenon up to now. That field had easily been exhausted by passing thoughts about the fact that while there is an infinite variety of combinations of elements, the elements themselves are constant, and therefore, by the law of probability, a significant similarity in the combination of elements in some objects, people, or events completely unrelated and quite distant from one another was entirely possible. "A remote likeness," in this case, rather a likeness of two distant objects than simply an insignificant resemblance. But in an infinite series, there was the possibility of identity—yes, a curiosity, a trick of nature... like the trick of nature that by the same law of chance, we can become witnesses of such curiosities. Witnesses and nothing more. We have no responsibility for it. A remote likeness shouldn't disturb us at all. In fact we could say that any type of likeness or resemblance should delight any normal person not given to pondering the abyss ("I should have your worries..."—a reasonable response!). After all, a child is delighted by every similarity as his first mode of cognition, and the tender little whiskers of his first concepts stretch out from the still immeasurable "I" to the still measurable world... The adult too can be delighted by finding his own relationship to the surrounding world, his unity, even his fusion with it, in occurrences of similarity.

Now the surprising word "suddenly" can be used.

And suddenly Monakhov was terrified. He was shaken by this railway car resemblance... It was the justification of that false foot he put forward from the very beginning of our story. Although, in the broad sense, of course, not "suddenly." He had long been patiently led toward this "suddenly" by his unfathomable life. It was as if he had been unwinding a thread so long that he could no longer even see the ball: how much was there? Is the thread used up...? So, it *suddenly* seemed to him that it was stretched dangerously tight: was it stuck, or used up? A distressing question, and no one to ask it of. We don't attribute the same deep significance to the chance encounter in the car that Monakhov did; perhaps he exaggerated the resemblance... however, it's not for us to judge—it was *his* encounter, not ours. He took it as an indicator, however arbitrarily. That indicator signified that his life had described a circle. The theoretical spiral did not console him.* He had nowhere to put it. For him the only question was the quantity of circles he had described—wasn't this the third stop...? The third, not much consolation in that...

In any case, it was precisely at this point of his life, which had already turned into a stage, that Monakhov stopped to look around. This justification of that false foot he put forward from the very beginning of our story, which we'll call either "The Shadow" or "The Expert," or "The Wreath," or as we boldly wrote at the begining—"The Taste," or "A Remote Likeness." Before he puts forward the next, also possibly false, foot...

He came home, and they had a talk.

But Monakhov did not manage to start a new life right away.

Some time passed before his strange and radical intentions settled and took root in the consciousness of his loved ones (his wife) and took on an official and customary appearance: Monakhov was taking his routine leave, possibly with an extra month at his own expense, but would not spend it with his family, he would rent a room out of town where at last no one would keep him from digesting his experience. (In principle his next monograph, "Pendant reticulated constructions"...) But this could hardly be called an escape or a "vita nuova." Tolstoy... Monakhov said to himself, grinning wolfishly. But he was unjust to himself: had he not been unshakable in his decision, had his wife not been convinced of its unavoidability, had his superiors not grown accustomed to the idea... he would probably not be living at the dacha now, wrenched from the "cares of the world's bustle,"** with the prospect of living that way for two months...a practically impossible achievement! He would say: "I live opposite Pasternak's grave," and the word "live" sounded strange.

When he said this phrase for the first time, he wasn't sure he wasn't

---

* The spiral is the Marxist model of the dialectical pattern of historical development.

**From Pushkin's *Eugene Onegin*.

repeating it for the hundredth time. Multiples tormented him. Multiple thoughts, words, meetings. It all needed to be reduced, like a fraction. It had been time for him to leave. Solitude was essential for him. While he was still trying to achieve it, it was still a goal. He brought his things into the room, put out clean paper and reference books on the table, made tea... And underneath his brief childlike satisfaction at his independent set-up, he realized with despair that there was no solitude.

The landlady...but the landlady wasn't the point. This one-day-long fever of activity wouldn't be hard to cure. How to turn on the water, light the gas...this would pass. Something else bothered Monakhov in this much-touted place. He didn't know what it was, perhaps that it wasn't the way he'd expected it to be...but that too was an absolutely common occurrence: an appointed place is always like that—different from how you imagined it, and that's what's nice about it. Or maybe it didn't exist at all... Monakhov looked out the window and began to feel empty. It wasn't that it didn't exist at all: the pines, bushes, paths, barns—there was an adequate complement of all that. A certain plethora of detail, unformedness of the landscape, a general litteredness—that's after all precisely the nature of dacha surroundings, for scenery people travel farther, to the country. After all, one could like this disorder and weediness too, Monakhov in fact did like it, he knew and recognized its specialness. And nonetheless, it was as if this weren't a place or rather had already been one. Once. Not so long ago—Monakhov arrived and it was already gone. There was no place.

The way thoughts irritated him by their "already-thought-ness" and people by their "already-met-ness," as his whole life did by its "spent-ness," that was possibly how this place irritated him. It was exactly a "spent" place, as if it were moth-eaten (it was fun to imagine an insect that ate landscape...). But there was another nuance here. While the feeling of repetetiveness, already-been-ness, which possessed him in relation to people, thoughts, and feelings was his personal feeling which he experienced and nourished (in the sense of acquired), that is, while it contained the hint of being justly deserved (revenge for his unrighteous life...), he was guilty of this landscape's unsatisfactoriness only in part, in very negligible part. Someone had used it, had drunk up this nature, so that there wasn't any left for Monakhov. Monakhov didn't want to look out the window. A pine was a pine: bark, sap...but it too failed to live the peaceful self-assured life of a tree to which Monakhov was accustomed at home in the North—it was as if it were holding out as a pine but in its heart was already a board, fallen branches; a former squirrel ran along it with dead fur, the reanimated scrap of his aunt's muff. The view out the window had already been drunk up, there wasn't any color in its face, and Monakhov had two months to look at it, while seeking life and equilibrium. Plans! Fantasies...!

Who had managed to look the life out of it? Monakhov thought with hostility as he looked around. He actually gazed slowly so as not to get dust in his eyes in case it poured down from an incautious glance at the view of the woods, the hill, the field... It must have been the poet who lived here. Shortly before Monakhov. The landscape survived after his death only in the eyes of those who remained. That's how Monakhov explained the mute dissatisfaction that had been stirring inside him, unformulated. The abrasiveness of the poet's gaze, which had rubbed off the powder from the invisible wings of the surroundings, haunted his imagination, and although Monakhov only knew that poet's poetry slightly, he now almost vengefully decided to get it to read in order to be convinced that it was worth destroying this small place for. He remembered a photograph: in a quilted jacket, cap, and rubber boots, leaning on a hoe (which is what reminded him of the photograph), looking more like the gravedigger from *Hamlet* than its translator, he looks out in front of him, probably at this landscape the remains of which so displeased Monakhov.

Yes, this place had already been. Monakhov hadn't intended to describe it, but he nontheless missed it.

People, thoughts, feelings, and now this place—all of it had already been. Is it possible that I too have already been? That was the question Monakhov had not wanted to allow into his consciousness. And then someone else who had lived here before him up and took away the place that lay between him and his question, rolled it up like his own carpet...

"I live opposite Pasternak's grave..." Monakhov repeated, stressing the "live." No one had noticed the pun in this phrase, however weak it was. They smiled, as if shrugging their shoulders.

"A village of the dacha sort," he suddenly said.

"Recreation zone for workers of the Odintsov region" adorned the platform. "A saffron swath with a scythe—from the curtain to the divan..." Monakhov smiled. To get rid of this strange dissatisfaction with the place, he broadened his nodding acquaintance with the poetry. He didn't dare admit out loud that he didn't like the poems. They seemed to try too hard to be. What can you do if it isn't Mikhailovskoe*... is it really worth shaking the life out of the poor landscape... Although in a strange way it was the poems that had been written here that Monakhov liked best.

Only the church on the hill glowed with the same force as in the poems: "out of a cookie cutter." It delighted the eye. Out from beneath it, down the slope, up to the stream, descended the cemetery the poet was buried in. Monakhov decided not to go to the grave, the obligatory object of pilgrimage of every visiting member of the intelligentsia. Either he didn't want to be like everyone else, or he didn't consider himself one of the intelligentsia in that sense, or he didn't number all the rest among it, or he felt it was more original to "live opposite," or he didn't like cemeteries... This impulse wasn't sufficiently clear. Perhaps he was afraid of "rhyme."

---

* Pushkin's family estate

Symptoms, syndromes... "Rhyme" was his own concept which should be explained.

I've seen it somewhere, read it, heard it... It reminds me of something, I can't remember what... What a familiar face! Haven't I met you somewhere before... Oh, I told you that already... I know, I've already heard... All these everyday incidents, various turns of phrase which up to now had meant nothing, suddenly began to suggest to Monakhov that they contained more hidden senses than the normal person is capable of suspecting. Something would infallibly repeat itself the same day that up till then might not happen for years, as if it had been piling up all those years in order to fall out together... Let's say, he'd catch himself at an odd thing: going over the dusty heap in his desk drawer—photographs, receipts, notes... and suddenly begin to trim and glue, try to make the perfect composition until at the end of the day he had an intricate collage, a genre he had no understanding of. Not one piece of paper was left out! Monakhov found himself admiring the work of his own hands, got embarrassed, hid it under some things so that no one would see it (his wife). That evening she (his wife) asked him to cut out a pattern from a foreign newpaper—and with amused surprise Monakhov spent the remainder of the evening handling the same scissors and glue ("How good you are at it!"—Monakhov looked up cautiously—but of course she couldn't see through walls and drawers! "As a boy I was good at cut-outs..."). That was just the point, that to this day Monakhov, and he was absolutely sure of this, hadn't cut anything out for thirty years. The first time Monakhov clearly experienced this law was when he started driving. Having established habitual, standard routes for himself from which life rarely deflected him, he now knew for certain that if suddenly he had to go to some corner of the city in which he'd never been on some errand, also a somewhat unusual one—let's say, taking his wife's friend's typewriter to be repaired, then that meant that the evening of the same day he'd find himself in the same place for the second time in his life on a no less usual errand, accompanying the ambulance that was taking his son who'd suddenly gotten sick (it wasn't serious, thank God...) to an unknown hospital where there was a place, that place was in the hospital that was opposite the typewriter repair shop (and I was just there this morning! And didn't notice the hospital). And that's the way it was, if not every day, then every other day. And he'd never cut out anything after that time, or gone to that part of town again... Monakhov knew all the explanations for such coincidences, but boredom kept him from talking about probability. That was the whole point, that it was improbable! Yesterday he saw a dead horse in the middle of the street two times—this was now, in Moscow... when you meet a live one you're startled, but this—he saw one in the morning near the three stations and the other in the evening near Sokol (and what was he doing in Sokol? He couldn't remember...), as if that horse were being carried around the whole city so that he would keep bumping into it. No, he was quite normal. He never imagined things. But all of this happened so much that he couldn't remember a single example (including the ones cited), but he remembered that this law manifests itself everyday and keeps on *functioning*. And that hint is more than a hint; it's a *reminder*. What is it a reminder of?! That life exists independently of your existence. And if you, to avoid noticing your absence, stop reacting to life completely, it finds a way to remind you that it exists by means of this *rhyme*. You're lucky if it's not a direct hit. When you stop noticing these thing—you're lost... you can expect a hit... Monakhov hadn't become superstititious, he didn't try to explain incomprehensible things by primitive logical constructions, but he was put on the alert by such hints of existence, and passed the rest of the day a bit more cautiously and sensitively. The slightly worn-out fabric of his life, its sly meaning which is always hidden from logical necessity, shone through to him at such moments. It was enough for Monakhov to be on his guard, but not to try to grasp the fleeting secret sense in order not to completely destroy the frail fabric through which it yawned. And of course Monakhov fairly frequently froze in mid-word, in mid-gesture, suddenly catching that transparent moment behind the flash: it had already happened, he couldn't remember when, but exactly at such a point in space and time, at the same mid-word, it had already been! He remembered it precisely, he recognized that fleeting instant as already having been... time had made a complete circle and landed on the same point with Monakhov stuck to its rim quite by chance. Did this mean that time ended in him? Or should he be content with general (and his own) deliberations about timelessness?

The concept of the "rhyme" of time which Monakhov had formulated for himself was also the only way Monakhov now managed to perceive time as passing, as alive, as existing externally. He had no more memories. Of course, he could say: "I remember when..." and repeat something learned by heart as if it belonged to someone else and had never happened to him (how he, poor little thing, had fallen off the porch and banged his forehead... for proof he would point to the scar on his forehead and be almost astonished to find it with his fingers: there really was a scar... it was *on* Monakhov, but Monakhov himself didn't have it: the way a thread can stick to your jacket), and he grew bored with this theft of others' memories, because he really stole them, and not even from the self who had once experienced something, but from the next self who merely remembered what had once been experienced. No, he wasn't yet thirty-three... No, thirty-four. Wait, what year is it? Not the next one yet... ? Then nineteen seventy so and so... minus nineteen thirty so and so—was exactly thirty-three. But he hadn't had his birthday yet...

And again, he was absolutely healthy. Not senile. He could multiply three-figure numbers in his head. He could, if necessary, recall any excerpt from his past life with juridical exactitude. He remembered *everything*, without any gaps. If he needed to, he could recall it. But he *didn't* need to. And he didn't remember anything. He had no memories. Only reminders...

Rhyme. Bing-bing. It was even funny somehow. If one thing, then the same thing again. He didn't want to meet a second time a classmate whom he hadn't seen for twenty years till today. But he would meet one today. If he decided to go off to the bathhouse today—then he'd be there, and if he decided out of the blue to go off to Leningrad, they'd be on the same train.

That was why he didn't want to go to the cemetery to visit the grave, so as not to give fate an excuse to take him there again right away, for something closer to home. It wasn't that Monakhov thought exactly that, that would be an almost maniacal state of mind, but, we repeat, he was healthy, although the reluctance and the trepidation were there. And if he hadn't been dragged there, he wouldn't have gone himself... Svetochka descended on him (the look-alike...), and he absolutely had to show her that grave: she didn't believe he hadn't seen it himself and was insulted that he'd seen it but wouldn't make any effort for her... So his excursion to the cemetery with Svetochka turned out to be his "second" one anyway, even if only in someone else's consciousness. Fate didn't put the artificial non-visit on his account.

They wandered among the graves and didn't find the poet. "You've been there! How could you forget it..." Monakhov had stopped objecting. "Let's ask..." Monakhov was embarrassed to ask. That was something you were supposed to *know*. Now, searching, he looked at each grave with involuntary concentration. And not without curiosity: it was a long while since he'd been to a cemetery, thank God, a long time since he'd been at a funeral... This was in part a special cemetery, several graves attracted attention. But even when he hadn't gotten close enough to make out the name on it, Monakhov already knew that the next "famous" grave couldn't belong to the poet. And he would be right. And they would walk on. Monakhov didn't think about how the grave they were looking for would be distinguishable from the others, or why it should be, really... he was sure that it was *different* from the others, sure in advance, without having thought about it or troubling his imagination. The other graves were richer and poorer, but they were identical in relation to the one they were looking for unsuccessfully. How that grave should be distinguished—the question, perhaps inappropriate, would have puzzled Monakhov, especially since he had no special relationship to the poet. But, undoubtedly, without analyzing or going into it, the very expectation of a *different* grave meant distinguishing the poet from other mortals. Mortals indeed! Monakhov was touched and amused by the effort to extend life in a monument. Here was a monument he had been about to hasten over to hopefully... but closer up its hopeless proportions became clear—again not it. But marble and basrelief! A flowerbed! A little bench and a pedestal behind a locked gate... Too much. Monakhov looked at the basrelief—there was also too much face on that woman, it didn't express anything except respectability and wealth which the stone itself expressed anyway. On the gate hung a lock, heavy and solid. A splendid grave, the face of a splendid woman—the splendor *was* expressed. Monakhov couldn't find out any more, but already knew a lot. That thought about the resemblance of the deceased to his monument surprised Monakhov... It's true... the lock... what else, what other thoughts besides theft would that grave produce...? Monakhov passed it as if he had long been acquainted with the deceased, so clearly did her grave express her character. As if she were alive... He mentally repeated to himself the sigh of her satisfied relatives as they took leave of the basrelief: white marble, a lot of cheek, the red column, stately, probably like the torso of the deceased... Yes, what a resemblance! Monakhov was delighted. And the thought about resemblance didn't leave him. Here was another "non-poet's" grave, although it even had a high-flown verse of bald words carved on it, evidently written by the deceased... The way the author felt about his verse, and how his loved ones, who had chosen this verse to please him, felt about the author... Again a portrait emerged. Monakhov got excited: the images of the deceased were resurrected before him from their monuments, a little too typical, all in their characteristic roles—they acted their parts on the provincial stage of his imagination as if they were alive. He introduced them to each other... "What are you laughing at?" asked Svetochka.

"Just think," he said, "Many of them wouldn't like their headstones at all... I would never have thought that love could be so exposing."

"I don't quite understand you, of course," said Svetochka. "What's so funny about that?"

Indeed. Monakhov was embarrassed. He tried to explain. I mean, the relatives, out of love, trying to please the deceased, unintentionally put up something very characteristic, perhaps private, accidentally creating an image: perhaps of a man who liked acclaim too much, or put his heart into his income, or had a secret weakness for his own literary efforts... And they take his treasure—and exhibit it... Monakhov mumbled on a bit, more and more feebly and uncertainly. "We were here already," said Svetochka. They'd gone in a circle. "You're right," he said, suddenly looking at Svetochka and being struck by her immortality. Her every cell was young. She had already picked a flower from a grave and put it behind her ear. By some special irony she was wearing white shoes... He stroked her cheek the way you stroke an apple or a peach, not believing your fingers that they're like that. She completely misunderstood him and grew joyfully embarrassed. Immortal.

She was as appropriate in the cemetery as flowers, bushes, and birds are.

But Monakhov could not assimilate himself in the same way, feeling himself halfway between Svetochka and the grave. He would probably find more common topics of conversation with the underground inhabitants... And then when he decided the precious grave was enchanted and regretted that he hadn't asked the way right off, and, tired, tried to get out of the appendix by winding along a path that curled like a snail behind a row of young incompletely-drawn birches, again ended up in a dead end staring long and dumbly at a grey stone, a ridiculous profile, a facsimile... "There it is!" Svetochka exclaimed joyfully over his shoulder.

Now that's solitude...! Monakhov exclaimed mentally. When a man doesn't want to see people any more, it wasn't that he had anything against them—he doesn't want to see himself with them... For some reason at this grave that he'd finally found, he wasn't sorry for the one in the ground, he was sorry for himself. So sorry that he felt that sorrow almost as a lost happiness, and the surrounding world came right up to him, presenting everything alive that composed it: a leaf turned its velvety insect underside to him, a blade of grass unbent under him, a breeze from a branch rustling drowsily touched his cheek, the shadow of a cloud sliding past above stolled around, looking into all the illuminated corners... and he didn't want to leave this world for anything! He wasn't ready. For a second it seemed to Monakhov that the world had turned upside down, though he didn't duck his head: he seemed to be lying on his back, and everything above him was the puddle of the world which had been drained for him... Well, if it is—Monakhov rejoiced. Then it would still be possible that "over me would bend and rustle"...* then it would be possible. And nothing more would be needed. When you have that much—it's everything. That after death a person is granted the world of a tree is not so little. He has roots at last. The world comes to him so that he can look at it. A tree can't see as much as a person, but it sees a person as much as the person sees the tree... This strange idea wouldn't permit Monakhov to move, he thought he'd never leave the spot. He would really like that... he knew too well that he would finally move—an experienced despair broke in from the rear. "Recite me one of his poems," Svetochka asked in a whisper. Oh God! Monakhov howled to himself, having forgotten about her completely. And he moved on.

"Later," he said, completely without anger. This grave struck one by its poverty. The kind that seemed to befit a poet in disgrace... But no, not that kind! It was entirely on the level of the prosperous graves here, and even had a surplus of tasteful refinement. But still, what was this poverty, how was it expressed? Monakhov hadn't had a defined image of the expectation which unconsciously developed in him while he was searching. Now, having seen the grave, this image was lost forever: the grave was the way it was. His imagining was destroyed. It was its poverty of imagination that struck one: there was no railing, a fence made of poles—taste... a light grey, dust-like stone, unpolished—dignity... grass, a little lawn instead of a flower bed—modesty... a little row of those birch trees—the simplicity of greatness... a thoughtful canopy—the hint of a lyre... What else could be thought up and what avoided? Everything. To avoid disturbing it, everything. But if you disturbed it, then the poverty would seem like beggarliness. Because a monument to a genius cannot be a monument of genius... That's good. And this one was like that. True, the distance between him and his monument was somehow reciprocal and not so exposing... But even so. Wasn't it this profile on grey stone that made him freeze so nobly and stiffly in the last photographs

---

* From Mikhail Lermontov's poem, "I go out alone on the road" (1841).

while he was still alive? Wasn't this little fence of poles that showed strict good taste born of his solitary genius? And wasn't it from beneath him that the graves of old Bolsheviks poured down the hill and stopped as still as their white level stones on the green grass, even after death frozen into a battalion above the precipice...? And only the stream flowed on below as it had before him, independently of him, only poorer and shallower.

Everyone gets the monument he deserves.

The justice of such a conclusion crowned the bustle of the moments of trouble and distress of one's lifetime. Justice is the sole measure of time in units of one human life.

It was time to go. He still had to think about others' love for you after your death. Dizzying and impossible. Mama drinking tea, opening a jar of preserves from his lifetime, his wife sewing up her skirt, his son masturbating in the bathroom... The fuss of preparation for the Saturday trip to tend the grave—they look for it, find it... at the last moment they forget the package with the cultivator and the rake, but decide not to go back: it would hex the trip*...

Some one was approaching the grave. Two voices moving along the path Monakhov had made, not deviating from it... One was a dissatisfied and educated baritone, the other simpler, a simpering alcoholic speech. The dissatisfied one exaggerated his tone of strictness and discontent as if not completely believing his own ferocity, but not allowing anyone else to doubt it. The simple soul dishonestly imitated intelligence and future industriousness, which apparently consisted of the simplest relations to the future, that is, knowing everything in advance. "So I say, another culture won't arise here..." he said, justifying himself, and the word "culture" which didn't fit in his throat, separated and stuck in Monakhov's ear. "Culture..." the baritone repeated with a strange laryngeal screech. And they came in, cutting off Monakhov's and Svetochka's path of escape. One grey-haired and the other in a padded jacket... As if he hadn't expected there to be someone at the grave... as if there were never anyone here... Monakhov was embarrassed, but managed with a quick glance to see the haughtiness of the grey-haired one's profile, and now he compared him with the profile on the stone. His son... he thought. Clearly his son... the "son," as if displeased by the presence of outsiders, looked to one side, interrupting himself in mid-word: he shook a pole of the fence, wiped off his palm... Monakhov pushed Svetochka to the exit; the arrivals moved aside to let them pass. In the gateway, Monakhov, unexpectedly to himself, said "Goodbye," and the "son" nodded briefly like an examiner, and at once quickly zipped inside the fence. "Did you plant anything?" his displeased voice immediately boomed behind Monakhov's back. "Of course I did..." answered the gravekeeper.

Monakhov was touched for some reason. The son definitely loved his

---

* A Russian superstition.

father. And that businesslike caretaking was somehow just right, appropriate to a genius. Monakhov quickly walked along the paths as if he had long known the way, as if greeting the already familiar graves with short nods as he went. There's the property-owner... and there's the author of the verses... No, the cemetery was not the place to settle accounts with life, Monakhov thought. See how the dead cling to life and aren't letting go of it... Only motion has abandoned them; the rest—they still retain: position, tastes, vanity... even the love of those close to them and the recognition of their compatriots...

> I have died, while you still live,
> The wind, complaining with a sob
> Rocks the forest and the dacha...

he recited to Svetochka along the way to the house what he remembered.

> Not every pine tree separately
> But... tum-tum-tum... all trees...

"I've forgotten it," he said. Everything was especially windless and silent.

So it turned out that that grave did make an impression on him. His thoughts took an unaccustomed direction, he started noticing things around him the way he used to: a leaf, some small animal, a pebble he'd nudged with his foot... And he had someone to listen close by. At least she was someone with whom he could share the thought that strong impressions don't happen at all the way they do on stage: "he stopped dead," "he was thunderstruck," and so on... They appear gradually—things that happen at once are characteristically reactions of stopping short at the unaccustomed, the significant, or the force of an expected experience. A strong impression appears later, emerges, develops (in the photo sense)... Such were his deliberations, compensating both for his inadequacy of feelings as well as for his overflow of impressions. "Just like in love..." said Monakhov. Not right away. At first it seems nothing special, and then it turns out God knows what. Svetochka tensed.

Monakhov quickly reaped "his reward." For his sensitivity and impressionability. Revenge stood on the threshold and took the form of the schoolmate he'd met that morning—what could he do...?

"You know who else I met this morning!" he joyfully announced and, not waiting for a display of passionate interest from Monakhov... "Yes, Yaroshnikov!"

Monakhov didn't even make the effort to remember Yaroshnikov. His school friend was so old... He shook a worn-out "Beryozka" bag causing a three-rouble-sixty-two bottle to gurgle; Monakhov introduced him to Svetochka, and they went into the house: Svetochka, then the friend, hospitable Monakhov after them looking at their backs with despair.

From then on it was as if they'd had a script. Svetochka took the frying pan from Monakhov: "Where's the salt? Don't you have any onion?" The friend, tugging his greyish pompadour, talked on in a bass, looking at Svetochka to determine the degree of her relations with Monakhov, so far not taking him aside to ask how long he'd been "with her" and "how she was"; Monakhov finally began to recall something about him, in fact that already at school the friend had had a reputation "in that field." Now with a pot belly and greying hair he should somehow not be attractive because Monakhov didn't find him attractive; Svetochka was animated. Finally, she summoned the "boys" to the table. The friend proposed a long toast, inserting English words into it (it turned out he was in that field); Monakhov out of embarrassment hurried to take a drink and choked; Svetochka was all right, she didn't find the friend dreadful... Yes, he'd gone into isolation, Monakhov thought with despair, drank some more, and—let go. He was very surprised after a while to find himself telling a school adventure he'd remembered: how someone had stolen a tape recorder from the English office when recorders were still a rarity and they'd never found the thieves... "You mean you don't know who stole it?" the friend asked in amazement. "Do you?" "Of course," said the friend, but didn't reveal the secret. "Eet vas a marveloss stori," he added mysteriously. "Do you remember Asya? Oh of course, how could you not remember..." "What has Asya got to do with it!" Monakhov got angry for some reason. "He was in love with her," the friend explained to Svetochka. "In love...?" Svetochka said slowly, raising her eyebrows. "You know she died?" "No-o-o," Monakhov answered doubtfully; he tried to recall something unpleasant connected with the friend... was it that he'd once somehow been terribly jealous of him in connection with Asya... Yes, apparently he'd then tried to forget it and had. "How awful!" Svetochka exclaimed. "Cancer," the friend affirmed. "At first they cut out everything *there,* then they removed a breast..." Monakhov hadn't drunk in a long time, especially three-rouble-sixty-two... "This vodka is really terrible," he muttered and went out, knocking against the chair.

Having vomited, he went out on the porch for some air. There was a breeze above, but below it was still. The tops of the firs swayed, the wind rustled the needles. "Complaining with a sob..." Monakhov remembered and struck his fist painfully on the railings. "Damn it!" he said, shaking his hand out, and went back into the house.

But neither Svetochka nor the friend had disappeared; Monakhov was stupidly surprised by their presence and not very pleased. The friend was already sitting next to Svetochka reading her palm. "Yes!" Monakhov was delighted. "I remember! Twenty years ago he read *her* palm exactly the same way..." Monakhov didn't call her by name even to himself... (the shadow of *that* unpleasant memory flew past him with the rustle of a night moth, causing a shiver in his back. "Long eenaf, strong eenaf, put eet in," the friend was meanwhile telling her, laughing. Monakhov remembered that too, he told that joke *then* too about Longinov, Stroganov and Putyatin (the friend's name was Putilin, and he claimed the joke as his own). Svetochka didn't know English, she took German. What language had *she* studied. Monakhov couldn't remember. Of course she didn't know the one she studied, but anyway which was it? Did she understand the joke at the time?! Monakhov looked at "Put-it-in" maliciously and got up to put the kettle on.

"Let me do it," Svetochka took it away from him, "You don't know how." "What's there to know?" Monakhov said indignantly, "It's instant coffee!!" "Jew, put more grounds in," "Put-it-in" told the joke. Svetochka kept stirring the dry cup with a spoon. This seemed horribly tacky to Monakhov. "Who taught you that?" he asked with hostility. "It will have skin"* Svetochka sang out. "Are you sick?" she asked worriedly, handing him the cup. "Look how much skin... You're so pale." "Are you asking me, or did I get pale?" "Why are you taking that tone with me?" Svetochka asked guardedly. "You'll be late for your train," said Monakhov.

Svetochka finally got insulted and started getting her things together quickly with trembling lips. The friend, observing it all with silent understanding, also got up, not forgetting his "Beryozka" bag. "I have to go too," he said.

Svetochka rushed out without saying goodbye. "So we'll expect you tomorrow," said the friend. "Who's we...? Monakhov was taken aback. We already! He was amazed. "Have you forgotten, we arranged with Yaroshnikov..." "Oh yes..." said Monakhov. The friend was already hurrying. Monakhov had heard his menacing trot. He'll catch up...

He covered his eyes and swam, the room turned twice on its axis... "Huh? What is it?" He leaped up as if scalded. Someone was tapping at the window. He let in a tear-stained Svetochka. "I'm sorry, I'm sorry..." Monakhov couldn't bear women's tears.

Svetochka fluffed up the featherbed like foam. They lay down. Monakhov stroked her cheek which was cool from her tears... What had come over him? He was surprised. He'd hurt a little girl... Putilin too... A monster, of course, but after all quite good-natured. Svetochka kissed his hand. "What are you doing?" Monakhov gently took his hand away, and put it down on her breast. Her breast was tiny, childlike. He pulled his hand away as if he'd had an electric shock. Monakhov was horror-struck, as if his hand had fallen into a hole. "What's the matter?" Svetochka asked tenderly and put her hand down below. "Are you tired? Sleep, dear."

But in the morning he was glad that Svetochka was there.

He took her to the station and phoned home. "What? When? She was unconscious...?" he kept repeating senselessly. "I'm coming. Of course, I'm leaving right now."

Monakhov had to take this on his shoulders as a non-blood relative. He

---

* Russians consider that properly brewed coffee should form a kind of crust or skin

was not vexed by this and took it—in such cases you can't say easily and willingly, but readily. He was vexed rather that he hadn't been ready for this death. Not in the sense that he was shaken, no: he was, of course, sorry about Grandmother, but it was already inevitable, it was only a question of when (yesterday); it was not his grandmother. Monakhov was vexed with himself, that at last when everything was free and peaceful, he had spent these days wastefully, hadn't gotten any work done, hadn't reformed himself at all ... and the day before especially made him moan with shame, especially in front of ... yes, particularly her. As if he were guilty that Svetochka and Putilin had descended on him ... Did he search them out? Invite them? He *got* them ... In the final analysis, the i had been dotted, and he was a free man—then what's the fuss, then he wasn't guilty. He wasn't guilty that Grandmother had died! That was all true, but having put forth all these indisputable proofs, he turned out guilty over and over, for the one thing, the other, and even for Grandma ... He hadn't been ready. "The income of a profligate is equivalent to a short blanket..." he liked to grin wryly at this pronouncement, considering it appropriate to precisely this kind of situation. There had been situations like this (without Grandma) before. He had not managed to overcome his feeling of guilt with the hair of the dog right away. It somehow always seemed more convincing than simple lack of self-respect.

Who will wash her? Who will get the coffin...? Who will drown the kittens? The most tender-hearted person there is will drown them. Another wouldn't be able to... Grandma used to drown them.

Monakhov buried her.

So, hurray for the secondary character! He's the one who at least does something for the heroes who are busy feeling and living. He's the one who brings them the telegram, brings them home, and helps them out. Waited on from all sides, plugged in by wires of various sorts to light, water and information, they get the time and strength for all those thoughts and feelings appropriate to prose. A prose writer could really consider himself at the top of life's pyramid, ruling over the heroes themselves, if only he were waited on as well and invisibly in his own life as his heroes are. But he keeps having to attend to the things he's freed his heroes from—in his own life he's overloaded with the functions of secondary characters; he's far from free enough to have time to experience the life accessible to his heroes. Everything goes around in a circle making a ring: ruling over his heroes, he'll write a book for them which they read or don't read or forget in a taxi—he'll write it in the role of the one who brings them home or brings the telegram. And the prose writer gets tired, and his sympathies shift more and more to the ladies and drivers, drunk plumbers and even policemen mentioned by chance in passing who immediately disappear from the page. The insistent and egotistical life of the heroes begins to irritate him: where did they get the idea that they are the ones who live, and what am I supposed to do, not live?! I have no money, my families have disintegrated, and like Jesus I have "nowhere to rest my head."

It's worse than for Jesus, because in addition to it all I'm not Jesus, I'm mortal! On whom have I spent my life? Secondary birds have nests, secondary foxes have lairs... My hero goes in and out of his *own* apartment, the bastard even loses the key to it! After all, some secondary locksmith, however drunk and clumsy, will come and let him in, and there he is at home again... Of course I too could spend my time with someone dearer to me than my hero, but I have nowhere to go! In the next world someone will *write me* ... he'll torment me, of course, but he won't notice or understand what inexpressible freedoms of possession he'll reward himself with for it... The trouble is that even Hamlet will write Shakespeare worse than Shakespeare wrote Hamlet. Someone has already noted caustically that in the decline of Russian literature former characters have started expressing themselves, that the latest literature is being written by Bashmachkins and Pirogovs, Lebyadkins and Peredonovs.*
It's possible that he is correct in the critical sense as well, but for me he's right in the above-mentioned sense, out of the mouths of babes... I used to protect my heroes from death. Now I understand the great tradition of their destruction: they must not be left to live on, corrupted by the freedom that is possible only on paper. And anyway, what kind of an ending does it make...? The hero walks around the city in the morning, pink from the sunrise, with the wandering smile of an idiot, symbolizing the beginning of a new life, and is reflected in an asphalt puddle (because a street cleaning vehicle issued by a secondary character will certainly drive by on that page...). Where will he come out, having overcome the trivial obstacle (not even always encountered) made up of the dates and places of writing? Correct heroes die on the last page, for, grown soft in book space, they simply wouldn't survive if they went out the gate of the cover: there wouldn't be anyone there to bring them things, their decisive social come-down from the main to the secondary in everyday life wouldn't suit them at all. So that a fatal outcome on the page is even in some sense humane. But if they cross over and start running around in life, what will happen on the page? God forbid! Isn't that the problem we're having already? They'll get loose and start writing in their turn, and then their heroes will start writing in their turn? No, kill 'em! Just kill them at the end. Let the reader be sorry for them, but at least he won't want to imitate them. And God grant him happiness in his live, secondary life. But if you're not partisans of bloodthirsty romanticism, if you have, so to speak, already yielded to democratic tendencies and sympathy for the secondary character and prefer the natural school, even then there is a way to prevent your hero whom you've raised from the secondary from escaping beyond the bounds of artistry and book cover (which in the given instance is one and the same): put him back in the ranks of the secondary, humiliate him after his brief centrality, reduce him to such insignificance and dust that it will really kill him without you lifting a

---

* Some of the more grotesque heroes from the works of Gogol, ("The Overcoat," "Nevsky Prospect"), Dostoevsky, (*The Brothers Karamazov*), and Sologub, (*The Petty Demon*).

hand (that, by the way, is the way the best representatives of the natural school managed the problem, like Gogol). Such heroes at least in escaping the bounds won't escape their insignificance, they won't even pick up the pen. Because to pick up the pen is already to be a hero (which is why they pick it up in the first place, not having perceived the homonymic trick of the word "hero," literary heroes). For that freedom with which the author rewards his heroes is born of the freedom he fights for heroically in his own life, and then only in the act of creation! But actually there is no other freedom. The hero and freedom—there are no more inseparable concepts! And if he has understood, if he has experienced it, if he has been convinced that it exists (freedom!), then let him perish, that's what he's a hero for. For what kind of a hero is it that doesn't perish? What kind of a fate is it to tell everyone on line for beer, not believing it yourself, that it all actually happened! It did! See, it's even written down... you get out your drunken dog-eared documents (omnia mea mecum porto...) and among them the newspaper clipping transparent at the folds or the certificate of the prize money you drunk up in honor of the feat... For what kind of hero is it who sur-vives? (Language won't deceive! It will find the right verb...) But he didn't survive—he perished again, only this time not as a hero. It's not enough to perform a feat, you have to perish beautifully in order to become a hero. He is a hero who perishes beautifully. That is, decisively and finally, bestowing his triumph on people without having received "his reward." For what is there to do once the feat is already performed and homage has been rendered? Freedom shapes the hero, but that freedom is not the kind that can be used. It's freedom's business to appreciate. And that is not so little! But what is to be done afterwards with this leveled remainder of life? Where can you put it? Into a new feat? But feats aren't ready-made form that's kept in stock which demand only bravery and decisiveness to perform. There are many more brave and decisive people than there are free ones. But you can't keep acquiring freedom after freedom... Poets are the singers of freedom not because they write its praises, but because they perish. That's why people treat them as heroes, because they hang on to their freedom longer than everyone else and represent the value of perishing in themselves. Poets are the heroes of literature itself. They are no longer people, but neither are they characters. They are the boundary between life and the word. Free, nothing threatens them but success, a word equivalent to the word "survive." But success is not glory.

How much simpler it is in secondary roles... Who sticks a little landscape behind the heroes' backs, who gives the reader a break from the immobility of the heroes' lives? Who secretly takes a rest himself in a digression...? The author.

The car, which hadn't been used for three days, wouldn't start. Today, when it was so necessary. Monakhov tried everything he knew himself, followed all the advice which the few dacha passers-by gave him, among which was licking the battery terminals. "What's it like, acid?" asked the advisor. "I don't know," Monakhov answered in despair: when he licked it he only tasted boiled coffee and yesterday's cigarettes. His heart beat horribly. He was unhealthily excited. He was hurrying to comply. There was in this not only a readiness to help and support his wife and her family in grief, but even some kind of eagerness—to get rid of himself for awhile on such a noble pretext. The secondariness and responsibility of his role somehow suited him at once, it was good to use himself selflessly, on someone else's business. He hadn't died and his relative hadn't died, and there was no one besides himself to do it all... Death made everything as certain as death itself. Monakhov was needed, here he was; the car was needed, and it did start; a coffin, evidently, was needed... and Monakhov went for it.

On the way he realized that he couldn't remember the deceased, although they had seen each other fairly often and not so long ago. He only remembered that she had gotten sick when she first saw her granddaughter's husband, that is, Monakhov. She was lying face down across the bed with a white porcelain face, her mouth slightly open and gleaming with a row of gold teeth. She was lying not amiably but angrily and Monakhov couldn't understand how he had so frightened her, what she had expected to see instead of him, what manner of prince? "The Countess..." Monakhov remembered " the Queen of Spades" and smiled: the funny thing was that Grandma really was a countess... But after the first impression there was an interval of excessive politeness and tea drinking ("Would you like it a bit stronger?")—Monakhov discovered that he had forgotten the deceased while she was still alive. He didn't remember her, he *knew* about her. He knew that her husband had been shot (his wife's grandfather, the count) and her second husband (a prince, it seems) had also been shot after an interval of nine years; that she had worked all her life as a nurse (almost sixty years), was well known, our most titled doctors knew her and from the time she had stopped working to the day of her death she could call them and ask their help for someone (and they would give it). An utterly modest person... He suddenly remembered her hat of rice straw from Paris (why was it that out of everything that hat had survived...?)—it was even hard to imagine that you could wear it, yet she would put it on every time in front of the mirror, and when she walked away, it was really a hat, put on the one right way, the way it was in the old days. Granmother finally *emerged* in Monakhov's consciousness, in fact he heard her laughter—she laughed very youthfully and infectiously. Monakhov also thought that our memory for voices is much more exact than for faces. Mentally enumerating the dead people he knew, he remembered the voice of each one and each time shivered at how clearly he could hear it. Accompanying the voice the clearest of all was the smile, from the smile—to the ear, the cheek, and then the face too became clearly visible, now he could look in his eyes... at that moment Father turned away, averted his gaze, his face disappeared, and the hand remained... the hand was distinct and separate, it reminded him of the one lying now on the steering wheel, his own... Monakhov hadn't noticed this similarity before.

Grandmother laughed and told, for some reason very gaily, what they ate on their estate ("before the catastrophe," she would say laughing), they ate, it turned out, all the time and large amounts (and of course very well)—it was hard to believe it, looking at the thin little girl-grandmother, no, she hadn't been fat then either, she had been just the same as now... Then for some reason would come the story, told with the same bell-like laughter, about the arrest (I come into the cell: they tell me "Put on the samovar!" and I look around, where is it? But I was supposed to answer "The jam is under the table," so they understood at once that I was there for the first time), then about Solovki (she had gone to visit the count, who was a terrific lover of cats and kept seventeen, so when he would be sent from place to place he would put the cats in a sack and off he'd go to the new place with the sack), this was forty-five, no, forty-six years ago, and she would laugh again infectiously...

Grandmother, who was small anyway, completely disappeared in the coffin Monakhov brought. An ashen petal... But he'd forgotten about the ribbon and the slippers. She had her own shroud. She also had a little metal pre-revolutionary tooth powder box with earth from the estate (in the Pskov district) where she was born, the only thing that the old lady still retained, besides the hat. Monakhov, amazed, mechanically opened it, and closed it, even more amazed: the earth was *old,* also like ash. She had preserved this little box in order to be buried in *her own* earth. Monakhov quickly went for the ribbon and slippers and returned.

She was supposed to spend the night in a church. Monakhov went to the only one he remembered from the time an acquaintance of his had had his funeral there. But at the time he hadn't been responsible for organizing it, and now he didn't know how it was done, with whom he was supposed to arrange it, how to pay for it, etc. And it was getting on toward evening, he had to have time to return with the burial bus. Furthermore he had to have a death certificate, otherwise it appeared they wouldn't put her in the church. Monakhov's head was spinning.

The church stood in a quiet and empty Moscow side street that had been preserved. Already old, the trees around it had also been preserved. And starlings which seemed to have been preserved from Savrosov's * day made circles in the darkening sky. There was no service; he pulled at the door in vain. He went around—no one. He squeezed through the crack between the gates. An old woman in black was gathering some chips in the little yard and carrying them to the samovar... Rejoicing, Monakhov knocked on the gate. The old woman, neither hurriedly nor taking her time, opened the gates to him without fear. Monakhov confusedly and hurriedly, going into detail, fearing refusal, explained what the matter was, and the old woman listened, or rather, patiently waited for him to finish. Monakhov expected the same thing

---

* Alexei Savrosov (1830-1897) known as the father of the Russian school of landscape painting whose best-known work is "The Starlings Flew In."

he'd encountered today all day long, what we encounter nowadays when we need something absolutely essential (he had waited for the saleswoman in the funeral store for half an hour: "She's gone to the base")—with a slippery rude coldness on their contorted mugs. Having heard him out, the old woman said: yes, bring her, yes, she would be here the whole time, yes, she would open the gate for him... And no paper was necessary, no death certificate, his word was enough... Monakhov was amazed. The name? asked the old lady. What? Monakhov didn't understand. The name of the deceased? "Oh!" Monakhov realized happily and rattled off last-name-first-name-middle-name as if he were on a drill ground. "God's servant Maria," the old lady repeated. "All right, I'll remember." Monakhov's amazement grew into rapture. How simple... he told her—and that was all? My word and her word is enough? Is it possible that it was like that once? Is that why Grandmother laughed all her life... Monakhov went out of the old lady's yard into another time, another space. It seemed that the church held these trees and starlings and the side street around itself with a secret force... And it wasn't as it had seemed to him when he had come, that the church had been preserved because the corner of the city in which it stood had been preserved; Monakhov understood it differently now: now it was clear to him that everything around it had been preserved thanks to the church, because it was in its field. It was precisely a field (in the popular scientific current sense) that Monakhov felt around the church... but here, ecstatic, light, he crossed some invisible line—there was a honk of a car horn, the squeal of brakes, the driver shook his fist at him, a new skyscraper for high officials soared up, a policeman from the booth of the embassy of a new little country looked at him without censure... and Monakhov remembered that he had his own car but had forgotten and gone on foot—he went back and got into it submissively.

He did everything necessary. He had done absolutely everything. Grandmother spent her last night on earth in the church. Unfortunately, he told his wife, I absolutely have to be there... I'll go quickly, just there and back. And he went to Yaroshnikov's.

And he vaguely remembered how he'd ended up under the windows of Svetochka's dormitory.

The candle trembled in his hand. He supported it with his other hand, but it trembled anyway. The hot wax dripped on his hand. Monakhov felt this heat on his hand with a certain joy: a sign of life. The whole way he chewed gum vigorously, he only stopped right in front of the church—after all it was awkward to chew in church... and it seemed to him that he reeked a meter off; he tried to stand apart, not to touch anything or anyone. Memories of the previous evening merged, he tried not to break them apart through carelessness. The sense of sin, shame and an unclear conscience was so profuse and strong that it didn't need definition; it would be terrible if something concrete were to rise to the surface of his memory. That internal trembling that penetrated his unsteady body was enough. It seemed to him that the candle in his hand was crackling somehow especially loudly, not like the others', as if he himself, a splinter of sin, were smoking and fuming through the candle, and the taste in his mouth was monstrous, and besides all this it seemed to him that he smelled of dog... Last night he had had an attack of rheumatism, and attentive Svetochka had tied a clump of dog fur to his waist as a sure remedy... Since morning it had been drizzling, a rain hung in a fog like dust... That's what it was, it was from the dampness. Having found the reason, however, didn't much reassure Monakhov: it seemed to him as before that he was going up in the candle smoke and it smelled of dog not from the fur but from himself, and that he was standing here, a fiend of hell, and for some reason the ground hadn't gaped beneath him yet, but would any minute. The old ladies sang in angelic cracking voices: the one who sold the candles, the one who wrote out his receipt (there was still and all a receipt even here...) and the one from yesterday, the holy one... Monakhov was somewhat comforted by the unpleasant comprehensible priest who was rattling off "Nunc Dimitis" with such lazy boredom, not exactly swallowing his words, but managing to pronounce even a whole paragraph in one word made up only of vowels, so that Monakhov wondered for a second: is the priest in the same state too...? At this he shifted his position for security, as if moving from the place which should have gaped beneath him.

They said their farewells quickly, the priest impatiently shifted from one foot to the other by the coffin... Monakhov made an effort and also kissed the deceased on the forehead after his wife. It was as if this could set something right between them or change what had happened the day before... Feeling that special coldness, always unaccustomed, under his lips, he moved away, considering the strange taste that filled his mouth. This vivid kiss reminded him strongly of something fairly unusual, but very recent. What was it? An utterly unique taste. "The battery!" Monakhov suddenly realized, and he unjustifiably rejoiced at having guessed. (Again that morning he had tried hopelessly to start the car and hadn't succeeded... again he had licked the terminals). And then another, previous taste surfaced in his mouth... and again not right away... at first squinting, almost howling... he didn't realize that it was the taste of Svetochka... there... so that when the general taste of vodka returned, concealing all these subtle nuances, it seemed holy and sinless to Monakhov... But the whole rainbow of vodka-coffee-tobacco-Svetochka-battery-deceased struck Monakhov's dimmed and dessicated consciousness, as if the taste was the last live feeling still available to him. I can't hear, can't see, can't understand, can't feel... just taste!

But again the old women started in with their holy voices... and the priest was already leaving, with his briefcase. Only then, and then out of sheer luck Monakhov remembered with horror about the box with the earth... he rushed after the priest. He explained with difficulty, breathlessly, trying not to breathe inadvertently on the priest. The priest blessed the box, shifting his briefcase from one hand to the other, and again set off. But where should he put it, what should he do with it? Put it in the grave? Or sprinkle it on top? "Put it in there..." the priest said lazily. In where? "In the coffin!?" he barked as he walked off.

But they were already taking the coffin out to the bus. Monakhov managed to thrust it in...

And here he saw Putilin. "Here I am," he said, smiling a gentle, shivery smile. And seeing Monakhov's uncomprehending gaze of non-recognition, added: "I promised to help you." Monakhov didn't remember. Putilin was frozen, blue, damp, as if he had been standing there a long time. "Why didn't you come in...?" Monakhov asked distantly. "I didn't want to interfere..." Putilin said respectfully. "Listen...!" said Monakhov and swallowed, "is it true?" "What? What do you mean..." Putilin asked, frightened, even stepping backward a little. "Is it true that Asya died?"

Someone somewhere had gotten something mixed up... The rain slashed down, the fog didn't lift, and still the sun shone through like a rotten yolk. There was no sky. There was no God. There was no devil. There was no earth. A yellow, snotty clay slithered underfoot. At an angle, like barge haulers in harness, they pushed a heavy wagon with Asya's coffin made of welded pipes. The little wheels of the wagon wouldn't turn and left a flat toboggan track on the clay. "Bitch!" Monakhov hissed, meaning the blue devil barely able to stand on his feet by the gate who had given him this cart in exchange for the death certificate. In form, color, and size, the death certificate was like the student card Monakhov had had in his time. "Why do you need the certificate?" Monakhov inquired with irritation. "So that you bring the wagon back," the devil explained goodnaturedly. "Bitches!" Monakhov repeated. The coffin slid around, knocking against pipes. Out of the corner of his eye Monakhov saw his friend's legs covered with mud up to the knees, and was filled with a feeling of gratitude to him: "Putilin's a touching guy!" "But just what went on between him and her...?" There was no end to the cemetery. In his fist Monakhov held a crumpled paper the size of a tram ticket. On it was written "Plot 72," and they were now crawling past the 34th. "We'll rest at the middle," Monakhov decided. They stopped. Monakhov looked around: now in both directions the cemetery stretched to the horizon. You could see it all, because little trees were planted only in the first rows of graves and still weren't able to block anything. Beyond them continued the crosses, columns, stars. And it would be hard for anything to survive here—there wasn't even any grass growing. They had a smoke; now, here—it didn't seem blasphemous to anyone. Monakhov turned over the ticket: on it was written "Lavrik," "The brigade-leader, what do you think?" he said to Putilin. "Probably," Putilin agreed. "The cemetery is Khovanksy," he remarked. "So Khovan* is his last name" (Put-it-in, Monakhov remembered). "So the brigade leader is Lavrik... "And his soul which had been prepared for heaven was sent to hell along

---

*From *khovat'*, to put away.

with his mourners by mistake..." Monakhov added. "Saintly or sinful, alive or dead, what do they care?" Having had their joke, they went on. Their shoes were soaked. First their feet slid inside their shoes and then the shoes slid on the clay... The schoolmates remembered their lessons: static friction and kinetic friction... Monakhov felt very close to Putilin, like a brother. "Listen, I've been wanting to ask you for a long time..." "What?" "Oh, nothing important..." Putilin was silent, and then agreed: "Nothing important."

They finally reached the boundary. The crosses ended as well as the rows of fresh mounds. In front of them yawned empty graves. And they were digging. Finished, half-finished, just begun. The grave diggers in pairs stuck out of the graves, some from the neck up, some from the waist, some from the knees—at all stages of the cycle. Before them stretched a boundless wasteland—the future of that cemetery. On one side it was strewn to the horizon with rusty tin cans and a mixture of rags and paper which sometimes flew up and settled again like a special sort of bird. At closer inspection, however, the dump didn't quite reach the horizon: along the horizon it was edged with a cabbage field, but the blue-grey film of the day on everything and the visibility limited by the fog almost completely equated the cabbages with the tin cans; in any case, the impression that the cans were planted and grown in this hell was reinforced by the supposed presence of cabbage on the horizon itself. Here at the end of the path the wagons crowded into line. Three were already waiting for graves ahead of them. "It'll be a while," Putilin agreed. The first in line wailed for the last time over the deceased as their turn came, either from grief or relief. The grave diggers labored like prisoners, their naked bodies shone. Here and there on heaps of earth lay freshly emptied bottles. The grave diggers were so drunk and worked with such frenzy that they seemed not to intend to leave here, but to burn up here on the front edge. One grave digger in particular kept attracting Monakhov's eye. A youth, pudgy and sober, a Jewish boy who looked like a student, clearly couldn't keep up with the brigade's pace, and his naturally red, still childish, cheek was already blue from obvious heart insufficiency; the unspent despair of this moment showed in his eyes even more profoundly than his nation's thousand year one. What had driven him here, given his obvious domesticity, without the slightest trace of any kind of a fall? What idea could he have had of what he'd earn and *how* ... ? He was behind in production and felt the contempt of the brigade with his smooth skin, when every few tosses he would stop for breath again and again. The others' shovels flashed incessantly. "Perhaps he doesn't get out of the grave while they smoke and drink, because besides everything else he doesn't smoke and drink..." Monakhov thought listlessly. It was painful and unpleasant to look at the boy but you couldn't help looking at him. And here over this clay stood the final sign of equality. The grave diggers, the dead and their mourners and the drunken orchestra playing a damp hymn over the body, and the cabbage and the cans, the air and the water—all this already *understood* each other independently of itself. And over all this flattened, even bent, expanse, a man-lucifer-beast-head crook-god towered like a monument, and he must certainly have been LAVRIK. Lavrik, the god of death, stood on heaps of earth with his legs spread wide in their officer's boots on a height inaccessible to the dead and the mortal, slightly twitching his immobile knee and immobile smirk, slightly glancing at his furiously digging subordinates and his wards who looked like lost sheep. And the mourners at the end of their journey really looked as if they were going to the grave themselves. Lavrik was tall, slender, elegantly gaunt like a gangster, and he had no arms. The idea that an armless man ruled over the diggers transfixed Monakhov. That's right! "I wonder if they hold the vodka for him?" To hide his defect, his jacket was lightly, even gracefully, thrown over his shoulders like a cloak. And his face! His face was handsome, with regular, finely forged features, and from under the cap, which was lightly pushed back on his forehead, his eyes looked out mockingly and hopelessly with stunning blueness. So that, having caught their glance, Monakhov even looked at the sky: had it cleared? The sky was irreversibly grey. Lavrik knew that this was all, this was the end, and it neither depressed him, inspired him, or amused him. Monakhov had never seen a man with such a look. No humility, no despair, no hysteria, no posing, no grief—a life lived in uninterrupted power, ending in power which no one would ever overthrow. Had he gotten used to it in prison or somewhere else? In the eyes of his decaying face lived an undiminished intelligence which saw everything and knew everything without ever thinking about it. He perceived Monakhov's attention: jumping down lightly, or rather flying down like a bird, he stood before him. He nodded at the coffin: "Yours?" Monakhov realized what he meant and nodded at the people standing in front of him. "Couldn't it go faster?" "Where do you want your grandmother to lie?" "Isn't it all the same here?" Monakhov expressively gazed around at the abomination of desolation surrounding them. "It's not all the same," the king of darkness said knowingly. "Then whatever's best," said Monakhov. With a barely perceptible motion of his luxurious girlish eyelashes, Lavrik indicated his breast pocket. Monakhov understood. And as soon as his hand returned, leaving something over Lavrik's heart, he, like an angel, ignoring gravity, flew up on straight legs onto the same two heaps, only slightly waving the sleeves of his jacket, and took up his position there with folded wings. "Quick! Everyone to that grave! Grandmother's grave—at once!" he said, quietly and sharply, and there was no space between the order.... And it really took less than a minute. "Say your farewells," said Lavrik. And in this just and deserved world Lavrik seemed more appropriate to Monakhov than the priest had ... They opened the lid; from the hellish shaking along the clay, grandmother had slid onto her side, the absolution had fallen out of her hands, but they firmly held the little box with her father's earth. Monakhov even started: He seemed to remember clearly that he hadn't put it into her hands. Lord! he wailed. If you exist! May *you* be cursed! And the "you" which fully included himself, was so distinct!

How we bury our dead . . . neither earth nor death . . . what awaits us? That little box so shook him . . . As if grandmother knew that there would be no more earth like the earth in the little box . . . ! And she took it, the last thing she did, she took the sole living pinch of it into this profane clay . . .

The hammer banged. They lowered the coffin, let down the cloths . . . And then suddenly Lavrik grew arms—it was amazing! With a deft, caressing motion he drew out the cloth. And even said "Ashes to ashes" and "dust to dust" and "Sleep peacefully."

A peaceful, healthy, lively hatred boiled in Monakhov's heart. He had seen evil. He had no doubt. He understood that he was fully prepared to answer for his sins. But this he would never forgive. Yesterday's idyll of the dead who resembled their monuments infuriated him. That which we are approaching was neither a prospect nor a threat. That which we had come to was a fact.

I am dead, but you live on...

"She is dead," he thought.

1966, 1976, 1979

Afterword

Autobiography and Truth: Bitov's *A Country Place*

In the short paragraph Edward J. Brown devotes to Bitov, he describes Bitov's stories as "focused on the psychological experience of a character at the moment of intense inner agitation" during "minor deeply personal crises,"[1] and this summarizes critical thought about Bitov's work. I would like to outline here what I think Bitov's reasons are for writing his "deeply personal" stories; to show that these plotless vignettes "with an autobiographical ring," as Deming Brown says,[2] are Bitov's way of addressing what is unaddressable in print in the Soviet Union: the nature of truth in literature.

It is easy to be misled by the clearly autobiographical nature of Bitov's writing. His props and characters have certainly been assembled from his real life. "Life in Windy Weather" takes place at his in-laws' dacha in Toksovo outside Leningrad, and Bitov can show you the exact bend in the pathway where the hero's epiphany occurs. His family appears in his writing, and he himself is the point of reference for his author-hero, just as Levin and Pierre are for Tolstoy and Nerzhin is for Solzhenitsyn. To call this autobiographical literature is of course to take the point of view of, say, Dmitri Panin in *The Notebooks of Sologdin* who wants to correct the "inaccuracies" of Solzhenitsyn's portrait of him in *The First Circle*. In reading Bitov, then, it is instructive to examine the divergences from autobiographical, historical truth, and consider why Bitov introduces them.

Bitov explores the special nature of literary truth explicitly in *A Country Place*. The work consists of two parts: 1. "Life in Windy Weather" and 2. "Notes from the Corner." The first part has appeared both in English[3] and in Russian; the second has yet to be published in any language though it was written simultaneously with the first part, in Toksovo in 1963. The pair comprises a kind of inner duet: the fictional hero of the short story, Alexei, has his unspecified "work" to write; the "Notes from the Corner" are that hero's journal for the period described in "Life in Windy Weather." That is, the

"Notes" present the raw material for the story, though they too have been shaped—they're the hero's notes, but that hero explicitly identifies himself as "Bitov," not "Alexei," and refers to Bitov's real-life family.

If we begin with a reading of "Life in Windy Weather," we can then see what the "Notes" add to it. Central to the story is the metaphor of wind as creative inspiration, which is first established in the description of the hero's second-story working place in the unfinished attic of the dacha. The wind brings a storm, "a real squall," and Alexei imagines his attic as a ship with rafters for masts; then he changes the image to strings, seeing the attic first as a ship, then as an organ, and, when the wind falls and he notices the sharp angle of the roof, as a cathedral. "The sense of all this could have become the beginning of his work"—that is, the image of himself as writer sailing a stormy sea, allied with the cathedral and the organ, conjures up the Romantic poetic ideal. And the tin cans from previous years placed to catch leaking rain drops provide the realist ballast for his journey; they give him a feeling of "constancy and solidity."

In the second instance of wind, Alexei's son takes his first steps, causing Alexei to perceive everything with the heightened perception of slow motion.

Another instance of the wind metaphor occurs when Alexei's father drives him to town. As they pass the train platform, Alexei imagines a girl on it with her back to the wind, skirt blowing. "He didn't choose a face for her." He enjoys a bittersweet feeling at his image: he is at the beginning of the creative process and fragmentary, incomplete images emerge, are tested, and discarded almost unconsciously.

They cross a wind-swept wasteland where there is no breeze. Alexei ponders his inability to communicate with his father. Then the wind rises again, reminding him of the platform/girl image, and this triggers a recurring nightmare fantasy of atomic war. He realizes that the fantasy has become habitual and therefore lost its formerly agonizing sharpness.

The fifth moment involving wind contains the hero's epiphany, the turning point in the story. Walking his one-year-old son, Alexei is struck by the accidental symmetry of the scene which integrates his thoughts and allows him to merge with the whole of it.

One might expect that to be the last use of wind, but the epiphany is not an end in itself, it is a necessary stage in preparing to write. The final use of the metaphor occurs at the very end of the story when Alexei walks his two visitors to the train. The wind is blowing toward town, and catches a piece of cardboard which it raises and turns over in slow motion. This description precedes the guests' departure. Alexei then turns homeward against the wind, and the exact same description is repeated verbatim. The repetition suggests that Alexei is now ready to write. The image which he captures and uses in his work is that cardboard in the wind: it's real, and emotionally neutral (unlike the bittersweet faceless cliché of the windblown girl on the platform); it's not habitual and "used up" like the fantasy of war, and so Alexei's experience of it (the first description) becomes part of his story (the second occurrence) as Alexei goes home to write, fulfilled now that the writing process has begun and will be irreversible, now that the wind of his epiphany has become concretized in a wind-image that is new and personal. Now he can be at peace with himself and his wife. The six major uses of the metaphor map a progression containing the crucial components of creativity: the artist; his images; the joy of intensified vision; his battles internal and external; synthesis in epiphany; and the creative distance to explicate that synthesis.

The epiphany is triggered by Alexei's son's pointing arm. His son helps cleanse his vision because he is learning to speak, exhilarated by the world and the names for its objects. The son helps the father to rediscover his unity with the natural world which in turn helps him accept his own father. But Alexei's father is associated with elements placed in opposition to nature, timelessness, and a fresh vision: he has the car, drives to and from the city, worries about leaving on time to beat the traffic, and talks in an artificial, second-hand way. Alexei has moved from the city to the dacha to write: he associates the city with "vanity" (in both the Biblical and the "empty bustling" sense) and with war. His bomb fantasy occurs on the way to the city, and there Alexei spends a pointless evening at an acquaintance's shooting at the cover of a German magazine with an air pistol. Having forced the host to lend him the pistol, he shoots at the tin cans in his dacha attic until the friend visits and takes it back to the city. The description of the gun "jutting stupidly from under his arm" is wedged between the two cardboard-in-the-wind passages. War is also brought to the dacha from the city when the in-laws visit. A "constant war is waged" around the son between mother and daughter, a counterpoint to the fathers-and-sons theme: "the forces are martialled," there is a "dense encirclement," and the "war moves into the battle." The war theme is carried out on the political level (the bomb); the interpersonal level (his father, his in-laws, and his wife); and the personal, internal one (toy suicide). The description of Alexei's "suicide" weapon recalls that of the duelling weapons in *Onegin:*

> Alexei [...] opened the barrel, enjoying the opposition spring of the cock and the coolness of the steel, put the lead pellet in and shot at the rusty can standing on the floor. He hit it. *(Popal)*

Compare Pushkin (6, XXIX):

> The pistols now have gleamed.
> The mallet clanks against the ramrod.
> Into the faceted barrel go the bullets
> and the cock clicks for the first time.
> The powder in a greyish stream pours into the pan.

And Bitov's *"Popal"* (he hit it) evokes Pushkin's *"I padaet"* (and he falls).

Bitov makes this same reference at the opening of *Pushkin House*. There too the hero suffers a mock death from a gun. This gun has a cigarette butt *(okurok)* stuck in the muzzle (a pun on Pushkin's *kurok*, the cock of a gun) and the brand is "North" which is "bad for him" parodically. Bitov's reference to Pushkin and *Onegin* suggests not only Bitov's relationship to his hero (Bitov is to Alexei and "Bitov" as Pushkin is to Onegin and "Pushkin") but also the problems of literary politics in Alexei's ideas about the term "formalism" which he tries out on his wife over tea in the course of his "ascent toward work." Alexei first gives his definition of formalism: "He's a formalist in matters of honor, for example, if you can't pay your debt at cards then it's a bullet in the head" (another reference to Onegin's duel about which Zaretsky is a "classicist and pedant"). Therefore, says Alexei, there can't be formalism in something new. In that case,

> they're using formalism for form which doesn't correspond to reality. But art has never been a copy of reality and is based on convention, on abstraction. If you say "Ivan thought such-and-such" it's an abstraction. Because who knows what he was thinking?

In Alexei's definition, formalism frees one to come closer to the living truth, "to escape into open space" (compare the epiphany in an open field), by liberating one from forms that are incapable of expressing what is new. The official view that uses "formalism" as a pejorative term suggests one dimension of the battles that impede Alexei's creativity. His dacha attic becomes his "fortress" where he is finally able to achieve an ideal: writing while living at peace with his son and his wife. The story ends with an image of love, "peace" and "happiness" in this contemporary version of Pushkin's "Distant habitation of work and pure delight."

"Life in Windy Weather" presents the process of the achievement of an ideal with all the elegant balance and densely connected images of the best traditional literature, suggesting that the ideal realm of the Romantics can be embodied in the actual daily life of a Soviet writer in Leningrad in 1963. The story is made fresh and specific by its seemingly direct autobiographicality, while it rings with Puskininian, Turgenevian, and Tolstoyan associations. But "Notes from the Corner" gives a very different reading of the same events and themes straight from the hero's mouth, or pen, or in fact, typewriter. Discussing his own writing, the journal-writer "Bitov" considers the formalist question from the writer's point of view.

In "Life in Windy Weather" Alexei defines the use of "he thought" in fiction as an artifice when he discusses formalism; later he wheels his son around the village trembling with the ecstasy of creation and thinks:

> There are three things no one knows about: what a child thinks, what a dying man thinks, and what Ivan so-and-so Ivanov thinks who is not you.

Afterword 369

The passage in "Notes from the Corner," then explains why Bitov values the autobiographical: the only thing you can know is your own experience; the only thoughts truly accessible to you are your own. So even the figure of speech must be unmasked as a lie—Alexei's romantic "pen" (quill) is in fact Bitov's typewriter (and note another connection to Onegin's duel in the analogy to Pushkin's realistic metallic pistols as contrasted to the arrow in Lensky's poem).

The "Notes" show us how Bitov transforms "life" into fiction. The simplest way is by changing factual details. For example, Bitov in reality has a daughter Anya, not a son, but evidently altered the fact to emphasize the fathers-and-sons cycle so important to Alexei's development in the story. In the "Notes" Anya says "Papa" for the first time, but in "Windy Weather" the son takes his first steps. In Bitov's creative process the experience that brings inspiration preceeds its verbalization and so Bitov emphasizes the child's first steps over its first words.

By juxtaposing the two texts, Bitov makes the process of "aestheticization" explicit. In part it consists in paring down multiple events and perceptions to an essence which can be expressed in one particular image. Alexei is annoyed by his father's talking about "all animals" on the basis of "one dog," and this principle determines the difference between the descriptions of leaves after the rain in the two texts. In "Windy Weather," the rain refreshes the leaves the way the wind inspires Alexei. But in "Notes," the leaves in the rain show that Bitov has developed a reflex, which he regards as part of the process toward death. In childhood he'd deliberately tried to develop habits to be grown-up. But, he says, reflexes replace consciousness, and this is his theme in the stories "Penelope," "The Garden," and "Windy Weather." The vivid individual leaf and its drop "has its aesthetic" not merely as a visual image, but by its association with artistic inspiration which in turn restores his love for his wife; this wholeness, this love, is part of the goal of his work. In the "Notes" the leaf image carries a movement towards death through the formation of ossified reflexes in which the aesthetic element is irrelevant.

Analogously, Alexei is pleased when his father says "You're getting gray;" it makes him feel grown-up. This emphasizes his positive identification with his father. In the "Notes," though, he says

> I've begun to age. In the beginning I used to boast about my gray hairs and the teeth I'd lost. I was young. But since I started to notice it wasn't just a matter of teeth and hair, I've stopped bragging.

The negative identification with his father's age and closeness to death is brought out, and then linked to his father's relation to Anya. While in "Windy Weather" the father has no contact with his grandson, in the "Notes" the grandfather is obsessed with his love for his granddaughter, taking unnecessary precautions to guard her safety. The life-giving aspect of his love is transferred to Alexei in the story, while the movement toward death is emphasized in the "Notes." The negative relation to the grandchild is transferred to the in-laws in the story in the context of blocking Alexei's creativity.

The city/country opposition in the story is related in part to the father/in-laws contrast. In the "Notes" the city is the source of the writer's political annihilation.

> The city makes me absolutely sick. I get colds in it, I suffocate there. I start to hate when I'm in it.

In his anger the writer "loses concern for the objective and for the representation of the world in its merciless equilibrium." The symmetry and distance of "Windy Weather" is a convention which the "Notes" disclaim in order to include the author's rage at literary politics and the problems of honesty they add to the writer's effort to achieve artistic truth. But he also meets his friends in the city who give him support. Bitov reads his "Notes" to them as they all get drunk. But later he rejects this elation. Rather than finding confirmation of his writing in the city, Bitov realizes he's out of touch with literary politics and has become a pariah: "They're all busy burying me, even my wife." Bitov is speaking of his first wife, the writer Inge Petkevich. The end of their marriage is chronicled in the "Notes." Fighting, they insult each other's creative methods. Thus the idyll of reading his work to his wife in "Windy Weather" is a recasting in ideal form of the illustory drunken communion with the friends in the city, while the rejection Bitov meets there clarifies the meaning of the toy pistol: brought back from an evening with acquaintances in the city, the gun signifies the hostility of fellow writers who politely ignore Bitov and try to avoid him because he's out of the ideological swim.

From these parallels it might appear that the fictionalized version is idealized and aestheticized, and is therefore untrue, while the "Notes" present the actual events and thoughts. This would certainly contradict the view of art presented in both texts, and ignore the distinction Bitov makes between a fictional hero and a writer's inner thoughts. By pairing the two in *A Country Place,* Bitov sets up a series of oppositions which are complementary: while the first text moves toward life and affirmation, the second dwells on death and despair. Their point of contact is in religion. The epiphany in the metro at the end of "Notes" provides the meaning in life that allows Bitov to write "Life in Windy Weather" in which he explicates that epiphany.

Rereading "Life in Windy Weather" in the light of the "Notes," we see the relationship of the organ and the cathedral in Alexei's "study" to the cupola of the sky in the epiphany in which Alexei "feels himself a god," and understand that Alexei's epiphany is religious, that the love at the end of the story is emblematic of a larger harmony. The story and the journal together form a complete cycle of life and death, of artistic and divine creation, and their complementary truths merge in religious love.

Priscilla Meyer
Middletown, 1984

Notes

1. Edward J. Brown, *Russian Literature Since the Revolution,* (Cambridge: Harvard University Press, 1982), p. 333.
2. Deming Brown, *Soviet Literature Since Stalin* (Cambridge: Cambridge University Press, 1978), p. 192.
3. *Contemporary Russian Prose,* ed. Carl R. and Ellendea Proffer (Ann Arbor: Ardis, 1981).